PANDAEMONIUM

1

PANDAEMONIUM

Christopher Brookmyre

WINDSOR
PARAGON

First published 2009
by Little, Brown
This Large Print edition published 2010
by BBC Audiobooks Ltd
by arrangement with
Little, Brown Book Group

Hardcover ISBN: 978 1 408 46094 8
Softcover ISBN: 978 1 408 46095 5

British Library Cataloguing in Publication Data available

Printed and bound in Great Britain by
CPI Antony Rowe, Chippenham and Eastbourne

For David MacDonald, David White and
Gary Hunter.
Be glad you went to PGS.

ADNAN'S QUICK-REFERENCE GAMER GUIDE

[CLAN AFFILIATION]
PLAYER NAME

[ADNAN'S MATES]
RADAR AKA RAYMOND GALLAHER
EWAN LAUCHLAN
CAMERON MCNEILL
MATTHEW WILSON

[HEIDTHEBAWS]
DESO AKA STEPHEN CONNOR
MARKY AKA MARKUS FLYNN
BEANSY AKA MICHAEL MCBEAN
FIZZY AKA PHILIP O'DOWD

[THE HARD TEAM]
KIRK BURNS
DAZZA AKA DANIEL MCINTYRE
ROCKS AKA PAUL ROXBURGH

[THE BEAUTIFUL PEOPLE]
JASON MITCHELL
LIAM DONNELLY
REBECCA CATHERWOOD
SAMANTHA COULTER

[BACK-BITING BITCHES]
YVONNE MCGUIRE
GILLIAN COLE
DEBORAH THOMSON
THERESA LEARY
JULIE MEIKLEJOHN

[GOD SQUAD]
ROSEMARY BRESLIN
MARIA PEARCE
BERNADETTE GELAGHTLY
CAITLIN BLACK

[SPLENDID ISOLATION]
MARIANNE SEVERIN

[MOSTLY HARMLESS]
MICHELLE SHARP
ROISIN O'HARE
RUTH ANDERSON
CAROL-ANN WELSH

[THE STAFF]
DAN **GUTHRIE**
STEWART **KANE**
HEATHER **ROSS**
FATHER CONSTANTINE **BLAKE**

[NOT PRESENT]
DUNNSY AKA ANDREW DUNN (DECEASED)
ROBERT **BARKER** (DECEASED)

Prologue

The Resurrectionist's Price

'We're going to Hell for this.'

It is one of the soldiers who speaks, talking almost under his breath to the similarly sculpted muscular redoubt standing beside him. Their arms are bare from the shoulders down, dark green sleeveless slips the only clothing between the skin of their chests and sweat-streaked grey tabards of body armour. Their biceps are taut from the weight of their weapons, or maybe that's just how it looks, because Merrick knows what those things feel like to hold; knows a weight in them that derives from more than simply mass and gravity. Those muscles are US military: built, trained and maintained. You could sling a feather duster across those forearms and the musculature would look just as pronounced, just as swollen and primed.

Merrick recalls a detached fragment he glimpsed surfing the digital channels, showing a poster from the Weimar Republic. It depicted an Aryan god of an athlete above the slogan: 'A healthy body houses a healthy mind'. To which some seditionary artist had added: 'but often a very small one'.

All of the soldiers in here look like gay porn. So much muscle on show, all of it glistening with moisture, fresh beads of sweat pooling for a moment, then suddenly swooping in rivulets in response to a slight movement, a shift in stance, and not infrequently a nervous shudder. It's the heat: that's why they're dressed that way. It's so hot in this place, so infernally hot, always. No amount of venting seems to make a difference. He's stood right next to the giant fans at the base of the intake regulation shaft, walked beneath the coolant transit vessels in the heat-exchange orbital, several miles of insulated alloys thrusting through a circular tubeway engirthing the primary accelerator chase. You can put your left hand next to the vent outlet, or up close to the transit vessel, remind your fingers what cool air feels like; but if you place your right hand a few inches further back, then they might as well be in any other room in the facility, as they'll feel no change. It's like the principles of conductivity have been suspended, or some inexhaustible energy supply keeps pumping more warm air in to replace every atom that gets cooled.

Merrick's going through tubs of Vaseline trying to reduce the chafing of his thighs and where his arms brush his sides, and that's just wearing trousers and a shirt, sometimes a lab coat. What must it be like for these guys, strapped, clipped, belted and burdened until they look like cyborgs and gladiators?

Not that the soldiers would be complaining. They didn't complain, they didn't argue, they didn't question. But that didn't mean they weren't sweltering, didn't mean they weren't blistered worse than Merrick, and most certainly didn't mean they weren't scared.

'*Going* to Hell?' replies the second soldier. 'We ain't going. We're standing down all border patrols and letting Hell come to us.'

They don't know he can hear them. They're talking in whispers and the sound of the machine—the incessant sound of the machine—would make it hard enough to catch anything below a shout from the other side of the chamber.

4

Merrick, however, is picking them up through his headphones from one of the directional laser-mikes he's deployed, monitoring a range of sound frequencies calibrated far outwith the spectrum of human hearing. He's also running all pick-ups through a counter-frequency interference filter, which cancels most of the frequencies coming from the tooth-rattling, pulsatile hum that is as unresting a constant of this place as the stifling heat. It's only with his headphones on and those filters running that he can escape it, can hear a human voice resonate like it would in a normal room in a normal building back in the lost innocence of the normal world.

Maybe he was mistaken, however, and the soldiers said nothing. Maybe all he heard was the words inside his own head.

We're going to Hell for this.

I'm going to Hell for this.

This *is* Hell.

Here beneath the world, held fast by adamantine rock, impenetrable. Here impaled with circling fire, yet unconsumed.

He recalls the words of a senior cleric a few years back, in a predictably alarmist harangue of Merrick's fraternity.

'One might say that in our country we are about to have a public Government endorsement of experiments of Frankenstein proportion—without many people really being aware of what is going on.' Thus he had warned the nation about the unchecked recklessness of those mad scientists, still grasping for that apple despite God having been quite unequivocal on the subject. Or as every monster-movie aficionado knows, 'there are some

5

things man was never meant to tamper with'.

This moral colossus had gone on to suggest that he might even be willing to help redeem the scientific community by stepping down from on high and granting an audience to a delegation of their representatives.

'In agreeing to such a meeting my only condition would be that the scientists were also willing to accept instruction from our Churches and peoples of faith on basic morality.'

Merrick still feels the smouldering embers of his indignation at the way he and his peers were being maligned as so many Mengeles, as Frankensteins unfettered by any consideration of morality, driven remorselessly by the pursuit of discovery at any cost. But now he would concede that perhaps it had angered him so much because, like a stopped clock hitting the right time, amid his automatedly dogmatic declamations the cleric had stumbled on to a nasty little truth.

There was a question you could never answer while it remained purely hypothetical, a measure of your character you could never record until it was truly put to the test. That question was: how far would you be prepared to go, what sacrifices would you be willing to make, and most pertinently, what values would you be prepared to compromise, in order to know that bit more, in order to glimpse that bit further than anyone had before you?

It was a question, a test that would only ever be truly faced by a tiny few; but not, he understood now, a lucky few. Those were the ones who would have to live with the consequences of their choice: to pass up seeing what was behind the curtain for personal ease of conscience, or to accept that an eternal burden of shame and guilt might be the price they must pay as individuals in order to secure greater knowledge for all—albeit with no guarantees that this knowledge would be a blessing or a curse.

Merrick knew the cleric was right, because so many had taken the latter choice. Where would we be otherwise? The myth of Prometheus, like all myths, had its root in a human truth. Scientists had forever defied the values of their societies in order to get that elusive further glimpse, but let's not sugar-coat it as a question of shifting mores and challenging attitudes. They had sometimes done what they knew to be wrong: horribly and hideously wrong. They had robbed graves, or paid the resurrectionists to do it for them. And when the likes of Burke and Hare got creative, they had asked no questions. The promise of that glimpse compelled them to override their morality. Merrick knew this now, knew how little that cleric truly understood with his debates over whether the end justified the means. It wasn't about justification. It was that the promise of the glimpse could obviate the very need for a justification. The glimpse could become its own supreme, unchallengeable justification.

The researcher sacrificing laboratory animals could justify his practices to himself on the grounds that the resultant understanding protected his species. Natural selection had put us in this superior position, he could tell himself, and his responsibility was to his own kind. But Merrick's compromise in this was something far worse than a reluctant vivisectionist's guilt. Maybe the Mengele comparisons weren't so hysterical after all. And the worst part was knowing he'd make the same decision, accept the same tainted deal, if the choice was offered over again. Galling as it was that the glimpse be so small, so needlessly small, and the shame he was party to so utterly unnecessary, if it was the only way to get a glimpse at all, he knew he'd still do it again.

So he'd have to confess that, in the end, that churchman was right, more right than he could possibly know. Look at the compromises he was party to, how far he had stooped here, what dominion he was genuflecting beneath in order to get that glimpse. How vindicated would the cleric feel if he knew what tainted hosts Merrick was prepared to get into bed with, just for a tiny chance to forward his research.

Here in this dark, opprobrious den of shame: this is its own punishment.

This is Hell.

He glances up from the console and takes a lingering look at his surroundings. The hardware. The boy-toys. Technology so beyond the state of the art that the private sector doesn't know it even exists, never mind the consumer. Weaponry that may not see a battlefield for ten years, if ever. Soldiers so electronically bedecked they look part-android. The mikes, the cameras, the computers, the arrays of screens, the banks of consoles bearing keyboards, tracking devices, laser-mapped 3D motion-capture grids. Not to mention enough medical monitoring and sensory instrumentation to give a hospital accountant a seizure were he to see it thus assembled in an NHS theatre. And all of it contained by walls of crisp white panelling like it's Moon Base Alpha. Twenty years ago, throw in Maria Whittaker in an unbuttoned lab coat and this would have been close to his idea of heaven.

The panelling has a distinctive sheen, partially reflective in certain light. It's almost like china. It was developed for heat resistance on the new generation of ICBMs, so it's very tough. It's also easy to clean. That's the thing here. Easy to wipe down. But there are places where you can still see live rock visible through gaps between the panels. The reality of this location, of this circumstance, can be masked off, but it's still there, inches behind the spotless veneer. Beneath the façade of science is a sin of selfish curiosity. Stains cannot be wiped away so easily from the live rock. The taint endures.

Merrick is slapped from his grim reverie by all of the screens giving that simultaneous hiccup he's never got used to, despite the regularity of its rhythm. The images all shudder like some digitally manipulated wave-pulse effect, accompanied by a high-pitched pinging sound. All attempts at shielding have been powerless to prevent it during the surge phases of the machine's cycle. Across the room, he sees Avedon adjusting the focus on a hand-held digital video camera: just in case they miss anything on the dozen other CCTV and infrared cameras. They're all digital; magnetic tape having proven . . . problematic. The white panelling in here is also lead-lined and thus supposedly anti-magnetic, but Steinmeyer himself has confessed that they still don't know what other forces the machine might be generating or even simply interfering with. Merrick just hopes nobody

9

in here has plans to father any future kids.

Steinmeyer is hovering restlessly, close to the table, inspecting the surrounding instrumentation with simmering disdain. He looks apt to start knocking things over, to go hauling out tubes and cables and clamps. He's got a headset mike in place so that he can communicate with the rest of the physics and bio teams, but he's been in here forty minutes and so far he hasn't uttered a word.

Lucius Steinmeyer: one of the leading scientific minds of his generation, but not one many people are likely to have heard from in a decade unless they hold sufficient security clearance. A man who thought he had long ago faced The Question when he accepted that only military resources could facilitate his ambitions. A man who remains haunted by a vivid dream he had, in which he was the person in charge of what was taking place here. Merrick could have sworn he had the same dream too, but now they're both wide awake.

Whatever Merrick might be feeling, he knows Steinmeyer's feeling it far worse. Merrick is merely head of the bio team. It's Steinmeyer's lifetime project that's been hijacked and sub-hijacked in a rude awakening to what the phrase 'eminent domain' truly means; *whose* domain, and more pertinently, whose eminence. The physicist has come to realise that after a decade in bed with the devil, everything up until now has merely been foreplay. However, he's not ready to surrender, not yet prepared to accept the renegotiated terms in which the glimpse gets smaller while the price gets higher. Steinmeyer is still fighting to wrest back control, and that, more than any practices doom-mongering clerics might find abhorrent, is

10

what makes him dangerous; *that* is what genuinely designates him a 'mad scientist'.

Bowed down over the consoles, Merrick's perspective is flattened so that the table looks like just that, with a number of metal objects sat upon it. It's only when he raises his head again that it resumes its true shape, and the metal objects reveal themselves to be welded and bolted into place. All around it, Merrick's equipment stands in wait, like so many siege engines.

He runs another systems-diagnostic. He knows everything is good to go. Everything has been triple-, maybe quadruple-checked. It's no more than a nervous fidget; no purpose to it beyond finding something to keep his mind occupied, keep his fingers busy. Glancing at what's cradled in those sweat-streaked arms, he hopes the soldiers don't have the same problem. What's making the systems-diagnostic more redundant is that he won't even be permitted to use half of this stuff, and of what remains, much of it might be unable to tell him anything anyway. On a trolley next to the table, for instance, there is a Swan-Ganz catheter for measuring pulmonary arterial pressure and an arterial line for invasive blood pressure monitoring, while next to those is an oesophageal Doppler for monitoring cardiac output. What he doesn't have—for they have thus far allowed him insufficient opportunity to determine—is any guarantee that there will be a heart, lungs, oesophagus or arterial system present to be monitored.

Steinmeyer checks his watch, and to Merrick's relief (but, he'd have to admit, slight disappointment) moves from the vicinity of the table and thus outwith the range of sedition and sabotage. He turns his gaze instead towards the door; not the main door, opposite Merrick's console, upon either side of which stand the two soldiers his mikes picked up, but the other one, the one at the south corner. The circular steel one. The blast-proof one. The mag-locked one, upon either side of which is posted a phalanx of six more soldiers.

All eight of them, as well as all six of the science and medical personnel, stiffen to varying degrees in response to the main door lock-warning alarm as it reverberates off the white walls. A blue glow emanates from the digital read-out topside of the double-width sliding main door, the LED panel's border flashing red in time to the first five pulses of the alarm. After that there's only the countdown: twenty seconds until the chamber is sealed.

At ten seconds, the two halves of the door slide together, but this happens any time someone comes in or goes out, so nobody's fazed by that. It's ten seconds later, when the tumblers drop into place on the other side, that always draws an anxious glance. Nobody likes to know they're locked into anywhere, but knowing what they're all about to be locked in *with* takes it to a whole other level.

One of the soldiers guarding the entrance slides a card through the swipe-reader inset in the wall to the right of the now deadlocked door, then lifts the telephone handset next to it. He's confirming the lockdown and submitting the auth code for the second stage. Merrick can't stop himself looking towards Steinmeyer. He's got one hand on his chin, his thoughts unreadable. He's still staring at the circular door, and as soon as the second warning alarm sounds, so is everybody else. It's another twenty-second countdown, but this time to opening.

'Okay, places everybody,' Merrick hears a voice say. 'Game time.'

It's the second phrase before he's fully aware that the voice is his own. He's functioning, putting himself into operational mode like any other piece of military-owned equipment he has deployed here, and even as he does he can feel his deeper self disengage, retreat into merely spectating from above like in some out-of-body experience.

He already knows that later he will review the myriad video files, and will see himself in the images, but he won't feel any of this, and there will be no footage saved of the view from inside his head.

The countdown hits five. The phalanx step into an altered formation, forming a V widening away from the door. Their weapons are no longer merely cradled, but levelled at shoulder-height, six little blue LED ammunition readouts describing the V shape, like a constellation, or the floor-level emergency lights on a commercial airliner. And at the apex, one big blue LED reaches zero.

There's a second of silence, or as close to silence as the sound of the machine can permit in this place. One last very pregnant pause. Then there comes the percussive chimes of the mag-locks disengaging, followed by a belly-shuddering thunk as eight impermeable steel cylinders retract into their housing within the giant disc. The final herald's trumpet blast is an indignant hiss from the pressure seals, before the big circular door swings smoothly and slowly open on its hydraulic servo-assisted hinges.

Merrick knows this door cost more than his house; maybe more than half his street. Given what's kept behind it, he also knows it's money well spent.

But right now it's open, wide to the wall.

At first, all he can make out are shadows and silhouettes, the shapes of several figures moving slowly in concert, like a procession. First to emerge fully into the chamber are two men in identical yellow radiation suits, covering them from head to toe. They move backwards, their gait a cautious, tentative shuffle, resultant of having no option to look at where they're putting their feet, of looking behind, or indeed of looking anywhere but at the subject. Two more follow, flanking the centre, this pair facing inwards, shuffling sideways. Their movement might be crab-like, but Merrick finds himself thinking of a tortoise: not the plodding creature itself but the name given by the Romans to a specific formation of their legionaries. This particular formation is completed at the rear by two forward-facing Romans, and it is in their visors that Merrick catches his first glimpse of what is being escorted at their centre.

The visors are one-way transparent, something to do with the light and radiation filtering, meaning in practice that they can see out but you can't see in. When you speak to them, this has the disorientating and inhibiting effect that you see only the reflection of your own face. And mostly they don't speak back much either. Not to Merrick anyway, nor Steinmeyer, nor anyone outside their own rarefied constituency. Down here, it's all about who you're answerable to, and the command chain has become rather tangled since they and their boss showed up.

Once all of them have emerged fully into the chamber, the structure of the formation becomes more apparent. It has a frame; maybe you could even call it a skeleton. One member each of the vanguard and rearguard has hold of a metal shaft, terminating either side of a stainless-steel restraining collar. A second, wider such hoop is thus tethered a couple of feet lower down by the Romans on the flanks. The remainder in fore and aft also grip metal shafts, but these will only connect to the subject if the other restraints become insufficient. They are five-feet-long electrified pikes, their business ends crackling like Space Dust on the tongue as blue static dances restlessly around the grey steel.

Merrick hears a low, breathy gurgle: not a growl, but bassy enough to be felt in his own diaphragm, and loud enough to convey that the noise would be fearsome were it to give voice to anger. He strongly suspects that driving a bolt through the skull in order to facilitate intra-cranial Doppler pressure-monitoring might just elicit that response, and that the subject, not having been formally consented, might wish to later register a complaint.

For now, the procession remains calm.

Merrick catches only flashes of movement in the shifting gaps between the yellow suits. He sees skin reflected in the visors. It looks flayed, livid, even steaming, like it's reacting to a drastic change in the ambient temperature or humidity. The first

15

time he caught such a glimpse, he reasoned that it was down to a distortion of the reflection caused by the visor's curvature and by light flaring on the glass. This time, he's got infrared cameras and humidity sensors waiting in place to filter fear and hysteria from hard data. Unfortunately, he's confident that the hard data will merely provide ample justification for more of the first two. The idea that anything organic could be hotter than the air in here is a truly unsettling one.

The yellow tortoise continues its palpably tense but necessarily unhurried procession, headed towards the table, flanked now by four of the armed phalanx. Two soldiers remain at each door; securing chamber access is their paramount objective, one understood by everyone now locked inside it to override their personal safety. If anything goes wrong here, then here and here alone it stays.

The procession stops a few feet short of the table, which at this stage remains concealed from the subject. At most, all that is likely to be visible between the radiation suits is the odd flash of stainless steel. There is no means of deducing how much the subject knows about what will take place next, no way of anticipating reaction and response.

A million white mice go meekly and unsuspectingly towards certain death, then one of them seems spooked and desperate, and you ask yourself: how did it know to be afraid? When it's a white mouse, chances are it detected some smell or sight it didn't like, or perhaps was simply anxious anyway. This, however, is no white mouse. The subject has no inkling what will take place in this chamber, but a specimen such as this goes nowhere meekly; and as for unsuspectingly, well, the steel braces kind of render that one moot.

With some alarm, Merrick notices that around knee height there is something unsecured and in motion, though it looks too thin and too flexible to be an arm. He is not comforted to realise that it is a tail.

From the centre of the formation Merrick hears a guttural, throaty rumbling, like a very large motorbike: idling, but the slightest throttle-twist away from unleashing far more power. He felt the last emission in his stomach; reckons this one is vibrating his chest until the sound falls away and he realises the palpitation hasn't ceased.

He's not here though, he reminds himself. He's only looking down, and looking down he hears his voice order Avedon to 'present the table'. There is a keening hum of gears as the table begins to rotate on its vertical axis. It tips eighty-five degrees until almost perpendicular to the floor, its shape distinct in grey steel against the white panelling, a horizontal brace bisecting the trunk at around two thirds of its height.

The subject sees it now: a cross, risen, elevated to dominate the room. The subject doesn't like this. There is a ripple through the formation, suggesting that the four Romans gripping the restraining shafts are not so much tethering the subject as merely hanging on like sailors in a storm. The other two respond. The pikes are applied. The storm gets worse for a while, then abates amidst a flurry of fizzes, crackles and winded-sounding groans (though no roars and no screams). The subject goes limp, the four escorts now supporting its weight. The air smells of ozone, and a sweet odour that reminds Merrick pleasantly of childhood for the few seconds it takes to remember that its source was a bacon-curing factory close to his school.

With the subject stunned, the escorts move swiftly to open the loops attaching its wrists to the metal band around its middle, then place them instead into the waiting clamps welded to either side of the table. A metal neckpiece is similarly bolted into place, then the feet are locked in position also.

'Subject secured,' reports one of the yellow suits. With his face concealed, it's impossible to be sure precisely who he is reporting this to, but Merrick knows he could narrow it down at least to being one of the soldiers. It sure as shit isn't him, or Steinmeyer, or anyone else on the scientific staff.

'Subject secure,' one of the soldiers in the phalanx acknowledges, then gives a signal to his colleague manning the swipe dock at the main door. Another countdown begins, but now it's not just the door that's on a clock. Whatever he's going to do, Merrick is going to have to commence now, and he's going to have to work fast.

'Restore the table,' he tells Avedon.

The subject writhes in languid disorientation as the table returns to the horizontal: not quite conscious, not quite oblivious either. He'll know when it's fully come round, because that's also when he'll discover how sound those welds are. Right now, though, it merely looks like it's in the last pre-waking throes of unquiet dreams.

Merrick first takes hold of the modified plastic clip that is the sensor end of the pulse-oximeter, and delicately levers it around one of the subject's

18

ear lobes. This particular piece of kit was checked on one of the soldiers an hour back so that hardware error could be ruled out if there is a repeat of the reading Merrick got on a previous subject. The device measures oxygen saturation in red blood cells by passing two different wavelengths of red and infrared light (normally through a finger, but that requires a willing patient) from an LED and comparing the different light absorptions demonstrated by oxygenated and deoxygenated haemoglobin. When Merrick first tried measuring this on a test subject, the results were so low as to be inconsistent with human survival. Ruling out knackered kit would open up other explanations. One was denser tissue make-up leading to a greater overall opacity, resulting in little of either wavelength getting through to the sensor. More dramatically, a second interpretation was that there was genuinely very little oxygen in the blood, and that it was therefore nitrogen or even carbon dioxide that was being conveyed instead. Thus instead of a standard human or even mammalian respiratory system, they could be looking at something closer to photosynthesis. Hence the expired gas analysers, though Merrick isn't much looking forward to fitting the mouthpiece.

He reaches to a tray and picks up an electroencephalographic sensor, placing it gently to the subject's temple, then applying a little pressure to make it fast. His little finger brushes the base of the protuberance just above, and he dares to indulge his curiosity by pinching gently with his thumb and forefinger also. It's hard, ungiving, solid. Tougher than bone.

19

Merrick places another electrode on the opposite temple, then reaches to a second tray and lifts the sensors he will attach to the chest. As he sticks the first of the little pads in place, he stares at the hairless, lightly crenulated plateau beneath his fingers, insulated from his touch by a layer of latex. Merrick finds himself taking off a glove in order to feel the skin directly against his own. It's tougher, like soft leather, a surface that feels as though it would be easily scuffed and scraped, but nonetheless hard to penetrate. He lets his arched palm collapse until it is lightly pressed, feeling for a heartbeat. At this, the subject opens its eyes and sharply turns its head to look into his.

Merrick would not care to describe what he sees in there in that moment, but he knows the results of one test, at least: that test an unlucky few must face. He couldn't say which action constitutes passing or failing, wonders whether any man could, but he knows this for sure: he will make do with the ECG, the EEG, the pulsox and at most the expired-gas analysers. He will not be attempting any invasive monitoring procedures without anaesthetising or analgising this thing, neither of which he has any idea how to accomplish anyway.

This inability is, of course, irrelevant, because even if he did know how, he would not be allowed to make an attempt. Monitoring and observation, as has been made unambiguously clear to him and his team, are the absolute extent of his parameters, the demarcation of which will be enforced, if necessary, by the twitchy-looking muscle-bound fuckers carrying the very big guns.

He checks the monitors. He's getting readings above the baseline from the ECG and the EEG.

20

There is cardiac output and there is intracerebral electrical activity. What that's going to tell him, beyond that the subject *has* a heart and a brain, he's not sure.

Merrick looks up from the table and finds himself locked in Steinmeyer's gaze. It is only marginally more comfortable than the last pair of eyes he just stared into, but Christ, what does Lucius want him to do? Steinmeyer looks to the main door, then back to the table.

'This is insane,' Steinmeyer says. 'This is completely fucking insane.'

'Lucius,' Merrick appeals, though he can see it's futile. His face is stone-set in a coolly resolute anger: no sudden, precipitate fury. Steinmeyer shakes his head. Something here has broken, something inside of him. He hauls off his headset and slaps it down on to a nearby tray, upending scalpels, lines and canulae on to the concrete floor.

Steinmeyer then strides towards the exit, but finds his way barred. The main door is no longer in lockdown, but there is a soldier between him and the swipe dock for his security card.

'I'm sorry, Professor Steinmeyer,' the soldier states. 'I'm not authorised to let anyone leave this chamber until I have full clearance that the procedure is complete.'

He doesn't look quite so coolly resolute any more. Merrick can see the sinews tense in the back of Steinmeyer's neck, and fears for a moment that he is about to do something rash. Just then, however, he hears the susurrus of the pressure release as the main doors glide apart. The soldier looks around quizzically, then snaps to attention and gives a salute as he sees Colonel Bud

21

Havelock stopped in the entryway, arms folded as he waits for the two halves of the door to slide fully home. The seven other soldiers also salute as he steps into the chamber.

The men in the radiation suits react not at all, their collective attention remaining intent upon the subject on the table.

With the door now open, Steinmeyer attempts to walk towards the passage but the soldier manning it steps across his path.

'Colonel Havelock,' Steinmeyer appeals.

'Sir,' the soldier barks, looking past the physicist, 'my orders are to secure the chamber until I have full clearance, sir.'

'Stand easy, Corporal,' orders Havelock. 'You have my clearance to let Professor Steinmeyer pass.'

'Sir, yes, sir.'

The soldier moves out of Steinmeyer's way with an exaggerated step, his eyes front and away from the professor the second the order is given. This leaves Steinmeyer with only Havelock to get past.

'Where you off to?' the colonel asks. 'Forget something?'

'I have no role here,' Steinmeyer replies. '*You* have no role here,' he insists, inviting Havelock's agreement like he's sure he knows how the army man feels about the issue. Turns out he's wrong.

'I would strongly dispute that, Professor. We both have a role here because we may be dealing with a threat to national and international security. This is the US Army. This is what we *do*. Now this ain't a war, not yet, but if it becomes one, it's men like me, men like Corporal Clark and the other soldiers you see right here, who'll be in the shit, fighting it. So if this helps us learn more about what we're up against, if this in any way helps save my men, if this helps us *win*, then goddamn right we've got a role here, and goddamn right so have you.'

'There will be no war unless you create one. We're the ones holding the door open, remember? The only barbarians at the gate are on *our* side of it.'

'Ah, bullshit, Lucius,' Havelock replies. There is frustration in his face, indicating that his concern is genuine. 'You've seen as well as I what's on both sides of the gate. What I've seen has given me serious grounds for worry about what would happen should ever the twain meet, and it's my job to worry about that shit. Yes, we're holding open a door: we're holding open *one* tiny door so that we can gather us a little intel that just might come in handy if it turns out that meanwhile, on the other side, they're getting ready to tear down the walls.'

'You will learn nothing from this here today,' Steinmeyer states calmly. 'This is superstition and barbarism.'

'This is *cancer*, Lucius. This is AIDS. Times ten. Times a thousand. This could be the greatest threat we've ever faced as a species. It's the Black Death and you're saying lay off being cruel to the goddamn rats. We cannot afford to be squeamish right now, and we definitely cannot afford men like you closing their minds to *any* possibility. *What's been discovered here alters our whole understanding of the nature of the universe*: those are your own words. There's nothing about this we can take for granted, so that's some pretty fucking bad timing for you to abandon the scientific

23

principle of observe-and-deduce.'

'You abandoned *all* scientific principles when you brought in Tullian.'

Havelock drops his voice again; looks like he bit back an initial reply, but this one, while quieter, is no less unequivocal in its import.

'That wasn't my call, but it ain't my place to second-guess it, and I don't get to pick sides. I'm on the side of the US Army—that's my job. But I'll say this much for Tullian: it ain't him who's backing away because he's afraid of being proved wrong.'

Steinmeyer gives the bitterest laugh.

'Tullian's not afraid of being proved wrong, because from his perspective, being *proven* wrong is conceptually impossible. I'd advise you to understand the danger inherent in that before it's too late.'

That's his last word. Steinmeyer walks through the main door and into the mouth of the entryway where, heading towards the chamber, is an unmistakable silhouette. No radiation suit, no fatigues, no lab coat and no uniform can cast that shape: only flowing robes, gathered about the waist by a cummerbund. The words 'speak of the devil' flash into Merrick's mind, but he dismisses them with an almost superstitious level of haste. We're talking closer to the other end of that particular spectrum, and the phrase is not one anybody around here would utter with any degree of flippancy.

The two men stop in the passageway; or rather, Cardinal Tullian stops, hands clasped, head slightly bowed in greeting. Steinmeyer makes like he's going to storm past, ignoring him, then changes his mind and halts. They look at each other for a moment but exchange no words. Steinmeyer evidently changes his mind once more, swallowing whatever he had stopped to say, and continues his exit.

Tullian watches him pass, waiting patiently should Steinmeyer decide he does wish to speak to him after all. He stays there until the physicist has turned the corner out of sight, before turning almost reluctantly and proceeding into the chamber.

His entrance through the doorway elicits a mirror image of Havelock's: the soldiers respond not at all, while the men in the yellow suits divide into two facing lines, each trio side by side, hands palmed, heads slightly bowed; the Vatican equivalent of ten-hut, Merrick guesses.

The subject responds also to this new presence, though pinned by the neck brace, there is no way of seeing the entrance from flat back on the table. Its head strains, trying to turn, the forearms testing the fortitude of the bonds. Logic tells Merrick that this is simply a reaction to detecting the nearby movement that was prompted by the Cardinal's arrival, but he nonetheless fails to find this explanation entirely satisfying or of any reassurance. He looks at the elongated nails, the parallel serrated saw-blades of teeth and again, in awestruck, frightened fascination, at what lies just above each temple.

Then Merrick looks at Tullian, striding slowly across the chamber floor, and feels only relief. He has endured the frustration of impotence, the resentment of being subject to the rule and authority of other parties, other bodies. Now he understands he's only been straining at the leash like the yappy little dog who knows deep down that it's the leash that's protecting him. It's at this point that he admits he is more than happy that other people have control of what is going on here, people who know what they are dealing with. And he doesn't mean the people with the big guns.

His misgivings evaporate as he realises his qualms were truly fear. He told himself he didn't want to be working on this on someone else's terms, but he can admit now that the prospect of working on it on his own terms would have been far worse. He is grateful, therefore, to defer to someone who knows the territory, someone who understands what he's dealing with. Merrick would never have called himself a religious man, but they say everyone cries for intercession in the deepest darkness, and the darkness didn't get any deeper than down in this place.

There's another guttural, idling ante-growl from the table. ECG and EEG show a slight rise, but Tullian isn't in line of sight yet. There are spikes when he begins speaking, though; or declaiming might be the word.

'*In nomini patre, Trinitas, Sother, Messias, Emmanuel, Athanatos . . .*'

Merrick sees the neck muscles stretch as the subject tries to locate the source of the voice. There's another spike on the monitors when finally it does, accompanied by an agitated growl: defensive, territorial, threatening.

'*Pentagna, Salvatror, Ischiros, principium et Finis,*' Tullian continues, moving closer still. Then from the folds of his robe he produces a crucifix, hanging on a chain around his neck, which he holds out at arm's length, less than a metre from the end of the table.

Tullian lets the crucifix fall, and from elsewhere in his robe produces a phial of clear fluid, which he holds out to one of the figures in yellow. He takes it in both hands and kneels in front of the Cardinal, presenting the phial above his bowed head. Tullian holds his hands apart, either side of the phial, and speaks, in English this time, his accent all but shorn of its American roots by its heightened register:

'Let these waters be sanctified by the power, the agency and descent of the Holy Spirit; Let descend upon these waters the cleansing of the Three who are One, and endue them with the grace of redemption and the blessing of Jordan, that Satan may be crushed under our feet, that every evil counsel directed against us may be brought to naught, and that the Lord our God will free us from every attack and temptation of the enemy.'

He gives another short blessing in Latin, while the kneeling man unstops the lid and hands him the phial. Tullian makes a pronounced, ceremonial sign of the cross with his right hand, blessing the subject. The eyes of the blessing's recipient follow the hand intently, its fury either ebbing or temporarily spent. The blessing complete, Tullian transfers the phial to his right hand, and gives it an equally pronounced and equally ceremonial flick with his wrist, sending a spray of the holy water on to the subject.

As soon as it hits that grey, crenulated skin, the monitors spike a new high and the chamber reverberates as Merrick finally gets to hear the roar he sensed those low grumblings warned of. It

27

overloads the audio, reduces everything to crackling white noise, shakes Merrick like a sapling in a gale. The ferocity is paralysing, accompanied as it is by a writhing, shuddering frenzy against the braces and cuffs that gives a terrifying measure of just what physical power is being contained. Even the soldiers flinch, a ripple of human recoil passing along the stocks and barrels of all those tightly gripped weapons. The skin fizzes, bubbles and blisters along a three-foot arc where the water has streaked it, and once more all of the welds are given a mortal proving as the subject struggles desperately to free itself.

This is when he appreciates what stern stuff Tullian is made of; sterner than him, maybe than Steinmeyer too. Merrick has come up against his limitations, said 'let this chalice pass from my lips'. Tullian is stronger than that. Merrick sees him shudder in the face of the roar, sees fright and horror in his eyes, and that makes him a stronger man still. Courage is not fearlessness. Courage is not even overcoming fear: it's being able to operate, to carry out your duty, in the face of it, in the grip of it.

Tullian sends a second arc of the holy water perpendicular to the first, describing a cross on the subject's torso. The EEG spikes again while the ECG flatlines, but this is because both chest sensors have popped off in the flailing, screaming tumult, adding the urgent whine of the asystole alarm to the cacophony.

And it gets suddenly worse. The subject . . .

The subject.

Come on. What is he trying to hide from himself? Who is he trying to kid any more? This is not a special effect. It is not a man in a latex mask. It is not even of this world, and he knows this for certain, as he has seen the portal it came through: one considerably more daunting than the mag-locked circular door.

The creature, then.

No. Say it. Say it. No mere creature. No refuge in feigned ignorance. He can't hide from what this is. *The demon.*

The demon ceases its screams, holding its head up as far as the neck brace will allow, the better to look straight at Tullian. Its jagged mouth opens again, but delivers no base primal cry. Instead, it bellows forth a twisting, gravelly, punctuated issue like a grim parody of Tullian's declamations. It stares at the Cardinal and snarls its venomous defiance. The language is unintelligible but all of its searing hatred is conveyed nonetheless.

Tullian chants something else in Latin. Merrick catches the words *'exorcizo'* and *'exorcizata'*. He has to raise his voice above the demon's foul retort, the whine of the ECG alarm and the growing, pulsing hum of the machine.

'. . . *et ipsum inimicum eradicare et explantare valeas cum angelis suis apostaticis* . . .'

The demon goes limp for a moment, just long enough for Merrick to begin to believe that Tullian's words have somehow quelled its dark spirit, until its rest is revealed as a mere gathering of strength before another assault. In its redoubled writhing, it pops a bolt on the band securing its left elbow. The band doesn't come fully away, but thus loosened it will allow the creature more purchase on the clamp restraining its wrist.

The men in yellow raise their shock batons, while

the soldiers level their guns. Tullian waves them both off, raising his hands and gesturing them all to hold. He then reaches once more inside his robes and produces, this time, an intricately ornate dagger.

'. . . *per virtutem ejusdem Domini nostri Jesu Christ . . .*'

The demon sees it, watches Tullian raise both hands full height over his head.

'. . . *qui venturus est judicare vivos et mortuos et sæculum per ignem,*' he shouts, his voice rising to a roar of his own on the last words as he drives the blade down into the creature's chest.

Blood so black, so lightlessly black, sprays from the wound, spurting like a fountain as Tullian hauls the knife free and up again. The demon strains at the wrist clamp until its own flesh tears and more black fluid pools around the base of the metal loop.

Tullian brings the knife down once more, still calling above the noise: '*Deus, Agios, Resurrectio.*'

Again.

'*Aeternas, Creator, Redemptor.*'

Again.

'*Unitas, Summum bonum, Infinitas . . .*'

Again. Again. Again. Again.

Until, with the creature unmoving but for ever-gentler twitches, silent but for a deflating moan of final breath through its throat and the splash of its jet blood upon the concrete floor, he desists, and breathlessly utters one last word of Latin:

'*Amen.*'

Transports of Delight

I

There is a smell of sulphur dioxide. It is stifling, engulfing, invading every breath of what was already stale air.

'Biohazard detected. All personnel evacuate. This is not a drill. Repeat, biohazard detected. Alert! Alert! Alert!'

Brimstone, they used to call it: the stench of Hell. Volcanic, something redolent of the bowels of the Earth. Certainly bowels and earth are the two things that leap to Adnan's mind as his eyes threaten to water in the face of this olfactory assault.

'Mother of Christ, that is evil,' says Deso. 'That is pure evil.'

'It's fuckin' hellish,' Marky agrees. 'Jesus God.'

'Seriously,' Deso rejoins, 'if a factory had produced that, the fuckin' EU would have them shut doon for being in violation of aboot ten different environmental regulations.'

'Ach, yous are all just jealous,' says Beansy with a satisfied grin, wafting more guff from the seat of his toxic trousers with a near-regal wave of his hand. 'There's nane of your puny wee arseholes could generate a bouquet of such variety or potency. Come on, take it in, draw it all the way down and savour the sophistication. Mmm. I'm getting canal water, I'm getting burst bin bag in August, and ooh, a subtle top-note of Saltcoats beach at low tide. Exquisite. And there's plenty more where that came from.'

'Fuck's sake, Beansy,' Radar warns, 'I'm telling

33

you: if I smelt that comin' oot of me, I'd be straight doon tae the nearest parasitology unit to make sure I didnae have a deid Komodo dragon up my Ronson.'

Adnan's eyes are streaming now, but it's more from the laughter than from the fumes. He can't see the screen on his DS, couldn't concentrate anyway because he's doubling over in his seat.

Deso gets to his feet in the aisle and reaches towards the neat little hammer that's fixed above the pane for breaking the coach's windows in an emergency. Then he pretends to collapse before he can make it.

Fizzy puts his hands to his cheeks and goes: 'Noooooooooo!'

Deso fucking loves this stuff. Everybody's falling about, pishing themselves. It's almost worth putting up with the smell of Beansy's farts for the sake of the laughs and the carry-on. Almost.

One row forward of Deso, Cameron gets to his feet, leaning across Ewan to slide open the vent panel above the window, and while he's vertical, he reaches to the overhead shelf and cranks up the tunes a wee bit as well. Pretty decent portable speaker rig he's got up there, just a shame it's Cam's iPod they're attached to. Fucking emo stuff: it's a wonder Cam never committed suicide or turned into a fucking vampire. Some of it's all right, though: the one playing just now has a good stomp on it that makes an appropriate soundtrack for travel. Deso finds himself nodding his head to the rhythm, but he's as much nodding in approval of the vent getting slid back, because he knows what that's about. Oh yes indeed.

Cameron takes a look down the front, checking

34

none of the teachers are choosing this moment to cast a backwards glance over their responsibilities.

Beansy is on to it as well. 'Yo, wastoid,' he shouts across the aisle. 'You're not blazin' up in here.'

Cameron shoots back a finger-on-lips gesture, eyes indicating the dangers lying towards the front and rear of the vehicle, though he's grinning as he does so.

'Tubby bastard's probably just afraid we'll blow a hole in the bus when we light up,' says Ewan, 'given the amount of gas he's just pumped into the atmosphere.'

Deso hears the strike of the match, sharp and distinct through the music, the engine and the babble of thirty-odd voices up and down the bus. It's one of those sounds that school trained him to notice from any distance and to isolate within the widest spectrum of foreground volume. Some folk were like that with sweetie wrappers: they could hear you trying to secretly open a packet of Fruitella in your pocket from the other side of the playground, and they'd be in your face demanding: 'Geez wan, gaunny, eh?' before you'd slipped the first sleekit swedger between your lips. Deso had honed a different skill within two months of first year, his tuck-shop funds proving insufficient to finance a nascent nicotine habit. If you wanted a drag, you had to cadge it from one of the older guys, and with so many eager gaping mouths coveting the same few fags, you had to be first on the scene to be in with a chance.

He doesn't smoke now, though; not fags anyway. Had to give it up halfway through first year when he made the football team. If you got caught having just one fly draw, you were out for good, no parole. He hasn't puffed a cigarette since, but a wee bit of doobage now and again, that's a different story. Not incompatible with midfield creativity either. Look at Russell Latapy: nobody was telling Deso *he* never liked a jay.

Deso sees it getting passed from Ewan to Cam. It's a well skinny wee doob, but that just shows Ewan knows his game. Very little smoke, crucial in reducing the chances of detection, and not just from the teachers. A far greater threat is the jay getting spotted by the inhabitants of the back row.

Aye, some things don't change. It's fifth year, they're not kids any more, but the big men have still laid claim to the back seats, same as they did in first year; same as they did in fucking primary school. It is inevitable that Kirk, Dazza and Rocks will clock the joint eventually, and Ewan knows passing it to them for a wee toke is like making a sacrifice to placate a potentially vengeful deity. However, the trick is to get it shared around the rest of them for a while first. If it ends up with Kirk too early, it won't be coming back, and not out of greed, but power. The prick would hang on to it and smoke it right down to the roach purely to demonstrate that nobody had the balls to take it back off him. Fucking wank that he is.

It's only a few moments before there's a more welcome smell drifting Deso's way, dispersing the last traces of Beansy's violation. Then a cupped hand thrusts back towards him through the gap between the seats and the window. Deso takes it more swiftly and gracefully than those relay guys ever manage at the Olympics, and pulls it to his lips. Oh yes.

The smoke is almost invisible as it drifts its way

down the bus, detected by most, identified by some. Marianne recognises it as immediately as she recognised the music, though in both cases this is despite interference from closer to the front. Gillian and Deborah and their little clique have their own iPod playing in competition, showcasing 'Ibiza Club-Ned Anthems Volume 103'. It's the same stuff that's always blaring out of the open windows of souped-up chav-mobiles when they pull up at traffic lights. She's often wondered whether the little guys at the wheel are secretly hoping you'll lean in as you walk past and say: 'Your tunes are the bomb, mate. You must be cool as.'

The smell of blow is one of the few things to penetrate the fug of perfume and body spray enveloping this section of the bus. If the collective scent could be bottled, it would be called Trying Too Hard. Marianne hopes they've brought dental mints too, because even all that eau-de-teen-queen isn't going to mask what's on their breath.

'Eeuugh,' splutters Yvonne, looking with distaste at the green bottle. 'Is white wine no' meant to be chilled?'

God's sake, some front she's got, Gillian reckons. Never brought anything more intoxicating than a packet of Lockets and the cheeky cow is slagging *her* contribution?

'Aye, sorry,' Gillian responds. 'Hang on till I get my ice bucket out of my bag. If you don't want it, pass it on.'

'I didn't say that,' Yvonne clarifies with a giggle. 'I've just got more rarified taste than you plebs.'

'What are you talking about?' asks Julie. 'It's been decanted and everything. Right into that

Appletise bottle.'

Yvonne hands the bottle to Theresa, who helps herself to a long swig.

'Aah,' she says approvingly. 'Liebfraumilch. Shitey German sweet white wine served at room temperature with just a hint of three different shades of lipstick.'

Julie has taken the bottle next, and spills a little on her chin as she laughs at what Theresa just said.

It was quite funny, Gillian would concede, but the lassie better be as ready to break out some vintage swally when they get there as she's ready to break out the cheeky patter.

'Still tastes better than Buckfast,' Gillian asserts.

'You're tootin' there,' Yvonne agrees. 'Michael McBean could do a big grogger into the bottle and it would still taste better than Buckfast. I think those monks must make that stuff to drink as a penance.'

'Whereas if Liam Donnelly did a big grogger in it, you'd be the first to drink it,' Debs suggests.

'No I would not,' Yvonne replies with a blush that is only partly fuelled by indignation.

'Of course she wouldnae,' agrees Gillian. 'Different story if he *came* in it, right enough.'

'I still wouldn't be the first to drink it, though. I'd be lucky if I was third behind you pair.'

They all laugh, though Deborah silently notes that Yvonne didn't *deny* she would drink it. It's always worth storing such ammunition, especially on a trip like this. You never know who you'll end up sharing a room with and therefore how dirty you might need to fight in five-way conversations at two in the morning.

She notices Gillian glancing back and across the

38

aisle. Gill's got a smirk on her face when she sees Deborah's caught her. Deborah smiles too and steals a peek over the back of their seats. The subject is he of the supposedly coveted jizz (even when diluted in warm Liebfraumilch), Liam Donnelly. He's gorgeous, but let's face it: the only way she, Gill or Yvonne were likely to get near his bodily fluids *would* be if he spooged into a bottle. Him and his equally pretty pal Jason might be on this same coach, might be in the same classes, but it didn't seem like they attended the same school. They were aloof: that was the word, one she finally understood when she saw them glide down a corridor like it was a catwalk, somehow disconnected from the world of damp duffle coats and dinner-hour tribal warfare that everyone else was stuck in. For years before that, she had assumed it meant something to do with being gay, mainly because it rhymed with poof. In a way that was a measure of their status: they were fey and preening enough for 'poof' to be the more readily applicable description, but they had this disdainful maturity about them that meant even the hard cases seemed to regard slagging them as a self-defeating exercise.

They had their female equivalents in Rebecca and Samantha, two more of the Beautiful People who had always managed to come across as more grown-up and sophisticated than some of the staff. They hung around out of school with the same crowd as Liam and Jase, but it wasn't clear whether or who might be boyfriend-girlfriend among them. Even the ambiguity of their relationships was as much an indication of their status as their fevered speculation reflected how

Deborah and her pals were still daft wee lassies.

'I heard she's had a Brazilian,' says Gillian, indicating Rebecca. 'My cousin works at a tanning place in Hamilton, and she says she's been in and had it done.

'A Brazilian?' asks Yvonne. 'I've heard she's had an Argentinian, an Australian and two Poles.'

'I bet she's had more poles than that,' Deborah says, seizing the chance to trump Yvonne's joke.

Deborah steals a look to make sure she hasn't been overheard, feeling suddenly anxious, not to mention distantly guilty. She knows her remark was based on nothing but a kind of vicarious wishful thinking. She just made it up to sound bitchy but she feels like she'd actually be jealous if it was true.

She is relieved to spot that Rebecca is oblivious. She is sitting on her own, neckband cans plugged into her iPhone, head bobbing to the music and the rhythm of the bus as she stares serenely out of the window. It would look like a carefully considered pose if it wasn't that Rebecca probably looked perfectly composed even when she first woke up each day.

Samantha also has a double seat to herself, as do Liam and Jase. It is a further demonstration of their aloof self-assurance. As far as the rules apply to everybody else, only complete sad-sacks end up sitting by themselves. Odd numbers unavoidably meant some folk would be sitting alone in the row behind or across from their mates, but if you weren't situated adjacent to your pals, you would settle for sitting next to someone you weren't that friendly with rather than end up conspicuously on your Jack.

Apart from the Beautiful People, the only folk sitting in true isolation are the weirdo loner Matthew Wilson and that creepy English Goth, Marianne.

Marianne's only excuse is that she is the new girl, but she isn't that new; otherwise why would she be on the trip? You hardly need grief counselling if you barely knew the person who's dead, do you? She'd been here most of a term, joining after the summer holidays. Not just your Matalan bulk-issue Goth, either. Definitely weirder. Some of the ones you saw hanging about the town made you think there must be 'emo-look' pages in the new Next Directory, whereas Marianne's gear seemed to have come from a Victorian jumble sale. She looks like she'd smell of rickety houses and old ladies' perfume, but nobody is venturing close enough to verify this.

Then, of course, there is the music, some of which Debs can hear coming from further up the bus: probably courtesy of Cameron McNeill. He isn't a Goth or an emo but he is definitely trying to make some kind of pathetic statement by playing that stuff. It's a total pose. Nobody really likes listening to that depressing and tuneless racket; it's like the Emperor's New Clothes. They just think it makes them dead cool if they say they don't like the *X Factor*, and then there is an ascending scale of alternativeness according to how weird the stuff they *claim* to like is.

With this thought, Deborah climbs across Gillian and into the aisle so that she can reach to turn up her own music, drown out all that gloom. Soundtrack to a bloody horror movie. Wasn't this trip supposed to be about making everybody feel

41

less depressed? If so, the staff should have stipulated that it was to be a strictly Goth-free venture, confiscated Cameron's tunes and completely barred Marianne from getting on the bus. It's not like she would be missed.

Now *there* is a conundrum: did being a creepy weirdo who nobody wanted anything to do with turn you into a Goth, or did being a Goth turn you into a creepy weirdo who nobody wanted anything to do with? Christ, even Rosemary and the God-squadders have all found somebody to share a seat with.

*   *   *

'Have you both got a copy of the latest CYG news-sheet?' Rosemary asks, turning around to thrust a sheaf of yellow A4 pages at Caitlin and Maria. Sweet Jesus, Caitlin thinks, in the horrified knowledge that it's not a question. Rosemary personally compiled, printed, photocopied and distributed the newsletter, not to mention writing most of its content, so she knew fine who did and didn't have one. Knowing Rosemary, she probably kept a register.

The CYG: St Peter's Catholic Youth Group. Caitlin started going to meetings back in second year, after being misinformed that it was Justice and Peace. Instead she found Rosemary's big sister Vera presiding over what she regarded as 'an umbrella group for all school involvement in Catholic causes'. This had nominally included Justice and Peace, which was why her conscience kept dragging her back, but in practice the CYG meetings under Vera's direction mostly comprised singing hymns and taking turns to demonstrate how much more vehemently pro-life you were than the previous speaker.

Caitlin stopped going more than a year ago, but Rosemary still talks to her as though she's part of the fold. She has never been sure whether this is intended as an inclusive gesture or an ongoing punishment. Either way, it has a horrible tendency to rub off, leaving even certain teachers under this embarrassing misapprehension. She's long had to tolerate being regarded a quiet little goody-two-shoes, but she draws the line at this.

Rosemary hands her two copies of the sexy and sizzling CYG news, leaving it incumbent upon Caitlin to pass one along to Maria. Wonderful. This is an act of complicity that Maria will unavoidably interpret as Caitlin saying: 'I'm just as far from the trendicentre as you, so let's all be dweeby little church mice together.'

Caitlin can feel the heat in her cheeks as Maria takes the paper from her hand.

'Thanks, Rosemary, I've not read this,' Maria says politely, and Caitlin feels something in her gut turn to stone.

'Which topic would you like to discuss first?' Rosemary asks.

Caitlin gapes, unable to stop her mouth falling open as she contemplates the projected length of the journey ahead.

'If no one has a preference,' Rosemary goes on, 'I'd like to start with Pope Benedict's universal indult restoring an individual priest's permission to celebrate the Tridentine Rite.'

Caitlin swallows, her throat suddenly too dry to speak. A guilty wee voice inside her head, the same one that always told her to log off MySpace and get back to studying, nags her that she ought to learn from Rosemary's example. They were always being told that if they found religion boring, it was because they weren't giving enough of themselves to unlock its rewards. Caitlin is well versed in knuckling down and getting on with even the least engaging tasks. If she can sit down to an hour of calculus, she should be able to apply herself to anything. Maybe she should read the signs, try that bit harder. This is supposed to be a retreat, after all.

However, as she listens to the subsequent discussion, she feels like something inside her is being denied, something that makes her want to scream. To avoid this outcome, she decides to try and zone out. Too bad Maria has the window seat, so she can't just lose herself in watching the road go past, but she can stare at the sheet in front of her without reading it, like she does with her missal at mass: take her imagination for a trip while the words become meaningless squiggles in her field of vision.

She's almost back at the Barrowland watching Jimmy Eat World when Rosemary crashes the gig and hauls her back to the bus.

'And what do you think, Caitlin?' she asks, leaning over the seat.

She's about to mumble 'I don't know', in lieu of 'fuck off', but she knows from experience that a disinterested response will not be enough to deter Rosemary from further attempts to drag her into the discussion.

Okay, she thinks, you asked for it.

'To my mind,' she begins, 'the term "universal

44

indult" is the first thing that calls for analysis. How universal are we talking? If we discover intelligent life on a distant galaxy, and it turns out they're Tims, does the Pope get to call the shots? What if they've got their own Pope? Do they have a Pope-off to decide it? They're both alpha primates, after all. Would it be bare-knuckle, or would it be like Gandalf versus Saruman using those papal croziers?'

They leave her alone after that.

*   *   *

'I can only apologise, Father,' Kane overhears Guthrie telling Blake as another gale of cackling laughter billows from amid the pounding dance music and the ever-swelling cacophony of teenage voices. 'They're a damp disgrace.'

Kane feels sorry for Dan Guthrie. The deputy head is wound tight enough at the best of times, but the strain on his blood pressure over the next few days could be catastrophic. He's the most sincere and well-intentioned man Kane has ever worked with, but with the burdensome side effect that he holds himself and everyone around him to the highest ideals, and consequently takes the most trivial things far, far too seriously.

'They're teenagers, Mr Guthrie,' Blake replies, an explanation that would be enough for anybody else.

'But behaving this way when they're supposed to be reflecting on the death of their fellow pupil? They're a damp disgrace, that's what they are. Unbelievable.'

Guthrie is unable to even use the word 'damned'

45

in front of the priest, low as it might rank on the sweary scale. This would be fine if it didn't look like it was costing him something each time. There were plenty of folk who never swore because they never felt the desire to express themselves thus, but Guthrie, the poor bastard, clearly wanted, *needed* to swear: every oath censored, every unworthy feeling suppressed, every thought unspoken seems to add to the torrent that is straining against the flood barrier.

Sorry as Kane feels for Guthrie, he feels sorrier for his old pal Con Blake, or *Father* Blake, as Guthrie still unwaveringly insists on calling him, despite his having been school chaplain for nearly three years. He must feel like somebody's maiden aunt whenever Guthrie is around, trying to shield him from—and apologise for—all of the uncouth and inappropriate (i.e. normal) behaviour of the St Peter's pupils.

Blake is conspicuously uncomfortable with the deputy head's unstinting deference, given the vast experience gap in terms of the years they have each put into their respective jobs. This discomfort is greatly exacerbated by the fact that Guthrie's deference comes into the same category as his not swearing. An anxiously self-conscious young prelate couldn't fail to disappoint the idealised expectations of such an unreconstructed trad-itionalist, but that wasn't going to stop Guthrie bowing and scraping nonetheless. As long as Blake wore that collar, he was untouchable.

Kane hears a retaliatory salvo from the boys at the back, upping the volume on the latest from some troupe of American self-harm fetishists resourcefully plundering the album collections gathering dust in their divorced parents' lofts. Funny how the same ideas keep coming around. Used to be each generation discovered the Beatles: maybe each generation will now also discover back-combing, mascara and The Mission. Fair play to them: the genre hasn't merely stood the test of time, it's even got Dan Guthrie to his feet. Bus-aisle moshing, however, is unlikely to feature high on his list of intentions.

*   *   *

Adnan senses the danger just a moment too late. He's trailing a few paces behind Radar, crossing a short bridge over a river of toxic slime. The cross-hair of his reticle fixes on his companion, giving him a stat readout on his Heads-Up Display: armour, health, weapon, location. On the other side of the bridge lies a wide, empty cavern, deep in the gloom of which he can see the glow of a blue keycard, sitting on a raised plinth.

Radar's charging around totally gung-ho since he got hold of that plasma weapon. Adnan is sticking with the shotgun, as Radar has hoovered up all the plasma cells. Unhindered and unopposed, he is making a beeline for the plinth, but moments before he reaches it, Adnan sees what Radar doesn't: an unhindered and unopposed route to their objective at the rear of a large, gloomy cavern.

'Radar, it's a trap!' he cries, by which time Radar has already bounded on to the plinth, and they are immediately beset on all sides by the biggest ambush of Stygian spawn Adnan has ever seen. There are Bull Demons, Pain Elementals,

47

Cacodemons, Mancubii, Hell Knights, Revenants and a veritable swarm of Lost Souls. Radar starts spamming plasma in a circular arc, haemorrhaging health points as fast as he's spending ammo. Adnan gets a few good blasts off with the shotgun, then strafes sideways in search of cover behind some boxes. It's only as he gets up close that he spots they're of the exploding variety. Schoolboy error. A fireball hurled by a lowly imp—oh, the ignominy—connects with the combustible crates and reduces him to chunky kibbles.

'Gibbed,' he reports.

Radar's demise isn't long in following, his defiant but suicidal stand finally ended by a disembodied-head-butt.

'That was mental,' Radar laughs. 'Ridiculous overkill. You said this was a custom map?'

They are playing a home-brew port of *Doom II* on their DS Lites, the game engine modded to run on the handheld machine and the net code updated to support wireless multiplayer. It is a museum piece of a game, about all the Nintendo's puny processing power can handle by way of first-person shooters, but there's a reason why everything that has come since has owed its dues to this original; the same reason he and Radar have been playing this for the past hour in preference to thirty-odd other games on their data cards: it's still the best.

'Custom, yeah,' Adnan confirms. 'Not part of any of the original games. My cousin Tariq made this map at least ten years ago, when he was a student. Folk always end up jumping the shark when it comes to creating their own maps. He claims this one *can* be successfully completed, but I don't

48

believe him.'

'I suppose the clue is in the map being titled *A Slight Case of Over-Bombing*,' Radar observes.

'Aye. Though you wouldn't get a student called Tariq typing the words 'over-bombing' into a computer these days unless he fancied forty-two days' detention without trial.'

'Tariq. He's the one that went on to be a physics hingmy.'

'Particle physicist.'

'That's it, aye. I take it he employs a wee bit more subtlety these days?'

'I'd like to think so, but it does worry me, playing this, to see how much he seems to enjoy seeing things blow up.'

'Fancy another crack at it?'

Adnan is about to ask 'why not?' when he senses a different kind of danger, but in this instance, he's just in time. It's the sudden clarity of Cameron's music that he latches on to: the interference of Deborah Thomson's mindless aural chewing-gum has suddenly ceased, and you generally don't get a wish like that granted without complications. He lifts his eyes from the miniature LCD screens and looks along the aisle. Still in gaming mode, he pictures a reticle and a HUD superimposed upon his vision, the stats readout corresponding to the subject in his imaginary cross-hairs, which change colour from green to red to denote a fix on the target that is stomping through the coach.

NAME: DAN GUTHRIE. WARRIOR CLASS: DEPUTY HEADMASTER. STATUS: ARSEHOLE. STRENGTH: MORAL FORTITUDE. WEAKNESS: WOUND TOO TIGHT.

Adnan envisions a danger level to the right of his

49

field of vision: a column of horizontal bars, the stack moving from yellow through orange and into red as it ascends.

Adnan elbows Radar by way of giving the edgy, but there's no means of inconspicuously warning anyone else. Worst caught out is Beansy, who is kneeling up on his seat with his back to the aisle, deliberately jutting his arse into the passage and wiggling it exaggeratedly in time to the music. Guthrie is standing right over him, looking like he is sorely regretting the passing of the years and the passing of the human rights legislation that have denied him the right to boot that arse as a moral imperative. Instead he looks at the luggage rack and locates Cam's iPod speakers, then, after a brief moment of bafflement in attempting to negotiate the interface, simply yanks out the jack.

It's impressive how a precipitate absence of sound can be as startling as a sudden loud noise. Bodies stiffen, heads turn, reveries are abruptly truncated. The words 'who the fuck . . .' are reflexively spat forth and just as reflexively silenced as the answer to this question becomes apparent. Somewhere in Adnan's peripheral vision he sees Fizzy hurriedly flicking a small white object past Marky's head and towards the grille above the window, before folding his arms in a singularly self-defeating gesture of innocence. Fortunately for him, Guthrie is concentrating his blazing eyeballs on Beansy at this point, in a sweeping arc of boiling disapproval that also takes in Deso's copy of *Maxim* as well as Adnan and Radar's gaming hardware.

'The whole bunch of you are a damp disgrace,' Guthrie shouts. If they were in a hall or a

50

classroom, there would be some serious reverb, but the engine, the road and the tightness of the space mute his bellows a little. Nonetheless, his harangue does silence the place, and makes those other sounds seem that bit more quiet and distant in the pause that follows. 'Have you forgotten what you're doing here?' he demands. 'Have you no respect? Can you not relegate your own trivial gratifications just for a while, and maybe turn your thoughts to something other than your shallow, shiftless selves?'

Guthrie is sweeping the beams again, all target eyes averted just before contact can be made. Everybody is doing the chastisement charade: kidding on they are chastened and ashamed in the face of this admonishment. Whatever gets him to drop it and fuck off back down the bus. Prick. Nobody's forgotten why they're here, which is why nobody is feeling genuinely ashamed or genuinely chastised. He's the fud that's lacking respect, because he's the one using Dunnsy's death as an excuse to read the riot act.

Guthrie takes a step further towards the rear, past Adnan's row, and a glance back reveals that, in fact, not everybody is doing the dance, nor averting their eyes. Sitting in the centre of the back row, flanked at a respectful distance of one empty seat either side by his two loyal and ever-present wingmen, is Big Kirk. He's staring directly at Guthrie, not so much with defiance as with a patronising scrutiny bordering on malicious amusement. Guthrie might have missed this, or might at least have had the option to pretend he missed it, were it not for the fact that Kirk has just brought a lit filter-tip cigarette to his lips and is

51

drawing deeply on it as he draws a bead on his foe; or maybe victim would be closer to the truth.

Kirk, it has to be said, is every bit as much of a prick as Guthrie, and to his fellow pupils—being unrestrained by human rights legislation—a far more dangerous one. Still, when one prick faces off against another, there's a certain satisfaction to be had in the anticipation that at least one of them will suffer as a result of the encounter, and if you're really lucky, both. In this instance, though, there is little prospect of mutually assured damage. This is an impossible moment for Guthrie, and Kirk knows it; knew it as he watched him make his angry way along the aisle; knew it as Guthrie performed his histrionics and meted out his tongue-lashing; knew it and relished it as he pulled his fag-bearing left hand from out of sight behind a seat and drew it to his mouth.

Kirk may be a St Peter's pupil, but he's no schoolboy. He was taller than all his peers and half the staff when he was thirteen, an advantage Adnan can never recall him wearing with lightness or grace. In the intervening years, as well as adding another few inches, he has filled out with muscle and even more attitude. He's not brawny—it's his mate Dazza who's got 'the guns'—but there's a taut, sinewy solidity to him that every guy in class has had the misfortune to perceive at some point, whether unavoidably in PE or as a consequence of failing to observe a respectfully wide berth in a corridor. Like just about everybody else, staff and pupils alike, Adnan was hoping he'd leave at the end of last year and maybe get a job clubbing seals or something. Unfortunately he had shown up again in August, having done disappointingly well

52

in his exams and come to two worryingly realistic understandings. The first was that if he had come this far without bothering his arse, then if he put in a bit of effort he could probably get some decent qualifications; and the second was that he could now take not only all of the pupils in a square go, but also all of the teachers too—perhaps even simultaneously.

Thus, as he draws slowly on that cigarette, it is understood by both parties—as well as all interested onlookers, of which there is now an enthralled host—that Guthrie's authority, as adult, teacher or even deputy head, only cuts ice if Kirk is playing the game.

In this one seemingly endless draw, he sucks the fag until it burns right down to the filter. Under the circumstances, his decision to exhale the smoke downwards from his nostrils rather than forwards from his lips seems almost non-confrontational.

'The driver could put all of us off, right here, right now,' Guthrie says, the measured tone of his voice serving only to convey how much anger he's trying to keep a lid on. There's also something deliberately neutral about it, almost an appeal to reason. Whether he meant to or not, he has all but acknowledged the reality of this power balance, and only in doing so will he have any chance of securing Kirk's cooperation.

'Wouldn't want that, sir,' Kirk says. Then he nips the fag against the heel of his boot and offers the dead stub to Guthrie on the palm of his hand.

Guthrie bats it away angrily. He turns again and takes a couple of paces back down the aisle, then stops and snatches the DS Lite from Adnan's grip,

Radar's too, before reaching up and pocketing Cam's iPod for good measure.

Yeah, that sure won you back all the face you just lost, dude. Big up Mr Guthrie, Deputy Dan, the G-Star. You da man.

Radar remains frozen, his hands still in place from where his DS had been untimely ripped, his face a study of catatonic incredulity.

'Can't believe that bastard stole our kit, Adnan, man.'

Adnan's eyes remain trained on the aisle, his imaginary HUD showing the danger level column recede into the yellow as Guthrie retreats towards the front. Father Blake moves into the cross-hair as he stands up to let Guthrie back into his seat.

WARRIOR CLASS: SCHOOL CHAPLAIN. **STATUS:** HALF DECENT. **STRENGTH:** OPEN-MINDED. **WEAKNESS:** DOUBT.

'I don't know what to do without my box,' Radar moans. 'I might need to read a fuckin' book or something. Are we nearly there yet?'

Adnan pans his imaginary reticle across the aisle to fix on the profiles of the two other teachers accompanying them on the retreat: first Mr Kane (**WARRIOR CLASS:** PHYSICS TEACHER. **STATUS:** HALF DECENT. **STRENGTH:** BRAINY AS FUCK. **WEAKNESS:** NON-BELIEVER AT A TIM SCHOOL); then Miss Ross (**WARRIOR CLASS:** ENGLISH TEACHER. **STATUS:** QUITE TIDY. **STRENGTH:** ALWAYS CALM. **WEAKNESS:** FATHER BLAKE).

'It's all a game, Radar,' Adnan says, smiling to himself. 'Boot it up in your head instead.'

*　　　*　　　*

54

Rocks is staring out of the window, waiting for Dazza to respond. You'd think it was fucking trigonometry or something.

Rocks didn't mind that Guthrie had cut off the music somewhere around Inveraray—it was shite anyway—but there was another couple of hours to go and the silence had started to get to him. That was why he decided to suggest a wee game.

He hadn't expected Kirk to join in, but he was beginning to wonder whether Dazza was blanking him as well. Wouldn't blame him, given that any conversation was going to have to take place across the space of three seats: two empty and one full of brooding self-indulgence.

'Okay, Rebecca Catherwood,' Dazza finally says.

God in Govan. Took him all that time and *that's* the best he comes up with?

Rocks glances down the bus at Rebecca, looking, as per, like she just stepped off the cover of *Red* or *Marie-Claire* (way too classy for the lads' mags, that lassie), and can't help but laugh.

'Fuck's sake, Dazza, that's not the game. *Anybody* would shag her. The idea is to find out how much of a munter you'd pump just to get your hole.'

'Oh, I get you now,' Dazza confirms, blood having apparently been extracted from stone. 'Right.'

'For instance,' Rocks begins, then looks down the bus for a good example. His eyes alight on wee Michelle, sitting close to the front, mousy and bookish. She wouldn't get a second look most of the time, but neither is she a pure hound, so for all of that, she's the perfect candidate. 'Michelle Sharp. Yes or no.'

55

Dazza takes a moment to cast an eye over her, his face screwing up in slight confusion, as though Rocks has either made a mistake or baffled him again.

'There's no way she's even had her tits felt, never mind given anybody their hole.'

'This isn't about plausibility,' he explains to Dazza. 'The name of the game isn't could ye. It's *would* ye.'

Dazza looks at Michelle again for a moment, then grins. 'Aye.'

'Yeah, me too,' Rocks agrees, giggling. 'Now: your turn.'

Dazza's face takes on a look of intense concentration, then a sneaky wee smile appears at the corners of his mouth.

'Julie Meiklejohn,' he says.

Rocks needs no time to pick her out among the rows. She is chubby and loud, laughing open-mouthed and inelegantly along with that shower of harpies she hangs about with. On the other hand, she's got big bouncy tits, she looks like she'd be game, and they say fat lassies are grateful.

Rocks and Dazza look at each other, glints forming in their eyes. They answer simultaneously: 'Aye.'

Both of them burst out laughing, knowing it's true.

Rocks snatches a glimpse at the Big Man to see whether he's letting any light through the curtains, but the miserable prick is still just staring ahead, got this blank, unreadable expression on his coupon, just one from his repertoire of scary faces. Well, fuck him. Going about in a mood the whole time isn't going to bring Dunnsy back.

'I'd shag a bathroom plughole if there was enough hairs around it,' Rocks declares.

'I'd shag the hole in the Rangers defence,' Dazza replies.

'I'd shag the hole in the ozone layer.'

'I'd shag a barber's floor.'

'I'd shag two caterpillars glued round a hole as long as they were hairy wans.'

'I'd shag Beth Ditto . . . on her bad week.'

'Too far.'

*   *   *

Adnan and Radar are earwigging, on the sniff for some embarrassing admission or merely uncircumspect sexual bravado that they can file away for discussion later. It's always therapeutic to be able to take the piss out of these people in their absence, especially if you've been under their boot-heels, as is an inevitability at some point over the next few days. Throughout this latter part of their discussion, Rocks and Dazza are talking loudly enough to suggest they don't mind being overheard. It can be a canny call to acknowledge a joke from these guys, especially when it is actually funny, not least because it clarifies that you were 'laughing with' rather than 'laughing at'. Adnan glances back and scores some eye contact from Daniel McIntyre, Dazza to his inner circle. This is a calculated risk. There's always a chance of eliciting a highly counterproductive 'What the fuck has it to do with you?' response, but it's more likely that he'll notch a couple of 'wee Adnan's all right' points.

Indeed, as it transpires, he moves a little more

into credit at one branch of the Bank of Bam, and this established, his eyes alight briefly upon the HQ: Kirk Burns.

WARRIOR CLASS: UNDISPUTED BEST FIGHTER. **STATUS:** FUCKING MENTAL. **STRENGTH:** HARD AS FUCK. **WEAKNESS:** NONE DOCUMENTED.

Big Kirk seems oblivious to the hilarity, his eyes trained on a fixed spot to the fore like there's a TV down there. His face is set like stone, a calculating contemplation etched so intently upon it that makes Adnan very relieved not to be its subject, but less comforted as he steals a look down the bus to confirm who is. His reticle gets a lock on Matt Wilson, sitting alone in a double seat one row behind the teachers, who are under the impression that they are protecting him.

WARRIOR CLASS: LONER. **STRENGTH:** INSCRUTABLE. **WEAKNESS:** KNOWN ASSOCIATE OF ROBERT BARKER. **STATUS:** ENDANGERED.

*   *   *

'Seriously,' Gillian insists. 'My big sister Tracy heard she gave Dazza a wank at Jason Mitchell's party after the Halloween disco.'

'Who, *Katherine*?' Deborah asks, with an incredulity borne of this sounding too good to be true, as well as an odd little fear that it might be. Katherine Gelaghtly is in sixth year, but she's resitting French so she's in Deborah's class for that. Her wee sister Bernadette is sitting next to Rosemary a few rows in front, with all that that entails, and Katherine has given off every impression of being just as uninterested in the opposite sex; not to mention just as ill-equipped to do anything about it if she was. Yet here was a credible rumour that she'd gone a lot further than Deborah had ever dared, which was almost as dismaying as the implication that she had been invited to one of Jason's parties—something Deborah had *definitely* never managed.

'Yeah, Katherine,' Gillian confirms with a delighted giggle.

'Heard from who, though?' Julie asks. 'If she heard it from a guy, then the truth is probably that she groped it through his jeans at the most.'

'Tracy says she told her to her face.'

'Mistake!' observes Yvonne.

'Wow,' says Julie. 'And you know what that means.'

'What?'

'Well, by the same token, if she admitted to a wank, it might even have been a blow-job.'

'How come nobody's heard about this from the guy's side?' Yvonne demands, sounding like she is also surprisingly eager to debunk it, and not in defence of Katherine's virtue either.

'Getting a wank off Katherine Gelaghtly maybe isn't something you'd want to boast about,' Julie suggests with a cackle.

'No, I don't think that's it,' Gillian responds. 'Our Tracy says your man Dazza is actually quite mature when it comes to his dealings with girls. Mature enough to know not to burn his boats by blabbing, anyway. I mean, it's not the same as if somebody was daft enough to give a wank to a clown like Beansy or Deso. They'd tell everybody.'

'Beansy would take an advert out in the *Evening Times*,' says Julie.

'Only if he couldn't raise the funds to hire one of

those airship efforts,' adds Gillian.

'How far do you think Bernadette's gone, then?' Yvonne asks. 'Maybe the God-squad bit is just a really sneaky camouflage for being a cock maniac.'

'Jesus, so how much of a slut would that make Rosemary?' asks Gillian.

They all crease up. Deborah laughs too, but she can see it getting daft now, and she wants to head that off. It's more of a thrill when it's a realistic appraisal, especially when it serves as a conduit for rumour, substantiated or not. She stretches in her seat, hands up in the air, and rolls her head around her neck, using it as an excuse to look about and remind herself of the field. She spots her top candidate right away—kicking herself that she needed a reminder, in fact—but completes the stretch for cover.

'What about Marianne?' she suggests. 'How far do you think she's gone?'

'Marianne?' asks Julie. 'The English Goth lassie?'

'Yeah, the new girl,' Deborah confirms, though Julie not being sure who Deborah is talking about doesn't bode well for the emergence of any goss.

'I bet she's gone all the way,' Julie opines, confounding Deborah's pessimism.

'Why?'

'I saw her in the changing rooms at Gleniston baths. Lacy black knickers, quite see-through. Landing strip as well. That's not stuff you go in for unless you're expecting somebody else to see.'

'Or touch,' Gillian suggests.

'Or tongue,' adds Julie.

And Deborah feels it again: that mix of vicarious prurience tinged with jealousy. She is glad to hear

60

Marianne disparaged but at the same time wishes Julie had witnessed her wearing huge granny-pants, off-white from a thousand wash cycles, on top of a bush like a burst couch. As it is, she is left with this discomfiting feeling of being somehow smaller, being somehow left behind.

Oh, make up your minds, ladies, thinks Marianne, having overheard every giddily overexcited word. Why is it that every girl who's had more sexual experience than you is a slut, and every girl who's had less is a square? Chalk another one up to Catholic education. Nah— probably the same across all denominations, just as long as they're British.

Marianne had readily identified Deborah Thomson and Gillian Cole as projecting-insecure-bitch material within a week or two of starting at her new school. It was hard to say, therefore, whether she had opted to generally disregard them before or after they decided that their clique should ostracise her. What she does know for sure is that *her* ignoring *them* has bothered them a lot more than them ignoring her. The crucial difference was in the practice: her ignoring them has consisted of, well, ignoring them; whereas their blanking her seems to be rather a theatrical undertaking. And nothing says you're ignoring somebody quite like going out of your way to tell them about it.

'Okay, my turn,' says Gillian. 'Caitlin.'

Must be calibrating the sexual-experience barometer, Marianne reckons. Had a few hits towards the racier end and now they need to balance up by zeroing in on a bookish L7.

'You kidding?' Yvonne asks. 'She's never got off

with anybody.'

'How far do you think she would go, though?' asks Deborah.

'Good-night kiss and no tongues,' Yvonne says with a glib confidence. 'Doesn't matter. There's no way any of the boys would be interested anyway.'

*   *   *

Rocks allows himself a second lingering look at wee Caitlin, seeing as Dazza seems happy taking his time about his own assessment. He then turns to look across Kirk and waits expectantly for Dazza's verdict. They both nod at the same time, laughing again.

'Doesnae score high on the plausibility scale, though,' Rocks concedes.

'Ah, see, you never know, though. Sometimes it's the quiet ones that surprise you. But purely hypothetically? Fuck aye, I would. Probably a tidy wee bod underneath there, no' like some of the chip-shop casualties you see. If it was on offer, I'd be in about her like a dug with a bucket of mince.'

'Seriously?' Rocks says, hoping it doesn't sound like he might be seeking advance approval in the unlikely event that he and Caitlin were to hit it off.

'Well, I'm not saying she's top of my wish-list, but I thought we were just playing what-if. I'll tell you this, though: give it a year or two, and out of all the girls in our year, Caitlin could well be one of the ones you'd most want to be going out with. Just because she doesnae say much doesnae mean she's got nothing to say. Lassie like that, folk never notice what's there.'

Rocks thinks of Dazza getting off with Katherine

Gelaghtly at that party; it was rumoured that he even shagged her that night. It was only when Rocks saw her in Geography the next week that he realised he'd been in her class for months without noticing her. The Katherine that showed up every day in school and the Katherine who had turned up after the Halloween disco were two very different girls. No wonder Dazza has taken a while to get his head round the idea of this game, and why he's taking so long to answer each time. Dazza's instruments of appraisal are far more sensitively tuned, and his plausibility gauge is set very differently to Rocks'.

Rocks still knows how he can really test him, though.

'Okay, I've got one: Rosemary.'

They both glance down the aisle, and for once, Dazza's verdict is instant.

'You're taking the piss now,' he says.

*   *   *

Caitlin watches Rosemary climb to her feet and grip the seat back for balance as she takes a few paces down the aisle. She's got that glower about her, a look of determined disapproval and simmering indignation that anyone meeting her for the first time would be alarmed to learn is actually her neutral expression. She can do happy, but it's a forced happy, a dutiful, affected, 'Jesus says I *must* be happy' mugging that's actually more intimidating than her frown. She has a crucifix round her neck, and umpteen Christian badges on her jacket: Pro-Life, SPUC, Silver Ring, True Love Waits and, of course, that bloody fish. The

63

Silver Ring and True Love Waits buttons make Caitlin smile every time. They really ought to be accompanied by a more honest third badge, saying: 'Chance would be a fine thing'; or maybe simply: 'As if'. It's hard to imagine anyone *less* interested in sex.

Caitlin has heard it remarked of some girls that they were thirteen going on thirty. She would have said Rosemary was seventeen going on forty-five if it wasn't that Rosemary had already been forty-five for a good few years before she ever turned seventeen.

Rosemary makes her way forward a couple of rows, then leans over to talk to Deputy Dan.

'Mr Guthrie, sir, would it be all right if I got out my guitar?'

Fuck no, thinks Kane, before turning to share an appalled look with Heather, who puts a fist in her mouth and bites her knuckles.

'That's an excellent idea, Rosemary,' Guthrie replies. 'Singing some hymns would be most appropriate,' he adds, with a look to Blake for encouragement; or is it just to check the priest isn't wincing too?

'Whoa, whoa, whoa, steady the buffs,' Kane says quietly to Heather. 'Can we not have a vote on this?'

Guthrie gets to his feet, offering to help Rosemary take her guitar down from an overhead rack. Kane seizes this moment to send a what-the-fuck? look across to Blake, who holds up his palms in an apologetic gesture of helplessness.

'Keep it light, though,' Guthrie advises. 'Something to raise our spirits.'

Rosemary unzips the PVC carry case and

removes her six-string, placing one foot on an armrest and supporting the guitar on her raised knee. Then she starts to play, at which point there really is an outpouring of religious expression.

'Oh, Glory be.'

'For Christ's sake.'

'God almighty.'

'Mother of God.'

'Christ on crutches.'

'Jesus fuck.'

Rosemary strums a few bars, then launches full-throated into a hymn.

> 'It's me, it's me, it's me oh Lord,
> Standing in the need of prayer.
> Not my brother or my sister, but it's me oh
>   Lord,
> Standing in the need of prayer.'

Bernadette joins in with gusto, as does Maria a split second later. Caught in the epicentre of this beamer-quake, Caitlin wants the ground to open up. She feels her cheeks burning, wants to leap to her feet and yell: 'I am not with these people.' She stares at the floor with her head down, too mortified to make eye contact with another human being right now.

> 'EVERYBODY, it's me, it's me, it's me oh
>   Lord,
> Standing in the need of prayer . . .'

'Standing in the need of singing lessons, more like,' says Deso.

'Do you think if there was a God, he'd want to

listen to that pish?' Adnan asks.

'Christ, why could it not have been *her* that Barker stabbed?' Beansy moans.

'Fuck it,' says Radar, climbing over Adnan.

'Where you going?'

'I can take being without my Nintendo, but this violates my fuckin' human rights.'

Radar starts moving down the bus, looking out the window rather than at Rosemary in order to allay suspicion. She wouldn't notice anyway. She's so into her hymn that she even has her eyes closed.

Adnan pictures him as only a faint outline: Stealth mode power-up engaged.

Radar whips the guitar from Rosemary's hands and immediately turns around to block her, keeping his body between her and the instrument. With little room to manoeuvre, it's like trying to keep a beachball off someone in a phone box, so he offers it towards the nearest person, which turns out to be Caitlin. She can see the resignation in his face the moment he makes the usual wrong assumption about her being with the God-squadders, by which time the guitar is in her grasp.

'Thank you, Caitlin,' says Rosemary, reaching out expectantly and also making the same wrong assumption.

Caitlin turns round and instead offers it to the first outstretched hand. It's that Goth girl, Marianne, who Caitlin finds a bit scary, but she smiles conspiratorially as she takes possession of the guitar, and it feels like something is shared in a moment of mutual complicity.

Marianne, in turn, passes it on to Cameron. He steps into the aisle and stands up with it, striking a pose. Behind him, Adnan can see Rosemary still

66

trying to wrestle her way past Radar, with Guthrie getting to his feet once more at their backs. He's wondering if there's any way of getting one of these windows open so that Cam can lob the thing right out. As it stands, it's only a matter of time before it's restored to Rosemary's keeping, amid another loud reminder of how they're all 'a damp disgrace'.

Rosemary gets a foot around Radar's shin and draws upon the good Lord's strength to trip him to the ground, administering the sacrament of a sensible shoe up his arse as she stomps over his sprawled figure. Cameron gets an eyeful of this and suddenly decides the guitar is a hot potato. Fortunately for Cam, Deso must have remembered his asbestos gloves, because he gratefully takes hold of the neck and pulls the box across the seat back. Standing up with one foot on his seat and the fret-board gripped in his left hand, he lets rip with a finger-flashing classical intro of a virtuosity and accomplishment so unexpected that even Rosemary pauses in her tracks.

Deso clocks Adnan's look of astonishment.

'It's what you play when you don't have Nintendo,' he says, then breaks into a strum, nodding to emphasise the beat until people realise this is a cue to clap. Beansy cottons on first, then Cam, then everybody joins in, which seems to further restrain Rosemary, who just waits with her arms folded to see and hear what will emerge.

'I want my hole, I want my hole,' Deso sings, and is immediately joined, with ecstatic enthusiasm, by everyone to the rear of the bus. Everyone except Rosemary, obviously.

'I want my hole-i-days.
To see the cunt,
To see the cunt . . .'

Guthrie comes lolloping up the aisle desperately, trampling poor Radar in his panicked urgency to stem this sudden onslaught of musically accompanied damp disgrace.

'To see the cunt-a-ree.
Fuck you!
Fuck you . . .'

Rosemary all but falls on top of an appalled Liam Donnelly as she leans back to let Guthrie charge past. Liam loses his normally unflappable studied poise as he flattens himself against the window away from Rosemary, looking like he's afraid uncool is contagious.

'For curiositee,
I want my hole,
I want my hole . . .'

Guthrie has always looked like a heart attack waiting to happen, and Adnan strongly suspects the day could be upon them. Deputy Dan has forever been inclined to take daft weanish behaviour too seriously, but he's outdoing himself today by way of disproportionate response. They're singing a stupid song that's been a teacher-baiting staple of bus trips since primary school, one that most staff have always had the good sense to ignore. Who knows what's going through that increasingly ruddy head of his; must

68

be something about underlining his authority ahead of reaching what he suspects will constitute an uncomfortably informal environment. And talk about closing the stable door after the horse has bolted. They've already belted out the 'cunt' and 'fuck you' lines—what more is he hoping to prevent? A shaming rendition of 'The front of the bus, they cannae sing', perhaps?

He's got Deso in his sights now, though. Adnan images it: danger level in the red, a proximity detector pulsing concentrically, ETA running down in milliseconds. It's reading around 0.657 when Marky suddenly leaps up from his seat, having made a slightly disquieting discovery.

'Fuck, my arm's on fire.'

Fizzy has to duck as Marky starts flailing his burning sleeve in an attempt to beat out the flames.

'Jesus, Mary and Joseph,' Guthrie says with a gasp, spinning on his heel and grabbing hold of Marky in one unbroken motion. He takes him down like it's a wrestling move, getting him on to the floor and smothering the flames by lying with his chest across Marky's arm. There's a huddle around them, everybody leaning in to see. A little smoke emerges from somewhere around Guthrie's neck as he lifts himself up to check that the fire has died.

'Are you all right?' he asks Marky.

Marky just lies there looking a little stunned, and it's anybody's guess whether this is more down to the shock of the conflagration or the force and rapidity with which Guthrie resolved the situation.

'Markus, are you all right?'

Marky nods, holding up his jacket sleeve. It's all

black and melty, the outer layer collapsed and shrivelled. He stares at it in an entranced daze, then his eyes widen as his features suddenly become sharply alert.

'Fuck!' he yells.

'It's okay, stay calm,' Guthrie says. 'Just take a moment.'

'Naw, look, for fuck's sake, the fire,' Marky insists, a panic across his face as he extends his arm.

'It's okay, it's out now,' Guthrie tells him, taking hold of his wrist and restraining him from his attempts to get up. 'We'll get this off and make sure you're not injured.'

'I'm not talking about my arm. The fuckin' *bus* is on fire!'

At which point everyone looks along the line of where Marky's outstretched arm was actually *pointing*, and sees that the curtains next to Fizzy are indeed now well ablaze.

'Where's the fire extinguisher?' Guthrie shouts.

Father Blake has reached it even as Guthrie speaks. He wrenches the canister from its strapping on the wall and bounds down the aisle, already spraying water towards the curtains before he reaches the fire.

It's the sudden leap into action from Blake that belatedly alerts the coach driver to precisely what is being wrought upon his vehicle. A glance in his aisle-view mirror presents a sight he cannot quite believe, which is why neither can he help but physically turn to confirm with the naked eye that, yes, the St Peter's kids have indeed set his bus on fire.

His eyes are only off the road for a second, but

it's long enough for the vehicle to start drifting just as it is coming into a bend. He overcompensates on the wheel as he returns to facing the road, causing the bus to fishtail as the sideways momentum is instantly brought into conflict with the forward drive.

Back in the rear section, the lurch has a whiplash effect, pulling everyone first one way then the opposite. It tosses them all towards the right-hand side, a section of which is now wet and smouldering.

Marianne, having been leaning into the aisle, is sent sprawling back across her double seat, giving her an extreme close-up view out of the window. Due to the sudden uncontrolled change in direction, the coach's forward momentum is pulling against the efforts of the engine and the traction of the tyres to drag it sideways towards the grey metal crash barrier. This previously substantial-looking steel restraint suddenly appears to consist of two flimsy-looking waist-high rails, about to face off against the mass and energy of a three-metre-high coach, and beyond this barrier she can see a five-hundred-foot, high-gradient slope down to the shores of a loch.

There's a percussive hiss of brakes and a scream from the engine as the driver drops the gears and ups the revs. The side of the bus scrapes the barrier with a foil-meets-fillings shriek and a shower of sparks, then from close to the front on the other side there sounds the most hideously dull and solid bang, the sound of the bus colliding very hard with something that did not give.

The bus comes to a sudden halt a fraction of a second later, the resultant jolt banging a few heads on seat backs and thus partially obscuring the sound and vibration of a second exterior impact. Sounds like it came from above.

There's a moment of complete silence, not even the sound of the engine, which has either stalled in the final stop or been killed by the driver. Nobody says a thing. It's like they all need a second or two before they can re-engage with anything or anyone.

Then an adult voice asks if everyone is okay. It sounds to Deso like it's somewhere in the distance; can't tell if it's Guthrie or Blake or even Kane. He hears a few responses, each gradually getting closer, like they're being faded up as his surroundings come back into focus. He puts a hand to his forehead. It took a bang but it doesn't feel sore. He looks up, sees everyone slowly reanimating: those sent sprawling picking themselves up, others just doing the same as him: a quick once-over to confirm nothing's amiss.

Then Deso sees Radar, still prostrate in the aisle, covered in tiny pieces of glass. He's lifting himself up from the floor, glass tinkling to the ground around him with every movement, and as he raises his head he becomes aware of blood running down his face. He puts a hand to it then looks dazed and uncomprehendingly at his darkly smeared fingers.

He pats his hair, dislodging further fragments of glass, and finds more blood pooled up there.

'Jesus . . . Radar,' Beansy says, frightened.

Radar kneels on the aisle floor and continues to pat his scalp. 'Not mine,' he says, with a very gentle shake of his head.

That's when he glances up, as does Julie, who screams.

72

The overhead skylight panel has been shattered by the impact of a deer's head, which is now jutting through the aperture, staring into the coach with its dead-black sewn-button eyes.

'Euh, that's bowfin',' suggests Cameron.

The deer's head is lolling at an awkward angle, still connected by an evidently broken neck to the rest of the animal. Father Blake takes a step underneath it, helping Radar get to his feet. It's still a hypnotic sight in its staggering incongruity, something of a bad Photoshop job about it. Deso is trying to imagine the caption when the head suddenly jerks and he just about shites himself, in common with probably everyone else. Another rivulet of blood is disgorged from somewhere down the beast's throat and runs out of its mouth on to Father Blake's head, after which the deer is still once again.

'Just a death rattle,' Blake says, a tremble of laughter in his voice indicating his fright and relief.

There's silence again, another frozen moment in which, this time, it feels like everybody's too scared to re-engage in case they precipitate some new shock. Then Beansy comes to the rescue.

'Venison tonight, folks?'

II

The light is beginning to fade as Sendak takes a walk through the main building, running off his mental checklist item by item. The bedrooms are clean and prepared, folded linen and fresh towels piled up on each bunk in a neat and compact stack next to the pillows. In every corridor, the floor tiles are freshly waxed and have been polished until they are partially reflective, giving a satisfying squeak as they come into contact with the rubber tread of his boots. The shower cubicles are all operational: no leaks, no drips, no busted safety thermostats on the twist-grip controls. Hot water is issuing on demand from every faucet. The heads are spotless, spare paper rolls in every stall. The tampon and sanitary-towel vending machines are fully supplied, and those new high-speed hand-driers working just as the rep said they would, which is convenient, as it saves him tracking the guy down and killing him in his sleep like Sendak said *he* would.

He makes a second circuit of the dormitory blocks, ensuring all of the fire doors in the link corridors are closed but swinging freely, and that none of the fluorescent tubes are blown or flickering. He replaced all of the batteries in the smoke detectors last month, and tested the fire alarm two days ago.

He checks the conference rooms and the library, his route then taking him through the reception area, where he makes sure all redundant notices have been removed from the pinboard and the water fountains are running free. Dollars to doughnuts they'll be clogged with chewing gum within twenty-four hours, but the best you can do is deal with the shit you *can* control. Sendak then proceeds to the games hall, where he goes into the store cupboard and tests the circuit-breakers, then into the main dining room, finishing up at the kitchen, where Mrs McKenzie is slicing mushrooms on an island worktop. Sendak looks at the containers full of chopped onions, peppers and tomatoes, ranged in front of her chopping board, and allows himself a hidden smile of satisfaction at her unfailing work-rate. Her husband dropped her off but twenty minutes ago. She is the human Cuisinart. She'd have dinner for forty prepared before Mr McKenzie made it back to their home in the village of Tornabriech, just twenty miles away.

'I don't know how that man of yours survives without you when you come here for three days at a time,' Sendak tells her.

Mrs McKenzie's chopping action doesn't slow or skip a stroke as she replies.

'Donnie?' she says with a chuckle. 'I'm only worried he gets done for speeding in his haste to get home. Three nights of takeaways and seventy-two hours' uncontested possession of the TV remote. It's when I'm around that he struggles.'

'Now, I *know* that ain't true. Man cannot live on Sky Sports and Indian takeout alone.'

'Has anyone done a controlled trial? I'm sure Donnie would sign up. When are our guests due to arrive, incidentally?'

'Any time soon. What you got planned for them?'

'I thought we'd dice them and make them into pies, as usual. If you handle the slaughter, I'll do the actual boning and preparing the meat.'

'Okay, but I think you should have a back-up plan. The authorities are gonna start to get suspicious if they keep sending us schoolkids and all they ever get back is pie.'

'Ach, Sergeant, you're never done worrying. But you do have a point, so I was thinking veggie lasagne instead.'

'Sounds good to me.'

Sendak makes his way outside through the dining room's external doors and begins a circuit of the outbuildings, taking an anticlockwise route around the compound. Shit, still calling it that. He used to think he would have to come up with a different way of thinking about the place, shake off the military terminology he couldn't help applying. That was before he accepted that after fifteen years a soldier, he'd be thinking in military terminology until his grave, so he may as well make it work for him. Hence he got comfortable letting everybody call him Sarge, and hence his playing in character a little sometimes for the paying guests.

He goes first to the barn, where he lets his horses, Loki and Mercury, eat from his hands for a few minutes, before tidying away some spilled bales and securing the ladder to the storage gallery. Then he takes the long route, along the gravel path, past the sports field and up the hill to the generator shed, where he makes sure it's fuelled and ready to kick in should the mains power drop out for any reason. Next, he makes his way back to the side of the main building, where he reads the dials on the twin oil tanks and ascertains that the fuel reserves stand at roughly what he estimated, confirming that there are no leaks, and pleasingly that there has been no further overburning since he made those recent adjustments to the heating systems.

Finally, he clears a few broken branches from the 'courtyard', as he likes to think of it—it's really just a clearing, hemmed in on three sides by trees and on the fourth by the front of the main building—

which gets used as a car park by visitors, or a turning circle for buses and fuel trucks. Then he trots up the wooden steps on to one of the pine decks that flank the entrance, where he leans against the handrail and watches the sun dip towards the trees atop Ben Trochart.

Everything is in order, as he knew it would be. Nothing overlooked, as it never is. Doesn't stop him checking, though; nothing ever will. Staying fastidiously in command of the shit you can control is never a failsafe against the shit you can't, and nor, in his experience, is it any consolation later on, but what choice does he have? In Sendak's world, the most he can do and the least he can do are exactly the same.

The low rays scatter red light, giving a rich tint to the colours of the forest and the hillside for a short while before they will all be turned to charcoals and blacks. He looks at his watch, which he has been relieved to observe has continued to work normally throughout the day.

It's only just gone four. It'll be fully dark by five. There's no cloud, no wind either, and a crispness to the air. Gonna be cold tonight, cold and clear, and he likes that. Not cold like back home in the Chicago winter, scary-dangerous cold: just cold, the kind of cold that makes the lights from the building take on a welcome glow, makes the food taste better, the beds feel snugger. Yeah. Nights like this, weekends like this: this is what he loves about this place; this is why he stayed.

Somewhere in the distance he hears the grumble of an engine and the squeak of air-brakes. He smiles. Nobody ever appreciates how much that hairpin bend sign ain't kidding. That'll be the bus, then.

*   *   *

Their destination suddenly appears through a break in the trees beyond another stomach-lurching bend. It's one of those places you simply cannot see until you are upon it, and as Kane has seen only one road sign to indicate its proximity, it makes for a somewhat unheralded, if still very welcome, end to the journey. Not having a clue how much of the drive remained had made the last ten minutes feel like an hour. The kids had calmed to a numbed and dozy near-silence. Their early high spirits would have died a natural death anyway, but the fire, airborne ex-deer and close-skirting-of-a-five-hundred-foot-plummet-to-certain-death combo had fairly put their collective gas at peep.

The driver had, with a credible display of conviction, expressed his intention to stop the coach and abandon the journey at Inns of Cluach, the nearest village after what young Adnan had described as 'the Volvo-to-venison interface'. Surveying the considerable interior damage, including the loss of the skylight through which a large dead animal was now jammed, he threatened to declare the vehicle unfit for purpose, though Kane could only imagine what manner of vehicle the driver *did* consider fit for the purpose of transporting this shower right then.

There was a very tense little interlude, with the coach parked in the village's disused petrol station and the kids disgorged into a snaking gaggle precariously close to the roadside, throughout which the continuation of their whole trip remained very much in the balance. The scales were tipped back in their favour by a combination of factors.

One was the intervention of Guthrie, who appealed to the guy's sense of duty and obligation in his own inimitable fashion: ie piously sincere to the point of aggression. He explained, quietly and at length, the tragic circumstances underlying why the St Peter's kids were on this trip, and in a gambit that evidenced either remarkable audacity or a complete lack of self-awareness, beseeched the driver to therefore be that bit more forgiving of their behaviour than he would normally consider it reasonable to ask.

The other factor was the intervention of Kirk Burns in climbing unbidden on to the roof and hauling down the dead deer, at a stroke removing the aspect of the vehicle's condition that the driver was least looking forward to addressing. Kane wouldn't claim that this was of itself decisive, but it certainly made it easier for the driver to do the right thing.

They had to leave poor Prancer at the side of the disused forecourt. Given the driver's very evident squeamishness, Kane thought it wise not to relay the irrepressibly insensitive Beansy's less-than-half-joking suggestion that they 'bung it in with the luggage and eat the fucker when we get to Fort Trochart'.

His mate Deso had then, in Kane's opinion, gone one better.

'Fuck that,' he argued. 'Stick its heid on the engine grille, then write in its blood up the side of the bus: "St Peter's Gleniston—Don't fuckin' mess".'

*   *   *

The coach comes to a halt in a wide clearing before a pine-fronted, one-storey modern construction, a fibreglass signpost at the head of a short path identifying it as the Fort Trochart Outbound Facility. The sight of big double-glazed panes inset within expanses of interlocking nutty brown wood piques feelings of rich relief and pleasant surprise in Heather Ross. It's not just school parties that come here, she remembers. When it's not full of urban weans being acquainted first-hand with what mountains and rivers look like, it probably plays host to City types learning how to pretend they don't hate each other for the sake of corporate morale, and those people don't like their back-to-nature experiences too authentically Spartan.

She had been braced for faded seventies functionary brutalism, envisaging flakingly aged Formica fittings, off-white NHS-style bed-sheets and a sour smell off the shower curtain. Instead, this place has something of the Scandinavian woodland idyll about it, though she guesses it might be pushing it to expect outdoor hot tubs and a fridge full of gravadlax. A moment's fantasy, picturing herself lolling in a wooden tun beneath a glorious tumult of bubbles as steam escapes into the cold clear air of a pine-scented glade, is brutally punctured by the image of Beansy and Marky sploshing in either side of her, making their own flatulent contributions to the froth, and trying to see her tits through her bathing costume.

80

Never lose sight of what you're doing here, she reminds herself—not even for a second.

The coach's doors open with a hiss, which sounds like the pressure release they're all feeling from being stuck inside it so long. Kane gets out of the double seat and steps aside to let her be the first off the bus. Guthrie, meanwhile, steps into the aisle and starts barking out instructions.

'I want you all to wait for the driver to empty your bags from the luggage hold, and then once you've retrieved your belongings, I want you to form an orderly line *outside* the premises.'

Heather climbs down the stairs and feels a restorative drop in temperature. The air is still and cold and smells quite deliciously of pine. After several hours of diesel fumes, over-applied body spray and recycled farts, it's so refreshing it's almost like she's drinking it. She takes a couple of big, deep lungfuls, watching the wisps of her breath linger in the failing light before evaporating. Then she walks around the side of the vehicle and faces the building.

There's a man standing on a raised area of decking, short and black, elbows rested on a wooden balustrade, casting an evaluative gaze towards the coach. He stands up straight and begins walking as soon as he sees her. He's wearing a short-sleeved polo shirt though it must be about two degrees, and despite the casualness of his attire, something about him quietly and un-pretentiously states 'military'. She has to revise her impression as he approaches, because the nearer he gets, the taller he appears. He's not huge, maybe about five-ten, but the proportionate effect of his stocky build made him appear shorter from a distance. There is a thin scar snaking from in front of his ear around to the back of his neck, less obvious on his skin than where it carves a passage through his shaven hairline.

'I'm Sendak,' he says, extending a firm and taut brown hand.

'Heather. Heather Ross.'

'Welcome to Fort Trochart. You guys had an interesting trip?'

Heather glances back at the coach. She can't see the top of it here on the ground, but is guessing he had a different view from up on the decking. She also guesses he doesn't miss much.

'A fire, a minor crash and a woodland fauna fatality. Welcome to St Peter's.'

*   *   *

Guthrie is standing in the centre of the reception area, holding up a sheet of A4 paper.

'Now, just everybody hold your horses. I've drawn up a room allocation list, so I want you all to wait until you hear who you're rooming with, then do not proceed until everyone in your group is—'

As soon as they hear this, the kids charge purposefully past him towards where Sendak just indicated the bedrooms to be located, wielding bags and rucksacks to buffet each other out of the way. Guthrie is like King Canute, being swamped by the waves.

'Listen, come back this minute,' he demands, with a conspicuously diminishing faith in the chances of this happening.

Heather sends a roll-eyes amused look towards

Blake, seeking him as a confederate. Blake acknowledges it with a bashful smile, but feels uncomfortably exposed in doing so. He's reluctant to be seen to undermine Guthrie, and tends to be far more obedient and deferential towards him than the kids or his staff have ever been. The deputy head just invests so much respect and authority in Blake—neither of which he feels he is due—that he feels obliged to repay it in kind; it's the least he can do by way of acknowledgment and apology for not being the kind of priest Guthrie would like him to be. What's really putting him on the spot, though, is that neither does he want to rebuff Heather, especially not by coming across as boring Father No-Nonsense.

If it had been Kane, he could have pretended not to see, or even batted it back as another instance of his old friend trying to get him into trouble. Kane knows he's not Father No-Nonsense; in fact, it's what else Kane knows about him that has them going fifteen rounds every so often. Heather is different, though. He's only known her since he became school chaplain, and in that time hasn't had many opportunities to let her find out what he's really like beneath the dog collar and beyond the altar. Why he should care so much about this is, of course, the source of a whole other kind of anxiety; one he doesn't like to think about, but one he has of late spent an increasing amount of time not thinking about.

Kane, who is among the last to get inside with his bag, observes Guthrie's futile entreaties and places a gentle hand on his shoulder.

'You'd be easier herding cats, Dan,' he says breezily. 'Just leave them to it. Fight the fights you

83

can win.'

'I've allocated these groups with some considerable thought, Stewart,' Guthrie argues. 'Best to keep certain individuals apart.'

'Aye. That'll work,' Kane replies with a chuckle.

'You won't be laughing if the only bed left for yourself is in a room with young Master Connor.'

Kane catches sight of 'Master Connor' amid the throng bustling through the reception area. His first name is Stephen, but even the staff—Guthrie excepted—have been calling him Deso since about second year. He and Philip 'Fizzy' O'Dowd are burping loudly in each other's faces as they proceed, cans of Irn-Bru and Vimto having supplied the ammunition.

Kane promptly grabs the list from Guthrie's hand.

'Come on, everybody, you heard Mr Guthrie. Hold your horses, there's an allocation plan.'

Blake smiles, knowing this is pure theatre from Kane. He glances to Heather again, reckoning this constitutes safer ground for sharing a joke, but it seems she didn't get it. She's looking askance towards the ongoing scramble down the corridor, clearly wondering what trials the sleeping arrangements may have in store.

'Don't sweat it,' says Sendak with a grin. He's leaning against a wall, sculpted arms folded against his equally sculpted chest, his back flat to the upright to make room and let the last of the stampede pass. Most of the kids have squeezed themselves into the corridor, only a few stragglers bunched up behind the bottleneck in reception. 'There's separate accommodation for the adults. Individual rooms, higher spec. Our consolation for no longer being so blessed with youth.'

'Is it in a remote part of the complex?' Heather asks hopefully.

'Indeed, at a greater distance than most nocturnal noise can travel.'

'I'm already feeling like we're in very good hands, Mr . . . sorry, I didn't catch your surname.'

'Sendak *is* my surname. For what it's worth, my first name is Max, but that's by the by.'

'Everybody calls you Sendak?'

'No, but you guys can if you like. Everybody else calls me Sarge. Come on, I'll show you to your rooms.'

*   *   *

Caitlin is one of the first girls to reach the bedrooms, not through being fleet of foot but rather sharp of eye sufficient to notice the small sign at the junction of a link corridor directing her to 'Female Accommodation'. Just about everyone ahead of her had simply barrelled through (or been helplessly driven by the Gadarene rush) towards what they would soon learn was in fact only the Male Accommodation end of the block.

As she rounds the corner, she can hear shrieking, laughing and arguing, slightly muted by being behind a set of heavy fire doors that denote the only barrier between the two sections. Spirits are high, but let no one fail to understand that what they are currently about is a serious business; and who bags the best rooms is considerably less important than who ends up sharing with whom.

Only those perceived as having been directly affected by the incident were offered places on the

85

trip: that meant those who had actually witnessed it and, of those who didn't, those who were close to the parties involved. Out of Caitlin's close friends, only Claire had been in the social area that day, but she had gone down with appendicitis on Wednesday and gave up her place to someone else. A lot of people were in a similar situation, isolated from the security of their normal social circle. It would be wisest to room with a group of girls none of whom were particularly close, as they'd give each other a bit of space; while the scenario to avoid was to end up playing gooseberry to a clique.

One of the first rooms she sees is a two-bedded affair. As she draws nearer the door and is able to see further inside, she observes that Samantha Coulter has been sharp of eye *and* fleet of foot. Caitlin looks away before eye contact can be made, so that she doesn't subject herself to the awkwardness or embarrassment of Samantha even thinking that she might have designs on the other berth in that room. They both know that the second bed is earmarked for no mere mortal. Try steerage, down the hall.

She sees the vanguard of the wayward gaggle pouring through the fire doors into the female block, and quickly skips inside a four-bedded room across the corridor. She unburdens herself of her rucksack, placing it on the bed nearest the window, and stands by, hoping for the best, bracing against the worst. A short few seconds later, Bernadette sticks her head around the door and, upon conducting a quick bed-count, hastily ushers Rosemary and Maria in to join her.

Oh God, no. No, no, no, no, no. She got here first, she had the whole deck to play with but she's

86

ended up bust.

It could have been worse, she tells herself. She could have found herself the designated whipping-dweeb in a room otherwise occupied by the likes of Deborah, Gillian, Yvonne, Julie and Theresa. So yeah, chin up, it really could have been worse.

Rosemary places her guitar case down on her bed alongside her holdall, from which she proceeds to remove a plastic two-litre bottle of sparkling mineral water. With the bag unzipped, Caitlin can't help but see inside, where her eye is drawn to a large-folio paperback volume entitled *Fifty Hymns for the Guitar*.

All right, now it *is* worse.

*   *   *

Deborah has found herself tagging along at the coo's tail with Michelle Sharp, hurrying their way through the building with a horrible, dawning sensation of having missed the boat. It's not a total catastrophe yet, but it could be, as it looks like everybody else has had a head start on getting the rooms sorted out, and now she could end up sharing with Michelle and God knows who else instead of her pals. Bloody hell. She's only just got over the fright of thinking her bag had somehow been left behind in Gleniston. She distinctly remembered leaving it with all the others alongside the coach in the St Peter's car park, but when they all got emptied out again in the clearing at Fort Trochart, it was nowhere to be found. Michelle was in the same predicament. By the time the last of the luggage had been lifted, the pair of them were left there empty-handed, with the

87

driver already having closed up the hold and buggered off somewhere.

They found him having a fly fag round the side of the building, which he put out with extremely bad grace before trudging back to the coach. Both of their bags were discovered to have slid in transit, and become lodged behind a wheel-arch bulkhead on the far side of the hold.

God, what a waste if she ends up with Michelle. Nothing against the lassie, but she wouldn't say boo to a goose so she's hardly going to be the life and soul, staying up late, sloshing back the swally and turning folk's hair white with her mental stories.

But oh, thank Christ. She sees Gillian up ahead, through a wire-meshed safety pane in the fire doors, Julie at her back. They're both turning to their left, her right, so she knows which way to make for.

She feels herself walk that bit faster, but she doesn't want to make it look like she's literally running away from Michelle, so she restrains herself. It's all fine, no rush. Gillian will keep her a place.

Seconds later, the sight that greets Deborah goes from dismaying to totally pathetic in the space of about two seconds. There's four beds, all taken. She clocks the situation, understands it's an 'if you're not fast, you're last' number: the hand she was dealt when her bag decided it fancied a wee wander around the luggage hold. It's a disappointment, a punch in the gut, in fact, but it's the others' reaction that's worse. Nobody says *anything*. It's not like she's due an apology or nothing, but this makes it all the more awkward.

There's this pitiful silence, everybody just standing with their glaikit expressions, not knowing what to say, all tensed up and kind of guilty, like they're afraid she'll start crying or like that way when you've just been talking about somebody and she walks in.

Actually, maybe not everybody's quite so glaikit: is that a hint of—fucking better *not* be—a smirk on Julie's fat coupon? Is as well. She's loving this, the fucking cow.

'First come, first served,' Deborah says. Got to acknowledge the practicalities and make out it's no big thing, because there's a weird vibe, like it's somehow turning *into* a big thing, and a big thing that's putting the four of them in one camp and her alone in the other.

'Doesn't matter where you're sleeping, the carry-on will still be in here, the five of us,' says Gillian. It's meant to be reassuring, but it actually makes Deborah's hackles rise. She feels like she's being talked down to, a charity case. She doesn't understand why, but she suddenly feels like she hates Gillian right now. She also feels a lump in her throat, which is pathetic, and something she utterly can't let develop. If anyone notices her voice tremble, never mind shed a tear, it's a disaster. This is so weird. Where's this all coming from?

She manages a smile and swallows before speaking. 'Bloody right,' she says. 'I chipped in for that carry-out. I'll find somewhere to dump my stuff and I'll see yous all back here in a wee minute.'

'Aye, okay,' says Gillian.

'See you in a bit,' Theresa goes.

And it would have been fine, but then Julie weighs in.

'I saw a bed free in Marianne's room.'

That's all she says. She doesn't add anything, doesn't lay on any emphasis, but there's something about it that's definitely meant as damage, maybe just the fact of underlining to everybody where Deborah is going to end up.

She feels pure acid welling inside, a no-holds retort, but stops herself saying it; stops herself losing it. If she says something, she's just further underlining that she's the sad-case here, papped out the club and stuck with Marianne. Besides, if she has a go at Julie, she's as good as having a go at all of them, because once it's over, it's Julie who's going to be on the same side of the door as the other three.

'I'll phone if I need rescued from being a human sacrifice,' she says.

'Aye, okay,' says Gillian.

'No lezzin' it up with the vampire, but,' goes Yvonne.

'We'll be checking your neck for bite marks in the morning.'

'If it's a lezzie vampire, it's no' her neck you'll need to check,' goes Julie.

Deborah withdraws from the room quickly but not, she hopes, conspicuously so, turning away so that they can't see her face is burning. The tips of her ears feel hot, which only happens when she's got a pure beamer or is totally raging. On this occasion, it's both. Who were they calling a fucking lezzie? She must think more about sex than any of them, than all of them put together. And as for Julie, Deborah might not have done it yet, but at least she was in with a chance. That fat hump was never getting a shag. Fat ugly boot was the one that *looked* like a lesbian. Aye, maybe that was it. They did say the folk who'd something to hide were the first to be making accusations. Though even if Julie *was* a fat ugly lesbian, she still wasn't getting a ride, not even off of another fat ugly lesbian.

'It's shite, but, innit?' says Yvonne.

'Aye,' Gillian agrees, but she's relieved that Deborah is gone. It was weird: she felt a bit guilty, but at the same time resented feeling that way, and wished Deborah would just fuck off and not stand there making everything awkward.

'Is she really gaunny be stuck with Marianne?' Yvonne asks. 'Or is that a wind-up?'

'Straight up,' Julie replies, with a look that is about ninety per cent appalled and ten per cent delighted.

'It was the only room left with any beds free,' Gillian confirms.

'No surprise, I suppose,' says Theresa.

'Need to watch Deborah doesn't get, you know, infected with the Goth virus,' Yvonne says.

'If she comes out in the morning dressed in fishnets and her hair dyed jet black,' adds Theresa, 'we need to stage an intervention before she starts to self-harm.'

'Aye,' Gillian says, joining in. 'Anybody hears her humming a My Chemical Romance song, that's it, she doesnae get back in this room. We have to stop it spreading.'

They're all pure gutting themselves now, and Gillian doesn't feel guilty. None of them do. Every one of them knows it could have been them and is grateful it wasn't, because every one of them also knows it's devil-take-the-hindmost, no quarter asked or given. No fun being in unless somebody's out.

* * *

Kirk is taking his time, ambling down the corridor in no hurry whatsoever, when through an open doorway he sees a sight that stops him in his tracks. He's a dozen or so yards behind the scrambling and jostling morass. The squeaks of umpteen sets of trainers on the floor tiles is matched in pitch and volume by as many overexcited voices, making claims, shouting instructions. Daft fucking weans, so they are. Wasting their efforts too, some of them. Dazza's near as bad. Kirk can tell he wanted a head start in finding their digs, and now his face is tripping him because Kirk delayed them and they ended up at the back of the crowd. Like that matters, fuck.

Kirk had a wee bit of business to attend to outside, and he wanted to make sure all potentially prying eyes were safely out the way, indoors in the reception area, while he got on with it. Dazza's nose was further put out of joint because Kirk wouldn't say what it was—just told him and Rocks to stay put and keep the edgy while he nipped round the side of the building and found a good spot to plank the wee zip-locked bag. And now he's even more pissed off because Kirk's stopped to smell the roses a wee bit. Well, he can just pull his knickers back out the crack of his arse. Kirk's got a bit of business here as well, a bit of business with the fucker who's standing inside this room

92

with his back to the doorway: Matt weirdo cunt Wilson.

Aye. Well seeing he's on his tod in there. Nobody wants anything to do with him, but what's annoying is that that's actually how the fucking oddity likes it.

Kirk drops his shoulder bag to the floor, so that Matt turns round and sees him. He looks away again immediately, which is how Kirk knows he's been noticed. That's as much eye contact as you'd ever get from the boy anyway: just wee glances to absorb the minimum amount of information about the social aspect of his environment. That's what it said in the paper, anyway, in a piece he read about a guy that made him think of Matt. Asperger's Syndrome, the guy's condition was called. Kirk doesn't know if that's what Matt's got, but he certainly recognised a few of the symptoms. Big fancy name for what used to just be called being an ignorant cunt. 'Good with numbers, not with people,' that's what he overheard one of the teachers say about Matt. So, what, is he meant to be fucking Rain Man or something? Kirk's not buying it. There's something calculating and cold about the bastard. He's not some harmless doo-lally numpty like Davie O'Hara: that boy's soft in the head and soft in the heart. Everybody likes Davie, and Kirk had handed out a couple of panellings to folk that tried to rip the pish out of him. But Matt is a different story. Unlike Davie, he isn't weird thon way that he looks like his mammy dresses him. There's something precise about his clothing and appearance that's worse than those preening fuds Liam and Jason.

Kirk had never really noticed him much until

93

maybe a year or so back. He went to a different primary school from Kirk and he wasn't in any of his classes until third year. You *wouldn't* notice him, that's the thing. More like you become gradually aware of him. It's creepy, anyone being so quiet, blending into the walls. Kirk doesn't like mouthy bastards either, but there's a happy medium, and this freaky cock comes across like he's above talking to anybody—which made it all the more galling who he *did* fucking talk to.

Naw. Matt's a far different story to wee daft Davie. This yin knows what he's all about. That's why Kirk isnae buying all the shite about him being just caught in the middle of what happened to Dunnsy. He's a sly bastard as well as a smart one, and Kirk's fucking well on to him now.

He stands with his arms folded, just staring, watching to see what Matt will do. He's got his back to the door still, looking down at his bed where his rucksack is parked, but he's not taking anything out of it. His head is down but Kirk guesses he's not looking at the bag or the bed. He'll be staring at the floor, looking for a reflection or a shadow that will tell him whether Kirk has moved away. Shiting it. Good. Get used to the feeling, ya weirdo prick.

Then a voice intrudes into the moment.

'You finding yourselves rooms all right there, boys?'

It's Mr Kane, subtly making everybody aware that he knows the score.

'Getting there, sir,' says Dazza, giving Kirk a look that's asking for a skelp in the dish, still fucking sour-faced that Kirk had held them back.

Kirk lifts his bag from the floor. 'Cannae find the

bellhop,' he says. 'I'll be writing a strongly worded letter to the management.'

Mr Kane gives him back a thin smile, not letting him walk away thinking they can both kid on he never saw nothing there. Fuck, why did it have to be Mr Kane? Guthrie, bring it on—he'd mix it with that purple-heided wannabe sergeant-major bastard all day, and the more authority he tried to wield, the less seriously Kirk took him. But Mr Kane was different gravy, the one guy he genuinely didn't want to get on the wrong side of.

Kirk walks away, resisting the temptation to have a look back; at Mr Kane *or* Matt Wilson. No need to incur unnecessary complications. Nothing's changed: that fucker's time is coming. All the better, in fact, if he knows it, and has a wee while to dwell on that. Aye, sleep well not knowing when or where you're getting yours, ya weirdo cunt.

*   *   *

Beansy drops his guts again about two seconds after dropping his bag. It's a quiet one, and he says nothing, just waits for them all to notice. Delayed response is always the funniest, and this one's a stoater. Deso's halfway through saying something about Rosemary's guitar when it stops him in his tracks.

'Fuck's sake, Beansy, that's out of fuckin' order. You dae that once more and I'm gettin' the fuckin' fire extinguisher, all right?'

Marky's next to get a warm noseful of the bouquet.

'That smelly bastard's like one of those animals that has to mark oot its territory.'

95

'If it's territory he wants, he can have a fuckin' room tae himself if he keeps that up,' says Fizzy, but he's laughing as he says it. They all are, with a cumulative effect on Beansy, who can feel himself starting to lose the place. There's tears coming out now and everything.

'Oh fuck, this is serious,' Marky observes. 'He's managed to make his *own* eyes water.'

Beansy lets himself fall back on to the bed, the laughter tightening his guts and making him cough with it now. It's not so much the carry-on in here, as this coming on the back of what just happened along the hall, which gets funnier every time he pictures the moment again. He and Deso clocked that Liam and Jase had nabbed this big four-bedded room to themselves, so the pair of them wandered in to claim the spare berths just to see the disgusted and disbelieving looks on their coupons.

'Yeah, right,' Liam said, once he had got over the initial horror and slipped his fanny-pad back in or whatever.

'Whit?' Deso asked, face like butter wouldnae, actually starting to take stuff out his bag, the mental bastard.

'No fucking way,' Jason gives it. 'Find somewhere else. Now.'

'There's nowhere else,' Deso told him. 'It's a full hoose. If you wanted a room to yourselves so's you've got peace to poof each other, you should have taken thon two-bed effort up the hall next to the swing doors.'

'Handy for the lassies' toilets as well,' Beansy added. 'Case you need spare tampons or that.'

'The male section isn't full,' Liam replied, arms

96

folded so he looks even more like a lassie in the cream puff. 'There's more girls than guys on this trip, or can you retards not count?'

'That why you two have overspilled into the boys' corridor.'

Jase just sighed at this point and looked at the ceiling, like this was just boring the lacy pink panties off him now. The game was a bogey, as he'd finally sussed that they were only doing it to take the rise.

'Come on,' Deso urged, packing his stuff back into his bag and lifting it again.

'Aye,' Beansy agreed, then turned to Liam on his way out the door. 'As if me and Deso actually wanted to share with you two up-yourselves boring bastards anyway. We'd get better conversation oot the lassies—and less of it about clothes and make-up.'

Liam closed the door behind them with a highly satisfying slam, which is when the giggles started to set in.

Lying on his bed, Beansy's still coughing and wiping his eyes when big Kirk fills the door frame, Rocks and Dazza at his back. He's got that game face on, serious as fuck, which kills the laughter. Beansy recognises it as the put-on game face, as opposed to the genuinely-on-the-brink-of-bleaching-some-cunt game face. This is potentially more dangerous, because in the case of the latter, you're probably all right as long as you're not the one who's pissed him off. When it's put on, it's because he's about to lay down the law, and any challenge to his authority must be met with full force, or else every fucker would be taking liberties.

'Right,' Kirk says. 'Get yourselves tae fuck.'

'Aw, come on, gie's a break, big man,' Deso appeals. 'There's four of us, and we were here first,' he adds, looking to Rocks and Dazza, who can occasionally be appealed to when they know the big man is out of order. Dazza is glancing to the ceiling, looking fed up. He's not exactly ready to die for the guy right now, but doesn't look like he can be arsed arguing either.

Kirk responds by simply staring at Deso, nary a word spoken. Deso stares back, not feeling defiant, simply unable to restrain himself from conveying his anger at this moment. Kirk is a cunt for doing this: not just for muscling them out, but for bringing the threat of violence into their midst after what happened to Dunnsy.

He remembers a fight on the beach on a school trip to Girvan in second year: him and Beansy, a square go. Cannae mind what it was about, just shite that had been building up for weeks. Shook hands a wee bit later, mates again for the trip home: back when a fight ended in a burst nose and a squiggly walk from getting a boot in the sack. Violence is something else now, not wee boys incompetently trying to panel each other.

Suddenly Deso's back at school, looking at the spreading, lapping pool of blood on the grey tiles in front of the lockers. It disappears again. Feels like he didn't even have to shake the image himself; like something else kicked in and blocked it. The flash was so vivid one second, then the next, he couldn't picture it if he tried.

Deso sighs and turns around, muttering as he begins repacking his bag.

There are several resigned 'fuck's sake's emitted

around the room as big Kirk and the boys step proprietorially inside. Beansy meanwhile makes his protest felt by means of his own specialised silent form of emission.

'Aw, in the name of fuck,' blurts Rocks, closing his eyes like it's stinging them. 'It's bowfing in here.'

Kirk tuts, shaking his head. It's only a fart, they all know, and the smell will be gone in a minute— maybe ten minutes; fuck it, half an hour—but it's provided the excuse Dazza and Rocks need to back out of this.

Dazza taps Kirk on the shoulder. 'C'mon. Let's leave these clatty bastards to gas themselves,' he says, offering Kirk an out that won't look like a climbdown.

'Good shout,' Kirk says, accepting. He knows everybody is under no illusions regarding the fact that he would prevail if he chose to, but it's not worth it, especially not with that niff to contend with. 'Don't know how these fannies are gaunny be able to sleep in here without firefighters' breathing apparatus,' he adds, walking out.

There's silence for a few seconds, everybody bursting to laugh but calling canny until the big man has moved a respectful distance away, hopefully out of earshot.

Marky breaks first, falling on to his bed and shaking it as he buries his face in his pillow to stifle the sound.

'I never thought I'd say this . . .' Fizzy begins, but Beansy shushes him, finger over lips.

'Wait for it,' he urges. 'Listen.'

They hear Kirk's reprised order from down the hall: 'Right. Get yourselves tae fuck.'

99

Jason's response echoes after it, muffled by distance and intimidation: 'Fair's fair. We were here first.' His voice sounds as pathetic as his reasoning.

The third voice is Dazza's, low, harsh and unequivocal:

'There's two of you fuds in a four-bed room. Don't give us your shite.'

Beansy steps into the centre of the room and takes a bow.

'Who da man?' he asks. 'Who da man?'

'You da man,' they all reply.

He high-fives Marky and Fizzy, but extends Deso a hand to shake, reducing it to a single index finger as Deso reaches to grip. Deso knows what's coming, but figures Beansy has earned it. He grabs the offered finger and pulls.

*   *   *

Blake can hear shrieks of laughter and the ring of enthusiastically exchanged abuse. He's not sure if it's bouncing its way through the network of corridors or traversing the internal courtyard separating the kids' dormitory block from where the teachers have been allocated their single rooms. Sendak may have been wrong, he reflects, pulling his clothes from the zip-toothed maw of his rucksack: their host said the kids would be at a greater distance than most nocturnal noise can travel, but he'd never heard the St Peter's lot in high spirits. There was that 'nocturnal' qualification, though. They had just got off a coach after a very long journey and were like a newly shaken bottle of ginger right now. At night-time,

100

they'd keep it a little lower, if only to avoid giving Guthrie reason to patrol.

He hopes so anyway, if he isn't to be kept awake half the night. It isn't so much the noise he fears as the distracting awareness of once again being on the outside of someone else's good time. It seems daft, but while Kane and Heather were expressing their relief at being told they had their own rooms in a separate block, Blake actually felt disappointed, though not surprised. He understands why, as teachers, they need their privacy and a respectful degree of isolation from their charges, but for a decade, Blake has known little *but* privacy and isolation. The fact that he's considering the grass might be greener amidst fart gags, supermarket cider and juvenile moonlit reverie suggests he may have known it too well.

Five years in study and training, seven years a priest. Wasn't he supposed to be over this by now? Or was it an ongoing test of strength, commitment and character? Rome to Royston, South America to South Lanarkshire: he had always been around so many people, all day, every day. He was immersed in their lives, in their works, in their troubles, their aspirations, their pain, their losses, in their celebrations and their joys.

He had once been a shy person, skilled at secretly keeping his distance, able to communicate without engaging, without risking himself. To do what he did as a priest, though, he *had* to engage, had to open himself and share all of those other people's emotions, heedless of whether he might get hurt. It felt like he was giving each of them a little part of himself, and there were times when he would be exhausted but amazed that he could still find something more to give. Those, in fact, were the best days. So why, at the end of even those days, *especially* at the end of those days, upon being faced with a small, neat bedroom, did he feel the way he does now: that the room seems empty? That there is something missing, and missing from himself?

He takes out his little green toilet bag and checks inside to make sure his can of shaving foam hasn't burst open and covered everything. It only ever happened the once, but after tasting it on his toothbrush for a fortnight, he's always afraid of unzipping the top and finding himself facing a repeat. All is well, despite the minor collision endured by the bus. He goes to stick it in the bathroom, and reminds himself that a further consolation for not being an excited teenager this evening is that he won't need to go creeping down any darkened corridors if he wakes up in the night and needs to pee.

Blake opens the bathroom door, and walks inside, which is when he discovers that it's not the bathroom door. He has come through what turns out to be an adjoining door into the next room, in the centre of which Heather is in the process of changing her clothes. Her bra and midriff are exposed, but her face is obscured by the rolled-up polo-neck she is pulling on, which is why she didn't see the door opening.

She hasn't heard either, which provides a moment during which Blake could just possibly withdraw again unnoticed. He doesn't seize it, though. He's afraid it would look even worse to be caught like a peeping Tom, grabbing an eyeful and then scuttling away.

'Oh, Jesus, sorry,' he says, by way of announcing himself and owning up just before she gets clear of the polo-neck and sees him.

She doesn't start, just laughs a little with embarrassment, though this embarrassment seems more to do with how the polo-neck has left her hair plastered to the side of her face than at being caught underdressed.

'Thought this was my bathroom door,' he explains.

'Well, now we both know,' Heather replies.

Having done the honest thing and let himself be caught red-handed, Blake retreats and closes the door gently but firmly. He stares at it, his heart thumping so loud he's afraid she'll hear it, already feeling the conflict and confusion get revved up as her words keep looping in his head. Christ. Had she just screamed, had she just tutted with annoyance, had she just muttered 'For God's sake' in rightful indignation, he'd have gotten a light sentence: maybe ten minutes beating himself up over an accidental moment of mutual mortification. Instead she had batted him something sufficiently ambiguous as to condemn him to spending at least the next hour dissecting her reaction, at the end of which he would be none the wiser.

Then he'd have to say mass, with her watching.

III

A brace of static pings cause his monitor to degauss, the second shuddering the image like a boulder dropped into a millpond just as the ripples of the first have finally cleared. Those were bigger than normal, and he knows what the bigger fields mean: each one heralding yet another new arrival through the Dodgson anomaly.

Merrick pulls himself back from the computer, and it's only as he disengages from the trance-like state induced by so long immersed in the data that he realises his head is splitting with pain. He hears a guttural, rumbling cry from outside the lab, across the corridor in the controlled area they've started referring to as TLV. On the other side of the room, Avedon seems oblivious to the sound, remaining intent on the microscope's imaging monitor. This tells Merrick that he has no idea how long the cries have been sounding out, exacerbating his headache, as he was in the same detached state up until a few moments ago. Now, it's like someone scraping the inside of his skull. He can do that these days: phase out the sound of the animal noises like he's learned to zone out the permanent hum of the machine. It's a purely analgesic process: the damage is still being done, and it hurts like crazy when he withdraws, but zoning out the noise does mean he can work through it.

He's been working through a lot of things of late.

Avedon steps away from the microscope and makes towards the supply cupboards that take up the full length of one wall, the other three lined with sinks, workbenches, machinery and a fume cabinet.

'Can you throw me some Brufen out of there?' Merrick asks him. He needs something for his head, though the water he swallows the tablets with will be just as important. The bottle beside his PC is empty, and he recalls there was barely a mouthful in it when he sat down. This prompts him to look at his watch. He's been at the computer for nearly four hours. His clothes are damp from sweat, so he must be pretty dehydrated. Who would have thought you could spend so long in the north of Scotland without ever feeling cold?

Avedon chucks him a blister pack of pills. He pops two into his palm and goes to a sink, where he pours some tap water into a glass beaker.

Avedon remains at the supply cupboards, evidently perplexed.

'Is there a problem?' Merrick enquires.

'We're out of oleum.'

Merrick feels the headache become that bit sharper as an involuntary tension seizes him. He's clenching his fist around the pills with one hand, gripping the beaker too tight with the other. He feels threatened. Avedon is getting at him.

Then he realises that Avedon is merely looking for oleum. It's his own conscience that's pushing his buttons.

Oleum. Hazardous material. He can picture the decal on the jar: the little hand, the test tube, the descending droplets, the cartoonish wavy lines indicating a harsh, corrosive reaction with organic material.

Warning. Avoid contact with skin.

Danger.

The test tube. The droplets. Little wavy lines. Looked like the hand could just be giving off a smell, a 2D depiction of perfume. And in truth there had been a smell. Wavy lines too: of smoke, of gases. Screaming. Screaming he *couldn't* zone out. Screaming he'd be hearing forever.

If the road to Hell is paved with good intentions, then what did it say that he had been tempted down that path by holy water?

What he witnessed in the test chamber had spooked him on a number of levels, so much so that it took him days just to make sense of his memories. He felt like he had to sift through the data collected by his own senses, disentangling and interpreting it like any set of lab results until a coherent picture could be assembled. He was still so reeling from the fear, shock and astonishment that he needed time to get his analytical head back on.

Holy water had burned the creature's skin: real Hammer horror movie stuff, and it had happened before his very eyes. The fact that the skin belonged to a horned demon bolted to the table did make this particular sub-phenomenon seem minor to the point of incidental, but the utter enormity of what they were dealing with was too huge to compute, so he had, almost by scientific instinct, homed in on one detail that he *could* try to make sense of.

What if, he pondered, it was water itself that caused the reaction? As far as he could ascertain (access to the holding area remaining highly restricted, with an information seal almost as tight

106

as those on the mag-locked doors), the specimens were being given water to drink. That suggested there couldn't be a complete aversion, but internal tissue could react differently from external. He knew from painful experience that chopped chillies, for example, could be swallowed without damage while the fingers that carried them to the mouth could suffer a chemical burn from the contact, to say nothing of what happened if you rubbed your eyes or worse, went for a piss.

He took a skin sample from one of the expired specimens, then tested it against a number of substances: tap water, holy water, an acid and an alkali, these last two of corresponding pH. The results were even more perplexing than he had anticipated. Both the acid and the alkali inflicted visible damage to the skin, while neither water sample—sacred or profane—produced a reaction. Not only did this suggest that simple water wasn't responsible for the damage he'd witnessed in the chamber, but it indicated that holy water only reacted with *living* tissue. The ramifications of this were dizzying, but he knew he couldn't draw any conclusions without comparison tests on a live subject.

The term TLV—The Little Vatican—had initially been coined by Steinmeyer out of ill-tempered flippancy, but it was more accurate than he could have anticipated. If the Vatican was indeed a state, then its outpost here was like an embassy, accorded full diplomatic status. The US Government might hold the note on this facility, and it might be sited in Scotland, but when you stepped through those doors on the opposite side of the central corridor, you were as good as on

Roman soil. Cardinal Tullian had even consecrated the ground, carrying out some ritual at what had to be a record altitude below sea level. Sacred ground didn't have to be the high ground, it seemed, but whether that went for the moral distinction as well as the physical was a matter for debate. Certainly, nobody would be calling any of The Little Vatican's house guests to supply endorsements.

Gaining access to a live subject proved a prolonged and delicate process of negotiation, the key to which was keeping his frustrations in check. It might seem surreal to Merrick that the facility's scientific personnel were having to go cap-in-hand to a bunch of priests in order to gain access to specimens procured through their own experiments, but not only was he quickly learning to redefine his concept of reality on a daily basis, he had also learned to accept which realities around here were genuinely unalterable. Chief among those was the way the military operated. Their purpose was, first and foremost, security. Therefore, as they saw it, the moment the first of those creatures was brought forth into this world was the moment their role here ceased to be the running of an R&D facility and transformed into a threat-containment operation. Priority number one, at that point, was garnering intel on what the full scale and nature of that threat might be.

To that end, as well as consulting the science personnel, they had called in the base chaplain, who immediately declared it to be way above his pay-grade, in respect of *either* of his employers. Neither the chaplain nor the scientists were in the position to offer any kind of informed assessment, but in the padre's case, he was at least able, as he put it, to 'point them in the direction of a man who could'. With the world of science incapable of similarly recommending someone with comparably superior credentials, it was the American Cardinal Terrence Tullian who swiftly became the US Army's senior adviser on what they considered to be potentially the greatest threat they might ever face.

To be fair to the military brass, it wasn't a difficult choice. For their part, the science personnel offered, at best, frank admissions of ignorance and, at worst, in the case of Steinmeyer, histrionic displays of outrage. By contrast, Tullian offered information, experience and cold, measured certainty, which had been in far scarcer supply than the military could tolerate. Unlike everyone else, he was able to assure them that he knew precisely what he was dealing with, which was always going to be music to their ears, but he played an even sweeter tune when he offered to bring in his own personnel and effectively take charge of the threat. This gave the military a role they were far more comfortable with: they were content to let someone else accept responsibility, as long as they knew they had ultimate control. They were used to peacekeeping, used to securing borders and maintaining stability while a reliable, autonomous infrastructure was established beneath them. Tullian gave them that, and in exchange they gave him complete control of the specimens—at least while they were alive, after which they became official (if ultimately disavowable) property of the US Government.

Tullian insisted that only his people were

permitted to be in direct contact with the specimens, and was anxious to restrict circumstances that would bring non-Vatican personnel into close proximity. This was to prevent what he described as 'spiritual contamination'. Merrick had encountered some unusual, uncommon and improbable Health and Safety stipulations in his time, but this was the first time he had seen the threat of possession cited as an occupational hazard.

The fact that it actually seemed a *credible* threat nonetheless proved no deterrent to Merrick's burning experimental quest. After much patience, greater delicacy and a degree of deference closer to grovelling than diplomacy, as well as the submissions, each in triplicate, of four different drafts of a formal experimental protocol, he eventually procured permission to carry out his live-subject study.

When he stepped through the door of what Steinmeyer was always bitterly reminding everyone used to be the Alpha Labs, he was left under no doubt that he was now on Vatican property. The fixtures and fittings were largely the same as in the Beta Labs across the corridor—even the initial layout was symmetrical—but from the logos on the keycards for the electro-locked doors to even the screen savers on their computers, the iconography served to stress that this was all under a very different—and some might say higher— jurisdiction. Tullian and his staff were using this part of their allocated area as office space, confirming what a priest once told Merrick at a friend's wedding: that in day-to-day operation, the Catholic Church was more bureaucracy than theocracy. However, it wasn't only the former Alpha Labs that the Vatican staff controlled; it was what lay beyond them, above them and beneath them that represented the true extent of the Cardinal's delegated power.

Merrick was welcomed into the LV offices by two priests who were to be his escorts throughout the test, as agreed on the final draft of his experimental protocol. Monsignor Kharkov and Father Tanner, as their photo-IDs announced them, furnished him with one of their yellow suits and left him to put it on while they verified the agreed contents of his inventory. He declined the garb, a certain scientific chauvinism compelling him to point out that all Geiger readings taken around the creatures had been negative and the radiation suit was therefore unnecessary. That was when they reminded him that radiation was not what the suit was intended to shield him from.

They did not suit up themselves, he noted.

'We will be remaining outside of the contamination radius,' they explained.

It occurred to him to ask how they measured such things: a possession compass? He held his tongue, though. He didn't want them taking the huff and cancelling the experiment; and frankly he had little right to be irreverent, when so far these guys had demonstrated a far deeper understanding of the phenomena they were all dealing with than anybody across the hall in the Beta Labs had managed.

They led him beyond the office complex, through a mag-locked door, into a wide, steel-walled corridor. He was inside the secure section, taking the same journey as the specimens, and would enter the chamber precisely as they had: from the Alpha side, accompanied by his own Vatican escort. At this point he was glad they weren't wearing their yellow suits to complete the effect, not to mention the steel tethering shafts.

He passed a code-locked security door on his right, the top of its formidable outer frame bearing the legend: 'Containment Pods—Extreme Caution'. Stealing a glimpse through the bulletproof glass observation panel, he saw a wide aisle flanked on either side by a row of steel grids, each one securing the front of a small cell.

It was a long walk to that second mag-locked door, longer still as he understood that its distance corresponded to the length of the chamber housing the pods. It used to be a testing range for experimental weapons.

The original containment area had been the brig, on the opposite side of the corridor, consisting of a mere four cells. Merrick couldn't get hard data on how many live specimens were currently in containment, or how many had come through the Dodgson anomaly in total. Steinmeyer estimated the latter figure to be upwards of a hundred.

On one wall of the corridor there was a small arsenal of Decoherence Rifles visible inside an electronically locked, keypad-operated cabinet. Kind of like 'in case of emergency break glass', except the glass was unbreakable and you needed code-clearance to get hold of the hardware. Merrick wondered whether the priests had it; he sure as shit knew the scientists didn't.

When the countdown ended and Merrick stepped inside the chamber, he found that the experiment was already set up in accordance with

112

the agreed protocol. Tullian was waiting a few yards from the subject, which was clasped and bolted to the cross-braced table. It was a smaller specimen, attended correspondingly by only two yellow-suited priests and a detail of a mere four soldiers. The subject was shorter and less muscular than Merrick had seen previously. Its horns were only budding, though there was the same snarling defiance and crackling aggression about its visage.

Merrick placed his materials on top of an aluminium trolley while Kharkov and Tanner set up the recording equipment. Just the two cameras this time: one standard digital video and one infrared, both stationed a few feet in front of the trolley and trained carefully on the subject.

Merrick then approached the table slowly and connected the first of his sensors. The subject scrutinised him intently, trying to twist its neck to keep an eye trained on him wherever he stepped. Up close, the creature looked rather scrawny, its skin taut against wiry sinews in a manner that reminded him uncomfortably of concentration-camp inmates.

Merrick glanced towards his escort, catching Father Tanner's attention.

'You're giving them water to drink?'

Tanner nodded solemnly.

'And that's causing no burning effects, right?'

Another nod.

'Okay. So what are you giving them to eat?'

Tanner immediately broke his gaze from Merrick and directed it towards Tullian. Merrick didn't catch what Tanner saw in response from the Cardinal, but deduced that it wasn't permission to speak. Instead he clasped his hands and bowed his head, almost as though he had been switched off.

After a silence long enough for Merrick to accept that he would receive no answer, Tullian spoke, calmly but gravely, in that odd accent of his, one indicative of many years spent speaking in foreign tongues and talking of higher things.

'They feed on souls, Dr Merrick. Thus there is no nourishment we could *or would wish to* offer them.'

'So they're not fed?' he responded, trying to ensure that his tone conveyed only incredulity and enquiry rather than outrage or accusation. 'It's been months for some of them.'

Tullian closed his eyes solemnly for a moment, and when he opened them, he wore the burdened expression of one charged with conveying news of bereavement.

'They also feed on each other,' he said.

'I see.'

'No, you don't, and you ought to give thanks for that. Dr Merrick, I have little doubt you have already seen sights enough in this place to haunt your dreams forever. I appreciate that the jurisdictional inequities necessary to my involvement here must have chafed harshly with your fraternity, but trust me, your end of the deal is not without its privileges, and not having witnessed that particular sight ought to be prized among them.'

Merrick glanced back at the creature, suddenly paying closer attention to the rows of pointed teeth bared across its snarling mouth.

'I'll take your word for it,' he said.

Merrick approached the creature bearing the first test phial, which contained plain water. The liquid rippled inside the small vessel, agitated by the tremors of his hand. He was unsteady with trepidation, shivering in the chamber's humid, blasting heat, more apprehensive on this occasion than the first time he encountered one of these things. Was this because he knew what he was doing was wrong? He couldn't afford to think about that. He had to proceed. There would be no second chances at this, and he *had* to know.

The first splash upon the demon's skin was of a liquid not listed in the protocol: his own sweat. It was running in rivulets from his forehead into his eyes, and as he wiped them with his free hand, a few droplets whiplashed clear of his fingers and landed on the creature's abdomen.

There were no observable effects.

Taking a breath and steeling himself, he then extended his arm over the table and poured a small volume of water on to the demon's thigh. Observing no dermatological reaction, he quickly looked at the creature's face for a response. He saw only anxious curiosity amid that constant simmering aggression.

As part of the agreed protocol, he then handed the phial to Tullian, who would bless it right there under the rite of exorcism, so that they could be sure it was the same sample of water. Even a difference in mineral properties from a phial bottled in Rome, for instance, would have to be accounted for as a possible explanation, and that wasn't what they were testing here.

Merrick returned to his trolley and retrieved the next phial: a strong alkaline solution. It was as he picked it up that he realised he had not brought the protective gloves he used when preparing it.

The thought vividly magnified the reality of what he was about to do.

Behind him, Tullian began his declamations, chanting the rite. As Merrick approached the demon once more, the loud calls for a purge of evil sounded like an admonition towards himself.

His hand was still trembling even as his wrist remained locked, awaiting the will to rotate it and pour the solution. In the end it was the danger that his shaking would spill it on to his own fingers that prompted him to act.

'That Satan may be crushed under our feet, that every evil counsel directed against us may be brought to naught.'

The alkali hit the demon's skin with a blistering hiss that was immediately drowned by the creature's screams. Not roars this time. Screams. High, keening, an electrical jolt through the calcium of your bones.

'Free us from every attack . . .'

He couldn't do this again, couldn't visit this harm.

'And every temptation of the enemy . . .'

But he couldn't give up, couldn't *not* do it. He needed to know.

He reached for the phial of acid . . .

Now, these weeks later, the screams still echo, still scrape his bones and gnaw at his soul. But the data they heralded reverberated even more disturbingly. Tullian had handed him back the phial at the end of the procedure, allowing him to retest the same holy water sample on dead skin. It still had no effect. The acid and the alkali had the same corrosive impact whether the subject was dead or alive: the only difference was that the

116

effects on the dead sample weren't accompanied by screams of pain and an anguished wail from somewhere deep within Merrick's conscience.

Holy water on living tissue, however, had proven more damaging than any hazardous chemical.

The questions were only beginning. Did holy water burn other creatures, or only these ones? If so, why? He had checked the sample before and after the blessing, and at a molecular level it was unchanged. Did the incantation alter the properties of simple water at some level we could neither measure nor detect? Would the rite work if performed by anyone? Did it have to be a priest? Did it have to be a *Catholic* priest?

It was exciting, but in the most nightmarish way. Either his observations denoted the threshold of a whole new frontier of science, or they marked the barrier where the scientific paradigm reached its limit. What was truly disquieting about this was that if science couldn't offer explanations, then nor could it offer solutions; while what did offer solutions was more worrying still. Our world was in danger of being overrun by these marauding demons, and it was only things he had shunned and scorned that might offer hope: that might offer, to use the now frighteningly appropriate word, *salvation*.

With this thought returns the recurring fear, the one that stalks him every second he remains in this dark and damned place: Here beneath the world, held fast by adamantine rock, impenetrable. Here impaled with circling fire, yet unconsumed.

All his life, *he* shunned, *he* scorned.

He rejected, even ridiculed, the word of God, the very idea of religion. Now he's confronted with damnation, torment and demons in a sweltering furnace beneath the earth. Wasn't that what the Bible said would happen? How's that for cause and effect?

A world overrun by demons. *His* world. Perhaps only his. For what if this truly is Hell, *his* Hell? What if he had died but didn't know it? Wouldn't this be the journey that took him there: his unique, personal journey? He recalls some of his many possible deaths: a near-drowning at fifteen; on board a 757 tossed like a toy by an electrical storm above the Rockies. Then one more vivid than the rest: almost falling asleep at the wheel on a rain-lashed night nine months ago, on the drive north, on the road to here. He can still see the view from the windscreen. Lights everywhere, flickering and indistinct: white shapes stretched and pulled by random refractions in the rain and spray before being temporarily shrunk to points and discs by the wiper blades . . .

What if he hadn't snapped awake before that bend?

Perhaps you didn't go from your world to Hell: perhaps you brought it to yourself, made your own world *become* Hell. No moment of death, no judgment at the gate, no banishment with your fellow damned; but instead watching, close-up, helpless, as the decisions you had made, the things you had embraced not only proved powerless against, but in fact *precipitated* the advent of Hell on Earth.

Mass Effect

IV

'God our Father, renew the living spring of your life within us and protect us in spirit and body, that we may be free from sin and come into your presence to receive your gift of salvation. We ask this through Christ our Lord.'

'*Amen*,' they all respond.

The room is warming up by the second, condensation beginning to form on the inside of the glass and disappointingly clouding out Adnan's view through the windows, where he had previously been able to make out Orion.

A makeshift altar has been constructed at one end of the room, just a low-standing coffee table draped with ceremonial cloths and adorned with standard-issue holyware: a crucifix, a chalice, a bell, a bowl of corpse-substitute wafers and a copy of the *Christianity User's Manual*. Father Blake is got up in white vestments, arms outstretched and chest proud, like he's waiting to hug a really fat relative who he secretly doesn't like. Making his posture more bizarre is the fact that he's kneeling, so that he's not towering four feet above the top of his Playmobil Happy Priest Altar Set.

Everyone else is sitting roughly in a circle with one flattened end around the focus of the proceedings. Some are on chairs and sofas, but most are cross-legged on the floor, leaning back into the spaces between the paired legs of the ones who have bagged seats. For once, it's not the hard men and the cool kids who have secured the prime spots, as none of them wanted to turn up too early to this gig. It's mostly the God squad and the staff who have those privileges, though there is no sign of Mr Kane, which Adnan finds ideologically satisfying but at the same time slightly annoying. If he had to turn up for this shit, why should Kane get a free pass?

'May almighty God cleanse us of our sins, and through the Eucharist we celebrate make us worthy to sit at his table in his heavenly kingdom.'

Maybe it's the growing warmth, maybe it's his fatigue, maybe it's the fact that where he's leaning back, his shoulder is in contact with Caitlin Black's leg and she hasn't recoiled it in a deliberately conspicuous show of disgust, and maybe it's a combination of all of the above, but Adnan would have to admit he's actually finding the mass quite pleasant. There is a very mellow vibe around the room: no tension, no aggro, nobody being a pain in the hoop, everybody quietly contemplative. There is something cosy and genuinely communal to it, like how he'd always been told religion was supposed to be. However, there is also something inescapably ridiculous about it, kind of the elephant in the room that's being steadfastly ignored by the faithful. Really. There's Blake in his superhero costume, striking crazy poses and talking in this elevated semi-singing register that *so* isn't the guy's normal voice; like he's channelling or something. Meanwhile everyone else is nodding here, bowing there, all in unison, all on Pavlovian cue, and chanting like they're entranced, their own voices altered, their delivery uniform and unsettlingly identical.

'I confess to almighty God,' they all chant, *'and to you, my brothers and sisters, that I have sinned*

through my own fault, in my thoughts and in my words, in what I have done, and in what I have failed to do . . .'

Shit, that doesn't leave much space for plea-bargaining, does it? Sins of thought, sins of speech, sins of deed, sins of omission. Forgot sins of respiration and sins of spatial occupation, but otherwise we're all owning up to being a shower of spherical bastards: bastards any way you look at us. However, our damnation is not a done deal, there is hope:

'And I ask blessed Mary, ever virgin, all the angels and saints, and you, my brothers and sisters, to pray for me to the Lord, our God.'

Yeah. The blessed virgin, the angels and the saints got our backs.

It was at his dad's insistence that he and his two younger sisters went to Catholic school. Like many devout Muslims in Scotland, faced with the absence of their own faith schools, he decided he'd rather entrust the education of his kids to Crusader infidel Christian hardliners than to the scorched-earth godlessness of the non-denominational system. Besides, the Muslims and the Catholics might disagree on the divinity of Jesus and the veracity of Mohammed's secretarial skills in transcribing the word of God, but they had as much in common as divided them, mostly concerning who and what they disapproved of. This, according to Adnan's most recent calculations, was pretty much everything, especially if it could be described by the words 'enlightened', 'forward-looking' or 'fun'.

His dad would be less than delighted to hear that sending him to a faith school was what really accelerated his apostasy. Having been immersed so thoroughly in one religious culture, to be then plunged in close-up alongside another served to illustrate how arbitrary your allocation of faith was. The stork drops you down one chimney in Gleniston and you're a Muslim, down another and you're a Catholic; each with their own silly outfits, bizarre rituals and absolute certainty that their way is right. The Christians who were vociferously railing against Islamic extremism were precisely the ones who would have turned out hard-core fundies themselves, railing against the Crusaders, had they been born in Jordan rather than Jordanhill.

Despite the glass steaming up, Adnan can tell it's going to be clear tonight. Being so excitingly removed from urban light pollution, he knows the seeing will be different class, which is why he's already set up his telescope in the room he's sharing with Radar and Matt.

Most people had never known quite what to make of Matt, but he had gone from enigma to borderline pariah since the incident. Nobody could possibly blame him for it—at least, nobody rational, which unfortunately ruled out the folk most likely to give him grief about it—but there was an inescapable sense that he was tainted by his involvement nonetheless. Adnan had seen something of the same phenomenon back in second year when Radar's mother died. Everyone steered clear of him for a long time, and while part of that was because they didn't know quite what to say, it was also as though they feared bereavement might be contagious.

Adnan had always got on okay with Matt. They

124

were both geeks in their own different ways. Matt, however, was not one to pour forth his geekish enthusiasms, whereas Adnan didn't care who he bored or baffled. What a lot of the chuckleheads at school didn't appreciate was that you didn't have to be gibbering away incontinently with lame jokes and stolen patter to be good company. They always needed vocal affirmation of their own presence every thirty seconds or they got twitchy and self-conscious. Adnan felt relaxed in a room with Matt because he understood Matt felt relaxed in a room with him. He knew that just because Matt didn't say anything didn't mean he wasn't listening. That, in fact, was the big mistake people made about the guy. They assumed, because he was quiet, that he was withdrawn into a world of his own, when in fact he was probably the most attentive and keenly observant person among them. It was Adnan's bet that Matt had everybody's number, and they should all be grateful that he didn't say much, because if he did, he'd nail them to the walls.

*   *   *

This is about as much as Rocks has enjoyed being at mass in living memory. He's not paying any more attention than normal, but with everyone in a circle, the view is a lot better than the usual offering of the back of somebody's head, so he's able to reprise his assessments of the talent as practised on the coach journey. Informed by Dazza's experienced perspective, it's like seeing some of the lassies for the first time, which prompts the less comfortable contemplation of

125

what it might take for them to reciprocate.

Rocks envied the informed and dispassionately practical nature of Dazza's appraisal: the voice of experience, the words of a man who knows what he's talking about. Dazza's built like a boxer, and has always got girls interested in him: older girls, that is, students and the like. Consequently, he's seen a lot more action; more than enough to adjudge what level any given female is likely to be operating at.

Not that Rocks would be getting assigned to a high weight-class himself. If it turned out that the apparently demure Caitlin or Michelle *had* had their tits felt, then that would place them further up the sexual experience ladder than he had notched so far. (Unless you counted the time he got off with Christine Higgins at Dazza's birthday party and managed a fleeting brush of her blouse before her hand shot up with the defensive ferocity of a karate block.)

It's about lack of opportunity, he reckons, the absence of situations that would allow you to actually talk to lassies properly. Water, water everywhere, but not a drop to drink: there were girls all around you in every class, every day, but when did you ever get the chance to be around them when you were both being yourselves, as opposed to just gender-regimented schoolkids? Plus, as he was latterly learning, there is a price to pay for being a mate of Big Kirk's, aside from the standard one of perennially getting jumped by the Gleniston Young Team. The problem is that the girls tend to assume he is a bampot, and consequently he places a premium on potential opportunities to explain otherwise. That's why he

126

has high hopes for this retreat: it will take everybody out of the normal context. Nobody has to behave the way they're assumed or expected to, which means the Michelles and Caitlins of this world might well get their tits felt, and the Paul Roxburghs of this world might be the ones doing the feeling.

His big brother had said as much, based on the experience of his own senior school years. Joe told him about weekend retreats to some place in Ayrshire called Chapelstane Hall: school trips that are no longer on offer largely due to the sorts of abuses in which Joe and his peers had enthusiastically indulged.

'It was hilarious. The teachers thought they were really making a breakthrough because the likes of me and my pals seemed to have come over all happy-clappy, but we were only there for smuggled drink and the chance to meet lassies from other schools who would all be sleeping under the same roof. Or not sleeping, and not under the roof much either. Some serious action went on under the stars around that place, let me tell you.

'This retreat should be a particularly valuable opportunity,' Joe had encouraged him. 'Sex and death always go together. Part of the natural rhythm. Believe me: it does something to people, especially girls. If you cannae get a burd pumped after some poor bastard's just snuffed it, seriously: cut it off.'

*   *   *

Kane can hear the droning chants of the dutiful but disengaged from where he's standing in the

127

reception area. He's got a folder open on the counter in front of him, but he's staring at the huge panes instead, which are functioning almost like giant mirrors due to the star-dotted blackness beyond. The light is soft and low indoors, but it's mostly reflecting back and making the sitting area seem twice the size. Observed from distance, the facility must look like one of those stars: a glowing light source isolated in an ocean of black, thus visible itself but not illuminating its surroundings.

There's little to see, but it's still a sufficient distraction when he doesn't particularly want to look at what's right in front of him. The folder is full of press clippings, mostly the tabloid stuff. At some point over the weekend, he's going to get them to talk about this. In the post-traumatic storm, with their recall confused and their minds censoring certain painful or horrifying details, there is a danger that the tabloid version of events has become the one that stays in their memories. Part of his job this weekend is to help them prevent second-hand, speculative or even outright made-up accounts supplanting the truth of their own experiences.

Normally, there would have been a grace period of several months before the papers were permitted to salivate over such *sub judice* details, but Robert Barker denied them that mercy by killing himself so soon after killing Andrew Dunn. That's when the tide of hearsay, distortion, simplistic psychobabble, revisionism and lies in Kane's folder was truly unleashed. They painted a portrait of a monster, some apprentice Dahmer so deranged, sadistic and terrifying, the papers almost sounded disappointed he wouldn't get the chance

128

to fulfil his early promise. Every last piece of classroom tittle-tattle was blown up, picked apart and spun as an 'insight' into the mind of a psychopath. There were stories going right back to primary school. Christ, the kid fucking killed himself a few days after murdering a classmate. Did we need to excoriate his childhood to underline how troubled he was?

EVIL.

MONSTER.

How many times—or how few—did the kids of St Peter's need to read those words before they became synonymous with Robert Barker and they started believing the dumbed-down, cheesy horror-flick version of their own narrative? Did those reversed-out block capitals in the headlines make the words more true? Maybe the textual equivalent of screaming them like that helped the editors compensate for how meaningless they were. Calling Robert Barker 'evil' told us nothing about him and nothing about evil. It read like some hysterical maiden aunt who can't deal with this beastly, frightful notion. 'He's a monster, he's *evil*, that's all I need to know, so shut the book, don't tell me any more.'

Kane is buffeted from his reflections as something suddenly hits the glass with a bang that makes him physically recoil. He hears a scuttling sound, a scraping of little claws on wood, and through one of the windows, he can make out the shape of a bird as it scrabbles drunkenly on the decking. He feels his heart race, with Blake's muffled mumblings the only other thing audible in the vicinity. It was the silence that did it: the sound of the bang amplified in his ears by virtue of there being so little else to hear. Like a pocket torch suddenly shone in the pitch dark: the fact that it is light at all can be enough to dazzle.

A different kind of dark, a different kind of silent. He's only a few hours from Glasgow, but it doesn't feel like this is the same country; maybe not even the same world.

He has just about recovered from the initial fright when a second sudden sound has him close to levitation again. This time it's a voice.

'Dumb birds. They do that all the time.'

Sendak is standing a few feet behind him, apparently having materialised or emerged from a trap door. Kane didn't hear one footfall, a swish of clothing or a solitary breath. Through the glass they both watch the bird take off with a slow and unsteady beat of wings.

'I've heard that if you put the silhouette of a hawk on the window, it makes them avoid it,' Kane says, figuring Sendak is the kind of man who will be able to confirm or debunk this theory.

'Yeah, but where's the fun in that?' he replies.

They share a grin.

Kane is suddenly conscious of the folder, still open at an A3 photocopy of a *Sun* double-page spread. His instinct is to close it, but not only would this merely attract Sendak's attention, it's a cert he's already clocked it, particularly as Kane has no idea how long Sendak has been standing watching him.

'Something smells good,' he says, by way of diverting small talk. It does too, particularly as all he's had since leaving Gleniston is a Snickers bar.

'Mm,' Sendak agrees. He sounds noncommittal, like he's not buying the change of subject. There's

130

a moment or two of that deep, enveloping silence, not even Blake's voice audible, then it's broken by a chant from the common-room congregation.

'Got some important work ahead of you,' Sendak says, eyeing the folder. 'Half the battle can be just remembering the truth. All that bullshit sure don't help.'

'I'm guessing you speak from experience.'

Sendak nods sombrely.

'Though in my case, it's always been the "official" version that I had to purge. It's gonna hurt those kids, but it's a hurt they gotta endure, because it'll save them from worse.'

'Like what?'

'Like guilt.'

'That's not such a big threat in this instance. I don't think they're under any illusions about who's to blame.'

'Yeah, but I didn't say blame, I said guilt. When you've watched somebody die while fate chose to leave you standing . . . it does things to you. That's why it's vital that you hold on to a reliable picture of what really happened. Trust me on this. As you put it just now, I speak from experience.'

*   *   *

'Lord, we have sinned against you: Lord, have mercy.'

'*Lord, have mercy.*'

'Lord, show us your mercy and love.'

'*And grant us your salvation.*'

'May almighty God have mercy on us, forgive us our sins, and bring us to everlasting life.'

'*Amen.*'

131

They respond dutifully but with a glazed-over, dopey compliance so wholly lacking in any feeling that Rosemary can barely conceive of it being any further from a true sense of spirituality. It's actually worse than when they were all younger and the usual numpties would amuse themselves by getting up to all sorts of childish carry-on throughout the proceedings. Now they're more grown-up, more polite, so everyone is quietly and patiently sitting through it: tolerating it; enduring it. They're not feeling anything, and what's truly eating at Rosemary is that neither is she.

Father Blake looks slightly embarrassed, as though he's feeling self-conscious about celebrating mass in such a huddled and in-your-face environment. Exacerbating Rosemary's disappointment is that this last is precisely the aspect that ought to be making it special: that 'mass unplugged', as Father Blake had called it, would bring people together in contemplation and prayer, in the name of their shared faith, like nothing had since the tragedy. Instead, right now she's feeling very apart from everybody, even her friends.

They'd all been given counselling, and warned that they might suddenly feel naked and vulnerable, especially in the midst of a noisy crowd like there had been on that awful day. They'd been warned also that there would be times when certain of their emotions seemed unbearably amplified. What had happened to her on the coach ticked both boxes. When Radar snatched her guitar, she was initially just annoyed and determined to get it back, but it was what followed that caused something to crumble. When the guitar started getting passed around, and by people she never previously suspected had anything against her, she felt no longer determined, just isolated. She suddenly wished she could feel part of the stupidity, and wished even more that it wasn't her guitar that had provided the occasion, because that seemed more than anything to place her further on the outside of it all than where even the deputy head was standing.

She was feeling more composed by the time they arrived at Fort Trochart. The prospect of some heart-to-hearts after dark might offer the chance to resolve a few things. The rules here would be different, and maybe you could let your guard down without fear of it merely inviting attack.

Then she got her guitar out, just planning to test the tuning, in case it had suffered from its recent misadventures. That was when she saw the graffiti.

She used to have this Jesus fish sticker on the sounding board, but its colours faded quickly and it looked really scruffy, so she tried peeling it off. Unfortunately, it wasn't just the inking that proved cheap and nasty, as the glossy top level came away and left a rough paper layer stuck to the wood. Upon this blank off-white oval, someone had scribbled, in thick marker pen: 'This machine kills heretics'. Someone's idea of a joke. She didn't understand exactly what the phrase was getting at, but she did understand that it was getting at her.

She flipped the guitar over and laid it on the bed so that no one might notice the sticker. Then she hurried off to the toilets and locked herself in a cubicle where nobody would see her cry, particularly not her friends.

It wasn't just that they saw her as Miss

133

Unflappable, the thick-skinned one who fought all their battles and whose faith was too strong to be concerned by what other people thought of it (especially when the other people were sophomoric mind-clones pathetically enslaved by the tyranny of cool). It was that, for quite a while now, she felt she couldn't talk to them about matters other than those pertaining to school or church. Lately she had increasingly come to feel that the people who knew her best were the last people she would want to be aware of what was really going on inside her head.

More happily, at least Caitlin had ended up in the same bedroom.

Caitlin always seems hostile towards her these days, and Rosemary has never been able to work out why. She hates the idea that she has done or said something to hurt anyone, even unknowingly, and has felt driven to somehow make amends. However, the more she's tried to seek her out, the more hostile Caitlin has become. It's like throwing petrol on a fire, in fact. But as fate would have it, the only room with three free beds had been one with Caitlin already in it. Maybe her hopes of everybody pulling together this weekend were too much to ask, and this was God's way of saying that it takes small steps. If this trip was the thing that pushed her and Caitlin closer together, then that would be something, wouldn't it? Perhaps it was a sign.

She steals a look across at Caitlin, seated on the other side of the room. She is one of the few who seems to be paying any attention, intently following the celebrant's words, unlike the majority of the small, zombified gathering. Yes.

134

Maybe they were already closer in ways they didn't quite know.

*   *   *

Maybe this is evidence that there really is a God, Caitlin reflects: that He's punishing her for her blasphemous thoughts by appointing Rosemary her personal evangelical stalker, and parachuting the holy trinity of she, Bernie and Maria right into her bedroom.

She's sitting with Adnan at her feet, wondering what on earth he must make of this stuff. She can feel his shoulder against her leg. It's not unpleasant. Back at school, any such contact would have her squirming, if only just from fear of what someone might say if they noticed. Here, the atmosphere already feels different. You can tell: people are going to be able to talk more on this trip; get to know each other, *get off* with each other, and she wouldn't mind one of those people being her. Would Adnan fit the bill? He's interesting, different, though a bit geeky; a lot geeky, in fact, but that might improve her chances. The cool ones aren't going to be giving the she-geeks like her a second look.

Caitlin glances around the room, amusing herself momentarily with the idea of assessing the possibilities. She sees Dazza, Rocks, Liam, all firmly in the 'wouldn't give her a second look' category. Then she spies Ewan and Cameron. They're definitely in the intriguing category, in that she wouldn't say no, but the question is, would they? Then her fun is cut short as the next male she claps eyes on is sternly returning her gaze. It's

135

Mr Guthrie, popping up like the Jiminy Cricket of her Catholic conscience, as though he can read her mind and is browbeating her for such inappropriate thoughts here during mass.

Sir, if only you knew.

It was a stick-on that Miss Ross and Mr Kane would be the teachers asked to go on the retreat. They were the two teachers best able to talk to the kids and more importantly, to get the kids to talk to them. And just as certain, given the choice of those two doves, was that there would have to be the biggest hawk as well, Guthrie, coming along to play bad cop. His eyes are darting back and forth, divided between reverent participation in the service and scanning the room in search of further signs of disrespect. She wonders which activity lights his fire more. Of the staff, the only one giving the altar undivided and devout attention is Miss Ross. Caitlin was unaware that she was particularly religious: the thing to look for among the staff was which teachers went up to receive communion during a school mass, because that was what separated the nominal Catholics from the genuinely practising ones. She doesn't recall Miss Ross being in the latter group, but right now she's got her hands clasped and her gaze locked on Father Blake with rapt attention.

Most of the time, Caitlin can just zone out during mass, let her mind drift so that the tedium passes quicker, but occasionally she can't help but pay attention, and that's when the sheer inanity of it really grates on her cognitive faculties. They're conditioned to nod their head whenever they or the priest says 'Jesus', but it's taking Caitlin more and more willpower not to shake hers throughout.

136

'We believe in one God, the Father, the Almighty,
maker of Heaven and Earth, of all that is, seen and unseen.'

AKA the Intelligent Designer. The Vatican had latterly decided it could accommodate evolution within its view of Creation (largely because it could no longer accommodate the embarrassment it was feeling by continuing to do otherwise), but it was adamant that an acceptance of evolution didn't preclude God having started it. Yes, God set in motion this astronomically complex process but knew all along, despite the infinitely branching possibilities created by an incalculable multiplicity of random factors, that the end product would be mankind: begging the question, if that was always the plan, why did he take the long way around instead of creating mankind right off the bat?

'God from God, Light from Light, true God from true God,
Through him all things were made.
For us men and for our salvation he came down from heaven . . .'

So, having waited nine billion years for Earth to form, then held off another four and a half billion for his chosen species to fully evolve, He blows his wad early by sending down his messiah during the Bronze Age? If he wanted us to believe in Him and to live by His Word, couldn't He have hung on another infinitesimal couple of millennia and sent his miracle-working superhero ambassador in the age of broadcast media and other verifiable means of record, instead of staking thirteen and a half billion years' work on the reliability of a few goat-herders in an insignificant backwater of a primitive civilisation?

137

'By the power of the Holy Spirit,

'He was born of the Virgin Mary, and was made man.'

Yeah, that seems to happen a lot with gods. The Greek myths are full of it: lonely virgin out on the hillside, gets impregnated by an, ahem, 'god', to explain why she's up the stick and there's no father in sight. Tracy O'Keefe should have tried that one when she had her wean in fourth year: It was a god that did it. He appeared on the hillside (or the Gleniston golf course, anyway), with a halo (okay, a gold hoop through one ear), and he cast a spell on her (got her fuelled up with Buckfast), then vanished back to his realm (ran off to boast to all his mates).

'For our sake he was crucified under Pontius Pilate . . .'

Welease Wodewick! Welease Woger!

'He suffered death and was buried.

On the third day he rose again in accordance with the Scriptures . . .'

Because those things *never* get rewritten after the fact.

'We believe in the Holy Spirit, the Lord, the giver of life.

Who proceeds from the Father and the Son.

With the Father and the Son he is worshipped and glorified.'

Wait a sec, didn't you say just a minute ago that you believed in one God? You've now listed three. 'Ah, but that's a Blessed Mystery.'

'We believe in one holy Catholic and apostolic Church.

We acknowledge one baptism for the forgiveness of sins.

We look for the resurrection of the dead . . .'
No we don't, surely. Not if we've seen any George Romero movies.
'And the life of the world to come.'
This will be world version 2.2, then, world 1.1 having presumably failed four and a half billion years of beta?
'Amen.'
Amen indeed.

V

General McCormack glances up restlessly at the row of clocks on the wall. They are all set to different time zones, each bearing two extra designations supplementary to its military one, as a courtesy to the other constituencies represented at the facility. The one showing local time thus reads London, GMT and Zulu, but by any name, it demonstrates inarguably that the meeting should have started five minutes ago. Not long in Tullian's world, but to a military mind, surely an aeon.

They are in the Command Room, which on three sides could be the interior of any military building in the world, but from the fourth is an elevated perspective upon why right now it's more important than any of the rest. A vast single pane of specially developed reinforced Plexiglas affords a view of live rock adorned with pipes, cables, vents, dials and LEDs, plunging forty feet to the observation platform, then thirty more to the floor of what has been christened the Cathedral. The nickname had been a harmless irreverence that in retrospect now looked like an odiously mordant perversion. Down below, sustained by this vast steel, plastic, copper and fibreglass respiratory system, and nurtured by billions of dollars' worth of research and technology, lies the greatest folly since the Tower of Babel.

The magnitude of its hubris has latterly been appreciated by the other men around the room, but the difference between Tullian and his military counterparts is that he is the only one to understand that the threat presented is not merely to man's future on this Earth, but to his ultimate fate in the life beyond.

McCormack may be visibly agitated, but Tullian, while concealing it better, is on tenterhooks.

'My arse is making buttons,' he recalls a joyously and unapologetically coarse Irish colleague once remarking as they awaited the outcome of a vote. The issue at stake had meant more to Cardinal Daly and thus Tullian had regarded it as merely a colourfully crude remark. Here, today, he appreciates how close to the literal it was.

People imagined that military battles only took place in fields of mud and rubble-strewn landscapes. In truth, wars could be won and lost around oak tables like the one he was seated at right now. After four decades a priest, he was used to decisions being in the gift of superiors; and just as accustomed to decisions being in the gift of another estate. In both arenas, the arts of judicious lobbying and subtle persuasion could always tip the scales, and though he had found that the volatile factors of arrogance and caprice were less pronounced when it came to the military, one could never rule out a change in the wind, so he was taking nothing for granted when the stakes were this high.

McCormack looks at the bank of clocks again. 'Goddamn it,' he grumbles. 'Where in the hell is Steinmeyer? If that sonofabitch can't be assed turning up to hear it from the horse's mouth, then he can't complain if he just ends up reading the news in his email.'

'He'll be here, sir,' urges Havelock anxiously, always Steinmeyer's advocate, even if Steinmeyer lacked the vision to notice this. The physicist had become so entrenched in his siege mentality that he saw enemies all around him and no longer had the sense to recognise who his allies were.

Tullian, despite his caution, can't help but feel relief seep in as he listens to McCormack's words. Hear *it*, read *the news*. This isn't a meeting, it's an announcement, and there's only one announcement it could be.

He thanks God and with this thought immediately feels his relief turn to a different kind of anxiety, that which always accompanies getting what you had prayed for: a vertiginous uncertainty as to whether God was acting in approval of your desire, or granting your wishes in order to teach you a difficult lesson. In either case, it marked the onset of a great and testing task. When your prayers were answered, it was not a resolution, but a beginning: God was not taking matters into His own hands, but placing greater trust in your own. Even an act of God can be futile if the will of man is weak in response. Thus Tullian endures a burden of expectation underpinned by the driving, hollow fear of what it would feel like to fail.

I was afraid, and went and hid thy talent in the

141

earth . . .

Cast ye the unprofitable servant into outer darkness: there shall be weeping and gnashing of teeth.

'I swear, Havelock,' McCormack begins, prompting Colonel Havelock to get to his feet and move towards the door, perhaps intending to retrieve Steinmeyer personally. His intentions are rendered moot as the professor finally makes his appearance, with the fraught and agitated air of a man who doesn't believe he can spare even seconds for anything not immediately pertinent to his own agenda. Unfortunately for him, this is likely to prove more than merely an unwelcome distraction.

Steinmeyer looks as frantic as he does exhausted. Tullian guesses he has barely slept in a week, sustaining himself on caffeine and energy bars, relegating rest to the status of unaffordable luxury. Like Tullian, he must know what's coming; must have known it for days, which is why he has lashed himself to the mast and clung to the helm before time runs out.

Tullian feels for him, quite achingly so. Steinmeyer is a passionate, driven man, whom he admires for qualities he sincerely aspires towards in himself. His desire is pure, his dedication is absolute and he has no thought for base rewards: not for glory nor riches, only for knowledge and truth. He has foregone both renown and remuneration, guided in his choices only by what will afford him the greatest opportunity to pursue his work, and cares not for posterity, wishing simply to bequeath a legacy that may be built upon by those unknown who will one day follow him.

142

Tullian wishes that in his church there were but a dozen cardinals of whom he could say as much.

However, the one quality Tullian can lay claim to that Steinmeyer lacks is the humility of knowing when something greater than your own passion should be deferred to, regardless of how altruistic you believe that passion to be. Steinmeyer has lost perspective through a process that began with his own selflessness—a difficult lesson that many a priest has learned the hard way—discounting the cost to himself of his work as of no regard. At the end of that path, unfortunately, lies a dark place where to further one's work, *any* cost becomes a necessary price, no matter what may be wrought in its extraction.

Steinmeyer was lost in that place, consumed by a quest, as Marlowe put it in Faustus, 'to practise more than heavenly power permits'.

He stands at the edge of the table for a moment, as though hopeful that he can pay his scant regard to the meeting and then swiftly be on his way again. General McCormack gestures to a chair, the strain on his patience vented with a sigh.

'You better have a seat,' Havelock urges. 'This is important.'

Steinmeyer casts an arch glance towards Tullian, the implication of which is unmistakable: if the cardinal is involved, then as far as he is concerned, it clearly *isn't* important.

The suffering physicist is consumed with anger to the point that it must be shrivelling his soul. Tullian has tried tirelessly to reach out to him, even just to help him talk through his grievances, but he's balled up too tight to accept any olive branches. His entrenched position is that he refuses to recognise any legitimacy to Tullian's presence here at all, regarding it as an affront to his scientific principles. Tullian can sympathise: he respects the boundaries between their respective domains, but it is for this reason that he deeply wishes he *did* have no business here, and that Steinmeyer's attitude was merely impolite. Unfortunately, the reality is that under the current circumstances, his obduracy is reckless, and worst of all, unscientific.

'We're shutting it down,' McCormack says, before Steinmeyer's back has hit the leather of the chair. 'There, Colonel Havelock told you it was important,' he adds with unnecessary spite, perhaps in retaliation for being made to wait.

Steinmeyer all but gags on the news, and while he searches for his voice, McCormack presses the point home.

'You can spare me the histrionics, Professor. This can't be coming as a surprise.'

Steinmeyer's nostrils flare as he fights to control his rage. Tullian feels his own pulse increase in the fear that the professor will do something rash, as they are surrounded by strong and dangerous men, most of whom are only marginally less tired and overwrought than Steinmeyer.

'Lucius,' Havelock implores, 'we appreciate you're gonna be angry, but don't go burning any bridges here.'

There is silence for a long few seconds, then Steinmeyer speaks.

'It's no surprise, General,' he concedes, though his tone implies that this is the only concession he's about to make. 'I realised you had suffered a terminal failure of nerve back on day one of the anomaly, when instead of massively expanding the scientific roster, you called in the chaplain. After that, it was only a matter of time.'

'Failure of nerve?' McCormack responds. He's very slow to anger, a difficult man to upset, but there is a growing exasperation to his demeanour that began long, long before this meeting commenced. 'You have no idea where your debts lie, Professor. It's only because of me that you were allowed to keep this freak show running. I'm the one who has kept the Pentagon in the dark about just how far off the reservation you've taken us here, and I may yet get handed my ass for it.'

'Well I'd sure hate this epoch-making scientific discovery to have a deleterious effect on your career, General.'

'It's not my career I'm concerned about. There will be no shortage of wars for men like me to fight if we don't put a lid on this thing. It's potentially the biggest powderkeg this planet has ever seen.'

'Which is why you shouldn't be "putting a lid on it". You should be escalating this operation: there ought to be ten times the number of scientists down here in order to understand what we've discovered. Instead you sent half the science staff away after the anomaly appeared because you didn't want them to see anything they might tell somebody about. We've made a discovery that could change our understanding of the nature of the universe, that could provide the primer for the Unified Theory, and since then all we've had down here looking into it is a skeleton staff. Opportunities like this need men of courage, General. It's all right to feel awe, but can't you dial down the fear? You're all so scared.'

145

'Damn right we're scared,' the General thunders, slapping the table with the heel of his palm and knocking over two bottles of mineral water at the far end. 'Scared of more than it would even occur to you to imagine. A lot of people are scared, people who have greater responsibilities than compiling equations or separating quarks and gluons. When I say powderkeg, you think I'm only talking about what's coming through the looking glass. I mean, did you ever notice, over the past few years, maybe the odd time you lifted your head up from the particle accelerators, that there are one or two folks out there in the world who tend to get a little bit exercised over the subject of religion? So don't you see how the ramifications of our little science project might just make every government on the planet a teensy bit nervous?'

'We can't halt our quest to further our understanding on account of the superstitious fools who wish to wallow in ignorance. Knowledge is the antidote to superstition, General.'

'Yeah, Professor, it would work like that, because people would read the fine print and sift through the scientific interpretations, wouldn't they? Jesus Christ, man, can you imagine what kind of hysterical apocalyptic shit would be unleashed upon the world if just one of those things got out, or if people even just started hearing *rumours* about what we've found here?'

'We don't *know* what we've found here,' Steinmeyer replies furiously, his bloodshot, caffeine-strung eyes bulging in his indignation. 'Finding out what we've discovered is the point of the exercise. It's called science.'

'No, Steinmeyer, this has turned into something

146

way beyond goddamn science, and you're too intoxicated by it to admit you're out of your depth. You came here looking for the fabled graviton. You even warned me that if you could merge gravity with the other three forces, it might warp the fabric of space-time and create a miniature black hole. But you ain't telling me you were expecting any of *this* shit.'

'Well I sure as hell wasn't expecting the Spanish Inquisition. This was a scientific operation—'

'It *is*—and always was—a *military* operation,' McCormack reminds him.

'Quite, and yet you've handed the reins to the Vatican's spook patrol.'

Tullian doesn't rise to the bait, though he did have to bite back a fleeting desire to say: 'No one expects the Spanish Inquisition.' Much as humour could, in his experience, be entrusted to defuse certain situations, this wasn't one of them. Steinmeyer's anger was driven by the awareness that he had already lost this battle; it would only blow itself out once he felt he had made his point, so attempting to make light of the situation would be counterproductive.

'Instead of research and analysis,' Steinmeyer continues, 'we've got crucifixes and exorcisms. We're at the frontier of a new scientific age and your response is to deploy methods from the twelfth century.'

'You unleashed fucking *demons*, for Christ's sake,' McCormack blasts back. 'It's the clearest case of Eminent Domain I've ever witnessed, and I brought in Cardinal Tullian because we had moved into territory where he's the expert, not you.'

'Oh, spare *me* the histrionics. None of us knows

what we've "unleashed", because Cardinal Torquemada here won't let my people near the entities, at least not until after he's finished slicing and dicing.'

'Professor, with respect—which you seem disinclined to show anybody else—it's my strong opinion that what's pissing you off is not that I brought in Cardinal Tullian, but that since I did, the emerging evidence has been vindicating my judgment more than it has yours. The Cardinal is the leading—'

At this, Tullian raises a hand both to stay the General's defence of him and to indicate that he would speak for himself.

Steinmeyer already looks like he's not listening; or at least that he wishes to convey that he won't be. He stops short of putting his fingers in his ears and singing 'lalalala', but the intention is equally clear. Tullian responds by directing his words unavoidably towards him.

'I can only apologise to you, Professor, for intrusions and encumbrances that must seem as insulting as they do frustrating. If it's any consolation, I am, in fact, frequently embarrassed by the respective positions we find ourselves in. I am as awed and as respectful as anyone of your abilities and achievements, and I wish, I sincerely wish that I had nothing to offer here but my admiration. I am a greater student of physics than you might assume: I read your paper on superstrings and the unification of forces back in 1994, and followed your publications until you dropped off the radar. Having discovered what you are working on and encountered you here in the flesh, it would therefore have been my considerable honour to defer to your expertise—were it not that *I do know, exactly, what you have brought forth*. It is not a distinction I relish, but the truth is that I am the expert in the field your work has brought all of us into, and the body of knowledge I draw upon is not only thousands of years older than yours, but thousands of years older than even the church I represent.'

Tullian looks into Steinmeyer's eyes and sees a weary kind of scorn, the arrogant certainty that he had nothing to learn from parties he perceived to be at worst, enemies, and at best, obstacles. It's easy for him to recognise, as it's like looking through a mirror in time and seeing his own face reflected. Tullian had been just as arrogantly dismissive once too, before he came to learn that he couldn't afford to be. His task and his talent lay in reaching out to people, understanding them so that he could make them understand him. The tiny fragments that helped you piece together the greater truths could often be hidden in the least likely places, therefore there was nothing you could confidently overlook.

If only Steinmeyer knew how similar they both were, how much they had in common, and the extent to which they were striving towards the same truth. Like the physicist, Tullian had also dropped off the radar just as his star seemed on the rise, fading from view to undertake work that the outside world might never learn about. Having once been tipped to become one of the most pre-eminent churchmen in North America, he had been called to the Vatican in the late 1980s and promptly vanished from public life, never returning to an American diocese.

149

In truth, when he was summoned to the Vatican in 1988 and told he was being replaced as Bishop of Watercross, he feared it was a means of rebuke, especially when he discovered his new assignment.

A science graduate who had been pegged a moderniser and—whisper it—a liberal, he had occasionally piqued the dismay of traditionalists by giving voice to his embarrassment at the more primitive superstitions that attended the Church in some of its less culturally developed outposts. Most senior clergy he had spoken to shared his opinion that the veneration of tacky statues, particularly in Latin countries, didn't reflect well upon the Church at large, not least because it was uncomfortably close to idolatry, but there seemed an unspoken rule that voicing this to the laity was somehow disloyal. Doing so earned him a degree of suspicion in certain quarters, which was partly his intention, because it was a debate that he wanted the Church to have. Unfortunately, having such a debate was regarded as providing a spectacle for the entertainment of the Church's enemies, and thus he garnered no takers until he upped the stakes by publicly admitting to a general scepticism over Marian apparitions. He did not say outright that he didn't believe in them, but he did express that he considered it significant that the recipients of these visitations, and those of poltergeist, tended to be pubescent girls, undergoing a confusing and emotionally unstable time in their lives. (Contrary to some reports, it was not he who also drew the comparison between Lourdes and Fatima and the Salem witch trials: that was an academic who appeared on a discussion panel with him at a seminar held, as fate

150

would have it, *in* Salem; but nonetheless, Tullian's failure to contradict him was noted.)

The ensuing correspondence in American Catholic journals was joined by no less a figure than Archbishop Francis O'Hara of Chicago, speaking as a representative of the Congregation for the Doctrine of the Faith, the church body responsible for appraising the veracity of such miraculous visions. The Archbishop accused Tullian of 'grudging awe and wonder', of 'forgetting that God does not owe man any proof', and signed off by telling him that 'conditional faith is not faith at all'.

Tullian did not grudge awe nor wonder, and his faith in neither God nor the Church itself was conditional. It was absolute. To quote Father Benedict Groeschel, a priest with a doctorate in psychology from Columbia: 'True belief is a decision. It's also a gift. Accept the gift and you will make the decision.'

One didn't have faith *in* Christianity: faith *was* Christianity. O'Hara was correct: faith was absolute or it was nothing at all. Belief was both its own justification and its own reward. Thus it was embarrassing to suggest that God should be handing down vulgar trinkets in the form of mystical signs or miraculous interventions, and for His church to be offering theological bread and circuses. Equally, the practice of science and the quest for knowledge, for facts, was not a search for reasons to believe. *Blessed are those who have not seen, and yet believe*: John 20:29.

If you needed to feel wonder, wasn't Jesus enough? If you wished to thrill with awe at the presence of God, wasn't His creation enough?

151

This world, this universe? Tullian loved science—physics in particular—not because it offered proof, but because when you already had faith, then in science lay a deeper appreciation of both the hand and the mind of God.

There was a fashion for offering cosmological reasons to suggest that the insignificance of our tiny planet vanishingly reduced the likelihood of a divine purpose behind our existence here. This argument could be distilled down to: 'Space is much bigger than we thought it was a few centuries back, so the smaller we get in the big picture, the less likely it is that there's a God.'

In fact—and these most certainly were facts—the sheer unlikelihood of us being here at all, on this tiny little sphere, orbiting a minuscule star, in a minor planetary system two thirds of the way out from the centre of just one of a hundred billion galaxies, demonstrated entirely the opposite.

There was life on Earth because it was situated just the right distance from the sun in what was known as the 'Goldilocks zone' of the solar system: not too hot and not too cold, protected from asteroids by the gravity of Jupiter, and orbited by a moon just large enough to stabilise the planet's climate for the hundreds of millions of years necessary for DNA to develop. Our solar system itself was in the Goldilocks zone of the galaxy: far enough from the radiation field spewing from the vast black hole at its heart; close enough to the centre to allow the higher elements to form.

All of this, coupled with the infinitesimally precise fine-tuning of the laws of cosmological and subatomic physics that allowed the universe to exist at all, was a source of awe and wonder at

God's glory that dazzlingly outshone every other miracle, never mind every tacky Third World shrine.

All of this Tullian expressed in an impassioned and heartfelt letter to the archbishop that humbly sought to correct his misapprehensions, and though it succeeded in doing so, it unwittingly altered the course of his own fate.

Less than a year later, he received his summons—to come to Rome and work for the Congregation for the Doctrine of the Faith.

He interpreted it initially as a chastisement. He had always feared that his stance on Marian apparitions would come back to bite him. However, in an organisation as Byzantine as the Church, you never knew whose path you might have crossed, nor even the agenda you had become a part of. Thus such a reassignment could be a punishment intended to rein in an upstart, but just as easily it could be a lesson handed down by a senior figure who nonetheless agreed with you, but still thought you needed to learn greater humility. This would never be made explicit, however, as the lesson of the latter often required the belief that one was undergoing the former.

To this end, he was given several months of bureaucratic busywork: immersing him in the finest details of the Congregation's undertakings, methodology, reports and even expense procedures, until debates, seminars, science journals and his beloved Watercross Cathedral back in Massachusetts all became a sepia-tinted memory as he began to believe he had been banished to some kind of ecclesiastical gulag. Then, one stifling August afternoon, Archbishop

153

O'Hara appeared unannounced, handed him return flight tickets to Paraguay, and finally revealed to him the real reason he had been called to the Congregation.

'One is coming who is mightier than I,' O'Hara said. *'He will thoroughly purge his floor, and will gather the wheat into his garner; but the chaff he will burn with unquenchable fire.'*

Tullian was to become the primary filter through which all reported miracles, visions and apparitions had to pass before further consideration by the CDF. His remit, as the Congregation's Chief Scientific Adviser, was to investigate objectively but sensitively, then compile reports on his findings, which would be passed on for further consideration—or not, as the case frequently turned out.

He flew back and forth across the world, investigating weeping and even bleeding statues, glowing paintings, spontaneously occurring images of Jesus and (more frequently) the Virgin. He spoke to sometimes sincere, sometimes frightened, sometimes confused, sometimes conspicuously attention-seeking witnesses. He uncovered frauds and cranks, disclosing inventive uses of chemistry to effect miracles involving paintings and statuary, and on several occasions ensured that certain 'visionaries' subsequently received the medical and psychiatric help of which they were in genuine need. He exposed the human hands behind most of the 'spontaneously occurring' images, learned how frequently the outline shape of the Madonna and Child resulted when two conjoined branches were removed from a tree, and discovered just how subjective one's interpretation of any image could be once the beholder had decided what they *wanted* to see within it.

Of course, it didn't necessarily mean that these investigations ended with his report. His findings were sometimes 'taken under advisement' and a second investigator dispatched, to look into the matter further 'with a fresh pair of eyes'. The first time this happened, leading ultimately to the verification of a vision in Chile, he entertained the unworthy notion that part of the reason he had been appointed was that it added authenticity if the CDF could say that its most sceptical scientific investigator had examined the case (omitting, of course, what the sceptical scientific investigator's report actually said). However, this cynical thought failed to factor in the question of who, in that case, he thought the CDF were trying to convince. Though his sequestration had been revealed as an instance of head-hunting rather than punishment, he came to understand that humbly gaining a new perspective upon the realm of miracles and their perception within the Church was, perhaps purposely, part of the result.

Naturally, it often came down to politics or other such sensitivities: a localised boost to religious devotion could be both timely and expedient in a world increasingly beset by secular influences. The Church had many enemies, and Tullian came to accept that there were greater evils than an overzealous local priest exciting his parishioners' fervour with an old statue and some creative use of phosphorus. Sometimes, however, people simply needed hope. Even if the shot in the arm was synthetic, the hope it gave was not itself false. Sometimes, belief in something false was like a

155

temporary bridge to support pilgrims on the journey towards greater, true faith.

And very occasionally, he did encounter something that defied explanation and that made him tremble in recognition of a power greater than man's. Unfortunately, as he was to discover, that power would not always be a higher one.

By 1999, his continuing interest in physics had led him on to the emerging attempts to reconcile the Newtonian with quantum mechanics, most promisingly in the form of string theory, with its implications for the existence of six higher dimensions, albeit that these were imagined to be curled up smaller than an atom. Within this burgeoning field, the concept of membrane, or M theory, if true, had implications that were as exciting as they were disturbing; and in theological terms, had implications more profound than science had posed since Darwin.

In M theory, there were not ten but eleven dimensions, or 'branes', and rather than being minute, it was suggested that some of them might be infinite in extent. One hypothesis for the creation of the universe was. that these higher branes were in an eternal process of stretching and contracting, moving between energy states, with their collisions giving rise to new universes. There was a sophomoric atheistic argument regarding the vastness of the universe and its abundance of space supposedly making it absurd that Heaven and Hell might be accommodated somewhere else altogether. Tullian could imagine its proponents rejoicing at the notion of infinite new universes being created between the branes, when in truth this hypothesis only served to illustrate the plausibility of higher and lower realms existing in completely separate dimensions to our own. It was hardly a new concept to those of faith. What really excited Tullian about the membrane hypothesis was that it finally got past Einstein's necessity for a beginning of time—of time itself being created, like space and matter, in the big bang, with no such concept as time preceding it. M theory, while not fully implying a world without beginning as well as a world without end, did at least suggest the 13.7 billion years of our universe could be a mere blink in God's eye.

Truly head-spinning was that these other universes and higher dimensions, despite being infinite in size, might be less than an atom's width away.

One of the great questions facing physicists was why the force of gravity was so weak in comparison to the other three forces. The nuclear forces were strong enough to power suns and level cities. The strength of the electromagnetic force compared to gravity could be illustrated by pitting a toy magnet from a Christmas cracker against the gravitational pull of the entire planet and seeing which one wins the tug of war over a paper clip.

Nonetheless, the gravitational pull of our (and every other) galaxy was far larger than its mass dictated according to Newton's laws, an effect attributed to the existence of dark matter, the invisible entity that was hypothesised to account for up to ninety per cent of the universe's mass. However, according to M theory, gravity might in fact be as strong as the other forces, but appears weak in our three-brane world because some of it leaks into higher-dimensional space—meaning dark matter might have a more astonishing explanation than previously imagined. In M theory, because gravity was caused by the warpage of hyperspace, as well as leaking from our three-brane world into a fifth dimension, it could also pass *across universes*. A galaxy in a parallel universe would therefore be attracted across hyperspace to a galaxy in our own. Thus the gravitational pull of our own galaxy measured stronger than Newtonian physics dictated because there was an invisible galaxy behind it, floating on a nearby brane.

As Tullian put it in a letter to the now Cardinal O'Hara in 2002, the mass represented by these 'shadow galaxies' could equally be something more familiar. Dark matter, the missing mass of the universe, could constitute the traceable physical signature of the higher realm. Unfortunately, there was no reason why it couldn't also signify the physical presence of the lower one too.

Throughout modern Catholicism, there was all manner of half-cocked pseudo-philosophical nonsense spouted by people who professed to believe in God and in an afterlife (which most were too gutlessly coy to call Heaven), but not in Hell, and most definitely not in Satan. Tullian would have to own up to his own historical equivocation on the matter, and his reluctance to let human individuals off the hook for their values and decisions by handing them such a get-out clause as the existence of an external, autonomous and omnipresent source of evil. Nor was he ever comfortable with the suggestion that God would condemn even the lowest of his human subjects to an eternity of suffering: the idea that something so base and fleeting as a human being could provoke an inexhaustible need for restitution from the Eternal and Almighty was sheer conceit on the part of man.

However, very few would argue with the idea that evil exists in chaos. That it is in man's efforts to free himself and his world from chaos that he frees himself also from evil. The universe started in chaos, and the Second Law of Thermodynamics dictated that it would end in chaos too: entropy always increases. Therefore, if God had given man the free will to shape his own fate, was it in man's power—was it, in fact, potentially mankind's fate—to somehow damn himself? The existence of a darker realm, and of man's technological advancement towards being able to verifiably detect it, opened up some very dangerous possibilities. If man could detect it, he asked O'Hara in his letter, how long before he could *access* it?

A consequence of this idea of gravity leaking between dimensions, as Tullian read in one paper, was that 'quantum gravitational—and other—effects may be observable at energies replicable within large particle colliders, rather than at the Planck energy (10^{19} billion electron volts), as previously believed'.

It was the 'and other' part that truly disquieted him.

The paper explained how technology was reaching the limit of how much radio frequency energy could be used to drive particle accelerators. However, a new generation of accelerators was in development, harnessing laser power to create high-velocity gas plasma that carried particles in its

159

wake. So far, the lasers were only operable over very short distances, but even these could generate a thousand trillion watts (a nuclear power plant, by comparison, could only generate a billion). As this distance grew, so would the power available. This technology was developing by a factor of ten every five years, and would soon deliver a new breed of accelerators 'that would make the Large Hadron Collider look like a dinosaur'.

The paper was by Lucius Steinmeyer. It was the last thing he published before dropping off the map.

Across the table in the Command Room, the esteemed physicist looks like he's clinging on by his fingernails.

'With respect,' Steinmeyer says, his tone intimating that he holds anything but, 'myths and fairy stories are not comparable to data and evidence, no matter how many thousand years old. Science isn't a body of knowledge, it's a meth—'

'A method, yes,' Havelock interrupts. 'A method by which the true scientist has to accept what the data is telling him, even if it contradicts that which he has set out to prove. You've opened up a gateway and what's come through it are some angry motherfuckers with horns on their heads. Holy water burns their skin. They go fucking crazy if you show them a crucifix. Jesus Christ, Lucius, if it walks like a duck and it quacks like a duck . . .'

'It's duck enough for me,' says McCormack. 'And that's why we're shutting it down, forthwith. What's locked up downstairs is just what we caught when we dipped our net into the shallows. We have no idea what might be waiting in the depths. We are not ready for this, at any level. Not

160

scientifically, not militarily and not politically.'

Steinmeyer turns towards Tullian. 'You know, you should be on my side here,' he says, finally talking *to* him and not merely about him like he's not there. 'Surely if I've opened up the gateway to Hell, you're going to see business booming in the Catholic Church like it hasn't done for about five centuries. Do you really want to close the door on a chance like that?'

Tullian can't decide whether Steinmeyer's making an utterly desperate final gambit or merely lashing out like a drunk who knows he's about to be shown the door. Nonetheless, either way, he wants to get through to him, needs to make him understand. He needs to make all of them understand.

Tullian's letter in 2002 had been merely his latest regular digest of recent scientific matters. He had thought it a little self-indulgent in its laying down of so much rather speculative thought, and thus he wasn't even sure Cardinal O'Hara would give it more than a courteous once-over. He almost, in fact, deleted his ponderings upon dark matter as perhaps being melodramatic and lacking intellectual sobriety. Upon such tiny fulcrums do pivot the greatest turns of destiny. Before the year was out, he had been appointed a cardinal himself, such rank a prerequisite of his being granted access to artefacts and information that were among the Church's most securely guarded secrets.

In the secular world, people were increasingly seduced by the idea that the Vatican historically hoarded and suppressed any evidence that cast doubt on the veracity of Catholic doctrine.

161

Conspiracy theorists depicted shadowy and power-hungry cabals capable of the most ruthless deeds in order to protect the Church from the outside world discovering highly damaging truths. It made for exciting—if far-fetched—stories. In reality, this darkest of revelations—entrusted only to a select fellowship among the 'princes' of the Church—had been scrupulously kept hidden for centuries not for the protection of the Vatican, but for the same reason that any other state in the world would have classified it top secret had it fallen into their hands instead.

The Congregation for the Doctrine of the Faith had a remit to investigate the inspiring and miraculous, seeking traces of the hand of God. It had, however, undergone what was known in modern parlance as 'a rebranding exercise'. Prior to this, it had been charged with seeking traces of the hand of a darker power, and was known by a different name.

In 1950, Pope Pius XII had issued his epoch-making encyclical, *Humani Generis*, which shaped Catholic doctrine as it faced the world of the late twentieth century and played a large part in assuring this scientifically curious young prelate that he was on the right path. However, it also included the troubling requirement that all Catholics must regard the Devil as a person, all demons as real. This had always struck Tullian as being at odds with the bull's forward-looking purpose in preparing the Church for the greater malleability and open-mindedness that it would need in order to adapt in a world of accelerating scientific progress.

On a chilly November morning in 2002, only a

day after the solemnisation ceremony, Tullian was shown why he had been so hastily elevated to his new rank. In no dusty crypt but rather a spotless, high-tech and formidably impenetrable vault, he discovered what indeed existed in a shadow realm separated from our own by a barrier only an atom's width thick.

'Professor,' Tullian says, speaking softly so that he—and everyone else—will make a greater effort to listen. 'I have spent many years witnessing what undue import people can ascribe to the most trivial symbols, to happenstance and coincidence. Villages almost at war because a lightning strike has cloven a tree-branch and left a stump shaped like the Madonna and Child. It is apposite that you should have alluded to the Holy Inquisition. That most dark and bloody shadow upon the Church's history is replete with instances of mistrust, suspicion and hatred sparked by the merest suggestion of supernatural forces. All it took then was a rumour, a shape or shadow mis-seen in the firelight. Now think of what is being held in those containment pods. Were the world to see, as we have done, demons made flesh, living and breathing before their eyes, I fear a tide of madness and horror that no church, no army could contain. Consider in this world of—as you called them—superstitious fools: a reign of terror attended by the arrival of demons. It would itself create a self-fulfilling prophecy: people would hail it as heralding the end of the world, and in time, through the ensuing madness, it very well might be.'

'Hell on Earth,' Havelock says, his voice barely an awestruck breath. He sees it, McCormack too.

Steinmeyer, however, remains blind; and not so much blinded by science as blinded to all but his curiosity, his quest. Possessed, Tullian might even say, and he chooses his words with care. According to doctrine, the Devil cannot possess a person unless he is invited, and if Satan needed an instrument here in this place, he could not have found a better candidate than a scientist who did not believe in him and was driven by the purest motives.

'This is insane,' Steinmeyer protests. 'You're pulling the plug on something that could fundamentally alter our understanding of the very fabric of the universe.'

'It's purely precautionary,' McCormack replies, sounding as placatory as he can. 'It's just safest if we mothball the project at least until we know more about what we're dealing with.'

'Mothball?' Tullian asks, suddenly feeling like a trapdoor has opened beneath his chair. 'In my view it would be negligent to do anything but dismantle it.'

'Like I said,' McCormack responds, 'we all need to take a step back for a while.'

Steinmeyer is pressing his temples like his skull might come apart. 'You don't understand,' he says. 'You can't "mothball" it, because it's not something we can necessarily resume. We don't know what caused the Dodgson anomaly, let alone what the anomaly is. We don't know whether we opened a door or merely found the bell.'

'Well, a lot of folks are very worried about who's answering,' Havelock replies.

'That's the risk we'll have to take,' McCormack says, getting up from the table and thus signalling that the discussion is over. 'Shut it down,' he tells Havelock. 'That's an order, effective immediately.'

'Sir, for safety reasons, we have to let the reactor complete its cycle, which will take approximately twenty more hours.'

'Then shut it down after that.'

Steinmeyer holds up one hand in a final, futile gesture of appeal.

'If we let this close, there is every chance it will be lost forever,' he tells them.

Amen to that, Tullian thinks, though in truth he knows it is not something anyone would want left to chance.

For who can yet believe, though after loss,
That all the puissant legions, whose exile
Hath emptied Heaven, shall fail to reascend
Self-raised, and repossess their native seat?

VI

'The problem you have, Kano, is that you think we believe in this white-bearded cliché in flowing robes, stoating about on a cloud, and you say if science can't verify the existence of this flimsy straw man, then we must be a bunch of simpletons to believe in it.'

They're all gathered in Kane's room, where he invited them to share a nightcap. Kane and Blake are each sitting on single beds, Heather and Guthrie on chairs they brought through from their respective rooms. Heather is glad it was Kane who volunteered his quarters for the venue, as had it

165

been Blake, the interconnecting door would almost certainly have been noticed, and possibly even utilised in moving the furniture. It's bad enough she and Blake knowing about it, but the thought of the other two being aware would have her squirming.

She listens to Blake speaking and thinks back, beyond the awkward moment in her room tonight, to each of the encounters she has had with him. There is something perplexing about all of them, something not quite jarring but not quite fitting either. They all feel like deleted scenes: curios, sometimes interesting in and of themselves, but somehow unsatisfactory, failing to resolve anything, and therefore existing adrift from the greater narrative of both their lives. The question is, what does she want the greater narrative to be, if those deleted scenes are to make the final cut?

The bottle of single malt is probably the only thing distinguishing this gathering from the assemblies taking place right now in all of the other bedrooms. There's an almost juvenile sense of escape about the suspension of normal rules, ranks and other formalities, an appreciative awareness of how this gathering could not be taking place under any other circumstances. Even Guthrie has started to unwind, having now managed ten minutes without visibly stiffening in response to every echo reaching them from the kids' dorms.

'Science doesn't preclude the God I have faith in,' Blake expands, 'something eternal and transcendent that isn't subject to humanly verifiable rules of existence. Whether you're talking about evolution or the Big Bang, there's nothing in science to rule out a creator, and some of us are not so arrogant as to demand that He gives us a theological handout by way of proving his existence in a manner vulgar and obvious enough for us to make sense of.'

Guthrie is nodding along sincerely, looking like he might have hope for this drink of skoosh of a chaplain yet.

Kane, though, is smiling, loving this.

'Aye,' he says, 'the religious types are lapping up the beardy god in the sky right now. "Of course we don't believe in *that*, you silly atheists. We're down with the Big Bang, daddy-o." So let me throw you a bone. Let's say that the Big Bang was initiated by some kind of higher intelligence. What evidence is there that this being demands to be worshipped by its creatures? Your parents created you—do they demand to be worshipped?'

'Parents don't demand worship, and nor does God,' Blake replies. 'Parents give love, as does God, and they give guidance: they offer a way of living that will help you to live a good life. We choose to honour our parents, and we choose to honour God. You're relying on anachronistic connotations of the word "worship" here, Kano.'

'So what evidence is there that this being is good, or caring, or in any way motivated by a morality we might recognise? What evidence is there that this being has any interest in what is effectively a by-product, a trace element of the universe? What if this super-being is merely one of a race of super-beings, and is in fact the super-being equivalent of a teenager who created our universe one afternoon with his super-being chemistry set?'

'It doesn't change the fact that the existence of

God is not precluded by any of the absences of evidence that you mentioned.'

'The existence of God is not precluded by anything because it's non-disprovable.'

'And doesn't that tell you something?' Guthrie wades in, like he's exasperatedly explaining himself to a particularly obtuse third year. 'It can't be disproven. It's eternal, a thing of ultimate grace, and no matter what knowledge we arrogantly presume to bring to bear upon it, the truth of God prevails.'

Heather reluctantly decides to make her own intervention at this point, to avert the rage Guthrie is liable to fly into when he hears how this eternal grace and prevailing truth can be attributed equally to whatever bizarre deity Kane subsequently invents in order to make his point.

'Non-disprovable is a scientific term, Dan,' she says politely. 'In this context it doesn't mean quite what you've inferred.'

'What: non-disprovable doesn't mean something cannot be disproven?' he asks incredulously.

'It does, but it also means it can't be proven either. For something to be provable, it must also be disprovable. It's not enough to find evidence that supports your idea: there has to be, theoretically, a piece of evidence that would support a null hypothesis. For instance, gravity is disprovable. If I drop this glass and it doesn't fall, I'd disprove gravity. There's an experiment I can carry out or an observation I can make that will prove the idea either way.'

'Okay,' Guthrie says, taking it in. 'That's fine for something obvious, like gravity, but what about something more complex? What about evolution?

How is that disprovable?'

'Find a fossilised rabbit buried in a layer beneath a fossilised stegosaurus and you've disproved Darwin just like that. Kane is saying you can't do that with God.'

'Even if you could,' Kane says, 'it wouldn't make a difference. If the God hypothesis was somehow disprovable, and scientists found indisputable proof that there was no God, the Church wouldn't miss a beat. It would simply say that this emergent proof was merely a fabrication to lead man astray, thus instead proving the existence of Satan, and by extrapolation of God too.'

'And if God showed up here tomorrow,' Guthrie retorts, 'you'd be asking how we know he's not just a . . . what was it? Teenage super-being or some such drivel.'

Blake is laughing, though Guthrie wasn't trying to lighten the tone.

'Touché,' Kane says, before getting to his feet and finishing off the last trickle he's been nursing in his glass.

'It's coming up for midnight,' he says. 'I'll go and tell them lights out, for what it's worth.'

'No, no, I'll do it,' Guthrie says, also standing up.

Heather gestures to him to remain seated.

'With respect, Dan, that might be counterproductive. Play it canny,' she entreats, refilling his glass by way of further persuasion.

'Okay,' he says, though there is a restiveness about him as he sits back down.

'By the way, who do you all want in the sweep?' Kane asks, stopping at the door.

'What sweep?'

Kane opts to take the outdoor route to the dormitory blocks so that he can get some air, with the added advantage that he'll be able to arrive undetected by whoever's been appointed to 'keep the edgy'. It's a crisp, still cold that greets him: fresh enough to shake the bleary fug resultant of cosy indoor warmth, a full stomach and good single malt. You wouldn't want to be standing still in shorts and a T-shirt, but it's pleasantly refreshing on a brisk stroll such as takes him to the far end of the buildings. He steers away from the gravel, walking on grass to remain silent, an effect enhanced by his need to take it slow. It's really quite startlingly dark out here, even under a cloudless sky, until his eyes grow accustomed and the stars reveal themselves to his widening pupils like they're being faded up in an offstage control booth.

His way is further lit once he makes a turn at the north-west corner and comes in sight of the dormitory corridors' outside walls. Most of the windows are streaming light, curtains not drawn, some of the panes wide open, no doubt to vent smoke. There is one frame that stands out black, prompting Kane to check his watch in case it's later than he thought. No, not much past midnight. The dark window is therefore more suspicious than the smoking ones. There's just no way any of this shower has decided it would be sensible to turn the lights off and have an early night. He's not close enough to see very well, but it looks like the curtains are pulled back and the window open, so no, it's definitely not an outbreak of responsibility.

He makes his way quietly around to the rear fire exit and lets himself inside, allowing the door to bang at his back by way of giving everybody a heads-up to stash their booze and nip their fags. Kane then amuses himself by making a quick patrol of the boys' corridor, failing to keep a straight face as he observes the ridiculous spectacle of postured calm and order that has been rapidly assumed beyond each doorway. Marky Flynn is even pretending to read a book, for fuck's sake.

He returns to a spot roughly halfway along and addresses the whole corridor.

'Right. I'm not your mammy, lads, and I'm not here to say "lights out". You're all big boys now. Just don't kick the arse out of it—remember we've got a long day tomorrow. Nighty-night.'

Several boys reply, 'Good night, sir,' from inside their rooms, in a variety of giggling silly voices. Kane smiles to himself, making a counting-down gesture with his fingers. Four, three, two, one:

'Good night, John-Boy,' calls out Deso.

Damn it: he had Beansy in the sweep.

He is about to walk away when he notices that one door remains closed, and his geography tells him it's likely to be the room with no lights on. Kane approaches tentatively, his hand slowly reaching out to the handle and turning it, revealing the interior to be indeed in darkness. A thin and widening wedge of light streaks across the floor. It picks out only the edge of one bed. He sticks his head through the gap, at which point a pale-coloured shape flies at speed towards him.

It strikes him in the face and he bats away what turns out to be a pillow.

'Fuck's sake,' issues an irritated voice. 'Light pollution, man. Shut the bloody door.'

Stepping fully into the room, Kane sees Adnan, Radar, Matt, Ewan and Cameron gathered around a telescope, which is pointed out of the open window at the vividly starry night sky. It is at this point that Adnan spots who he's talking to.

'Oh fuck, sorry, sir. And sorry about the language too,' he adds, a smile in his voice though his face is in darkness.

'Don't rip the piss, Adnan,' Kane replies. 'How's the seeing?'

'Different class.'

'Aye, that's the middle of nowhere for you.'

'Take a look.'

Kane makes his way delicately to the telescope and peers into the eyepiece. He sees a bright circular disc, a hint of grey-blue around its edges.

'Venus?' he suggests.

'Good spot.'

'Looks like it's a ten-bob bus fare away, doesn't it, sir?' says Radar.

'Try thirty million miles when it passes closest,' says Adnan. 'And that's the nearest planet. The nearest star is Proxima Centauri, four light years away.'

'I'll leave you guys to it,' Kane says. He exits and closes the door.

Adnan gives himself a moment for his eyes to readjust, then makes some alterations to the telescope's position, keying in the corresponding coordinates on the computerised alt-azimuth mount.

'This is Polaris, the North Star,' he says.

Ewan has a look.

'It's actually two stars in binary orbit, but it looks like one because it's four hundred and thirty light years away.'

'Wow. So that means what I'm seeing here is actually . . .'

'Four hundred and thirty years ago, yeah. Shakespeare was live onstage when that light started its journey.'

'How did you get into this?' Ewan asks him. 'Did you get a telescope when you were wee?'

'Yes and no,' Adnan answers. 'I got a scope when I was wee because I was already into it. It was the winter that started me off.'

'Whit? Early dark? Clear skies?'

'No. When I was a kid, I hated being cold, and when winter was coming, I used to wonder why it had to. Was there any reason, maybe, why one year it might not, and we'd get the same weather all year round? I didn't understand why there had to be seasons. Then I found out it was an astronomy question.'

'Because the Earth goes round the sun,' Cameron suggests.

'No; well, partly. It's because of the Earth's axial tilt. During half our orbit, the northern hemisphere is closer to the sun, and during the other half, it's the southern. That got me thinking about what was in the sky as solid objects rather than just lights and dots. Got my first scope when I was ten.'

'I'd just have been using it to see in lassies' windaes,' Radar says.

'Only if you get turned on by looking at folk upside down,' says Matt, making one of his rare but insightful, if arcane, contributions.

'How's that?' Radar asks, but Matt doesn't answer.

'The image is inverted,' Adnan tells him, keying in a new set of coordinates. 'Doesn't make much difference when you're looking at stars. In space, there's no such thing as the right way up. Now, get a load of this.'

They take it in turns to have a look.

'It's Andromeda.'

'Is that a star? Looks a bit like a hamburger.'

'It's a whole galaxy.'

'Fuck, so it is,' Cameron says. 'Like a flattened disc.'

'The Earth wasn't flat, but it turned out the universe is,' Matt mumbles.

'Messier 31,' Adnan informs them. 'Two hundred thousand light years across. It's the nearest galaxy to here, and it's heading towards us on collision course at three hundred thousand miles an hour.'

'Fuck!' Cameron shouts, and dives theatrically out of the way, prompting much hilarity.

'Don't sweat. It's two and a half million light years away. We've got three billion years before impact.'

'Nothing can travel faster than light,' Radar says. 'I remember Mr Kane telling us that. So that means humans are never going to reach these places, are we?'

'Not travelling on a linear plane, no. In fact, the universe is expanding at such a rate of acceleration that the light from the more distant parts of it will never reach us. But that's only talking about movement in three dimensions.'

'Well what other dimensions could you be talking about?' Radar asks. 'The fifth one, with Mr

Mxyzptlk from *Superman*?'

'Physicists are increasingly accepting that there may be higher dimensions, as well as parallel universes.'

'Seriously?' Cameron asks, lifting his head from the scope and letting Ewan jump in.

'Straight up,' Adnan assures him. 'Our universe could be a four-dimensional island floating in higher-dimensional space, one of an infinity of islands, in fact. But the thing about this higher dimension is that if we could see it, if we could move through it, we'd have a very different concept of distance.'

'How?'

'Well, think about an ant on this duvet.'

'More like a flea if it's Radar's,' Ewan suggests.

'Shut it you, ya fudnut.'

'The point is, the ant is only moving in two dimensions: width and length. It can't access—and isn't even aware of—what is effectively a higher dimension: height. So if there was a group of ants on this duvet and you picked one up, it would look to its mates like it had dematerialised. You put it down again on the other side of them, and it looks to the ants like it's been teleported. But all that's happened is it's moved through a dimension the ants can't see and aren't aware of. We move in three dimensions, plus the dimension of time, but if there was a fifth dimension, the same effect could apply to us.'

'You could perform surgery without breaking the skin,' says Matt, grasping the principle and expanding on it in his familiarly skewed way. 'To a fifth-dimensional being, our anatomy would look like a cut-away diagram.'

'But how would we cover distance quicker?' Radar asks. 'The ant still has to travel—it hasn't taken a short-cut.'

'There's a limit to the analogy,' Adnan admits. 'But if you can imagine, our perception of three-dimensional distance might not reflect reality, just like the ant's perception of two-D distance. Look at this.'

Adnan takes a corner of the duvet in his hand.

'The ant is here, right, at one end of this wee universe. To get to the opposite corner, it's a long distance in two-D space, isn't it?'

'Aye,' Radar and Cameron agree.

'Now watch this.'

Adnan folds the duvet diagonally until the opposite corners are held only an inch apart. 'The distance in two-D space remains the same, but the distance in three-D space is much shorter.'

'Wow,' Cameron says. 'That's just . . .'

Adnan witnesses Cameron's awe in HUD-mode for a moment. He pictures the word **Overload** flashing across the screen, counter bars pulsing into the red zones at either side.

'We think of space as a place,' he continues, 'or even an absence of material, but scientifically you need to think of it almost like a substance itself. That's why parallel universes, if they exist, could be only a molecule's width apart from our own: a universe creates its own space.'

In Adnan's HUD, Cameron's head actually explodes.

*   *   *

Guthrie has a darkening glower about him, sighing

with a dissatisfaction that appears to be growing in proportion to his obvious efforts to refrain from expressing it. There's been a weird atmosphere since Kane left, exacerbated by it being his bedroom that they're sitting in. Kane had allowed Guthrie the last word and perhaps tactfully chosen that moment to withdraw, but he knew that Guthrie's values would be affronted that they were even having such a discussion at all. Consequently it feels to Blake a bit like Kane farted and then left everyone else to smell it.

'I should have gone for Beansy,' Blake says, harking back to the sweep to lighten the mood. 'Schoolboy error picking Roxburgh. Too grown-up these days, or aspiring to be.'

'Yep,' Heather agrees. 'That's why I went for Deso. Unapologetically juvenile. Dan's on a decent shout with Radar.'

But Guthrie's not going to be soft-soaped.

'With all respect, Father Blake, I think it's high time you stopped apologising for your church and started standing up for it. All this so-called atheism is just a fashion, a trend. They know the truth deep down and that's why they all change their tune as soon as they realise they *need* God.'

'They don't seem to be realising it in great numbers,' Blake replies softly. 'My growing fear is that I'm part of a dying way of life. How many kids who've been through St Peter's in your time ended up becoming priests?'

'That's just my point, Father. Secular influences: it's not trendy. But trends are localised. There's no shortage of priests coming through from the developing world, where they're less worried about their hairstyles, or what's being said about them on

177

each other's web pages.'

'Yes. The priesthood is a popular vocation where there's mass poverty, low literacy and limited access to communications technology. That isn't telling me the same good news as it's telling you.'

'Of course, there is a simple solution,' Heather ventures.

Guthrie turns towards her with genuine interest. It's clear he has no idea what she's about to suggest, which is entirely the point she's making.

'What's that?'

'Start ordaining women.'

Guthrie sighs with irritation, like he was genuinely hoping to hear something constructive but has instead merely received another 'anti-Catholic' jibe. However, it's Blake whom Heather decides to put on the spot about it.

'Why not?' she asks him. 'Do oestrogen levels interfere with the process of transubstantiation?'

'No, we're concerned that you'll start knitting in the middle of mass, or giving sermons about shoes.'

'Seriously, Con, why not?'

She's looking at him with something he just can't read. There's a mischief, a toying about her, and yet there's something else she wants from him, an invitation to break ranks on her behalf.

'Jesus didn't pick women. He created a priesthood of men.'

'That's the party line. What do *you* believe?'

'Any priest who declares in favour of female ordination would be doing so against the Deposit of Faith: the body of unchangeable teachings entrusted by Christ to his apostles.'

He hopes she hears his real answer, encoded in

178

the word 'would', but if so, she doesn't look satisfied.

'I think the Church would rather crash and burn than cave in on that one,' she opines.

'It would crash and burn if it did cave in,' declares Guthrie. 'Because it wouldn't be the Church any more. That's what the modernists and apologists don't understand. We can't start throwing the baby out with the bathwater. If we keep bowing to transient values just to be popular, then we end up giving away the farm.'

Heather puts down her glass, still with the best part of a measure in it, and stands up.

'*I suffer not a woman to teach, nor to usurp authority over the man, but to be in silence*,' she says. 'But in defiance of the Book of Timothy, being a teacher, I'm away to shout at Kane to get a shift on.'

And then there were two.

Guthrie pours himself another shot from Kane's bottle, while Blake braces himself for a sustained onslaught that he really can't be bothered with after a long day. Instead, however, Guthrie necks it in one and gets to his feet.

'I'm for my cot,' he says, stretching.

Before he goes, though, he puts a paternal hand on Blake's shoulder.

'Stand fast, Father,' he says. 'Take strength from the Lord. This church has endured for two thousand years, and it's had harder things to face in that time than the goggle box and the internet. It's God's will, and none can oppose it.'

Blake gives him a smile and a nod that he hopes look convincing.

I wish I had your faith, he thinks. I wish I had

your faith.

*   *   *

'How's things on the distaff side of the fire doors?' Kane asks.

'Calm,' Heather tells him. 'Winding down into late-night blethers mode. I'm just putting in an appearance for show: I think both sides know who's going to crash out first.'

'Aye. We can get our revenge in the morning, though. Wake them up early and kick in their hangovers.'

Heather realises he's only half joking. Despite dire announcements about being sent home instantly if booze was found on them, everybody knew it would still be flowing, even Guthrie. It was a matter of entrusting the kids to police themselves: it wouldn't be an issue unless any of them were daft enough to make it one.

They're walking slowly along the link corridor that forms an alternative route back towards reception, avoiding a trip back through the boys' corridor. It's fairly quiet, just the occasional burst of laughter.

'You're fifteen quid up, by the way,' Blake tells her. 'The sweep.'

'Oh, nice. I'll put it towards more malt. Actually, on second thought . . .'

'Yeah,' Kane says, a hint of a blush about him. She expected him to be unapologetic, even perversely proud of starting a rammy, but she sees something else. It's as though he's been caught doing something, and she thinks she knows what it is.

180

'I used to think that Guthrie got on Con's case, but I'm starting to realise: Dan's a pussycat compared to you.'

'It's not what it looks like,' he insists. 'Con and I go way back. We've been friends since before we were the age of the kids here. We like to butt heads, philosophically, but it's just a debate, albeit an endless one.'

'It looked like more than that to me,' Heather says.

'Don't worry about it—there's no animosity, I can assure you.'

'I believe you. What I saw was the opposite of animosity. You were impassioned. It was like Blake's an alcoholic and you're his best friend staging an intervention.'

Kane opens his mouth as though to offer a denial, then lets out a regretful sigh. Busted.

'You guys were at school together. Catholic school. But one day you saw the light and you've been trying to save him ever since?'

'That would be one way of looking at it,' he concedes. 'Except I don't tend to regard it as being me that had a conversion. It was growing up talking to Con about things that set me on my heretical way. He was always a deep thinker about these matters; about all matters. Smartest guy I've ever known.'

'But if the smart guy turns religious, you reckon something's gone wrong? Doesn't that seem a little arrogant?'

'It would if that was the whole story. Someone once said that "the reason smart people believe weird things is that they are skilled at defending beliefs they arrived at for non-smart reasons".

181

Usually that reason is that they were told this belief at an early and impressionable age by someone they trusted to tell them the truth. Then decades of reinforcement weave a web that is very difficult for the individual to pick apart because it's like performing surgery on yourself. With Con, I'm determined to keep picking at the web for him, stop it from hardening.'

'Because you think a "non-smart" reason lies at the heart of his faith. Sorry, but that still sounds incredibly arrogant.'

'Like I said, it's not the whole story.'

'I heard he was once engaged before he decided to become a priest. Is that part of the story?'

Kane has a glance back along the corridor, as though checking there aren't a dozen kids sneaking up on him. They're approaching reception. With a troubled look on his face, he nods towards a couple of couches, and they sit.

'Blake met this girl Gail in second year at uni, met her through me. She and I were at Strathclyde, Con was at Glasgow. She was studying law, but she said she'd no great desire to be a lawyer. Con was different: he didn't know what he wanted to do before he went to uni, then once he got there, he just knew he didn't want to leave. He enjoyed learning and he enjoyed teaching. By third year he was already paying back his student loan by tutoring kids for their Standard Grades and Highers. The guy just loved academia. He also loved Gail. The two of them were sickening, in fact, back then. I'd be going from one disastrous relationship to another and they were love's young dream.'

Kane grimaces a little, like he's suffering acid

reflux and will have to re-swallow something bitter.

'Just a fucking waste,' he says. 'Thinking of what he could have had. What *they* could have had.'

'So what prompted this dramatic change of path? Never mind that, what about Gail: if they were engaged, how did the poor girl take him ditching her to join the clergy?'

Kane swallows, and it's as bitter as he anticipated.

'She dropped dead on a squash court two days after Con sat the last of his finals. Undiagnosed cardiac defect.'

'Christ.'

'I can't begin to imagine what Con went through, and in my opinion, he never recovered. I think he joined the priesthood in the same way that men used to join the Foreign Legion.'

Kane's eyes fill, though he's talking about things that must have happened well over a decade ago.

'He would probably have described himself as agnostic before Gail died. We were both brought up Catholics, but the difference between us was that while I was happy to have extricated myself and given it up as a bad lot, Con was regretful that the Church couldn't answer his questions. He hadn't been to mass in years, but it was like he was always leaving the door open just in case the Church could improve its case. Then he suddenly finds himself trying to make sense of what had happened to Gail, contemplating the loss of this whole future that had been in front of him one minute and taken away forever the next. He needed to believe in something, needed to believe there was a reason or an order behind it, and a purpose for himself in the world after being cut

183

adrift. That's his "compelling but non-smart" reason for turning to religion.'

'But whether you like it or not, it was religion that got him through it,' Heather says. She speaks softly, trying to ensure it doesn't sound like she's telling him off or taking sides, but she's already conscious of wanting to protect Blake. 'You have to give credit where it's due. Con is happy in what he does. He's good at what he does. He could never get back what he lost, but what he's got today, he's got because of his faith. Maybe you should try to make peace with that.'

Kane says nothing for a moment, but it's like he's struggling to suppress a response rather than contemplating her suggestion. He opens his mouth to speak, then holds off again, looking at her as if to say she really doesn't understand.

'Tell me this, Heather,' he says, finally having collected himself. 'Where's the control group when people say faith got a person through something? How do we compare how that person would have got on in the same situation *without* their faith?'

'But if you're his best friend, the one who understands most what he's been through, shouldn't you of all people respect the decisions he's made, the conclusions he's reached? Even if you disagree with them, shouldn't you accept how important to him Con's beliefs are?'

Kane nods like this is something he knows is true, even something that bothers his conscience, but then fixes her with a look of unapologetic sincerity.

'If I believed *he* believed them, I would.'

Heather feels her mouth open slightly but nothing emerges. She's about to gently admonish

184

him again for the inherent arrogance in Kane's words, when she realises that they explain everything she's never quite understood about Blake.

'When we were debating tonight,' Kane continues, 'did you really hear what he said? He talks about "the God I have faith in", not "the God I believe in". Con has always had faith in the *idea* of faith. What he has is a meta-faith. Con isn't a priest because he believes. He's a priest because he wants to believe. Since Gail died, he's spent his entire adult life searching for something that will *make* him believe. And he's yet to find it.'

VII

November 12th 2002. Tullian remembers it more vividly than any other day of his life. It was, effectively, a second birthday: a day of being reborn, passing into a new world. A day when belief became fact and faith became reality. But not in a happy way.

He stood in an antechamber, having been silently escorted there by an elderly curate so imbued with a solemnity of duty that it was possible to imagine him having performed his role for a thousand years. Then he waited, alone, for almost an hour, before hearing a single pair of footsteps descend the staircase into the vault. He knew merely from the lightness of their gait that they did not belong to the man he expected, Cardinal O'Hara. Instead, he found himself confronted by the slight, octogenarian but

185

nonetheless daunting figure of Cardinal Carlo Parducci. Tullian was not ashamed to admit that he felt his pulse race, and briefly entertained the most paranoid fears that he had been lured down here for reasons better associated with the far south of Italy.

The laity and the media had talked of Joseph Ratzinger as being 'the Vatican's Rottweiler', but those truly in the know understood that it was Parducci who had long been the most feared man in Rome, the unseen power behind two of the preceding three papacies (John Paul I being the exception, with Luciani's efforts to marginalise Parducci's influence leading to the most squalid of rumours).

'Cardinal Tullian, peace be with you,' he said.

'Peace be with you.'

'I hope you breakfasted well, for it was your last meal on this Earth as you used to know it.'

That Parducci was speaking English, despite Tullian's fluent Italian, played a large part in salving his fears about what might be about to happen in this hidden and unwitnessed place. Parducci was extending a generous courtesy, and his tone was one of regret.

Parducci produced a key and pulled open the wide pair of wooden doors that dominated the antechamber. They revealed only a further door, this time of grey steel, its lock taking the form of an electronic keypad.

'What is this place?' Tullian asked.

'To put it in the context of your home country, Cardinal, this place is the Church's equivalent of what you may have heard referred to as Area 51.'

Parducci opened the steel door and led him

inside, into his rebirth.

The specimens were enclosed in glass cases to prevent decaying contamination from the air, and kept in darkness to preserve them also from light; the vault being lit by ultraviolet lamps on the extremely rare occasions when anyone was permitted to view it.

Parducci first showed him a skeleton, picked clean by the ravages of time but shocking enough in bearing a tail at one end of its spine, horns protruding from its skull at the other.

'This one came into the Church's possession in 1321, slain in the mountains of Bavaria. If you look closely, you can see the damage to its upper arm from a sword blow, though it was in fact killed by being run through. Little is known beyond that. It was sent here by Matthias, Bishop of Mainz, and its discovery precipitated a truly bloody period of witch-hunting throughout Germany.'

He then led him to a desiccated and partially mummified specimen, dried-out skin still stretched across its frame, a look of snarling violence still legible on its grimacing face.

'This one was entrusted to us by King James VI of Scotland—later James I of England—in 1590. Attempts were made to preserve it, but as you can see, the means available to our predecessors at the time were inadequate. This one was taken alive and observed personally by James, who eventually had it transported—under all secrecy—to the Vatican. James had seen the beast tortured but feared the consequences of killing it, in case this merely freed its soul to possess another.

'The experience had a dramatic effect upon him and consequently upon his country. Witchcraft had been a criminal offence in Scotland before 1590 but very little action had been taken in the name of the law. However, having seen this demon live and breathe, James became both obsessed and paranoid. Within a year, three hundred alleged witches were tried for plotting to kill him, accused of feats such as summoning a storm to drown him at sea and attempting to conjure his death by melting a wax effigy of him. In 1597, he wrote his treatise on "Daemonologie". Hundreds upon hundreds of people were executed as witches throughout his reign.'

Parducci's words barely registered as Tullian stared aghast at these revolting affronts and contemplated the hideousness of all that their existence implied—for the world and, indeed, for the cosmos.

'Your letter to Cardinal O'Hara suggested that the shadow realm could be but an atom's width away. Here lies proof that the border between it and our world has already been breached. Demons are not merely symbolic, Cardinal, not simple projections of our darkest thoughts and most fearful nightmares. They have been coming through into our world for centuries, most probably for millennia.'

VIII

'Caitlin,' Rosemary whispers, as loudly as she dares. There's been no sound or movement from Bernie or Maria for some time now, and she doesn't want to waken them, but she's sure Caitlin hasn't fallen asleep yet.

She'd been hoping she would be the first to flake out. There's no temptation when there's no option, and there's no option while there are other people sharing your room. Even in the dark, they're only feet away, sensing movement, hearing all sound. There's no option. No temptation. No temptation means not lying there saying decades of the Rosary, partly as a distraction and partly in prayer to Mary for strength. How many Hail Marys, how many decades of the Rosary, since it began? How many hours awake? How many failures? And afterwards, how many tears?

'Caitlin,' she tries again.

There's no response.

It's Friday night; no, Saturday morning now, technically. Saturday night into Sunday morning will mark her little anniversary. Six weeks clean. Six weeks since she last succumbed. It was getting more all the time, but she couldn't say it was getting easier. Some things required less and less effort the more you got used to them, but this was like holding your breath. The longer you held out, the harder it became.

She used to read about drug abusers and, despite the Church's message of compassion towards the afflicted—hate the sin but love the sinner—she couldn't help but feel they were weak and self-indulgent. That was before she found her own heroin. Closer to the mark, she used to think the same thing about homosexuals, who were 'called to chastity' according to the Church. 'This inclination constitutes for most of them a trial,' the Catechism said. 'These persons are called to unite to the sacrifice of the Lord's Cross the difficulties

189

they may encounter from their condition.'

Why couldn't they just call on God's strength and simply restrain themselves? she used to wonder. Now she knows.

This desire, it feels like a curse. She who has been so faithful, so devout, in every way that has been in her power; she who has never missed mass, said her prayers every night since she was three, given up most of her free time to church activities: she has committed a mortal sin. Knowingly, wantonly and repeatedly committed a mortal sin.

'Both the Magisterium of the Church—in the course of a constant tradition—and the moral sense of the faithful have declared without hesitation that masturbation is an intrinsically and seriously disordered act.' So said Pope Paul VI in *Persona Humana* 1975. She had searched for any update on the Church's position, or even a more liberal-minded interpretation of the previous, but as recently as 2000, the Scottish Catholic Education Commission's consultation document 'Relationships and Moral Education' reiterated that it was 'a very serious disorder that cannot be morally justified', while Pope Benedict had called it 'a debasement of the human body'.

She wishes she was still a child, wishes she was back in what that same document reminded her, longingly, was a 'period of tranquillity and serenity', undisturbed by 'unnecessary knowledge'. She barely talks to boys now. She sometimes tells herself that she finds them disgusting, with their crudeness and base obsessions, but she knows that she's merely deflecting the blame. What disgusts her about them is only what she sees reflected of herself: what they make her want; what they make

190

her *do*.

She has to make her sacrifice to the Lord's cross, and accept that she has a condition that, like homosexuality, must be seen as a call to chastity. Thus she has to limit her interactions, keep her dealings with boys as stilted and functionary as possible. She can't let them give her imagination anything to feed upon, because that's how it starts. A moment of flirtation, a lewd comment, a stolen look: the slightest thing can be the seed, the germ. That's how temptation works.

It is a relief to be here, to be on retreat. Perhaps God knew she needed respite. Three nights in a room with three other girls. Three nights with no option. She's been looking forward to it, knowing it will ease her over the six-week mark and beyond.

So why can't she sleep?

Because a retreat is not enough. Three nights' respite is not enough. She needs to talk to somebody, but there is nobody she *can* talk to: not about this. She can't confess it either, can't tell a priest. Not Father Blake, certainly, and not Canon Daly either. He's known her since she was about five, spoken to her three times a week at choir practice and what have you.

Bernie and Maria are not an option. Nor is she going to ask Caitlin: 'Hey, do you touch yourself?' But Caitlin does seem spiky on the subject of the Church these days, and Rosemary has a sudden interest in discovering why. She wants to hear a dissenting voice: not that of a person who was always ambivalent or even hostile to her faith, but a person who used to be as devout as she. If she could talk, just talk to someone who might have a different perspective, she's sure that would help.

191

But help how? Help because basically she wants someone to say what she's done—what she wants to do again—is all right? Who could tell her that, with any authority, when the Catechism is so clear on the matter, and has been for centuries? Isn't she like a drug addict wishing the authorities would just legalise heroin rather than dealing with her own problem?

It's *not* all right. That's why she's suffering. It's not rocket science. Sin leads to suffering. She sinned, ergo she is suffering.

So why, when she is *not* sinning, does it feel like she's suffering more?

'Caitlin,' she whispers a third time. 'Are you awake?'

*   *   *

Jesus, take a hint, Caitlin thinks. Yes I'm awake, but hasn't it occurred to you that, after three attempts, I'm either asleep and ought to be left alone, or *pretending* to be asleep, and thus attempting to convey the same message all the more strongly? Yes, Rosemary. I'm awake, but no, Rosemary, I don't want to have an in-depth late-night conversation about the latest pronouncement by Pope Benedict, the Novus Ordo, the Tridentine Rite or whatever other tragic shit you are disturbing enough to even *know* about.

For heaven's sake, girl, someone needs to remind you that you're seventeen, and you don't get to do this twice. Do you think an 'ever-loving God' would want you spending your adolescence alternating between anger and misery as a bunch of joyless old men in silly outfits tell you what to

192

disapprove of and what to feel guilty about? Yep, good thing all the big issues Jesus cared about, such as poverty, tyranny, inequality and oppression, had been eradicated: that left the Church free to concentrate on piddly little issues that they personally had hang-ups about, like homosexuality and birth control.

At this most difficult age, feeling awkward, misshapen, spotty, graceless, uncool and confused, all of it ultimately down to sex, it transpired that the only guidance an all-powerful super-being from a higher plane could offer on that baffling subject was: 'Try not to think about it. Put it out of your head until you're married.'

Why, thank you, Father, thank you, your Eminence, thank you, your Holiness. Thank you, Lord. That really saves us from the maelstrom of post-pubescent female emotions. Caitlin could picture a cross instead of a Nike swoosh: 'Just *don't* do it.' And what with them all being guys, they would be a lot of help dealing with what she has been going through of late. But then, it wasn't just religion that was useless when it came to this kind of thing. Who *do* you talk to about having this weird mix of fear and fascination with the male member?

It's been haunting her for ages: stalking her fantasies, killing them stone dead. She's seventeen years old and in no hurry to have sex; let's face it, she would be grateful enough for the chance to walk, never mind fly. But even her thoughts and daydreams (not to mention her last-thing-at-night dreams) in which she plays out soft-focus and strictly soft-core scenarios about meeting the right boy, are being increasingly derailed. She envisions

193

kind words, solicitous acts, soft lips, tender arms, and even, sometimes, delicate hands in delicate places—then up it rears, the serpent from the depths, the inescapable reality that lies in the extrapolations of even the most idealised imaginings.

That thing's got to hurt. It's got to do damage, and not just some rite-of-passage, largely symbolic damage in breaking the hymen. She's never been able to use tampons, and they're the size of cocktail sausages. There is no way that is ever fitting. And yet . . .

She lies there some nights simply wondering what it must feel like; and not only what it feels like to the touch, but what it must feel like to be male, to *have* that appendage. How can it be flesh and yet supposedly so rigid? Is it like muscle that's become calcified? Surely that can't be pleasant. And how can the softness of a kiss, the softness of an embrace, the tenderness of caressing, give way, give a willing place to this brutal, unyielding thing?

Maybe when it doesn't seem scary any more is when you know you're ready to do it. It's difficult to imagine ever feeling that way, but then right now it's hard enough to imagine just having a boyfriend. She got off with her cousin's next-door neighbour Carl last Christmas down in Southampton, and apart from officially 'going with' Radar in Primary Five, that's been the sum of her love life. In the movies, Christ, in bloody *Hollyoaks*, they're always having parties or hanging out in places where they can meet each other. How is she meant to find the time or the opportunity here in reality: studying for all these exams every night, working all day Saturday for a little cash she

194

seldom even has the chance to spend?

Then, of course, there is Sunday, a valuable chunk of which is sacrificed every week still going to mass because she is too chicken to tell her mum and dad what she really believes (and in particular what she really, really doesn't).

Yeah, quite the rebel. Quite the fearless heretic. Maybe the reason she is so sore on poor Rosemary for her ongoing assumptions is because she is too cowardly to tell anyone the truth. It's difficult, though. She's not good at confrontations, and she doesn't want to hurt her parents' feelings or in any way let them down. On the other hand, it's increasingly starting to burn that she is written off as a shiny-haloed goody-two-shoes. Yes, she's quiet and polite and she works hard: it's who she is, but it's not *all* she is. It especially pisses her off that people think because she's well behaved that she must also be dutifully religious. However, that doesn't piss her off as much as the fact that, in the Church's sin-seeking and ever disapproving eyes, she is far better behaved than she'd sincerely like to be.

*   *   *

Deborah actually finds it a relief when Miss Ross comes by and tells everyone it's time to go back to their own rooms. The vibe is still weird, uncomfortable, nothing like she imagined it would be. There's not even been much drinking: everybody's tired after the journey, and the consensus seems to be that they should save themselves—and the stash—for tomorrow night, when that Sergeant Sendak guy said they could set

195

up a disco.

Julie's really been getting on her tits. She just won't let up about Deborah sharing a room with Marianne. It has obviously been some kind of personal triumph for the chubby cow, and she's seriously kicking the arse out of it. It's all lesbian this and muff-dive that. God's sake: get some new patter, ya fat ride.

It's not just Julie, though. Everybody's happy to join in, even Gillian, and though they're all acting like it's Marianne they're taking the piss out of, Deborah can't pretend they don't think the joke is on her too.

She makes her way back to the two-bedded room, where she is greeted by the sight of Marianne dressed only in two towels, one tucked around her torso and a second wrapping her hair. There are wet footprints on the floor tiles. She's just out of the shower, having opted to grab one late at night when they're bound to be quiet. Smart move, Deborah thinks. It will be mobbed in the morning, unless she gets up before everyone else. Maybe she should set her phone alarm accordingly—she'll be wanting out of this room as early as possible anyway.

She's hopeful that the vibe will be different in the morning. They're going out on some kind of hike, so not only will there be none of this 'we're in, you're out' carry-on, but Julie is likely to be struggling to keep up. Plus, a night of listening to the tubby boot's desperate patter while she's trying to get to sleep would remind Gillian why it's Debs she usually hangs out with.

She should set the alarm for seven: half an hour earlier than Miss Ross told them they'd need to get up. She knows there's a fair chance she'll prize thirty more minutes in bed over feeling fresh when it actually comes to it (especially if they're going to be tramping about getting sweaty and mocket), but she'd like to have the option.

Deborah gets out her phone and hits the unlock code, intending to set the alarm, but finds it still on camera mode from the pics she took in the other room. On the tiny screen, she can see Marianne drying her hair, the topmost towel obscuring her face—and her line of sight—as she rubs vigorously at her straggly Goth mane. The lower towel is on the move too, the motion of her arms working it gradually free.

Deborah feels this sudden thrill, a sense of opportunity, and instinctively presses the Shoot button as the towel drops, revealing Marianne's skinny tits and modest wee bush. She only gets a glimpse, but she estimates that she's naturally light on the thatch rather than manually kept in trim, and that Julie was probably lying about having seen her naked at the baths. Marianne reaches a hand blindly downwards, trying to retrieve the towel, then, not finding it, resumes drying her hair for a few seconds before bending to secure it again.

Feeling her pulse race and her head spin a little, Deborah stares fixedly at her phone and pretends to text, making out she wasn't looking. The picture is a good one: well lit and not blurry, with the goods all clearly on display. She feels something flush through her, fears her cheeks are glowing and may give her away. What if Marianne glimpses the phone? she wonders. She goes to save the photo so she can clear it from the screen, pressing the corresponding button with her thumb. At the top of the resultant menu, above Save and Delete, is the option 'Send to'.

She thinks immediately of Gillian. A picture of any classmate in the scud would be social dynamite, but given that it's the creepy Goth weirdo, nobody would value this more. Oh the things they could do with it: pass it round, get it on Bebo. And the best part is, not only would Marianne be the last to know of its existence, but she couldn't even prove it was her, as her head was obscured.

Aye, she's totally got to send this to Gills. There's close to no signal round here, but maybe just enough for texting. Aye. A wee gift, flying from room to room over the airwaves: something secret just between them. It would get Gillian texting too: establish a special wee line of communication tonight so that they wouldn't be so separate. And wouldn't that put Julie in her place: Gills quietly texting Deborah in the dark instead of paying attention to all her rambling shite.

She selects 'Choose recipient(s)', being very careful to select Gillian and only Gillian, but hesitates when it comes to pressing Send, a sudden onset of anxiety staying her hand. It's that sudden, vertiginous sense that there's no going back: she's doing something she won't be able to undo. A single tiny action of her thumb, setting a zero to a one inside the mobile, will commence a sequence of events that would be further and further out of her control.

She can see Gillian immediately sharing it with the others: no secret stifled giggles and quiet wee texts, but instead cackling it up with Yvonne,

198

Theresa and Julie, the source all but forgotten. No, the source would not be forgotten: quite the opposite. Jesus. She suddenly envisions the hidden implications of what she'd be bringing down upon herself. Taking secret pics of another girl in the buff: it's actually Debs who's the lesbian. Even if they didn't believe that, even if they knew why she had really done it, it was in their power to pretend otherwise. She'd done it herself often enough: wilful misunderstanding, watching your victim squirm as her truthful and reasonable explanation is rendered irrelevant. This means what we want it to mean: that was the rule.

She cancels out of the Send menu but finds the file has autosaved. That's okay, she can delete it manually later. The main thing is she has stepped back from the brink of catastrophe. She puts down the phone like she's putting down a loaded gun. Relief runs through her, but it's not total: there's a new anxiety creeping in; or rather, a new perspective upon an established occasional worry.

Why *had* she really done it, she asks herself? That thrill had come over her before she even understood why, and she had acted upon it instantly, way before it occurred to her what she might do with the resulting photograph.

A familiar debate gets rehashed in her head. She's never done thinking about sex, speculating about sex: strictly heterosexual, boy-on-girl sex. However, it occurred to her recently that those speculations have never been about guys, only other girls: how far they've gone, what they have and haven't done, even whether they stylise their pubes, for fuck's sake. And now she's sneaking pictures of Marianne's nude torso. Does this mean

. . . ? But if it did, wouldn't she feel differently about her friends? Surely she'd be aware she wanted to feel physically closer to them; surely she'd have caught herself thinking she wanted to kiss one of them? She could not remember ever imagining kissing a girl, and the thought right now makes her go icky. And yet, there she was a minute ago, wishing for a kind of intimacy with Gillian, a secret bond, and feeling all vulnerable and excluded because she's ended up in the wrong room.

*   *   *

Marianne climbs into her cosiest pair of long-sleeved and long-trousered pyjamas, then blows her hair dry so she won't look too much like Helena Bonham Carter when morning comes around. She hasn't traded a word with Deborah, though her room-mate has at least progressed from demonstrably ignoring her to genuinely seeming rather withdrawn and pensive, the latter an extremely uncharacteristic condition for someone who didn't even have hidden shallows. She'd sat there rapt with her phone, like it was the Oracle at Delphi, then come over all ashen-faced like said Oracle had revealed to her the emptiness of her soul—by text.

After dinner, Marianne had sat alone, reading, while everyone else scuttled in and out of each other's rooms and pretended to themselves that they were in some lame teen movie. Too bad it wasn't *Scream*. Nah, she didn't mean that. Not entirely. Thirty per cent, at most. Maybe forty.

Roisin had asked—politely and charitably—if

she wanted to come next door where they were playing cards, but she declined, preferring to spend a little time on cards of her own. She didn't want anybody being 'nice' to her. Sure, it was a little sulky and masochistic, but in self-harm terms, it put her at the way-healthy end of the emo scale.

This is her fourth secondary school, due to her mum's job moving the two of them around. She has to go where the contracts are, keep the money flowing in. Her dad pays child support, but in her mum's eyes, that has to be supplementary—she never wants to be in a situation where she is relying on anything from him.

That is another reason why her mum keeps upping sticks and completely relocating. Her dad was—is—an alcoholic; a recovering one, these days, but in the past an occasionally violent one. It wasn't extreme; didn't have to be. He hit her mum twice, or twice that Marianne is aware of; on both occasions just lashing out, as opposed to sustained attacks. Her mum said she'd only forgive him once, and she was as good as her word. He hasn't fallen off the wagon since the divorce and is entitled to stay in touch with Marianne, but Mum doesn't want to make that easy for him. A change of address every year or so seems to be part of the strategy.

It's always Catholic schools she gets enrolled in, even though her mum doesn't go to mass or send Marianne there either. She can't remember her mum ever going, in fact, though she knows she used to. She got Marianne baptised, but by Mum's admission, that was largely to placate her grandparents. Yet every time they moved, she insisted on a Catholic school. It was some kind of tribalism, a running to what she knew because it offered a form of security amidst the unfamiliar. When you keep having to relocate to new places, you need the reassurance of certain things being consistent, even if they are consistently crap. That was why McDonald's was so successful. People didn't really like McDonald's, same as her mum didn't really like Catholicism, but when you were new in town, at least it was a known quantity. So that'll be a Quarter-Pounder and a Communion Wafer meal-deal to go.

But after four schools in five years, she's long since done with making an effort to be liked. Thus, she'd rather be alone than be tolerated, and she'd rather be creepy and unnerving than popular.

Her hair dried and tied back for the night, she settles down at the head of her bed, cross-legged above the covers. Having carefully arranged a couple of books on the occult where Deborah is likely to notice them, she then gets out her tarot pack and begins sifting out the major arcana from the deck. She has dealt ten of them into a Hagall spread on the bedcovers and is poring over them when her room-mate returns from brushing her teeth and performing her ablutions.

'What are you doing?' Deborah asks with a combination of scorn and anxiety.

'Tarot.'

'Oh no, cool the jets. You're not trying to summon up spirits. That stuff pure freaks me out. My cousin did that once: had a seance, and all sorts of weird stuff started happening. I was terrified. The house has had a weird atmosphere ever since. My auntie ended up asking Canon Daly about it. He said it was very dangerous stuff and you shouldn't be meddling in it. It's a sin, in fact.'

'I don't think a bunch of girls getting hysterical at a sleepover constitutes dabbling in the occult.'

'You weren't there. Maureen contacted the spirit of Kurt Cobain, and—'

Marianne tries to maintain a straight face so that Deborah will keep going, but she can't hold back from laughing.'

'Kurt Cobain? Are you serious?'

'Aye,' Deborah insists. 'It was the anniversary of his death . . . what's so fucking funny?'

'I'm just trying to picture Cobain in the afterlife. He's jamming with Jimmy Hendrix and Freddie Mercury, John Bonham's on drums, but he blows them all off because he'd rather go communicate with some daft teenagers in Gleniston.'

Deborah looks slightly crestfallen and a little confused.

'I thought you were into all that stuff.'

'Oh, I'm "into it" all right, a lot more seriously than your cousin. Which is why I know what I'm doing. It's not about summoning up dead pop stars.'

'So what is it about?' Deborah asks.

Marianne suppresses a smile. Come into my parlour, said the spider to the fly.

'Dive over and I'll show you.'

Deborah does not dive, but approaches gingerly as Marianne gathers in the cards. She climbs on to the far end of the bed, taking great care to tuck her nightie over her knees and avoid exposing her knickers.

Marianne deals out a new spread, four cards in a diamond shape with three more above and three below. Deborah watches each new card with both eagerness and unease, particularly when the Death and Devil cards are placed down. Marianne had, in fact, kept these to one side while poring over her previous spread, then slipped them in close to the top after shuffling the deck. They were her trump cards in this particular game. (Technically, *all* of the major arcana were trump cards, but when it came to freaking out someone like Deborah, these two were indispensable.)

'Death?' Deborah says.

'We'll come to that,' Marianne replies, denying her the standard reassurance that 'it's not what you think it means'.

Marianne spends a long time poring over the spread, partly to let Deborah's anxious imagination get to work, and equally to choose which cards will form the most appropriate basis for the cold reading she's about to give.

'Is this supposed to tell me about my future?' Deborah asks doubtfully.

'It's supposed to tell you about yourself. The cards can decode truths that are locked away inside you, if you know how to read them. There are truths older than history, things that remain true once you strip away all the trappings and fripperies of modern society, or of any society: truths about the essence of a person.'

Marianne points out a card, the left-most of the three closest to Deborah. It shows a woman, naked, kneeling by a pool beneath a bright yellow star.

'This is The Star. You see the woman holding two jugs: from one, she is pouring water into the pool, and from the other, she is pouring it on to the land. This represents harmony, balance, generosity and trust. But look alongside it: we have The Moon. Another pool, but a troubled one, and beyond it stormy seas. Instead of the woman and her tranquillity, we have dogs howling, and a lobster emerging from the water: a creature with a hard shell that lurks in the depths. The Moon's face betrays concern, in contrast to the woman's serenity.'

'What does it mean?'

Marianne cocks her head sympathetically.

'It tells me there's two sides to you that are very closely related and yet manifest themselves in completely contrasting ways.' She adjusts her posture, placing her hands palm-up in her lap in an aspect of openness as she cues the first Barnum statement. 'It suggests that you are a very considerate person, selfless at times, keen to offer whatever you can to those around you, and yet there are times, though you hate to admit it, when you're aware of a selfish side to yourself. And it's not like nasty selfish, more like sometimes you just think: "Sod everyone else, I'm having trouble handling things and I need to look after me right now."'

Deborah's face is troubled, her forehead wrinkled up as she takes this in. Marianne can just about detect a hint of a nod. Marianne says nothing, confidently bides her time for another couple of seconds. Here comes the confirmation, the magic words:

'What else?'

'Well, the jugs of water here symbolise generosity and trust: giving without expecting anything back. Yet on the Moon card there are these stone pillars, symbolic of defensiveness, a barrier against the

205

stormy seas beyond. It tells me that sometimes you fear you are too honest and open about your feelings, afraid you've given away too much, revealed yourself to people who may not be trusted. It also suggests you sometimes have the feeling that other people are having a better time than you, or getting on better at whatever they're about, even though you know you shouldn't complain about your lot.'

Deborah's visage is a study in concerned concentration, her eyes widening in disquieted response to how much she is recognising. She's no doubt starting to feel very spooked about how Marianne can know this stuff about her inner feelings, but that discomfiture always comes in tandem with a compelling curiosity to hear more, if even just to find out *how much* Marianne knows.

'What about the Death card. And that Devil beside it.'

'We'll come to that. There's other things you need to know first, otherwise you might find those parts too disturbing. Look instead to the other card in the line nearest you. That's The Lovers.'

'Adam and Eve?' Deborah asks.

'Among others, yes. On this occasion it's you and me, in a way.'

Deborah looks up like a startled deer. Marianne takes note.

'No, not the lovers. I'm the serpent in the tree, representing new knowledge. You're leaving behind a state of innocence. You're apprehensive, but it gets much more exciting when you succumb and try the forbidden fruit. Do you want to? Should I go on?'

Deborah looks like she's not sure, but curiosity

206

inevitably wins out over her fear of being exposed. 'Please,' she says, a little uncertainly.

'The Lovers represents doubt and difficult choices, as well as temptation and desire. It's a significant card at our age. Passion, desire, affinities, all these things are welling up, and not just the sexual side, though we'll get to that. Passion about music, for instance, desire for certain clothes, for an image. Things you want to identify yourself with: trends, singers, groups of people, individuals.'

Marianne lets this hang while Deborah nods with enthusiasm. Then she allows a pained look to fall over her face.

'What?' Deborah asks.

'Again, there's the Moon card casting a shadow. It represents fantasy and imagination, but also fear and apprehension: the things we dream up are always scarier than the real. In this case, alongside The Lovers, the conflict is sex.'

Deborah stiffens a little.

'It tells me you think about sex a lot. In fact, you sometimes worry that you think about it too much.'

Deborah nods absently, in a way that suggests she's barely aware she's making such an affirmation.

'You're really interested in sex, more than you think other people might be, and you know that's okay, because it's just how you are. But you're very daunted by it too. You have this mix of longing and trepidation. Something about it is confusing you, really confusing you, and that confusion is the thing that makes you most frightened and insecure. It represents the aspect of yourself that

207

you're most afraid of other—'

Marianne cuts herself off as she hears Deborah breathe in sharply, a look of distressed accusation forming upon her face.

'How are you doing this?' she asks, her expression rapidly collapsing into one of anguish and panic. 'How could you know? You mustn't tell anybody, oh Jesus, please don't tell anybody.'

Tears form in Deborah's eyes, accusation abandoned in favour of pleading. Panicking a little herself, Marianne realises she just stepped on a mine. What the fuck? All she has given Deborah is a series of Forer effect gambits that could equally apply to anybody, the last of these—sexual curiosity—being guaranteed to hit home with anyone in the whole dorm block. She can't tell her this, though, as she'll really fall apart if she thinks she's been tricked into revealing . . . well, whatever it is she thinks she's revealed about herself here.

'I'm not telling anybody anything,' Marianne says, insistently. 'Tarot readings are as confidential as confession.'

'But *you* know—that's enough. How did you get inside my head? Oh God, what else have you seen?'

'I've seen nothing that you didn't show me,' she says truthfully. She needs to walk Deborah back, but without giving the game away. 'And nothing that you've shown me isn't true about any of us. Who isn't confused when it comes to sex?'

'Not like this, though. You can't tell anybody about this. If you do, I'll just deny it and say you're making it up, and who are they gaunny believe?'

Marianne briefly considers offering further reassurance but realises it won't be necessary:

Deborah's words are by way of overture.

'It's that . . . you're right, I do think about sex. I haven't done it, okay?' she insists.

'Me neither, actually.'

'It's just . . . when I think about it, I think about . . . other girls doing it. Not me doing it with other girls,' she rushes to add. 'But I wonder about what other girls have done, or if I'm imagining something, it's some other girl or woman I picture doing it. I'm just terrified this means maybe I'm a, you know, a . . . a . . . I think I'd have to kill myself if it was true and folk found out.'

Deborah breaks down now, tears really flowing. She puts her hands to her face and bows over. Marianne suddenly feels dirty for having solicited this. She just wanted to frighten her a little by living down to Deborah and her moronic pals' worst expectations of the creepy Goth chick.

Marianne reaches quickly into her bag and retrieves a paper hanky, which she waves under Deborah's bent head until one of her hands grabs it.

'I think you've got the wrong end of the stick,' she says. 'You said you picture other girls doing it, not you doing it with other girls. I'm the same.'

Deborah looks up and stares at Marianne fearfully through reddened eyes.

'I don't mean I'm worried I'm a lesbian,' she clarifies. 'I'm the same as in I've not done it, so I can't realistically imagine myself in these situations. When I do, I can't take the fantasy seriously, which kills the thrill. You need a proxy, a plausible surrogate.'

Deborah is still staring at her, now even more expectantly than during her reading. Christ knows

209

how much and how long she's been beating herself up about this, and Marianne knows why. Unfortunately, for the same reason, she won't take the explanation coming directly from Marianne, but she'll probably accept it from the cards.

'You see this card here, just above The Moon? That's Strength. See the way the woman is restraining the lion? There's compassion there as well as inner strength, but in you that's combined with the Star card: openness and giving, and that can render you vulnerable. People close to you can take advantage of you, yet they'll never know the times you passed up the chance to take advantage of them. You have a tendency to be too self-critical and consequently you want other people to see the best in you. You've created this disproportionate fear of being a lesbian because it would destroy you in the eyes of the people whose respect you seek most. However, the Strength card suggests you're better than that: inside, you know that you don't need their approval, and you resent the things they would try to hold over you.'

Deborah dabs at her eyes and nose. When she pulls the hanky from her face, she looks as though an intolerable weight has been lifted, though she's not the only one experiencing relief. For a worrying moment, Marianne fears Deborah's going to lean over and give her a hug, but she's just running away with herself.

'That is . . . amazing,' she says quietly. 'How can you know all this about me? How can you tell so much from these cards? Don't take this the wrong way, but are you, like, into witchcraft or something?'

'I'm into magic, and I'm into myth,' Marianne

says, gesturing to the books that have by now fallen on to the floor. Deborah picks one up, a book of demonology, detailing nightmares and demon myths across five continents and fifty centuries.

'Do you . . . *believe* . . . in things like this?' she asks.

'It's not a question of believing, or of whether something is factual. Myths endure because they are true: what they tell us about ourselves is true, and sometimes myths were the way we instinctively understood these things before science and philosophy broke them down and explained them. Have a look at this.'

Marianne reaches for her bag and pulls out her beloved third volume of Neil Gaiman's *The Sandman*.

'A comic?'

'Not a comic, *the* comic, and this is my favourite story, about my favourite story.'

Deborah looks on, confused, as Marianne flicks through the book to *A Midsummer Night's Dream*, as commissioned by the Sandman from Shakespeare as part of a deal. It is performed by Shakespeare's own travelling company before an audience that has passed through a portal from another dimension: Oberon, Titania and Robin Goodfellow among them.

'There,' she says, finding the speech bubble she's looking for and pointing it out.

'*Things need not have happened to be true,*' Deborah reads aloud. '*Tales and dreams are the shadow-truths that will endure when mere facts are dust and ashes and forgot.*'

'You getting it now?'

'Kind of,' she says thoughtfully. 'Can I borrow this?'

'Long as you know what you're dabbling in. I mean, it starts with comics, but this time tomorrow you could be wearing all black and listening to Muse.'

Deborah gives her an 'aye, right' smile and climbs into bed.

IX

. . . nine months ago, on the drive north, on the road to here.

Lights everywhere, flickering and indistinct: white shapes stretched and pulled by random refractions in the rain and spray before being temporarily shrunk to points and discs by the wiper blades. Nothing holds its form or position long enough for him to focus. The closest thing to a constant is the perforated blur of lines on the road, stuttering just out of syncopation like a slowing zoetrope. They flicker and blur, sometimes lost for a second, smeared out in water and the glare of oncoming headlights. A second is a long, long distance at this speed. How far can he travel in that time? He works it out: needs something to keep the wheels turning in his mind. He's doing eighty: inner dial shows one-twenty in kmh. Divides 120,000 by sixty, does it again. Thirty-three point three three three recurring. Another truck to overtake. The spray is blinding, the wipers flailing indignantly at maximum speed, reminds him of a woman walking off in a snit,

212

elbows pumping. It takes eight seconds to pass, two hundred and sixty-six metres throughout which he can see only the shape of the truck and the nearby twinkle of its sidelights.

Finally past the lorry, he takes a curve and sees the windscreen explode into a white glow. Fucker had his lights on full beam.

'Dip don't dazzle.'

Merrick recalls that from some public-information campaign way back; can't remember where, can't remember when. He should *try* to remember, though: another mental exercise, another little project to stop his brain from trying to shut down.

He is just so tired.

The dazzle at least caused him to flinch, seeped just a little adrenalin into his system, but it's going to have its work cut out counteracting all the melatonin. The dark is not helping keep his eyes open, nor is the rain, the headlights, the need to squint, the inability to stay focused upon a point or an object. He needs sunlight. He needs the rain to stop. He needs about twelve hours' uninterrupted sleep.

He's got the fan blowing, taking the temperature down as low as it will go. His fingers feel stiff from the cold air jetting around the steering wheel. The outside temperature is about five degrees, but the heat from the engine means the fan can only blow so cold: it's not an air-con system. His eyes feel bloodshot from the dry air inside the car, the lids getting intolerably heavy. Every time he narrows them to peer through the rain, it feels easier to let them fall fully closed than to open them wide again.

He should pull over, find a lay-by, get out, waken up. He'd be drenched, though, in moments, and still have two hours' driving ahead of him. Plus he's on a clock and already running late.

They gave him zero notice. He was supposed to drop everything, which was an eventuality he always knew he might have to face working for the MoD, but which in practice he had found impossible when such a scenario was finally precipitated. Thus he took time he couldn't afford to try and collate his unfinished work into a form that his successor, if he had one, could comprehend.

He left Dartmoor eight hours ago, having been all but escorted out of the building and pointedly reminded not only that his work there was over, but that he was only ten hours from being in breach by failing to report for duty at his new post. The option to make his own way to Ben Trochart was the only courtesy about it. The alternative was to go on a chopper that was leaving within an hour of his being reassigned, which would have precluded any opportunity to put his work in some kind of order and ensure that certain crucial documents were backed up. The prospect of just having to drop his research was anathema; the idea that the project itself might simply be abandoned one he couldn't begin to contemplate.

What was so precipitately important? He worked for the Ministry of Defence, but you didn't get emergencies in research. Nor did you get rushed to a room and made to sign the Official Secrets Act, especially when you thought you already *had* signed the Official Secrets Act. ('Not this version you haven't,' he was assured.)

214

There had been 'an incident' at the Orpheus complex. That was about as much as he could get anyone to tell him. This confirmed a buzz on the grapevine in recent days that dozens of personnel had been pulled out of the place, and as such was perhaps the only recorded instance of a rumour about Orpheus proving well founded. It was a US-leased, MoD-owned site in the Highlands of Scotland, a former nuclear command complex that had been recommissioned as a research facility after the Cold War. Its location and scale deep underground naturally made it the subject of endless speculation among bored MoD lab-rats, to the point where it had become a running joke, a byword for the technologically super-advanced or downright impossible.

'We're waiting for Orpheus to finish Beta on that one,' was a common way of saying something couldn't be done.

The one thing he did know with any certainty about it was that it was mostly a physics hive, so why were they hastily summoning up a biologist? Dwelling upon that might have provided another exercise to stave off sleep, had it not been that he'd already been pondering it for most of the drive and come up blank.

His eyes are closing; it ought to frighten him how involuntary this seems, but it feels so beckoning, so comfortable. It'll be okay. Just a few seconds' rest, ten seconds, three hundred and thirty-three metres, surely he can risk that. NO. He snaps them wide, breathes extra deeply a few times, sourcing oxygen, gives his head a shake. The windscreen is a membrane, fluid and warping, stretching the light, smearing the shapes, blurring the white lines. He's

215

squinting, narrowing his eyes in an effort to shield the pupils, keep them from contracting so that he can see better into the rain-filled darkness. Maybe if he closes one eye and thus keeps it dark-adapted, then he can open it and close the other next time the oncoming lights are too bright. He tries. Yeah. Closing one eye feels good. It feels too good. He wants to close the other one too.

He hits a straight length of road, an interchange. There are streetlights for the first time in however many miles. He can see the road stretch out, unbending, must be half a mile. Six hundred and sixty-six metres would be twenty seconds. He can close his eyes for twenty seconds. The road is straight. He doesn't need to steer for twenty seconds, doesn't need to look for six hundred and sixty-six metres. He can just, yes, that's it, just . . .

NO.

Fuck no.

Did he really think that? Jesus Christ. Jesus Christ. That settles it.

He sees the sign for a lay-by, indicates, pulls in. He gets out, steps into the rain, teeming down in plunging streaks picked out against the towering lights flanking the interchange.

Jesus Christ. It was that close.

He lets the cold of the rain lash his face, run down his collar, feels the material start to cling against the skin of his chest. He'll get there wet and cold, but he'll get there alive.

Twenty seconds, six hundred and sixty-six metres. Jesus Christ.

X

Fizzy is telling a ghost story, supposedly about the place they're staying in, or what previously stood on the site anyway. Deso knows for a fact that Fizzy had never heard of Fort Trochart a week ago and probably couldn't find the place on a map right now, to say nothing of the fact that the boy's concept of 'historical knowledge' means being able to name players from pre-Fergus-McCann-era Celtic teams. He's adapting some old pish to the circumstances, but fair play, it's appropriate for the time of night. They've all settled down and the noise levels have dropped all over the place, so quiet, creepy stories are a good shout.

The main light is off and the curtains are open so they can see the stars.

Beansy has actually dropped off. All you can see of him is a big lump under the duvet, huddled against the wall beneath the window. Deso just hopes his arse is pointing that way, though the clatty bastard can probably fart so hard that the recoil off the wall will shift the bed. For every action, there is an equal and opposite reaction, as Mr Kane would tell them.

Beansy was first in and out the bogs for a wash and brush-up before nighty-night, and the dozy bastard was asleep by the time the rest of them got back. Marky noticed he was conked when Beansy never responded to a question, and was all for them having a bit of fun: putting Beansy's hand in warm water so he'd pish himself, or drawing a cock on his head with a magic marker.

217

'Naw, we're no' having any of that shite,' Deso had argued, in a way intended to convey that he would not be partaking and therefore did not expect to be on the receiving end either. Marky concurred quickly, realising what a dangerous situation he was leading them all into. Everybody would have been sitting awake the whole night, frightened to let themselves fall asleep before anyone else. Fuck that.

Ghost stories are decent craic at a time like this, but as Deso's lying there, he can't help wishing he'd brought a guitar. His fingers are fidgety: he's moving them under the duvet, feeling an imaginary fret-board and hearing the tune he'd be playing, really softly. He opted not to bring one in case it got damaged and because it was one more thing to carry, but now he's thinking it'll feel like a long time before he gets another wee fix. Ordinarily, he might have been in with a chance of borrowing Rosemary's, but he reckons it's safe to assume that boat's sailed now.

He feels a wee bit bad about that business, in fact. Feels especially guilty about what he wrote on that sticker. It'll come off, he knows, and it seemed funny at the time, but lying in the dim light with the atmosphere quite mellow, he finds himself thinking about what it looked like from Rosemary's point of view. If somebody wrote something on one of his guitars, especially taking the piss out of something he held dear, he'd take it very personally. It was hurtful. Cuntish, to be honest. He doesn't want to go as far as owning up and apologising, but he ought to make it up somehow. Be that bit nicer to the lassie tomorrow, let her know he thinks she's all right, so she'll understand it wasn't malice, just carry-on.

And he does think she's all right, matter of fact. All the hymns and God patter is a pain in the stones, but she's not as bad as some. Thon pal of hers, Bernadette, for example: fucking wee nippy sweety that yin is. Bernie seems the type that's religious just so she can have a moral justification for being in the huff with everybody: take the religion away and she'd still have a face like fizz. Rosemary's the opposite. She always seems burdened: an unhappy clappy. She goes on about the Good News and organises charismatic masses, but none of it seems to be bringing a lot of sunshine to the girl.

Fizzy's building up to his spooky climax.

'. . . and all they found was her shawl, the same one she'd been found in when she was abandoned on the doorstep as a baby,' he says. 'Totally. True. Story.'

Deso and Marky burst out laughing at this final declaration.

'That's fuckin' shite, Fizzy,' Marky declares, still laughing.

Fizzy just grins. Couldn't give a fuck.

'Not true, and not scary.'

'Jumbo fail,' Deso agrees.

'Can you do better, well?' Fizzy asks, clearly hoping that Deso can.

Deso thinks for a moment, and realises he just might.

'Aye,' he says. 'I'll tell you something really scary, and scary because this *is* true. No word of a lie, and you can ask when we get back because it happened to my uncle.'

'No word of a lie, you got shagged by your

uncle?' Marky says.

'Fuck off. This is serious. My uncle Iain and my aunty Margaret live out in Perthshire, middle of nowhere. A place nearly as remote as this. One night, about two in the morning, the doorbell rings, wakes them up. Uncle Iain goes downstairs and opens the door, and there's a man there, about the same age as himself. The man says: "Sorry to trouble you, but any chance you could give me a push?"

'Uncle Iain goes, "Fuck off, I'm in my jammies, it's the middle of the bloody night." He slams the door and goes back to bed, tells Aunty Margaret what it was. She goes spare. She says: "Don't you remember that time when my appendix burst and our Land Rover broke down on the way to hospital? We knocked on somebody's door and I'd have died if that guy hadn't given us a push. Get back down those stairs and help that man oot."

'So my uncle gets oot his bed again, and just as he's walking down the stairs, he realises it has been five years *to the day* since Margaret's appendix went. He's thinking, "Oh fuck, man," as he approaches his own front door. Then he opens it, and guess what he sees?'

'You getting shagged by the wee man?' Marky suggests.

'I'm serious, here. He opens the door, and he can see nothing. No man, no motor. But he can hear this noise, this wee squeaking noise. Eeeee. Eeeee. So he goes, "Is anybody there?" Nothing, just eeeee, eeeee. So he calls out louder, "Hullo, mister, are you there, are you still looking for a push?" And that's when the eeee noise stops and he hears a voice. It's distant, like just more than a

220

whisper, saying: "Aye . . . Over here . . . on the swing."'

Deso lets this hang for a second, then starts pishing himself with laughter.

'Oh, fuck you,' Fizzy tells Deso, then he and Marky start lobbing pillows at him.

'Fuckin' arsehole,' Marky says, but he's laughing as well.

Then one of the pillows misses Deso and wallops into Beansy. He doesn't respond. No half-conscious retaliation, no rolling over, not even a grumble or a snore.

Something isn't right.

Never mind snore, Deso can't hear Beansy breathing, and Beansy does *nothing* quietly.

'Beansy?' he asks.

There is still no response. Deso urges Marky and Fizzy to drop the pillows, give it a rest. They go quiet, exchange looks.

'Aye, very good, Deso,' Marky says. 'You're just trying to freak us oot.'

'Shhh,' Deso insists. 'I'm not. Something's no' right. I cannae hear Beansy breathing.'

Without anyone having to suggest it, they all hold their breaths. They can hear nothing.

'Fuck,' Fizzy lets slip.

Deso slowly approaches Beansy's bed, reaching a hand towards the pile of covers. Just as his fingers touch the duvet, he hears a fierce, throaty growl outside the window, and looks up to see a pallid, grimacing, demonic face snarling behind the glass. There are horns at the temples, seeping gouges on the cheeks, the features humanoid but viciously distorted.

Deso jumps back in response, clattering into

221

Fizzy and Marky, sending all three of them into a tangled sprawl on Deso's bed.

When he looks at the window again, he sees the demon pull the flesh from its own face.

Deso almost closes his eyes in fearful revulsion before noticing that the demon's arm is clothed in puffed-out nylon. The flesh is revealed to be a mask, beneath which is Beansy's grinning coupon.

'*That's* how you give somebody a fright, Deso.'

Bonnie Brae

Bonnie Brae

XI

It's only when a voice speaks to him directly that Merrick realises he's lost himself: staring without seeing, hearing but not listening.

'Two more entities for the collection,' the voice says. 'Not quite the kind of bestiary I had envisaged when I set out.'

It's Steinmeyer, standing next to him on the observation platform, from which they can look down on the floor of the Cathedral. They'd have a perfect view of the anomaly itself if there weren't a dozen soldiers and yellow-suited priests in the way.

Merrick would have been startled to notice anybody was beside him; that it's Steinmeyer adds a deeper level of discomfort. The guy is unravelling. He's been falling apart before Merrick's very eyes, or would have been had Merrick not been avoiding him in order to spare his eyes that distressing sight.

He has no idea how long Steinmeyer may have been standing there. The chief physicist is staring intently, as focused and calculating as Merrick had been disengaged and drifting.

They're shutting it down: Merrick got the memo. He hadn't seen Steinmeyer since learning this news, and hasn't been looking forward to discussing it. It's been hard enough making peace with it himself.

Merrick says nothing, worrying too much about his own response: will it convey how uncomfortable he is to be around Steinmeyer? Will saying nothing do that more? Will either response finally elicit the breakdown Steinmeyer's been so inexorably hurtling himself towards? At least he's being vocal today. Often he comes into the Beta labs and stands like he wants to talk, then says nothing. He's fuming, simmering, like there's so much inside needing to come out that he can't decide how to begin. So he doesn't begin. Then after a while he leaves, and you're very glad he's gone.

'I thought our most exotic captures would be new types of particle; or if not new, then perhaps very, very old, but never apprehended before, even for a nanosecond's duration. Kaluza-Klein echoes. Proof of extra dimensions greater than the Planck length, thus lowering the energy necessary to recreate the unification of the forces. Tangible evidence of the graviton, that was my wildest dream.'

He sounds reflective, even resigned, but he's been like this before. It's like watching a log drift serenely on glass-like waters just ahead of the hundred-foot falls that will plunge it to be consumed in the raging churn below.

Merrick has to reason with him, but not argue with him.

'We've got tangible evidence of something even more remarkable,' he offers.

Steinmeyer looks at Merrick with a pitying regret, like he's telling a child the truth about Santa Claus.

'We've got nothing,' the physicist says. He nods downwards, towards the soldiers and the priests. '*They*'ve got it.'

This could be the moment the log topples over the edge. Merrick searches for something

226

placatory to offer. 'I guess we both knew that when we signed our souls away. Secrecy was always a big part of the deal, but it's the knowledge that counts, not who bags the trophies—or even who gets their name on the paper.'

Steinmeyer nods, more to himself than in agreement.

'Ever heard of Giordano Bruno?' he asks.

'No,' Merrick confesses.

'Precisely.'

'Who is he? What's his field?'

'He was a sixteenth-century Italian philosopher, scholar, playwright, astronomer, teacher, magus and poet. Undoubtedly one of the great minds of his time. He once wrote: "Thus is the excellence of God magnified and the greatness of his kingdom made manifest; he is glorified not in one, but in a thousand thousand, I say an infinity of worlds."'

'Did he precede Copernicus?' Merrick asks.

'No. He was born five years after Copernicus' death. But how's this for a man preceding Newton and even Einstein: "There is no absolute up or down, as Aristotle taught; no absolute position in space; but the position of a body is relative to that of other bodies. Everywhere there is incessant relative change in position throughout the universe, and the observer is always at the centre of things."'

'That is indeed prescient,' Merrick agrees. 'So why doesn't history remember him? Too far ahead of his time? Prophet in the wrong land?'

'He was burned at the stake as a heretic by the Inquisition on February 17th 1600 in the Piazza Campo di Fiore in Rome, and his books placed on the *Index Expurgatorius*. He was offered the opportunity to recant his heresy, but he stood by his belief in a heliocentric universe, and that God and nature could not be separate and distinct entities. His life and work were consequently all but erased from history.'

'See, I don't think the US military go in for immolation. Maybe if Sarah Palin had got in,' Merrick says, trying a leavening of humour as he fears where this is going.

Steinmeyer is still placid, even laughing a little, but his eyes remain fixed on the Cathedral floor—he doesn't look at Merrick—and his mind doesn't stray from its track.

'Bruno was a difficult character. Not so deftly politic or circumspect when the situation behove it. He was all but chased from court by Queen Elizabeth in England because he made her feel stupid. But do you ever wonder why the Church, why the whole of Christian Europe was so in thrall to a Greek pagan who died three hundred years before Christ? Why not only the Inquisition, but kings and scholars wouldn't countenance any idea that was at odds with Aristotle?'

'It's hard to shift the paradigm,' Merrick suggests.

'Exactly. People prefer the world to conform to established truths. They like the idea that some smart individuals have already thought through all there is to think about certain issues, so they don't have to worry about them. It's why we accept authoritarianism: it's comforting to believe that someone else is in charge and knows what they are doing. Copernicus was resisted and Bruno reviled because people don't like someone throwing all the balls back into the air. The reason the

Inquisition had free rein to wreak their tyranny wasn't because they were all-powerful. They had free rein because people were happy to let them.'

Merrick sees it.

'They're shutting us down because the world isn't ready to know about this.'

'Quite,' says Steinmeyer. 'Tullian isn't where the pressure is coming from—he was just brought in because he could be relied upon to provide it. He's a convenient tool, being used by the military to achieve their objectives. We think of military generals as strategists when in fact they are, first and foremost, shopkeepers minding the store. Resource management is literally half the battle: they know what they can and can't afford in terms of deployment, engagement and, most of all, force depletion. After Iraq and Afghanistan, the last thing they want is a new engagement, and the way they see it, this could be opening up not merely a new front, but a new war, one unlike anything they've encountered before.'

'When you put it that way, it's a wonder they let it get this far. But that only covers why they're shutting it down. Where does the fate of Giordano Bruno come into this?'

'Under what happens next. It's safe to say they won't be handing out any Nobel prizes for what was discovered here. Nobody is going to be allowed to know about it.'

'I always knew that when I signed up,' Merrick says, though he knows it's no consolation to either of them. 'The opportunity to work on something as amazing as this was its own reward. But I guess that's going to make it hurt all the more to have to suddenly drop it all.'

'You think that's what's going to hurt?' Steinmeyer asks, once again with the calm, pitying regret that tells Merrick he's missing something. 'How do you think it's going to feel when it all gets tossed in the fire? Did you sign up for that? Because they're not just going to shut this thing down, they're going to erase all traces that it ever happened.'

'They announced they were "mothballing" it, not abandoning it,' Merrick says, suddenly embarrassed by his own naivety as he hears the words coming from his mouth.

'It will be wiped from the hard drive of history. What we've learned here will not leave this place. If nobody is able to follow our work, then as far as science is concerned, none of this ever happened. All you will have to show for it is a memory in your head, one you might start to question the veracity of after a few years, until you start to wonder if it was just a dream.'

Merrick, staring down at the assembly below, now sees the soldiers' fatigues for all that they imply. He recalls being quick-marched to that room back in Dartmoor, signing a version of the Official Secrets Act that few people would ever know existed: 'the most binding non-disclosure agreement outside of *Cosa Nostre*', as the supervising officer described it.

'If I talked to anyone about this, I'd go to jail for a very long time,' Merrick says.

'You'd go to jail, yes, but not for talking about this—not officially. It would be for some other breach they cooked up, because if they throw you in jail for talking about this, they'd be lending your story credence. No, they'll trash your professional

230

reputation too, give you the Roswell treatment.'

'You're not saying you believe Roswell was a military cover-up. Or is there something you're not telling me?'

'No. I'm saying they'd ensure anyone who talked about this place had as much credibility as some internet conspiracy nut. This will be buried and what we found here lost forever.'

The professor doesn't say anything further, just continues to stare intently towards the anomaly, but Merrick hears one more word, and that word is 'unless'.

The contrast between Steinmeyer's demeanour in recent times and the collected figure standing next to him now is as complete as it is disturbing. Merrick recalls seeing something like it only once before, in a colleague who committed suicide days later. A policewoman he spoke to said it was very common: once they have made their decision to kill themselves, the turmoil ceases and they can seem utterly calm and untroubled. Steinmeyer right now is as placid as Merrick has ever witnessed. There's not merely a stillness about him, but a profound sense of resolution.

They say that out in the deep ocean, a tsunami could pass under you in a rowing boat and you'd barely notice a bob. That's what this feels like.

Steinmeyer finally turns and looks Merrick in the eye.

'The world needs to know what happened here,' he says. 'Whether it's ready for it or not.'

XII

Deso gives his boots a stamp on the hard, dry earth, then jumps on the spot a couple of times to warm up a wee bit. It's pure Baltic, but it's clear and still, no wind, so once they get moving it'll be fine. Better than fine, in fact: a cold, sunny December morning and a cracking day for a trek with your pals. Pity there's a bunch of wankers coming along too, to say nothing of Deputy Dan, but you cannae have it all ways. Everybody is kitted out in waterproofs and walking boots, plenty of them sufficiently shiny and new-looking as to indicate there will be a lot of blisters on show later. Deso's got his rucksack already on his back, eager to go, but a lot of them still have theirs sitting at their feet on the ground.

The Sarge guy, Sendak, is looking at his watch. It's five past nine, according to Deso's. They must be waiting for stragglers, but he can't work out who: too many bodies milling about in a crowd. He sees Samantha fussing over her hair, trying to tie it back in a way that's practical but still looks like she could be on an album cover or at least a catalogue for mountaineering gear. The lassie's a doll, sure, but it must be hard work worrying about how you look every minute of every fucking day.

Big Kirk is slotting a packet of fags into the wee upturn of his woolly hat. It looks like a hand-knitted effort, a real present-from-granny number that would be getting slagged mercilessly if it was on anybody else. Not that it looks good on Kirk: he probably selected it especially, knowing it looked

232

daft, because it was one more thing that served to emphasise how the normal social rules didn't apply to him. Prick.

Deborah is farting about with her phone, as per, though it seems to be the camera aspect she's concerned with rather than texting folk twelve feet away to tell them what's happened in the five seconds since she last spoke to them directly. She's standing next to Marianne, which is a bit of a turn-up. Deso wonders what the score is there.

Beansy is bouncing about in front of the pair of them with a big stick. What the hell is that daft bastard up to now?

'Check it, Marianne,' he's saying. He's draped his arms over the ends of the stick and has assumed a posture of crucifixion. 'I'm Marilyn Manson.'

Marianne gives him the finger. There's something very sexy about the way she does it, Deso reckons, but maybe that's just him. Cannae ask anybody else to compare notes, unfortunately, due to the threat of a slagging.

Deso then notices a bit of movement towards the back of the group, hurriedly approaching from the main doors, unseen by the crowd. He realises what it is and lets out a horrified scream, startling staff and pupils alike.

'Aaaah! Paki with a rucksack! Everybody down!'

They all turn in time to see Adnan jogging up to join the group. He rolls his eyes and looks for a moment like he's about to take the huff. Then he yells out *'Allah hu akbhar!'* and pretends to detonate himself. Deso scrambles to 'save' Marky, pulling him to the floor as several others make their own dives for cover.

Guthrie looks fucking appalled, miserable fud

233

that he is, but at least he spares them all the lecture. Adnan's participation snookered him: he'd have been gearing up for a wee self-righteous tantrum about racism and religious prejudice, but the Muslim being in on the joke has fair buggered that for him.

Sendak and Mr Kane share a wee glance of tolerant amusement, before the Sarge gives them their marching orders.

'Okay, let's move it out, people.'

Sendak leads them forward across the single-track road and into the forest, following a path between the trees that opens up directly opposite the gateway into the Fort Trochart Outbound Facility.

'Where is—or was—the fort, incidentally?' Kane asks.

'Long gone,' Sendak replies. 'Nothing left but the name.'

Deborah takes a step to one side as the line passes, snapping a photo of the complex from a sufficient distance to get the whole place in the shot. Beansy has looped his rucksack over his stick, Dick-Whittington-style. He hops up on to a large tree stump for a moment and steps off, obliviously getting in the way just as Deborah's phone-camera clicks. It takes a special kind of talent, she thinks, to be that much of an arsehole even when he's not trying.

Beansy scuttles back to the pack and begins singing as they progress.

'Yo left, yo left, yo left, right, left . . .'

Most of the boys pick up the cadence.

'Yo left, yo left, yo left, right, left . . .'

Happy that they are now in synch as his rhythm

section, Beansy sings over the top of them, to the tune of *Yellow Submarine*:

'We all live in a Catholic housing scheme, the walls are painted green, Michael Fagan shagged the—'

Guthrie cuts him off with a hand over his mouth.

'That's enough, McBean,' he says sternly, which to Beansy is fucking rich coming from him. Beansy's dad told him Deputy Dan used to be on his supporters' bus to Celtic games, and was as enthusiastic as anybody for belting out the rebs.

Just ahead in the vanguard, Sendak sighs.

'Gonna be a long day,' he opines.

'Oh yeah,' agrees Kane.

*　　　*　　　*

'Okay, next victims, let's go,' Sendak calls, prompting Marianne and Cameron forward.

Kane has a look over the edge, getting the all-clear sign from Blake at the bottom, while alongside him Heather helps the newly descended Deborah detach herself from the harness.

The group have been taking turns to execute a gentle abseil down a rock face, two at a time. They're almost done, but Kane predicts the pace is about to slow as the more reluctant candidates are running out of other people to hide behind and will probably require some persuasion. Kane would bet the house on Julie Meiklejohn being last. It uncharitably occurs to him that she might provide invaluable impetus to speed the other fearties up if someone points out the greater risk of the line breaking after it has been subjected to the stresses of supporting her. Not nice, he knows,

235

but it's the release provided by such thoughts that helps him stay professional. They don't care to admit it, but being human, teachers are inevitably going to like some kids more than others, and Julie is one plump chick who is never going to be described, by way of compensation, as having 'a nice personality'. He can vividly imagine the processes that got her that way: the teasing and bullying that toughened her up and taught her how to locate other people's vulnerable spots. Maxwell's equations said that the amount of energy in the universe could never increase or reduce, but it seemed pain and cruelty multiplied like bacteria.

Guthrie helps Marianne into the harness while Kane assists Cameron, then Sendak attaches them to the lines.

'You've seen it twenty times now,' Sendak reassures them. 'Just kick off, and the line will only play out when you want it to, okay? So you go as slow or as fast as you need.'

Marianne bounces off gently, taking it a little at a time. Cameron, not wanting to be shamed by a girl, kicks away more ambitiously and panics at the sensation, going by how tentative his second kick appears.

Sendak has a look down, satisfies himself that the latest pair will manage, though they won't be breaking any speed records.

'So, how did this thing go down?' Sendak asks quietly.

It takes Kane a moment to realise what Sendak is referring to. Kane gives him a look, seeking confirmation that this is so.

'Hey, if you don't want to talk about it, that's

cool,' Sendak responds, misreading. 'I understand.'

'No, no. Talking about it is supposed to be why we're here.' Even as Kane says this, he realises how hard that is going to be. All they've discussed so far has been people's feelings, and only in the most abstract way. It's like they'll have to approach it by degrees, peeling away the protective layers one by one.

'Andrew Dunn—the kids called him Dunnsy— got in a fight with Matt over there.' Kane nods to his right, where Matt is now the only remaining male. 'When I say a fight, more like . . .'

'Matt started a lot of fights by the provocative act of being shy and awkward, right?' Sendak suggests.

'You got it. The other kids don't know what to make of him. He is very, shall we say, emotionally self-sufficient, and they can't deal with that. He can seem very aloof . . .'

'Which doesn't always go down with attention-seeking teens.'

'Exactly, that being a very apt description of wee Dunnsy. He was a little guy: short, tendency to overcompensate in terms of aggression and volume.'

'A hard-case wannabe,' Guthrie chimes in regretfully. 'More combustible than the bigger men because he had more to prove. Not a bad lad. Not a bad lad at all.' Guthrie swallows. This is hurting. It's as much as Kane has witnessed him discussing any of the particulars of that day. 'But a bit too eager for a fight. Tragically too eager,' he concludes, his face threatening to crack.

'I don't know precisely what precipitated it and I don't suppose it matters, but Dunn set about Matt in the corridor where some of the pupils have their lockers. It's a busy spot at break time, as you can imagine. A lot of kids milling around, and one of them happened to be Robert Barker.' Kane sighs, a dozen tabloid headlines screaming in the face of his thinking. 'Barker was . . .'

'Troubled,' Guthrie says, relieving him. 'He was in the year below this lot: younger in years but very much older in terms of experience. His father was put inside for murder when Barker was ten. Mother an IV drug abuser, dead loss. String of equally useless and varyingly abusive junkie boyfriends. Barker was a deeply disturbed kid. Randomly violent and self-destructive. There was a ferocity about him that was as frightening as it was tragic. He was a poor wee boy, really. Just a poor wee boy.'

Guthrie looks away over the tops of the trees. Kane can tell he's holding back tears. This is the other side of the deputy: he can be the most indignantly censorious and morally exacting figure much of the time, but somewhere beneath it is one of the most compassionate men Kane has ever known.

There was a simplistic mentality, as embodied by the tabloids, which saw a kind of closure, if not justice, in Barker's subsequent suicide. Guthrie was one of those who most keenly felt it instead as the compounding second blow of a greater tragedy. Both Guthrie's strength and his vulnerability—Kane couldn't call it weakness—lay in that he thought Barker could be saved, and it was his job to do it.

Kane has a look over the edge to see how Marianne and Cameron are progressing. Both taking it very cautious, just about halfway. It's no

238

surprise: Goths and sporting activity generally don't mix; though Kane anticipates their descents will look rapid in comparison to some of the last half-dozen, including, as it does, Yvonne, Gillian, Theresa and Julie.

'So how did Barker come to be involved in this fight?'

'Matt had the closest thing anybody could describe as a rapport with Barker,' Kane explains. 'Essentially two loners who each recognised another person who generally liked to be left alone. I think Matt may have stuck up for him on occasion—verbally, of course, not physically—but I don't know whether Barker would have even been aware of that. I wouldn't read much into it: they weren't buddies or anything. Matt just provided an excuse, and that's only working on the assumption that Barker even noticed who Dunn was attacking.'

'He brought a knife to school and he intended to use it,' Guthrie says. 'Matt just helped identify a target. Or maybe Dunn identified himself as the target by getting into a fight on that particular day. See, it was a disastrous combination of events. The latest junkie boyfriend stabbed Barker's mother. He went to stay with his uncle, the dad's brother, until she got out of the hospital. Then when the junkie boyfriend made bail, she let him move back in. That was the day before it all happened, but we knew nothing about it.'

'He was a bomb waiting to go off,' Kane adds. 'He brought a knife to school and he was stabbing somebody with it one way or the other.'

Marianne and Cameron have reached the bottom. Sendak waves over to hail the next pair.

Julie, Yvonne, Gillian and Theresa start jostling, trying to force each other to the front, but their efforts are rendered moot as Matt and Roisin amble dutifully forward.

'We should have seen it coming, though,' Guthrie says, once the two new descendants have kicked away. 'Between the school, social services, police, whoever. We should have seen it coming, just like I should have been on the spot that day. I was just round the bloody corner, ticking off some fourth years I'd caught trading cigarettes. If I'd been in the locker corridor or the social area, like I'd normally be at interval, I could have intervened before . . .' He sighs, still tearing himself apart.

'You're not fucking omniscient, Dan,' Kane tells him, but he's not listening.

'Every night since, every night, I think about how it could have been different. I was on my way to the locker area, as usual, but I was too late. If I had left my office a few seconds sooner or a few seconds later, I'd have missed those fourth years and I'd have been there and Dunn wouldn't have attacked Matt Wilson. Or if Dunn had decided to come the bully boy with Matt the day before, on a day when Barker wasn't stalking the halls with a knife. There's so many other ways it could have unfolded, so many different paths that would have led somewhere else, somewhere better.'

'No,' Sendak says. 'Right now, there's only the path that took you here. You start trying to see what was down the paths not taken, that way madness lies.'

Guthrie nods acknowledgment to Sendak for the sentiment, but Kane can tell it's not going to stop him punishing himself. What he hasn't mentioned,

240

and what it does nobody any good to know, is that Barker came close to expulsion on a number of occasions, and Guthrie always argued against his exclusion. He believed education—and mainstream education, at that—was Barker's best chance, perhaps his only chance. He believed he could be saved. Maybe he could have been, before his junkie mum got stabbed by her junkie boyfriend, then took him back in and triggered Barker's meltdown.

Pain multiplies. It multiplies in little ways, like Julie Meiklejohn going from bullied to bully, and in enormous ways, like Robert Barker's rage, the aftershocks of which they are all still suffering.

Kane looks at the tears forming in Guthrie's eyes, and at the sorrowful understanding in Sendak's, and wonders whether compassion can multiply too.

XIII

Of all the properties of physics that had fascinated and beguiled him down the decades, one of the most enduringly astonishing was the way photons of light, having rebounded from one human being, could subsequently fail to find the eyes of another once he was deemed to be insufficiently important.

Nobody looks twice at him as he makes his way through the vast, vaulted chamber. Soldiers and technicians are loading crates and dismantling equipment, though it is only the peripheral and auxiliary devices that have been authorised for removal at this stage. He walks behind two of the grunts, already invisible to them though his role here has not been formally concluded. He became invisible the second McCormack gave the order to shut down the operation. He still has his keycards, his title and his limited authority, but to the military, what remains of his relevance can be calculated by the countdown to the machine completing its cycle.

'Mothballing the operation?' muses one of the grunts. 'I'd fill the entire fuckin' place in with cement. Gonna have nightmares the rest of my days after this shit.'

'I hear ya, buddy,' his comrade agrees. 'I'm thinkin' of puttin' in for a transfer back to Basra for some peace of mind.'

He makes his way to the control and monitoring HQ on the floor of the Cathedral. It's deserted: rows of unmanned consoles and dormant monitors, identical screen-saver images dancing on all but one. The exception is displaying the countdown to the end of the cycle. There are thirteen hours, twelve minutes and nineteen seconds remaining until the shutdown process can be initiated.

He glances across at the thing between the cubes, shielding his eyes so as not to look directly into the red-shifted glare of the anomaly, the storm of light that so many people feared was a gateway to Hell. He knows otherwise, though. That's why he has to act.

One of the soldiers glances back, but his presence on the control floor doesn't merit any further interest. He's just someone taking a final, not-so-sentimental look at a spectacle they would be obliged to disavow for the rest of their lives.

242

And it is quite a spectacle. Despite the squabbling over certain sensitivities, there could be no question that Cathedral is the correct word, for science can surely have its cathedrals too. But like in any cathedral, there could be blasphemy. There could be sacrilege: sins against what was holy, betrayals of what was sacred. And there could be iconoclasm.

He strides along one of the rows, waking up all of the screens, and begins keying in new values to various fields. Confirmation is automatically sought from the computers for every action, but certain of his alterations trigger more than an electronic enquiry as to whether he is sure. Override codes are requested and supplied, escalating to a flashing advisory that 'PARALLEL GRAVITATIONAL REFLEX COMPENSATION MUST BE DISABLED BEFORE POLARITY RESET MAY BE APPLIED'.

He toggles the corresponding setting from AUTOMATIC to MANUAL to DISABLED, prompting a code-clearance warning that 'THIS OPERATION IS IN BREACH OF RECOMMENDED SAFETY PROTOCOLS'.

He supplies the code and executes the command, beginning a new countdown of his own, synchronising with his personal timepiece. 'POLARITY INVERSION WARNING: POLARITY RESET IN 09:59.' Then he calls up the inversion-abort authorisation and alters it to something keyed in at random with his eyes closed, copying and pasting it into the confirmation field so that even he doesn't know the code.

No way back now.

As he makes his way towards the main exit, there

is a grumbling, surging sound, somehow filling and trembling the rock cavern. The two soldiers he overheard earlier turn in response towards the giant black cubes either side of the anomaly.

'What the hell?' asks the first.

'No,' assures the second. 'No more Hell. Shuttin' it down. That's just the death rattle.'

They pay him no heed as he hastens past, heading back towards the labs, where he can take cover against the coming storm. He checks his watch: less than nine minutes, then the machine will undergo a modification that is going to make mothballing it a little more difficult than General McCormack hoped.

XIV

Rocks is sitting on an old upturned tree trunk, Dazza alongside him, casting evaluative glances over the assembly. The abseil was a real rush, though it's long worn off in the time they've had waiting about for everybody to get their go. Nonetheless, he feels pretty good: still has a sharp memory in his legs of what it was like to kick off the rock face and swing out for a few yards at a time. He is very pleasantly relaxed as an after-effect of exhilaration, and it seems to be a widespread phenomenon. There's a really good vibe about the place: nobody nipping each other or ripping the piss. Even Beansy seems quite subdued. The only cloud on the horizon remains the big man, who is standing a few feet in front, focused predictably on Matt as he makes his descent.

'Fuckin' weirdo cunt,' Kirk mutters. 'That lanky bastard was always making excuses for Barker.' He puts on a whiny voice, more by way of insult than mimicry. ' "It's a sin for him, his da was a bastard and his maw's a smackheid." Weirdo cunt.'

'His dad *was* a bastard,' Rocks argues, getting fucking sick of this. 'You never heard the stories about him? Fuckin' psycho.'

'Like father, like son then,' Kirk retorts.

'Is that not what Matt was trying to say?'

Kirk turns round and shoots him a threatening look.

'Whose fuckin' side are you on?' he demands.

Dazza intervenes, standing up from his spot on the tree trunk.

'We're all on the same side, big man. Just not so sure Barker was on Matt's side or Matt was on Barker's. Barker was on Barker's side, and that's all.'

But Kirk isn't having it.

'Shite. Dunnsy's dead because that weirdo prick couldnae fight his own battles and Barker was his back-up. Well, I'm Dunnsy's back-up—and the battle's not finished.'

Kirk stomps off, batting away Dazza's attempted restraining arm.

Dazza looks to Rocks as if to ask 'What are we going to do?'

'Somebody needs to talk to him about this,' Rocks says.

'We all need to talk about this,' Dazza replies. 'That's why we're here.'

Rocks glances at the rock-face again, in time to see Matt suddenly spin and tangle, ending up

245

hanging upside down. He doesn't panic, and nor does the Sergeant up top, who just calmly calls down some instructions. Matt hangs there a moment with one foot tangled above him, the other tucked behind his knee, a slightly bashful smile on his coupon. He's a cool customer, the Matt boy. Enigma probably sells it better than 'weirdo cunt', though Rocks can understand why Kirk finds him frustrating. What he doesn't understand is why the big man hasn't learned, after all these years, to leave the boy to get on with it.

*   *   *

It's getting on for lunchtime, or so Kane's stomach tells him. His watch says it's only eleven, though. Must be all the fresh air and exercise. He's absolutely Hank, but determined not to break into his packed lunch until Sendak gives the order.

They have just cleared the treeline, climbing towards a plateau, from which they have a view down into the valley between it and the larger Ben Trochart. He can see a river snaking through moorland where it isn't swallowed by forest, snow-capped peaks in the distance beyond. There are no roads to be seen, no buildings, not even cultivated fields: no visible evidence of human settlement.

'It's beautiful,' Heather says. 'Makes you feel . . . I don't know . . .'

'Insignificant,' Kane suggests.

'I was going to say inspired.'

'How about blessed?' asks Blake.

He and Kane share a glance: touché.

'It is beautiful,' agrees Sendak warmly. 'It's also cold, cruel and extremely unforgiving if you don't

246

treat it with respect.'

Heather fixes both Kane and Blake with a warning stare.

'First one to make a female comparison gets a boot in the peas.'

*   *   *

Adnan takes in the view from the plateau and instantly renders it in HUD mode, like it's a giant game of *Civ* or *Age of Empires*. He pictures a little cursor arrow clicking an icon in the front of his field of vision, then clicking again on the banks of the river and instantly constructing a fort. Further buildings spring up alongside, before being surrounded by troops and war machines, enthusiastically laying siege. He grins with deep satisfaction and takes a mouthful of Irn-Bru from the can he's been handed by the alien impostor who has kidnapped Deborah and replaced her with someone quite affable.

Deborah takes the drink back from Adnan and accepts an unwanted cereal bar from Cameron, who is sitting between her and Marianne. At Deborah's prompting, Marianne has got out her tarot cards and is explaining Cameron's choices, though because of the breeze she's just getting him to turn over the top cards one at a time. His first card is The Fool.

'The Fool is taking a step over a precipice,' she explains. 'We're most of the time too cynical, too insular or just too scared to take a step into the unknown. But if we don't, then we never explore, never expand our horizons.'

Gillian and that lot are about fifteen yards away,

though their ostentatious cackling is audible even over the gentle wind and the murmur of umpteen different conversations. They're being extra noisy for her benefit, Deborah suspects: it's not paranoia, she's done it herself often enough when she's been among them. It's bound to have put a few noses out of joint that she didn't come scampering over to them at breakfast (where they had grabbed a table for four anyway), or out on the hike this morning. She knows from experience that there's no fun dangling possible exclusion over someone who doesn't want to be included in the first place.

It isn't a statement she's making or anything, though she's aware they'll be dissecting it as such. Well, it probably is, but the point is it's not aimed at them; it's not about them. It's about her. That's what she realised last night.

It took her ages to get to sleep, but in a good way. A lot of things seemed clearer after her long talk with Marianne, and one of those was that it was a much more enjoyable experience to talk to Marianne than among that little coven. It feels easier to speak with other folk too, maybe because she's actually listening to what they're saying for a change, instead of looking for nuggets of embarrassment, sifting out reasons to slag them off.

This, though, sparks a moment of obsessive-compulsive anxiety, as Deborah asks herself whether, in the midst of so much emotion and revelation, she got around to deleting that picture. She's fairly sure she remembers doing it, but now that she's thought about it, she needs confirmation. She pulls out her phone and surreptitiously checks. It's gone, but it still makes her shudder to think how close she must have come to disaster, to doing something unforgivable to Marianne and calamitous to herself. It also seems amazing how far she has come from the person she was this time yesterday.

While her phone is out, she decides to have a look at the pictures she has taken this morning, and gasps a little at the first, snapped just as they were leaving the FTOF. It's Beansy with his bag dangling from a stick over his shoulder as he steps, smiling, off the edge of a stump and into thin air. She glances from the phone to the card in Marianne's lap and sees exactly the same composition. Marianne lifts it to put it back in the pack, but Deborah stops her.

'Look,' she says, showing her the phone.

'How appropriate,' Marianne observes. 'The Fool. Couldn't have picked a better model.'

'I didn't choose anything,' Deborah says, a little disappointed (but in another way a little relieved) that Marianne doesn't find it spooky.

Deborah nudges the joystick on her phone to view the next pic as Marianne invites Cameron to turn over another card. The shot shows Matt hanging upside down by one foot, his other tucked behind his knee. Cameron reaches for the deck and turns over the Hanged Man. Again, the composition is identical, right down to the curiously serene smile on his face.

'Marianne,' she says, showing her the phone again and trying to keep a tremor from her voice.

'Fuck,' Marianne responds, this time leaving Deborah under no doubt that she does find it spooky. 'That is . . . that is out there.'

'Jesus,' Cameron agrees. 'Hey, Adnan, mate, you gotta see this. Let's hear your quantum physics explain this shit.'

Marianne shows Adnan the two cards as Deborah passes him the phone.

'That's the order Cameron just drew these, too,' Deborah tells him.

Adnan has a look at the two images. The similarity of the composition is unsettling, he would admit.

'Are you familiar with tarot cards?' he asks Deborah.

'Not really. Marianne showed me some last night, but . . .'

'But you have seen them before?'

'Yes.'

Adnan nods. 'Pattern recognition,' he says. 'It's one of the human traits that helped us get out of the caves and make it to here.' He points up at the sky. 'We see faces in the clouds because we latch on to things that make sense in the chaos. Seeing those cards last night is what prompted you to push the button when something resembling the same images appeared in front of you. No mystic forces required.'

Again, Deborah feels a mixture of relief and disappointment.

'Isn't there room in your scientific world for a little magic?' Marianne asks.

Adnan sits up straighter and smiles, a response that Radar knows him well enough to read.

'Aw fuck, you've set him off. Don't go there, Marianne.'

'No, I'm interested,' she insists.

'You're familiar with Aleister Crowley, I take it?'

he asks. Marianne nods. 'Well, as someone said of his supposed wizardry, "the only problem with magic is that it doesn't work".'

Marianne laughs. Adnan is pleased to see that she has taken it in good spirit; more pleased that she appears to have a response.

'It's true, from a practical point of view, but he missed the point. Magic is about the realm of the imagination, about exploring the human subconscious.'

'So you'd admit it's all just . . . metaphors and symbols.'

'Kind of. But that's selling it extremely short. Look.'

Marianne reaches into her backpack and fishes out her book on demonology.

'You bring books up mountains?' Cameron asks.

'I bring books everywhere. You never know when you might get a quiet five minutes to read.'

Adnan almost apologetically produces a Michio Kaku paperback from his own bag, just popping it up for a second as a gesture of solidarity to Marianne and a two-fingers to Cam.

Marianne flicks through her volume, showing Adnan several plates depicting different demons from a variety of cultures. He sees demons with pitchforks, with horns and pointed tails; some demons crawling on walls, others with wings, hovering in the air.

'These are from all different societies, different religions, different eras,' she says. 'Empires that rose and fell . . . and yet they all have their own myths of the same thing. Ancient Greece, Mexico, China . . . Often very similar demons too. You can say they're purely symbolic, just an image or an idea that spreads between humans. But why did that same image spring up independently in cultures that have had no contact?'

'That doesn't mean there *is* such a thing as demons, though,' Adnan argues. 'The idea could be something primal, something hard-wired to the human sub-conscious that—'

Adnan cuts himself off as he realises he has just echoed what Marianne already said.

'See? Magic.'

'I guess that's why gods and demons don't show up on each other's turf. We have Bernadette at Lourdes, and the kids at Fatima or Medjogorje seeing Mary, but little kids in European villages never see Vishnu or Ganesh or any of the multitude of Hindu gods, while nobody in India has visions of the Madonna.'

'We all have localised myths of the same archetypes,' Marianne says. 'Creation myths, mother goddess myths, rival sibling myths.'

'Like the one about the son of God who was betrayed and killed, only to rise again, and through whose resurrection all mankind could achieve eternal life?' Adnan suggests, eyeing Marianne closely to see how she likes her heresy. 'Name of Osiris?' he continues. 'Worshipped in Egypt fifteen hundred years before Christ?'

'Son of Geb, the sky god, and Nut, the earth goddess,' Marianne says, letting him know this is not news and that *he* is on *her* turf. 'And if you want more Christ antecedents, you've got Prometheus—bringer of light to man, similarly punished by being brutally hung up and his side pierced.

'All over the planet, we've been telling ourselves

the same stories since the dawn of time. You can say they're only stories, only "metaphors and symbols" as you put it, but I think they're more than that. Myths are like truths we somehow knew about the universe and about ourselves but didn't quite understand, and didn't always even understand why we knew them. For instance, civilisations all over the world worshipped the sun as a god that gave birth to Earth. Thousands of years later we discovered that the Earth *was* actually created from the sun as part of the debris that was whirling around it four and a half billion years ago.'

Adnan wears a strained expression, reluctant but duty-bound to disagree.

'I take your point, but they were worshipping the wrong sun.'

'Here we go,' Radar says, flinging himself backwards as if in recoil.

'Our sun isn't actually hot enough to fuse hydrogen to helium. The sun that "gave birth" to us died billions of years ago in a supernova, which created the higher elements that make up our solar system. And that means that every one of us here is literally made of stardust.'

Marianne simply stares at him for a moment, with an expression he can't read at all, and which he fears for a moment will turn to one he has seen on dozens of faces before, most frequently Radar's. Then she speaks:

'That is the coolest thing I have ever heard.'

Adnan says nothing, but his honest response to what she said would comprise precisely the same words.

'. . . and somebody used the word whirlwind—Michelle, it was—to describe what we're all going through, because we're feeling so many things at once, almost like forces out of our control.'

They're all gathered—everybody—in a tight circle, seated on the ground with their lunches digesting inside them. With the landscape rolled out beneath them it feels to Heather like they're on a separate plane, higher than the world, detached from their normal reality. Blake chose his moment well. If they can't talk about this here, then they may never talk about it at all. His voice is mellifluous but natural, infusing the atmosphere with calm. He speaks softly but audibly over the breeze, without resorting to that elevated priestly register all men of the cloth could slip into: he wants them to know he's talking with them, not at them.

'We're all feeling loss,' Blake continues. 'We're all feeling pain. We're all feeling shock. We're all feeling anger.'

Heather can't help but glance at Kirk, and notes that she is not the only one. His arms are folded and his face is stony, hard-set, determined not to betray any emotion.

'And all of that is right. All of that is what we need to feel, in order to get through this. We need to feel it, but we need to express it too, because you'd be amazed how many of us here think we're the only one nursing a particular feeling, or harbouring a certain thought. It's only once it's out in the open that you discover you're not alone. Just say what you need to: it's why we're here. Don't

254

worry about what anyone thinks of you for saying it either: this mountain is like an extension of my confessional. What gets said up here does not come back down the hillside with us. Anyone who casts up anything spoken here today will be committing a grave betrayal of us all.'

Rocks looks across to the other side of the circle: all the heads are down, bowed more sincerely than during any prayer, hiding reticent faces. This could be the longest silence this lot has collectively engaged in throughout their entire school careers.

It stretches beyond a full minute, all of them left to their own solemn contemplation as the cold wind gusts about their ears. Father Blake offers no prompting, no pressure, though the longer it goes on, the harder it will be for anyone to go first.

Then a voice breaks the deadlock, just a few feet to Rocks' right. It's wee Caitlin, which might surprise some but not him. His money was always on it being one of the quieter, more dutiful ones that contributed first; the one time the loudmouths keep it zipped.

'I was there,' she says. 'In the hall, putting my chemistry folder in my locker. I can remember that that's what I was carrying. I can remember this sudden rise in a lot of voices, and seeing Andrew pushing Matthew. They both banged into the lockers right beside me. I can remember it really clearly. But then after that, it's like a curtain comes down inside my head. I was there. It happened right in front of me, but my mind won't let me think about it. All I can think about is . . . Andrew's mum and dad . . . I'm sorry . . .'

Caitlin fills up and can't go on. No one seems prepared to fill the void, keeping her grief in the

255

spotlight. Rocks feels for her, wishes somebody else would wade in, one of the teachers maybe. Then to his own surprise he finds himself speaking, just saying something to bail the lassie out.

'I was there too, and I wish I had the curtain thing Caitlin's talking about.' He's aware of Kirk's head coming up, flinching in astonishment and, no doubt, dismay. Fuck him, though. He's helping nobody with this bottled-up shite. 'I was on the other side of the hall when Dunnsy went for Matt. I started making my way over. I was gaunny pull Dunnsy away and calm him doon, but when a fight starts, there's always a swarm, and I never got there in time. Then I remember the swarm just melting away. It was so quiet. I don't know if it really was quiet or if it's just like my memory of it has no soundtrack and I see it in silence, no voices.'

Rocks can picture it all again as he speaks. He trembles, suddenly colder, like his body has just switched off whatever force-field was protecting him from the climate on top of a highland hill in December.

He catches Kirk's eye. The big man is looking at him like he can't believe he's doing this, like just talking about it is a fucking betrayal.

'I was scared,' Rocks says, as though in answer to Kirk. 'Or I thought I was scared, but it was mostly shock. Scared wasn't what I was feeling right then. Scared is what I've been feeling ever since. I used to think nothing that bad could really happen to you. You read about stuff, you see some horrible things on telly or the internet, but it never seems real. I know we're made of flesh and bones, but—'

256

He has to cut himself off. Despite Father Blake saying they ought to talk about whatever they need to, it feels wrong to articulate this. He doesn't feel he has the right to describe what he saw. You can't share this out. You can't ask anyone else to carry it.

He's seen a lot of blood at school. Who hasn't? If there's a fight, chances are somebody's getting their nose burst, and he's seen some bad ones. Dished out some bad ones, if truth be told. He was amazed and, to be honest, not a little ashamed when he saw how much Tommy Lafferty bled when he battered him in third year, but it was only blood, only fluid.

Barker didn't just stab Dunnsy, though: he gutted him. Rocks saw intestines, ribs and fuck knows what else spilled out on to the polished grey floor tiles. He learned a truth right then that he can never unlearn.

'We're just meat,' he says. 'So fragile. Since then, I've found myself jumping back at the kerb when cars go by too fast. My mum asked me to chip some potatoes and I couldnae do it because I got freaked out holding the knife. I'm amazed any of us make it this far. I'm amazed we got here as a species.'

He looks at Kirk again, and this time Rocks is the one glaring an accusation. Can't you fucking see this? he's asking. Kirk looks away, down between his feet, maybe just a little humbly.

Rocks has nothing more to say, but he doesn't feel self-conscious in the next silence; he feels wide open but not vulnerable. He catches Caitlin's eye and finds a look of teary solidarity.

'We're fragile, but we're also precious,' says

Radar. 'That's why it's so fuckin' unfair.'

Guthrie flinches, but gets a warning shot from Blake.

'Dunnsy wasnae even seventeen yet,' he goes on. 'Fuckin' Barker took away everything, not just took Dunnsy away from us, but took away everything he'd ever be. It's just so fuckin' . . . forever, man. No second chances. No saved games.'

'That's what I can't get past either,' ventures Dazza. 'I keep expecting Dunnsy to walk into a classroom.'

'There's a school of thought in quantum physics that says he has.'

It's Adnan who speaks, eliciting a glare from Dazza warning that this better not be him just geeking out at a time like this. But Adnan's not trying to be facetious or inappropriate: he thinks some of them may genuinely find this comforting.

'It's known as Many Worlds theory. In a parallel universe, Dunnsy is still alive and we never came here on this trip.'

'Oh, come on,' Dazza says irritably. 'Load of shite. This is serious, Adnan.'

'So am I. This isn't whacked-out fringe stuff. More physicists accept the existence of parallel universes these days than deny it. It's one of the possible implications of the quantum uncertainty principle. At every quantum juncture, the universe splits, creating an infinite number of parallel universes. Right here, where we sit, we are co-existing with infinite, slightly varied versions of ourselves and our world, and in one of those—in many of those, in fact—Dunnsy never died and we're doing something else of a Saturday

258

lunchtime. There's more evidence to suggest this than there is to support the existence of Heaven or Hell.'

'So where, physically, are these other universes?' Rosemary asks, suddenly wanting to get analytical now that her religion has been challenged. 'I mean, I've heard you ask where Heaven is when the universe is so huge. Where, then, is this multiplicity of universes?'

'It's right here. They're all right here in different waveforms. But it's like our perception is a radio and we can only tune into one frequency. We can only follow one branching path of our own reality.'

Dazza feels his hackles fall. He actually likes the sound of this: that he'd be better thinking of Dunnsy living out his life the same as the rest of them than thinking of him in Heaven, which has in recent years started to sound more and more like just a consoling thought for the living rather than a reality for the dead.

Guthrie's natural inclination to go on the defensive at Adnan's dismissal of Heaven and Hell is derailed by the tantalising nature of what this alternative offers. In another version of reality, he left his office a few seconds earlier, a few seconds later, never encountered the fourth years, and got there in time to intervene.

Deborah feels a shudder as she thinks of the parallel universe in which she pressed Send and shared that photo. She's ostracised, in lesbian hell, maybe looking at expulsion and even the sex-offenders register. One click, a no to a yes, a zero to a one, that's all it would have taken to split her universe into two vastly different paths.

'Is this maybe why we can feel people once

259

they've gone?' asks Michelle. 'Or why we sometimes say we feel like someone walked over our grave?'

A number of heads nod, a murmur echoing approval of this suggestion.

'No,' answers Matt, silencing it. 'There's complete decoherence. We can't interact with branching parallel paths.' He says it flatly, typically oblivious to the fact that he's slamming a door in the face of their hope. That's Matt for you, Adnan reflects: can't get a word out of him for ages, then he chooses to voice something that would have been better left unsaid.

'But you said last night,' Ewan appeals to Adnan, 'if we could move in the fifth dimension we could travel between universes.'

Adnan shakes his head, wishing he could tell him otherwise. 'Ironically, if we could access higher dimensions, we could reach the furthest points in space, but we couldn't reach the parallel version of our own reality that's right alongside us. Once it's gone, it's gone.'

There's silence again after he says this, leaving Adnan feeling like it's his fault. He lifted them for a moment only to drop them again, albeit with a lot of help from Matt. Thus he's unaccustomedly grateful when Rosemary wades back in.

'That's why Heaven is a much better concept,' she says. 'Because even Adnan would have to admit that there is a possibility that we can reach there and be reunited with our lost loved ones. Whereas there's no possibility of seeing them again in the worlds he suggested. Is that right?'

Adnan nods. He tries to be magnanimous and offers a little smile, but he's always uncomfortable giving up concessions to faith-heads. This is partly because he feels it's never reciprocated, but more so because it's like giving money to a junkie: you know they're just going to use what you gave them to make their problem worse.

'Well I just hope there's a Hell so that that wee cunt's paying properly for what he did. Fucker got off lightly.'

It's Kirk who speaks. Of course. Guthrie says nothing, reading it astutely. Kirk looks like he *wants* to be challenged, so that he can further rev up his moral indignation.

With Guthrie not biting, Kirk directs his stare at Blake, all but demanding a response. Blake just nods.

'Look, I'm not here to sell you some Jesus Juice on this,' he says. 'I could tell you how forgiveness will help you deal with this in the long run, but nobody's ready to hear that, not at this stage. We've all seen those front pages and we've all used those words: evil, beast, monster. But those words don't tell us anything. What Robert did was monstrous, nobody could ever deny that.'

'Here come the trendy excuses,' Kirk mutters.

'There's an important difference between excusing and comprehending, Kirk,' Heather intervenes. 'You say it's no excuse, that's your right, but Robert's upbringing is an inextricable part of what happened. This was someone who had known nothing but violence since he was brought into the world.'

'Evil breeds evil,' says Kane. Pain multiplies.

'I prefer to think of evil as simply an absence of good,' offers Blake. 'Like darkness is an absence of light. As I'm sure Adnan could tell us, darkness is the more prevalent state of the universe. Chaos is the natural state. Second law of thermodynamics: entropy always increases. Order always decays. All nature is war, Darwin said. The natural state of the universe is for things to consume other things, and not just biological life. Stars devour other stars, galaxies devour other galaxies. Good is us rising above natural savagery, and in doing so we burn like stars, illuminating the dark. But we can only burn for a finite time, so we have to burn as brightly as we can.'

'Robert will go to Hell, though, won't he, Father?' asks Bernadette, seeming to need assurance in the face of all this moral equivalency.

'Bloody right,' blusters Julie, proving the power of religion to bring people together: acid-dripping bitch-queen and God-bothering dweeb united in their desire to mete out eternal suffering. 'And Satan doesn't give time off for good behaviour.'

'I don't believe in Satan, Julie,' Blake replies softly. 'There are no demons with horns and pitchforks and pointy tails, and there is no "presence" of evil manipulating men. I believe in . . . I have faith in God. The God within us.'

Heather clocks this hesitation, connecting it immediately to what Kane told her last night.

'Satan is just a symbol we dreamt up for the worst that we're capable of,' Blake adds. 'I don't accept that evil is simply incarnated. Nothing is born monstrous. Monsters have to be created.'

XV

Tullian stared back and forth from the desiccated demon corpses to Parducci, feeling like he might burst from the torrent of questions welling inside him, but one preceded all its fellows.

'Why does this remain a secret? Why in a world corrupted by sin, ridden roughshod by arrogant godlessness, have you concealed such evidence of the truth of our church?'

Parducci nodded patiently, letting Tullian vent his incredulous frustration.

'These are the questions I asked also, when I was first taken here, the questions asked by everyone who sees this place. And I will first tell you what I was first told also: to consider the legacies of the creatures who lie here; of what was wrought in their wake. Hundreds of deaths, perhaps thousands, from a mere two such dark emissaries. The common man, even the common priest, is not equipped to deal with this knowledge. Nor, surely, would God wish for him to have it. God does not want men to come to Him through fear of monsters, but through love for His word.'

'But when His word is trampled and scorned,' Tullian protested. 'When the Church's influence is being squeezed out by secular forces in every corner . . .'

'Then we must learn from the Lord's example,' Parducci replied. 'Jesus suffered scorn, scourge and spittle, all of the time knowing he had at his disposal the power to turn all of it back upon his tormentors. He endured for a greater purpose, as

263

we must too. Even in torment, as the world turns its face from God, even as we may despair for our church's place in the world, it is our sacrifice that this horror, a mere phantasm to others, remains a reality *only to us*.'

'So it is our burden to know but to remain silent,' Tullian said, and even in saying so he understood that he was accepting that burden upon his shoulders.

'We must endure,' Parducci confirmed solemnly. 'But we must endure with vigilance, which is why you are here, Cardinal. We know what these things are and we know where they have come from. There is but one entity with the motive—and evidently the means—to have penetrated this barrier separating us from the shadow realm. We must be grateful that his successes have been few and the damage temporary. However, the greatest danger is not that he will redouble his efforts, but that man will do his work for him. As you have warned us, if scientists are close to deducing how it might be even *theoretically* possible to breach this barrier, then that is terrifying, because nothing will prevent them from pursuing such a course.'

Tullian immediately understood the truth of this. 'Scientists are like children told not to look in a particular room,' he said. 'Once their minds are set upon it, nothing will mean so much to them as their desire to uncover whatever is locked to them. No matter how disastrous the possible consequences, they regard their work as paramount, as though the pursuit of science constitutes its own moral imperative. The atom bomb proved that forever. Scientists pride themselves on objectivity, but they cannot be

264

trusted to be objective when it comes to the morality of their own conduct.'

Parducci nodded solemnly.

'You will therefore understand, Cardinal Tullian, that it would be futile to show them these creatures in the hope that it might convince them of what lies beyond the barrier and dissuade them from seeking to open it. This is another reason why we have never let the world in on this secret. If scientists examined these remains, they would entertain all explanations *except* the one that is obvious to us. They would say that these are simply another species of creature, nothing more. An evolutionary tributary, perhaps, that we have *projected* our fears on to, as the sight of horses glimpsed in the morning mist, their breath spouting steam, once gave rise to the idea of dragons. Then despite the physical evidence in front of them, they will dismiss the threat of demons as no impediment to their ongoing research.'

Parducci turned to him and gripped his hands as he looked deep into Tullian's eyes. 'Only when it is too late,' he said, 'when the seal cannot be unbroken and the blood has started to run, will they finally turn to us. And when that time comes we must be humble, we must be courageous, and we must be *ready*.'

XVI

Rocks is walking alone. He just dropped back and let Kirk and Dazza gain a bit of distance; can't be doing with what's going on with the big man just now. Nobody's really talking much anyway. Everyone is subdued compared to on the journey out, maybe a hangover from the solemnity of their discussion after lunch, maybe a bit of tiredness setting in too. It's still clear, but the sun is starting to dip.

He's aware of footsteps close by and turns his head to see Caitlin walking along just behind and to the right. She notices and gives him a timid, uncertain wee attempt at a smile, like she's half afraid he'll blank her. He wonders why she's walking alone; he thought she was pals with Rosemary and that lot, but he's sure they're way up ahead.

He wants to say something but he's worried that wee unsure look she gave him was just her being polite. It's a long-standing concern of his that the more studious and well-behaved lassies regard him as a bam. That was fair enough a couple of years ago, because he couldn't have given a monkey's, to say nothing of the fact that he *was* a bam, but he doesn't like the thought that that's what they still see.

But then she speaks.

'Hey,' she says, quite tentatively.

'Hey.'

'I just wanted to say . . . what you said up there . . . I really got it. I think the reason my memories are locked up is because my brain doesn't want to make sense of what I saw.'

'I didn't think there was anything to get,' he replies, self-consciousness making him feel he can't take credit for any insight in case she subsequently sees through him for being a fraud. 'Just a head-dump, really.'

'You said you're still scared. That's it. We all expect to be sad at this point, so we know what to make of that, but we don't expect to still be scared. We think that part's temporary. It wouldn't have struck me so much coming from a girl. Guys don't like to admit they're scared. And coming from a guy like you, it really hit home.'

'What's a guy like me?' he asks, trying not to sound too much like he's dreading the answer.

She blushes a wee bit. 'I don't know. Someone . . . not easily scared. Someone brave, I suppose, compared to me.'

'I used to be a bit of a bam. Doesn't mean I was brave.'

'Telling all those folk up there that you're scared—that's brave, if that doesn't sound too much of a paradox.'

'No,' he says, and manages a smile. 'Compared to all that stuff Adnan was talking about, it makes perfect sense.'

*   *   *

'Fuck! Check this,' comes a shout from Kane's left. He and Sendak stop and turn. Beansy is waving from the edge of the treeline, about a dozen yards from the path.

'What?' Kane asks wearily, already looking

267

forward to a warm bath and a cold drink and consequently in no mind to be entertaining any of Beansy's carry-on.

Beansy bends down to lift something. Kane really hopes it's not a dead animal. He can just picture the daft bastard with a sheep's head, chasing a few shrieking girls through the trees and thus bringing down a whole power of Guthrie-grief upon the lot of them.

To Kane's relief, Beansy holds up a rusted rectangle, though he fails to appreciate what is supposed to be so remarkable about an old sign-plate.

'It says "Mod keep out",' Beansy reports. 'Does that mean you're not allowed to play any of that shitey Gaelic music round here then? Or is it warning you that somebody *is* gaunny be playing shitey heedrum-hodrum music, so you'd better stay away?'

'Naw,' suggests Deso. 'It means you're not allowed in driving a scooter and wearing a raccoon-tail parka.'

'It's not "mod", ya stupit pricks,' grumbles Kirk witheringly. 'It's M. O. D.'

Kane turns to Sendak.

'MoD? This isn't army land, is it?'

Sendak gives him a hey-ho shrug. 'The name Fort Trochart not suggest anything to you?' he asks. 'Parts of this area been military land for centuries—but not as much as used to be. We ain't trespassing on a firing range, if that's what you're worried about. That sign must be fifty or sixty years old. Ben Trochart over there—that's still MoD land. Being why I took us out and around Ben Rudan.'

268

'So,' Heather says, 'how long are you hoping to hang on to the school chaplain position while going directly against church dogma and telling the kids there's no such thing as Satan?'

'I said Satan didn't exist?' Blake asks. 'You must have misheard. Are you sure I never said Santa?'

They're at the rear, making sure none of the stragglers falls too far behind and gets detached from the group. They've been walking side by side for maybe half an hour without saying anything, but that was because Guthrie was with them at that point. Heather couldn't help but be reminded of times when she and various boyfriends were making only minimal small talk while they waited for his or her parents to leave the room. As soon as the deputy decided to step up the pace in order to investigate whether Deso and Beansy were merely smoking or had in fact set fire to something, not only did she feel free to speak, but she sensed he'd been waiting for the same cue too.

'Actually, I'm cutting my own throat by telling the truth,' Blake admits. 'Maybe Guthrie's right and I should be going all fire-and-brimstone to at least consolidate my base, rather than reaching out to the waverers.'

'No. The kids actually listen to you. That's rare enough for an adult, rarer still for the school priest. There's no way in the world your predecessor, Father Reilly, would have been invited along on an occasion like this. There's no point in providing "spiritual guidance" if nobody wants any. The kids know you've got something to offer.'

'Yeah, but is what I've got to offer them spiritual? I mean, is there anything I'm giving them that I couldn't give them without the collar? That's what worries me. My big fear is that I can't reach the people I want to through my ministry, while I'm wary of the people who only want to reach out to me *because* of my ministry.'

'Who do you mean?' Heather asks, suffering a pang of paranoid concern that this might be his subtle way of warning her off turning into a priest-stalker.

'There are people who are quite definitely Catholics rather than Christians, hung up on the ritual and the institution. They're sort of Catholicism anoraks.'

'I thought we called those priests.'

'No. We're the crew of the *Enterprise*. I'm talking about the Trekkies here.'

'I got you now,' Heather says. Neither of them needs to name names, and he isn't just talking about Dan.

'They revere the institution: the ritual, the magnificence, the hierarchy, the history, the authority.'

'You're worried they're more enthused by the medium than by the message,' Heather suggests.

'That's it. I mean, you wouldn't believe the conversations I end up having. "Infallibility itself was not infallibly defined until Pius IX": someone actually said that to me. The circular logic of it is like an Escher painting. I've never known whether to find it amusing or disturbing. But it isn't that they're not interested in the message, it's that . . .' He winces, struggling to find the words. 'Well, take

270

these kids here. They still go along to church, but for most of them, their engagement is at the level of obligation. They're nice kids who want to do the right thing, and the right thing is going to mass, believing in God. They're nice kids already— they're not nice kids *because* of their faith. They don't need this medium to get the message, and consequently as they grow up, the medium means less and less to them, in the same way as it means *too* much to the anoraks.'

'But they were all raised in the Church,' Heather argues. 'Yours *was* the medium that gave them the message.'

'Kane would call it an unnecessary level of complexity: the values exist and function in society independently, so there's no need to bolt God on to them.'

'But aren't those values residual of our society's Christian heritage?'

'You could argue that, but you would only prove Kane's point—the residue is the essence, and that which was insubstantial evaporates.'

'If you believe that, why are you a priest?'

'It's not so much that I believe it as that I'm afraid it might be true.'

Heather recalls what Kane said last night: *'He's a priest because he* wants *to believe.'*

'Anyway,' Blake asks, 'why are you the one playing God's advocate?'

'I'm a Catholic,' she answers.

'But how much of one? I know you go to school masses, but you don't take communion. I notice these things.'

'What, do you take a mental register? I always feared Guthrie might do that, but I didn't know you did.'

'I don't.'

'You just keep a special lookout for me, then?'

He laughs, a little too quickly, like he's trying to conceal his embarrassment. She thinks she caught a glimpse, though. She thinks what he didn't say was:

('Something like that.')

Before the moment can grow awkward, she returns to his question.

'I'm playing God's advocate because I'm one of those nice kids grown up. I wish my religion had turned out to be as beautiful and amazing as I once had faith it would. I had faith that the questions would be answered, contradictions resolved.'

'Instead you got "blessed mysteries".'

'Instead I learned that priests weren't offering answers, just ever more sophistry-laden techniques for avoiding the questions—or for getting you to stop asking them.'

'And some surviving remnant of your faith sees me as the last hope? You want me to convince you?'

Heather doesn't say anything. First among the things she doesn't say is:

('Something like that.')

*   *   *

The light is dimming, and to Kane's mind the forest they are marching through is starting to seem more *Evil Dead* than *Midsummer Night's Dream*. He's guessing Sendak has taken them a circular route, as he doesn't recognise anything and has no idea whether they are still miles from the FTOF or about to happen upon it around the next bend. He goes to check his watch then remembers it still said eleven o'clock the last time he checked.

Sendak looks just a little concerned. He rubs at his scar, that long line like a sideways question mark with the curve cupping his ear and the tail going around the back of his head. You can hardly see it in most light, so the majority of the time you wouldn't even notice it was there, but Sendak has been absently tracing his fingers along it since lunch. Kane wonders if it's one of those injuries that plays up under certain atmospheric conditions, and really hopes it isn't one that plays up under certain psychological conditions.

'War wound?' he asks.

Sendak looks at him quizzically, confirming how unconscious the rubbing was.

'Oh,' he says, realising. 'Kind of. Finished my career, but it ain't no war wound. An accident on the . . .' Sendak touches the scar again, an action clearly triggered by the memory. '. . . base where I was posted. I was the lucky one. Two of my men got killed.'

'Shit. That's awful. What happened?'

'I can't talk about it.'

'I'm sorry. I understand.'

'No, I mean I can't talk about it, like, for legal reasons. As in highly classified.'

'One of those "you could tell me but you'd have to kill me" deals?'

Sendak smiles, but there's a micro-delay before he does so, as though it takes that time for him to decide consciously that a smile is the expected

273

response.

'That's it,' he says. 'It was in another life,' he adds soberly. 'A parallel universe.'

'So how did you end up here?'

'Took a long vacation after I was discharged. Liked what I found here. Worked out a way to make it permanent.'

Sendak's tone is slightly detached, just a little less natural than during their previous conversations. Could be simply that it sounds rehearsed because he must have been asked the same question a thousand times, but Kane wonders if it's just the paranoia induced by these darkening skies that is giving him the suspicion he's being lied to.

Sendak checks his watch, doesn't like what he sees.

'What time you got?' he asks.

'Bang on eleven,' Kane replies without looking. 'Watch must have stopped this morning.'

'Mine too. Eleven hundred hours dead. Got to be closer to sixteen.'

Kane calls back to Gillian, who is walking with Julie about ten yards behind.

'Gillian, you got the time?'

'You got the money?' she replies, prompting laughter from Julie, sufficiently disproportionate as to indicate quality sucking-up.

'Gillian,' Kane warns.

She looks at her wrist.

'It's . . . sorry, watch must have stopped, sir.'

'Stopped when?' Sendak demands.

Gillian appears a little affronted by Sendak's sudden sternness.

'Eleven,' she informs him, before looking at Julie

as if to ask: 'What's got up his arse?'

'Fourth time this has happened out here,' Sendak says, irritated. Irritated is good, Kane thinks, trying to assess his level of concern.

Sendak then stops and takes out his compass, which Kane finds altogether less reassuring. 'And look at this,' he says.

He shows Kane the dial.

'What am I looking for?' Kane asks by way of admitting he doesn't know one end of a compass from the other.

'The needle is pointing north.'

'Why is that bad?'

'Because that's due south. This has happened before too, except the needle usually just goes haywire. This time it's completely flipped its polarity.'

'Could we be on top of some underground power lines?'

Sendak gives a small shake of the head, looking away. Kane finds himself returning to the notion that there is something he is not being entirely truthful about.

Conscious of the approach of the permanently earwigging Gillian and Julie, Kane asks quietly: 'We're not . . . lost, or anything?'

'No. This is the same route I take everybody. We're less than a mile out, and I could find my way back from here blindfold. But something don't feel right. Let's pick up the pace, get everybody home.'

Sendak turns to address the whole group.

'Okay, people,' he booms out. 'This ain't no country stroll. Let's move like we got a party to get to.'

XVII

Merrick's ears have stopped ringing but there's still blood on the tissue each time he dabs either of them. Everyone he sees walking past has smears of it at least, and in some casualties it is still running profusely as they are helped to first aid stations. He had intended to go and get checked out himself when he thought he was the only one afflicted, but it's clear that it passed through the entire place like a shockwave, its epicentre in the Cathedral.

He was in the Beta labs when it happened. The ever-present throbbing, cyclical pulse had softened, its dwindling intensity like beating a tattoo of retreat. He knew the machine was in its final cycle before the shutdown process, and though it still had hours to run, he speculated that this indicated the onset of some advance procedure, perhaps the running-down of an auxiliary system. Quieter and quieter it faded, then there was a stillness he hadn't heard in this place in months. Despite his turmoil over the project being suspended, he could feel a big part of himself breathe out in that small moment of calm silence: the resolution of a conflict being over, even if he knew his own battle was just about to begin.

Then it was as if he was punched simultaneously on both sides of his head, while an enormous, massively amplified version of those infernal static pings ripped through the lab, shattering the glass on several monitors and instantly burning out the screens of the unshielded ones. His ears started bleeding and his legs gave way amidst a failure of balance and the onset of dizziness as extreme as though he'd been spun inside a jet engine. He cracked a flailing arm against a glass shelf as he fell, sending beakers and test tubes hurtling to the floor where they smashed and splattered their contents.

He sat slumped on the floor, too dizzy to move out of the way of the seeping fluids, expecting an alert to sound. He heard nothing. Absolutely nothing, beyond the ringing in his ears. For a moment he thought this was because his hearing had been damaged, but after a minute or so, as the ringing and the dizziness receded, it became apparent that there really was silence.

Then the pulsing returned, building up again as incrementally as it had faded, and some kind of equilibrium was restored. It was as though they were all waiting for this signal, this sound to reanimate them. In the silence there was fear, there was unknowing: had something gone wrong with the machine? But upon its resumption, in labs, in chambers, in tunnels and corridors, despite shock and a few injuries, everyone quickly resumed their duties, perhaps with even more alacrity—if that were possible.

The process is well underway, even before the anomaly itself has been closed: the systematic eradication of all tangible traces that this operation ever happened. The soldiers can't wait for this to be over, but they're not going to let their eagerness spill into impatience. They are being fastidiously methodical, albeit with demob-happy enthusiasm. Thus anything that obstructs their

277

progress will be harshly dealt with. All samples, all data, all files have been inventoried and will have to be accounted for, down to even the last fragment of the last test tube lying smashed on the laboratory floor. As Steinmeyer predicted, nothing will be permitted to leak from this place but memories, and even those might be cleansed. According to Lucius, there was a contingency in place whereby all but the highest-ranking soldiers would be told they had been unknowingly subject to a drug experiment, and left with the reassuring belief that nothing they saw here was real.

And where *is* Steinmeyer? He hasn't seen him in hours. Merrick harboured a growing concern that he was planning to do something reckless, and would confess that it was the first thought that came into his head when that wave went through the place, but then when the pulsing resumed, the thought evaporated. Perhaps, like Merrick, Steinmeyer is inconspicuously going about his own salvage project, his own means of ensuring that his work here is not lost, and maybe whatever just happened to the machine was part of it, a means of distraction.

Merrick's plan, in the initial phase at least, is considerably more low-tech. He's watching the corridor, both through the window on the door and via the CCTV monitor suspended on the laboratory wall, waiting for someone to come or go from The Little Vatican. There's been plenty of traffic through the corridor, especially after the wave, but no movement in or out of the former Alpha labs' card-locked door.

But now, finally, he sees what might be his chance. There's two soldiers coming down the passage. He recognises them as Harper and Velasquez. They're kitted out in full body armour, side arms holstered on their hips. They only get suited and booted like that down here when they're dealing with the specimens, and from the grim expressions on their faces, he suspects he knows what task this particular detail has been charged with.

Merrick goes to the door as they reach the entrance opposite. He's expecting to see them press the intercom and request entry, but one of them goes straight for the key-swipe. They have their own auth code. It's definitely what he thinks.

Merrick grabs an aluminium measuring rod with his right hand and grips the handle of the door with his left. The card swiped, they push open the door to the Alpha labs and proceed inside. Merrick waits for the second of the soldiers to enter, then briskly strides across the passage, sliding the rod between the door and its frame before it swings fully closed.

A few seconds is enough for the soldiers to clear the anteroom and enter the lobby, where they will present themselves to whoever is minding the store. Merrick nudges the door open slightly and listens out for voices: his green light to step just inside, out of sight.

'. . . been instructed to inform you that all Vatican jurisdiction over any aspect of this facility is hereby dissolved,' says Harper.

'Dissolved?'

'This is coming from the top. You are to cooperate in the surrender of all materials pertaining to any aspect of the work you carried out here,' adds Velasquez.

279

'But this work was carried out under the auspices of the Holy See. That it took place in your facility is immaterial. All documents and samples stored herein are now the possessions of the Vatican.'

'Not any more. When I said it came from the top, I didn't just mean our top. Cardinal Tullian has already signed off on this order, as you can see from the document. When you leave this place, it will be with only the clothes you walked in wearing. But first, you are required to escort us to the containment pods.'

Merrick hears them exit: sounds like two priests as well as the soldiers. After the door closes, he waits another few seconds, listening out for any further activity in the lobby. There's none. He moves rapidly to the front desk, where the main admin computer has been left logged on. There are noises coming from adjacent rooms: someone could walk in here any second, so he knows he'll have to be quick. He pulls a keycard blank from his pocket and slides it into the mag-writer slot, then issues himself a new pass.

Another fraught thirty seconds' work tells him where he'll find what he's looking for: The Little Vatican's video files of the experiments, as well as CCTV footage of the containment area. Like his own documents, they will have been scrupulously inventoried and the file tags cross-matched. He can't afford to have his own files show up back in the outside world, but if it looks like someone from the Vatican made the leak, then it becomes a different story. They also have a highly plausible motive for smuggling footage out of here: putting the fear of God back into the world—or at least the fear of Hell.

As he suspected, the files are not accessible remotely. He'll have to get them direct from the servers in the Alpha labs' AV room. He lifts the newly encoded keycard from the slot: he'll need it to exit the lobby and venture deeper into forbidden territory. But first he opens a wall-mounted cabinet and grabs one of their yellow suits, by way of disguise. Then, before proceeding any further, he retreats to the main door and retrieves the rod, which he had left there as insurance. The doors in this place didn't open from the inside without authorisation either, in order to trap anybody performing precisely the kind of tailgating stunt he just pulled.

He's in sight of the AV room when a priest emerges from a door off the same corridor, carrying a folder full of papers. Merrick gives him a cursory nod as they pass, and it takes all of his willpower to deny himself the reassurance of a look back to make sure the priest is continuing on his way.

By the time he reaches the door of the AV room, he fears he's going to be sick from nerves inside the suit. He staggers against the door and it falls open, card-swipe not required.

Merrick pushes the door closed again and takes a moment to steady himself. It was one thing sneaking into the TLV lobby, but as that priest passed him, it hit home that if he's stopped and caught now, he's going to jail. And if this is how he feels about walking past one priest, how is he going to cope when it comes to smuggling data past the military?

He asks himself how committed he really is to the noble goal of science. Committed enough to carry out the things he did in this place; committed enough to be complicit in the acts that took place in the test chamber. The compromises he has made, the resurrectionist's Faustian pact he entered into to steal that crucial glimpse: all of these become merely craven excuses for self-seeking amorality if he's not prepared to make a sacrifice of himself.

He takes a seat before the bank of monitors and plugs a USB-cable into one of the servers. Flash memory is so compact these days that he could leave this place 'with only the clothes he walked in wearing', yet have hundreds of gigs' worth of files secreted about him. Scary as that final walk would be, the real issue would be traceability, and he has that covered.

There's a lot of files. He can't take them all, but he only needs a sample: enough to prove what really happened here, and in particular his paradigm-shattering discoveries regarding holy water: again, another plausible motive for the Vatican to have made the leak.

He scans through the lists, finds the corresponding dates, and begins copying the files to his compact media player, a device that would normally be known as an iPhone in the outside world, where it might be permitted to connect to a comms network. As he waits for the data to transfer, he glances at the monitors, his eyes drawn by movement on one of the screens. It's the soldiers and their Vatican escorts: they've reached the containment area, the priests having donned radiation suits en route. Merrick moves to a second keyboard and toggles through the CCTV controls, pulling up images from the expanded brig on all of the screens and fading in the sound.

There are rows upon rows upon rows of those pods, but no movement from within. That, he is certain, is about to change.

Harper approaches a wall cabinet just inside the door: four rifles racked behind a mesh-reinforced glass panel, at the side of which is a combination keypad. He keys in six numbers. Nothing happens.

'Shit,' he mutters.

'You forget your code?' asks Velasquez.

'I know my code. We're in The Little Vatican: they got their own auth codes this side of the rainbow.'

'I'm Catholic myself,' Velasquez mutters, 'and I don't care if God strikes me down for saying it, but those guys creep me out almost as much as the *diablos*, man.'

Harper turns to the two priests.

'The use of decoherence weapons has not only been authorised, but explicitly specified. We need you to open these cabinets. *Now.*'

So he was right. Total annihilation. There would be nothing left, not even dust.

Decoherence rifles: they were Steinmeyer's price, what he sold of his soul to pay for his place here, with his hand on the controls of what the facility housed. Weapons so deadly, the army had never allowed them to leave this base. Their calculation of the risk-benefit equation had resolved that the threat of anyone else getting hold of such devices was far too great a price to pay even for the considerable advantage they would confer upon their own troops. It had been generally assumed that they would be decommissioned and buried before ever being fired in anger—but that was before the demons came through, and the military brass had reason to be a little less trusting in the efficacy of conventional ballistic technologies.

The rifles were so secret that even their naming was an act of misinformation, intended to cloud speculation should anybody ever be telling tales out of school. They had nothing to do with decoherence. Steinmeyer's field of interest was gravity, and in particular why it exerts such power despite its comparative weakness next to the other three forces. In the case of the electromagnetic force, this was due to the mutual cancellation of positive and negative charge. The greater strength of the electromagnetic force over gravity was such that if there was a difference of even 0.00001 per cent between the positive and negative charges within the human body, its atoms would be torn apart and instantaneously scattered into space.

Steinmeyer invented a weapon that created precisely that differential at a localised target; only for a nanosecond, but a nanosecond was all it took. The decoherence rifle was an abomination, but it was the price he had considered worth paying in order to facilitate the pursuit of his true ambitions. Now it was about to be used to erase the most tangible evidence that his greater work had ever borne fruit.

'I'd like to contact the Cardinal before you do this,' says one of the priests up on screen. 'There may be a rite that it is necessary to perform in order to cleanse—'

'Just open the goddamn weapons cabinet. No, second thoughts, just give me your code. You guys don't get to keep secrets here any more.'

The priest rhymes off a sequence of six numbers. Merrick can't see his face through the visor, but from the tone of his voice he can tell he's doing so with dignity and humility: no whining, no bad grace. Harper turns to the cabinet once again and keys in the code.

Still it doesn't open.

'Father,' he says gravely, 'I am warning you: you no longer enjoy any kind of special privilege or protection. You give the correct goddamn code, right now, or so help—'

Harper has glimpsed something behind the two priests, something that halts him mid-sentence. Velasquez turns his head to see what Harper is looking at.

Merrick watches on a different monitor, viewing the scene from another angle.

Oh God.

The barred steel gate on one of the pens is ajar. It's open only slightly, but in such circumstances that distinction has the same meaning as only slightly pregnant.

'The fucking code—*now*!' Harper yells.

'But that *was* the code,' the priest insists, a millisecond before something flashes across Merrick's screen. When he looks back at the first monitor, he sees Harper on the ground, one of the creatures clawing frenziedly on top of him. Velasquez unholsters his side arm and a shot rings out, but not before a second demon has hurled itself headlong into him, taking him down.

One of the priests makes a lunge towards a wall rack, where two of their electrified pikes are lodged alongside four more empty slots. He reaches towards the nearer shaft with both hands, but just as they are about to grasp it, another pike swings from somewhere unseen and shatters his visor with an electric crackle.

The other priest stands frozen for a moment, then breaks suddenly from his terrified stasis and turns to run for the door. He stops after one pace, halted by a shuddering impact. He looks down and sees another pike jutting from his midriff, a scaly talon curled around it.

'The demon takes a step back and angles the pike, lifting him off the ground. He jitters and trembles spastically, blue sparks dancing about the edges of the suit like an aura, before an eruption of blood spatters the inside of the visor.

Merrick watches as though hypnotised. It feels like he's stranded there, unable to move, though in reality it's all taken five seconds at most.

The pods are open. The fucking pods are open. On the monitors, he sees dozens of demons emerging from their pens, suddenly aware that their way is no longer barred.

Merrick looks at the door to the AV room, remembers how he fell against it. The red light is on next to the key-swipe, indicating that it's locked. He turns the handle. It opens freely. Fuck. Jesus. The key-readers are functioning normally, but the mag-locks themselves are dead. That pulse from the machine, that shock wave that had run through the entire base: it had disabled the magnetics. Every door in the complex is open.

He hears a gurgling scream from the speakers and looks up again in response. Before he can avert his eyes, he sees Velasquez's terrified face as his scream is choked to silence by a demon's claw emerging from *inside* his mouth.

Two screens along, Harper is being ripped apart.

Merrick hauls the headpiece and visor off the radiation suit and grips the desktop for balance. When his head stops swimming, a degree of clarity returns amid the fear and panic. He's got to sound the alert. He tears off the suit. It's no longer relevant that he's in deep shit for trespassing on the Alpha labs—none of that matters now. He has to let everyone know.

He uses the headpiece to smash the glass on the emergency panel and thumps the alarm button. There's a pregnant second while he waits, like the system needs to breathe in before it can call out its warning. The second becomes two. Three. He hits the button again, holds it down. Fuck.

Don't panic. Try another.

He opens the door, staggers into the corridor, repeats the procedure on the first panel he can find, only a few yards along.

Still nothing.

Oh no.

The alarm system has been disabled, the maglocks have been wiped out by an electromagnetic pulse and the auth codes have been changed on the cabinets storing the decoherence rifles.

Oh Jesus Christ no.

Steinmeyer.

He sees it, too late. Merrick thought he could convince the world of the truth with a few smuggled video files, but Steinmeyer knew there was one way of ensuring that the military couldn't suppress what happened here, one way of guaranteeing that further research would not only be permitted, but would become utterly imperative.

For this infernal pit shall never hold Celestial Spirits in bondage, nor th' Abyss long under darkness cover.

Chaos and Eternal Night

XVIII

Yeah.

It's all happening. Makeshift stage at one end of the dining room, speakers stacked either side. The man Sendak has some decent kit, Radar has been pleasantly surprised to discover. Must throw some parties up here for all the corporate wanks learning to be proactive hothousing go-getters. Whatever. Fuck them. Got a lighting rig, USB connector so that it can respond to the tunes: spinning ball in the centre of it, firing laser effects about the place. UV lamp to make all these peely-wally Scots look suntanned, and show up all the pooks on their clothes.

Found a big box of Christmas decorations in a storeroom. Bit early for that, you could argue, first week of December, so they've just draped the tinsel and laid off the flashing Santas and the like. The point is to make the place look fit for a party, and it does. Good as any effort they ever cobble together back at St Pete's anyway. Same old rolls of twisted crêpe paper they've probably been hanging since the place was built back in the seventies.

No sound system like this back in the San Pedro dinner hall of an evening, either. And no chance of him being granted control of it. This is the berries. Got his cans on, got double decks, got two litres of Merrydown transferred into a jumbo plastic ginger ale bottle stashed beneath the table. It's not a perfect colour match, but nobody can tell in the dark. Could do with some actual fucking records to play, but you cannae have everything. He's connected up the turntables anyway, just because it looks good. It's not *Father Ted* though: stuck playing the one song all night. The whole show's running off a laptop, and everybody with an MP3 player has had the chance to upload their stuff.

Yeah.

Radar's cued up 'Cloudy Room'. Perfect for the occasion. It's fucking Saturday night! Having a bit of it up on the stage, starting to move, tapping time with his fingers, bass drum, hi-hat, bass guitar, waiting for the big snare beat to kick in.

The big beat kicks in.

Has a swig. Mm. Pretty cool. Good move leaving it on the window ledge earlier, even if he had to keep checking every two minutes in case some bastard thieved it.

Yeah. Here we go. Tonight.

Gaunny be jumping. Gaunny be mental. Gaunny be the berries.

Or at least it will if any fucker shows up. Fucking typical, but. All that prep, all that anticipation, and he's the only bastard in the place. Right now, the party's spread out, happening everywhere *but* the dining room.

Ah, so fuck. They'll pile in here eventually, through those big double doors, and that's when they'll be requesting all their own shite music, so he's making the most of this while it lasts.

There's no going back from here, there's no going back from here.

*   *   *

'God's sake, how long are yous gaunny be?' Julie

292

asks. 'I can hear the music started already. We'll miss the whole thing at this rate.'

'Calm down,' Theresa tells her. 'We can hear music from about five other rooms as well, because nobody's left them yet.' She checks the time on her mobile. 'It's half-eight. The only folk in there'll be Radar kiddin' on he's a DJ and maybe Mr Guthrie. You want to get down there and shake it with the deputy?'

'I'm just sick waiting. It's only a pathetic school disco, and yous are all acting like you're going to some teen-movie prom.'

Gillian rolls her eyes, knowing Theresa can see her in the mirror from across the room and Julie can't. Teen movie prom. What is she like? They're just taking their time, enjoying getting ready. Julie's problem is she always looks a state and she *knows* she looks a state, so seeing other lassies getting dolled up just kind of rubs it in and annoys her. Well, good, because she's starting to annoy Gillian. All she did throughout the day was moan about how tiring it was. She wasn't wrong either: it was obviously so much effort hauling her fat arse up and down the hillsides that she didn't have the energy left to bitch about anybody, and when you take away slagging off other people from Julie's patter, that's when you realise her company's shite.

She could have done with Debs being around on the hike, she has to admit. That's been so weird, though. First all the vibe about getting split up in different rooms, and then the way she was blanking them. Or rather, it would have been easier if she *had* been blanking them: if it had been a pure obvious huffy act, making a big show of ignoring them. Instead, Gillian hadn't even

293

clocked her looking across or anything. She was all caught up with other folk, talking to people she'd normally have nothing to do with, like geeky Adnan, to say nothing of suddenly seeming all best pals with bloody Marianne.

Ach, maybe it *was* a huffy act, just a subtle one. Fair do's: she'd got the shitey end of the stick with the rooms thing, so possibly she was reminding them not to take her for granted. It bloody worked if that was the plan. Still, it was one thing to make out she wasn't bothered being away from them, something else to be actually hanging about with Marianne. Never mind, though. Party time. They'd all have a wee swally and a dance together and it would be back to normal.

'I'm ready,' Yvonne announces.

'You don't want to be going in yet, but,' Theresa warns.

'I know, but I can have a wee wander, get a look at what nick everybody's in, maybe grab some crisps and report back. You coming, Julie?'

'Aye.'

Yvonne and Gillian share a wee look in the mirror. She's a good girl, taking moaning-chops out the way for five minutes. First dibs on the voddy for Y, then.

Gillian reaches for the mascara wand, leans closer to the mirror. Her elbow catches the edge of it and gives it a dunt. The mirror is lighter than you'd expect: swings quite a bit and ends up sitting all skelly. She goes to straighten it, and that's when she notices a tiny wee hole, with light coming through it. There's sound too, the music from through the wall just a little louder now that the mirror has moved clear of the hole.

294

There's a flash of movement beyond, something flesh-coloured. She presses her forehead to the wall and closes her left eye, peering with her right.

'Oh. My. God.' Her last word is a whisper, as she remembers belatedly that the sound travels both ways.

'What?' Theresa asks.

Gillian doesn't speak, but instead makes a beckoning wave with her right hand, suppressing a giggle, her cheeks glowing with a combination of humour, embarrassment and delight.

'What?'

'Shh.'

Gillian points to the gap and Theresa takes a peek. Theresa springs back from the wall a moment later, her expression an incredulous mirror of Gillian's. Through the wall, she has just seen Jason and Liam in their boxers, obliviously getting themselves ready for the evening ahead.

Theresa helps herself to another swatch, then the two of them start playfully nudging at each other for control of the peephole.

'Hang on though,' Theresa whispers, 'does that mean they could have been spying on us?'

'No. It's only covered on our side.'

'Dirty bastard whoever it was did it, though.'

'Aye,' Gillian giggles, helping herself to another eyeful. 'Shameful.'

'Seriously, though,' Theresa goes on. 'You're a disgrace.'

'Me? How?'

'You've been at that mirror putting on your warpaint for ages. If you'd noticed the hole a bit sooner, we'd have got to see their cocks.'

*   *   *

'Oh God. Are you really sure about this?' Marianne asks. 'Feels like I'm doing Molly Ringwald on Ally Sheedy in reverse.'

'I'm sure, I'm sure,' Deborah replies. 'It's only make-up.'

'And hair,' Marianne reminds her. Marianne's pretty sure she didn't get the Ringwald-Sheedy reference, hopes she doesn't think it was some kind of lesbian thing. 'I'm just scared you're gonna freak out when you see the mirror.'

'I promise I won't.'

'I'll remind you you said that. Maybe I'll get you to record it on your phone, so I can play it back.'

'Oh, I'm excited now. Must be pretty dramatic if you're acting this way.'

'It's pretty dramatic.'

'Is it nearly done? Can I see yet?'

'Just another little lick of . . . And let me dab around the lines with . . . Keep still, that's it.'

Marianne breathes in. It was finished about three minutes ago, but she's been fiddling around the edges here and there, procrastinating to delay the moment when Deborah gets to see the results of her Goth-over.

'Oh come on, you've got to be finished by now.'

'Okay. Yeah, that'll have to do. Try and remember what you said, and no violence.'

Deborah steps away from the bed and has a look in the mirror. She gasps.

'Oh shit,' Marianne says, squirming.

Deborah just stares and stares and stares, speechless.

'I'm sorry.'

Deborah is shaking her head.

296

'It'll all come off. Five minutes. Got these great wipes.'

Deborah is still saying nothing, just staring, staring, staring. Whenever she's spent ages trowelling on the slap, the results have reminded her of the telly she had as a kid, when the picture tube started dying and her dad turned up the colour settings to compensate. Same face, only brighter. Every time she's ever looked in the mirror, in fact, she's seen the same face. Not now, though. Not tonight.

'It's amazing,' she says. 'I love the eyes. Like Cleopatra or something.'

'Yeah, but that's just you seeing it. Are you ready to debut the new you in public?'

'Absolutely,' she says, and she can't wait. 'I mean, you said Cameron's into this kind of music, right?'

'Yeah, but I'd stay off the subject if I were you, because it's going to take him no time to suss out that you're not.'

It's not about Cameron, though: she's just saying that for cover, a reason that feels easier to admit to. The real reason is that she feels like a different person, so she wants to look like a different person. A get-it-up-you as well? A wee bit. And yeah, actually it is a little bit about Cameron too.

*   *   *

Cameron hands Adnan a can of Irn-Bru and they clink them together in a 'cheers' gesture, leaning against the frames of the big windows in the reception area. It's pretty busy there right now, everybody in a kind of holding pattern between emerging from their rooms and actually venturing into where the party is supposed to be.

297

'You look in?' Adnan asks, referring to the fact that Cameron's trip to the improvised drinks bar—tended by the cheerful Mrs McKenzie from the side door of her kitchen—had taken him past the dining room.

'Aye. Still empty.'

They both laugh, not meaning Radar any harm. Mad bastard's in his element in there anyway, but there's a bit of a Catch-22. He's taking advantage of no bugger turning up yet to bang out a load of his own faves, but the problem is that he isn't going to tempt anyone into the hall while that stuff is playing. Glasvegas, for fuck's sake. Muse. Korn. That said, not all of what Radar's put on has been reveller-repellent: there's some good danceable stuff in there, but you've got to call canny.

Cameron just hopes Radar doesn't blow his wad too early by playing 'Mogwai Fear Satan' while there's still tumbleweed blowing about the place. He and Radar made their own dance mix of it on Radar's PC a couple of months back. Took them the best part of a weekend. Album version lasts sixteen minutes; theirs is pushing half an hour, but it's fucking amazing. Perfect for a night like this. He really, really wants to dance to it, lose himself in it, but it would be all the better if it wasn't fucking Radar, Ewan or Adnan he ended up dancing with.

Hence the cans of Irn-Bru containing nothing but Irn-Bru. A lot of folk are looking forward to getting leathered, and it's tempting for a laugh, but not as tempting as other possibilities. He wants to stay straight tonight, at least until being forced to accept there's no chance of getting off with anybody. So he'll probably be steaming by half-ten.

Radar's making a timely plea for company by flinging on 'Human', the floor-filler from the Killers. There's a bit of through-traffic in reception now, a few bodies piling into the hall. Cameron sees Ewan making his way towards him, Matt in tow. Ewan makes a subtle wee gesture for Cameron's benefit by circling his thumb and forefinger, which is when he notices Deso not so far behind. Ewan's been talking about scoring a bit of blow, and he must have got it sorted. Cameron isn't that fussed. Cannae be arsed going outdoors, for one thing, to say nothing of the hassle playing the ball-and-cups game with Deso, Fizzy, Marky and Beansy. As part of the strategy to prevent their collective stash getting 'taxed' by Kirk and his mates, they've been keeping the stuff moving between them, so that only two of them know for sure at any given time who is actually holding.

'Hey, Adnan,' Ewan says. 'Any chance of another wee look through your telescope?'

'Bet you that's what all the lassies say,' butts in Deso as he passes.

'Fuck off, Deso,' Ewan shoots back, laughing.

Adnan laughs too, though he thinks Ewan might be taking the piss. Folk can be a bit two-faced like that: happy enough to geek out one night, but wanting to act like they think it's a joke in front of their cooler pals.

'Seriously, but,' Ewan goes on. 'Any chance?'

And he *is* serious. WTF?

'You not prefer to get down with DJ RG?' Adnan asks.

'Me and Matt here want to mellow out, man, if you hear what I'm saying.'

Adnan does hear what he's saying, and he's not

299

sure he likes the sound of his most prized possession being entrusted to two guys with a stated intention of getting stoned.

'You won't see much just now. Too much light round here tonight.'

Adnan spots Marianne making her way into reception. Then he double-takes and realises there's two of her. Unless, fucking hell, that *is* Deborah.

Marianne catches him staring, looks back and gives him a smile. And that changes everything.

'Do you think we could see more if we took it outside, then?' Ewan asks.

Cameron has clocked the Goth-chick double vision. He and Adnan share a look. They've both seen interesting possibilities and Ewan is offering the opportunity for swift gooseberry removal.

'Yeah, absolutely,' Adnan says. 'If you take it to that clearing we came through on the way back from the hike, the trees will mask off all the light pollution from here. Go for it.'

*   *   *

Fear. The gravest fear. So many battles fought, wounds and scars to remember them by, never an enemy so terrifying, so bloodthirsty. No shame in this: no shame in running, in hiding.

So much slaughter. So much death.

Run.

Even if a way can be found, a way out of this labyrinth, he can never go home. He is in a different world now.

But he *can* survive.

*   *   *

'These things are just awful, aren't they?' suggests Maria.

'I know,' Bernadette agrees. 'Why do we need to have them? It's like some kind of indoctrinated ritual. It's Saturday night, so the young members of the tribe *must* all congregate and pretend to enjoy it.'

Caitlin is trying very hard to keep her mouth shut, though it's difficult to keep passing up these open goals. She's opted to accept her lot for the time being and try to be pleasant company, rather than seem huffy (or indeed look like a complete Billy No-Mates) by hanging about on her own tonight.

Since returning from the hike, Rosemary has actually been quite bearable: solicitous without being cloying. Caitlin wonders whether her lone-wolf routine on the walk sent a message, or is it that she's just feeling a little more tolerant herself due to her guilt about blanking Rosemary all the time.

'There *has* to be a party, there *has* to be a disco,' Bernadette goes on. 'It's like primary school again. Nobody's even interested. They're all out here instead of in the dining room.'

'Mmm,' is all Rosemary can bring herself to say. It's a murmur of agreement, one she fears may not have sounded too convincing, but Bernie's assumptions will prevent her scrutinising it for ambiguity. Rosemary doesn't even know what she feels about it; or what she's allowing herself to feel about it. The party looks pretty inviting to her: rich with the promise of something she can't quite define. Most people are still in the reception area, but the atmosphere even out here is . . .

interesting. Pregnant. Everyone looks so different dressed up; altered enough to be new to each other.

Well, most people do. Rosemary just looks dowdy in a different top. None of the boys is going to be looking twice at her; no danger of any memories to test her in the night when she gets back home on Monday. So why does that disappoint her? And why does the music and the perfume, the aftershave and hair-gel aromas tell some part of her that she could be wrong: that temptation could lie ahead, and that she deeply, deeply wants to succumb to it?

'Some of us are interested in more than acting like idiots or "finding boys",' Maria says.

'Who would want to "find" any of this lot?' Bernie asks. 'Bunch of morons and thugs. Michael McBean, for God's sake. Kirk Burns.'

'Shh,' Rosemary warns, glancing over Bernie's shoulder at where Kirk and his pals are gathered, the main man sprawled in a chair and his lieutenants perched on the arms. 'He's just over there.'

'Oh, so what? We're invisible to most people anyway.'

'Well, we can't be invisible to Paul Roxburgh,' Maria observes, 'because he keeps looking over here.'

Caitlin feels something racing inside her for a moment, then tells herself not to be daft. That they had shared a pleasant conversation was only proof that he was a little more polite and multifaceted than she had previously given him credit for. Maybe it's down to the rumour about Dazza and Bernie's big sister, and Rocks is merely

302

casting a speculative eye over Bernadette, wondering if it runs in the family.

If so, he's in for a disappointment.

'I really resent the way they look down on us,' Bernie rants. 'Just because we're not alcoholics or . . . out trying to have sex with everyone, it doesn't make us square.'

Caitlin can't hold off any longer.

'No,' she agrees. '*That* doesn't make you square.'

*   *   *

'In't that right, Rocks? Rocks? Roxburgh, this is Houston. Are ye fuckin' listenin' tae us?'

'Aye. Sorry. Whit?'

'Never mind. Who you staring at anyway?'

'I'm not staring at anyone.'

Rocks quickly checks Dazza's line of sight. Thank fuck: could be anybody in the milling crowd gradually making their way towards the dining room. Why is he so scared of Dazza sussing the truth, though? Does he think he'll be disappointed? Does he not want to seem ungrateful? All of the above, maybe.

Dazza has, after all, been laying a bit of groundwork on both their behalfs.

'Been chatting up Gillian Cole a wee bit,' Dazza told him earlier.

'I didnae think you liked her.'

'You re-educated me on the bus, remember, with the use of the would-ye scale. Nae danger long-term, but I'd be happy having a bit of fun with her when we both know there's no comeback. See, her and her pals are a good shout tonight. They know the score. If I was being harsh I'd say they're wannabes that are trying too hard, but the bottom line is they're up for a bit at a time like this. You want to go a wee bit further than you have before, then steam right intae Theresa or Yvonne. Just depends what you're looking for.'

This time yesterday, Rocks would have been champing at the bit. In fact, if Dazza had said this to him over lunch, he'd have been counting the minutes until the party. But back in their room after the hike, talking almost conspiratorially while Kirk was doing yet another of his disappearing acts, it sounded shallow. Pointless. Cold.

Just depends what you're looking for.

He can see Gillian and Theresa right now, sipping shitey white wine disguised as apple juice. He asks himself the would-ye question. The answer is no. Everything feels off: he needs to check his calibration. He asks it of Rebecca. It's too abstract. But that's the thing: does he feel nothing because it seems abstract, or does it seem abstract because he feels nothing?

Who are you staring at anyway?

He hasn't stopped thinking about her since the walk. The idea of feeling her up, seeing how far he can get, seems vulgar to the point of insulting. That's not what he wants tonight. Actually, he can't believe what he wants tonight.

When Dazza asked what he was looking at, he felt panic: not because he couldn't admit the answer, but because of the irrational fear that Dazza would suddenly see everything. For the past few hours, Rocks has been having thoughts he couldn't admit to anyone—except maybe her.

He goes to steal another glance but his view is suddenly blocked by the unlikely sight of Ewan

304

and Matt lugging a telescope towards the front doors. They make their way outside, exciting a degree of passing curiosity from all but one observer, whose interest in the spectacle is far, far keener.

'Check that,' Kirk says. 'Opportunity knocks.'

Through the glass, they can see Matt and Ewan heading away from the building, into the dark.

'Would you fuckin' leave it?' Dazza snaps. 'It's a party tonight. And I'm not missing it.'

'Dunnsy's missing it.'

'And if he was here, I'm sure he'd want us to be dishing out more violence instead of all that stupit bevvying and winching shite, eh? I mean, catch a grip. You want to ruin this tonight? You want to end up on the wrong side of that big Sendak bastard?'

Kirk averts his gaze, the fire temporarily quenched.

'Come on. You want to do something for Dunnsy? Let's party for Dunnsy.'

'Aye, all right.'

Kirk climbs to his feet and begins walking towards the hall, but not without another glance through the big windows at the departing stargazers.

'It's this way, ya zoomer,' Dazza says, tugging Rocks' sleeve as he fails to move from the spot. 'Honestly, you're wired to the moon. You coming?'

Rocks glances towards Caitlin one more time.

'I'll catch you up,' he says.

*   *   *

Blake watches Heather finish off her glass of wine

and get to her feet, stretching to suggest it was a wrench to leave the comfort of her chair. They're taking refuge from the revelry in one of the conference rooms, suggested by Sendak for its distance from the party. They can still hear the music pretty clearly, as well as the occasional yelp, shout and hysterical screech.

'You leaving us?' Kane asks, unknowingly voicing Blake's own disappointment.

'Somebody's got to go and help out our beleaguered deputy head. He must be like General Custer through there.'

'Nah,' Blake says. 'Those kids are perfectly capable of getting pished and causing a riot without any help from us.'

Sendak gets to his feet also, perhaps prompted by the picture Kane just painted.

'You guys chill,' he says. 'But you'll understand if I got a vested interest in my place not getting razed to the ground.'

Blake looks to Heather, holding the door open for Sendak. She looks . . . Well, yes, that. *All* that, in fact, as the Americans say.

'I think I'll go too,' Blake suggests, feeling strangely bereft as the door closes.

Kane loudly cracks the seal on another bottle of single malt and holds it up.

'Come on, Con. Do the wrong thing.'

Blake glances at the door. He'd just be following on like a wee lap dog. What could he assist with that Guthrie, Sendak, Heather and Mrs McKenzie couldn't handle? No. He'll spell Guthrie later. He can have one drink. Needs to ask Kane something while he's on his own anyway.

Kane pours him a measure, responding

obediently to Blake's cut-off gesture so that it isn't too generous. '

'Could be a taxing night,' Blake explains, 'and there is a balance to be struck between taking the edge off and becoming disinhibited. In charge of kids, I mean. Obviously.'

'Yeah,' Kane says, wearily enough to assure Blake he didn't pick up on his stumbling elaboration. 'One too many and there's always the danger you'll finally snap and end up beating Deso or Beansy to death with Rosemary Breslin's guitar.'

Blake has a sip, the reassuring warmth of the alcohol counterbalancing his anxiety about the subject he is about to broach. He can't even decide which aspect of it is unnerving him more: what he fears Kane might infer from it or what it's telling him about himself. It's all in how he couches it, though: if he plays it right, he can disguise his intent by making Kane think it's just the usual.

'Were you talking to Heather about me, by the way?' he asks, making it sound like a casual curiosity.

'When?' Kane responds, sounding slightly defensive. That's a yes, then.

'We had kind of a weird conversation on the way back this afternoon. Sounded familiar, like somebody had been briefing her on my areas of theological vulnerability. You wouldn't be using proxies on me now, would you?'

'Now, if someone else has been worrying at the same chinks in your armour, you shouldn't cry conspiracy. You'll end up like those nutters you get on internet forums, who start to believe everyone who disagrees with them is a multiple alias of the same guy.'

'What did you tell her?' Blake asks.

'What did you talk about?' Kane parries.

Blake sighs. This was a mistake, inviting Kane on to him like this. What was it he wanted to know, anyway? Or did he simply want to hear that Heather had been asking about him?

'She seemed to be under the impression that there were certain ambivalences about my faith. How do you reckon she could have reached such a conclusion?'

'I would refer the gentleman to the answer I gave above, and add that this should be telling you something about you, not about me.'

'Doesn't it strike you as a coincidence that she should have independently pinpointed this as an area for discussion?'

'Maybe you don't hide certain things as well as you think you do, Con,' Kane says. Blake tries to detect whether there's layers to this, but Kane has always had a better poker face than his. 'I didn't put her up to anything. And if it was up to me, I'd have warned her off trying to pin you down on what you actually believe, but as for identifying an ambivalence about your faith, that doesn't take a tip-off. It just takes five minutes' discussion before you start equivocating.'

'I'm not equivocal the way you like to portray it. There's complexities that you prefer to interpret as conflicts.'

'Well, faith versus evidence is a pretty big conflict in my book, and you're pulled all over the place by it.'

Blake feels a measure of relief at the feel of familiar turf. At least one aspect of this has come off okay: Kane thinks it's just the usual.

'I'm not: that's what you don't get. Faith isn't necessarily about ignoring the data and evidence, but about believing there's something else beyond them. Scientists had to believe in something beyond the evidence of conventional Newtonian physics in order to develop quantum theory.'

'But what is it you believe in, Con? We both know it's not some Old Testament bearded guy in the sky, so you can't hide behind that.'

'My idea of God is something far too complex to give you a pop-quiz answer. It's not even something that can necessarily be articulated in language.'

Kane sighs with exasperation, which was the effect Blake intended.

'Jesus Christ. The theists say God is this being who created the world in seven days. We prove that's rubbish, so they say "Well, God is actually something else." Now He can't even be defined in language? How far do you want to keep moving the goalposts?'

'Perhaps that's God's way of helping us win the argument. We can move the goalposts while you're anchored to the spot.'

'Weighed down by hard reality? Come on, Con. What is it you're hanging on to? I've heard you with the kids, telling them it's all metaphors and symbolism or stories that grew in the telling. I *know* you don't believe Jesus walked on water or fed the five thousand. Do you believe he raised Lazarus from the dead?'

'This again. You know I don't.'

Kane pauses. Blake sees what's coming just a little too late.

'So what about himself?'

Blake feels a little hunted, all of a sudden, and not just because of the corner he's been backed into. The moment he saw it coming, he recalled a hundred such previous arguments played out, always diverting before this point, and realised Kane has always been holding this question back. He could have hit him with it at any time, but never did. Why is he taking the gloves off now?

'Central tenet of your faith, Con. And it contradicts all the evidence, everything we know about medicine, about human—'

'What are you trying to prove here, Stewart?' he snaps back. 'How long have we known each other? Do you think you're suddenly going to change me? Why would you want to? I'm happy with who I am. I'm happy with what I do. I mean, what else is it that you think I want?'

At this point, the door opens and Heather walks back into the room, retrieving cash from her jacket for soft drinks.

Kane's eyes meet Blake's, answering every question that just passed between them.

*   *   *

Dark. Cold. Hunger.
 Seek light. Seek heat. Seek flesh.
 Fires in the distance. Beacon fires. Music.
 Souls.

*   *   *

Gillian is on the lookout for a few faces as she dances with Theresa, Yvonne and Julie. It's hard to make out who is who in the semi-darkness with the lights flashing and lasers playing around the walls and ceiling. They've done a not bad job, right enough: the main effect being that the place seems really busy, like there's far more folk in it than actually came on this trip. Her prior concern had been that with too few people it would end up looking like a party in someone's living room, rather than a club. The skin on her arms looks tanned and downy because of the UV, and they've even got some dry ice going around the stage, where Radar's up there, pure thinking he's it. Of course, it could always just be smoke, as she's heard Beansy and Deso and that lot have got some hash with them. She doesn't think they would spark up in here, though, surely, with Guthrie prowling around, but with those two daft bastards, you never know. She's not into it herself. Theresa and Yvonne claim to have dabbled, but Gillian's problem is the delivery system. Smoking just gives her the boak.

So far, she seems to be clocking everyone except who she's looking for. Liam, Jason, Samantha and Rebecca are not so much dancing together as ordering themselves into a protective formation to prevent anyone else getting close enough to start imagining they're attending the same gig. Roisin, Ruth, Carol-Ann and Michelle seem to be collectively dancing with Deso, Beansy, Fizzy and Marky in that indeterminate way that protects all parties from later claims that they were actually dancing with any given individual. But rather strangely—and not to mention annoyingly—two people who do seem to be unambiguously and exclusively dancing together are Paul Roxburgh and—God, she still can't understand it—Caitlin Black.

Leaving aside the fact that this is just wrong, what's most concerning her is the implications for her own plans. Dazza had been coming over very friendly earlier, making out that he and his pal Rocks would be interested in a dance and maybe a little more. Dazza usually went out with lassies much older than her, and though she knew he wasn't looking for anything serious, it could well open a few doors for the future. He'd mentioned Theresa and Yvonne as possibilities for Rocks, but Gillian reckoned it was the ideal scenario for Debs to return to the fold. Unfortunately, she hasn't found either Dazza or Debs yet, and Rocks appears to be out of the equation.

A gap forms in the crowd, three or four dancers moving simultaneously in the same direction, and she spies Marianne, dancing with Cameron. Good. If the Goth bitch is occupied (though Cameron must be fucking desperate), then she won't be creeping around Debs.

Then there's a change in the light, reds into blues, just as Marianne turns to her right and Gillian sees that she's not Marianne.

Julie registers too, immediately grabbing Theresa and pointing it out. Theresa looks shocked; Julie's just loving it.

Gillian feels like somebody stabbed her.

The cow. The fucking two-faced cow.

She remembers words spoken yesterday, as a joke.

If she comes out in the morning dressed in fishnets and her hair dyed jet black we need to stage an intervention before she starts to self-harm.

312

Too late for that: this *was* self-harm. Stupid bitch. What was this supposed to be: revenge? Well fuck her. She'd made her bed. No way back from here.

*   *   *

Dazza has all but had to drag Kirk over to dance with Gillian and her pals. Granted, big Julie is pounding the floor among them, but it's not fucking first year: you've got to be magnanimous about things like that. Be a gentleman: that's what experience has taught him. If you're polite to a lassie's fat munter of a pal, she'll get the impression you're soft-centred and sensitive. This in turn helps you get further with her sexually because she's less worried you're the type who's just going to blab to his mates. It's the kind of advice he's been passing on to Rocks, but the fly bastard's only abandoned him. Out of nowhere, man.

'I'll catch you up,' he said; next thing Dazza knows, he's cutting a rug with wee Caitlin, leaving him with Kirk, who is hardly Mr Charisma around lassies at the best of times.

Caitlin, though? What's the score there? Christ, now he remembers: yesterday on the bus, though it seems a week back now.

'. . . *give it a year or two, and out of all the girls in our year, Caitlin could well be one of the ones you'd most want to be going out with . . . Lassie like that, folk never notice what's there.*'

He was only speaking hypothetically. Daft bastard: it wasn't meant as a matchmaking suggestion. But fair play to him, and maybe it

313

reflected quite well on Dazza's own judgment. Course, the most action Rocks is likely to get will be a slap in the dish for trying to feel her tits, but as long as he's enjoying himself.

Seems like everybody's enjoying themselves. Gillian's face was tripping her a wee bit at first, but she's perking up. Even Deputy Dan looks quite vibed. He's standing to one side of the doors, arms folded but his head nodding a little to the beat. Dazza catches him looking across to Sendak, who's on the other side of the entrance. The Sarge gives a calmly approving nod, also in time to the music, as if to say 'everything is under control'.

Dazza's attention is then drawn to the ridiculous sight of Deso dancing with Beansy, the two of them acting it as usual. Bastards have got a stash, he's sure, but from the nick of them, he's also sure they've already tanned part of it. They sidle up next to Julie and Yvonne and start doing some weird figure-of-eight thing that the girls are happy to go along with. Then Beansy moves behind Yvonne and does something to the back of her neck that causes her top to fall open. She dances for a moment without realising her bra is fully on display, then does a double-take and clocks Beansy laughing. She pops the top off her bottle of water and pours it over him. Mad bastard just stands there and takes it, dancing as she drenches him. Then he starts pulling his shirt off, still dancing, doing it like a strip, while folk gather round about him, clapping and shouting.

Yvonne cools her ire and manages a smile.

'You've got bigger tits than me anyway.'

Belter, Dazza thinks. He turns to share it with the Big Man, but Kirk is gone.

314

Oh-oh.

He makes his way over to Rocks, offering wee Caitlin an apologetic smile for cutting in.

'You seen Kirk anywhere?'

'No,' Rocks replies. 'Did he come in here?'

Fuck.

*   *   *

Ewan and Matt are making their way to the clearing as Adnan suggested, taking it slow in the darkness. Ewan's eyes are getting accustomed but it's really fucking black out here and he's terrified of tripping over and dropping the scope. They can still hear the music from the party. Ewan smiles. It's 'Mogwai Fear Satan', Cam and Radar's dance-mix version. It's tempting to go back for the chance to have a bit of a bop to it with everybody; tempting, in fact, just to see whether Radar gets away with its full twenty-eight-minute running time before somebody mounts the stage and physically assaults him in their desperation to get something else played. However, if he can still hear it out here, that should be well mellow. Bit of blow, Adnan's scope, Radar's soundtrack, and Matt, the only guy Ewan knows who feels like great company without ever opening his gub.

*   *   *

Closer.

Beacon, yes, drawing them. Not fires: light. Heat. Music.

Closer.

Faster.

315

Adnan and Cam climb the stage to take in the view. Marianne and Deborah have done that girl thing of both going to the toilet at the same time. Adnan hopes it hasn't broken the spell. He's enjoying this so much. They stand behind Radar, gaze down upon a throng of dancers in silhouette and shadow. The music's building: beat is steady, but the layers of instrumentation are rising, filling out the sound. Heat's building too. Adnan thought it was just him, from dancing, but he sees Sendak open a door to the darkness and immediately feels a cool breeze blow through the place.

*　　　*　　　*

Beansy and Marky are dancing with Theresa and Yvonne. She took the unfastening thing in good spirit; they both seem up for a laugh. None of that snobby 'I'm not dancing with him' shite from school on evidence tonight. A wee flash of what he's got in his pocket has been taken in good spirit also: seems these fine ladies are up for that as well. Could be time to make a move.

*　　　*　　　*

Caitlin says something and gestures towards the door. Rocks doesn't quite catch it, but he nods. He thinks she's saying she's away to the loo. His first thought is just to hope she comes back. His second is to wonder what to be doing with himself in the meantime. He follows her off the dance floor and stops by the wall as she continues on through the double doors. A moment later she's back, looking at him quizzically.

'I said can we talk,' she tells him, laughing a little.

He follows her out into the corridor, where she turns left instead of right, away from reception.

'The big sitting area's that way,' he says.

'I'd prefer somewhere a bit more private.'

She leads him through a couple of turns and then stops at the top of a half-flight of stairs leading down to a grey door. She has a quick check left and right, then descends, opening it to reveal a supply room. He sees stationery, flipcharts and whiteboards, a projector for laptops. All that conference gear.

Caitlin looks back up the stairs at him.

'Are you coming, Paul?'

'Eh, aye,' he says, uncertainly. It's not a place you'd pick out for a cosy sit-down chat. He understands what all logical deduction is telling him is happening here, but is refusing to accept it: a little incredulous because it's quiet wee Caitlin, and also determined not to do, say, assume or even *think* anything that might bollocks this up.

'Rocks,' he says, to disguise that he's largely lost for words.

'What?' she asks.

'Everybody calls me Rocks.'

'Everybody calls me "that wee quiet lassie". Close the door.'

He does. Then she kisses him.

* * *

Rebecca's giving Liam the look he's been waiting for. Giving it to him a lot earlier than he had been expecting, in fact, possibly because, like him, she wants to get away from this infernal, endless track that seems to have been playing for the past fortnight.

He smiles his acknowledgment, keeping it cool, not wanting to come across over-eager. It's easier to pull off when it's a done deal. They agreed they'd take the opportunity presented by the party: slip away while all the wee diddies are kidding themselves they're clubbing it. On his way to the doors, he puts on a more businesslike face as he signals silently to Jason, still dancing. Even more uncool to appear over-excited to him. He gestures a key turning a lock. Do not disturb. Jason nods.

*   *   *

Gillian has been left dancing with bloody Julie now that Dazza's disappeared and Yvonnne and Theresa have fucked off with Beansy and Marky of all people. Bloody drugs. Deserve all they get.

She looks across the room to where the Goth doppelgänger version of Debs is now dancing with geeky Adnan, having swapped partners with Marianne. At least Cameron was halfway acceptable: you could almost, *almost* get away with the bloody Halloween outfit if it was purely a strategy to grab a half-decent-looking guy, and Cam just snuck into that category. But Adnan? They were still taking the piss out of him behind his back as recently as last week.

What a washout this is turning into. Somebody has to throw her a bone, surely.

318

Then she spies Liam and Rebecca leaving together, looking purposeful, and she wonders, she wonders.

*   *   *

Dazza's made it back to the room, but there's no sign of the big man.

Fuck.

He'd gone off alone last night as well, before lights-out, and of course it had been his furtive wee solo expedition that had held them up when they first got off the coach. Dazza got the impression he was planking something. Better not be hash, because he never let on to anybody that he was carrying.

He felt bad about having to come the hard man, trying to muscle Beansy and that lot out of their room (not so bad about those preening pricks Liam and Jason). It had been ages since they'd done anything like that, but Kirk was just edgy as fuck these days. You'd think he was the only one who lost somebody. They were *all* Dunnsy's pals.

*   *   *

Beansy finds Marky, Theresa and Yvonne waiting for him just along from the outside door at the back of the dormitory blocks. Had to nick into his room for a change of shirt, the other one being soaked. They look expectantly at him as he catches up, but this isn't the place, he decides.

'Need somewhere a bit more secluded,' he says. 'Anybody could stick their heid oot a windae and see us here.'

319

'You mean Guthrie?' asks Yvonne.

'Naw, I mean that cunt Kirk. Come on,' he says, and leads them on to the gravel path and into the starlight.

*   *   *

Dazza makes his way anxiously back into the dining hall. Still can't see Kirk. Can't see bloody Rocks either.

Something about this is spooking him.

Kirk's been acting weird for months, even before Dunnsy. There's been this latent volatility about him. What makes it worse is that he'd calmed down towards the end of last year, in time to get the finger out and pass a shitload of exams nobody would have expected him to give a fuck about. There was some incident with Mr Kane that Kirk won't talk about, but after that he seemed to screw the nut. He seemed to have changed. They all changed.

Rocks used to be more mental than any of them, but now all he wants to talk about is lassies, maybe realising his wild years have set him back in that particular game. Still pretty handy when it comes to it, but he lets folk take liberties now: seldom rises to the bait. It's a relief. Dazza cannae be bothered with aggro any more. Lassies don't like it—that's one of the things Rocks has cottoned on to. He seems to regard Dazza as some kind of mentor figure when it comes to women.

Kirk, however, just isn't interested in girls: never has been. Used to remind Daz of the joke about the definition of a Scottish poof: somebody more interested in women than in drinking and fighting.

320

These days, though, he couldn't say what Kirk *is* interested in. He'll have a toke, but he's not that bothered about drink. Maybe the odd can, but not into getting stocious. 'I don't like who I am when I'm pished,' he once said, which suggests he's worried about going postal, a very disturbing thought. The fighting is a comparatively rare occurrence these days, but at least in the past you could see it coming, you knew what it was about. Since the summer, he's been totally unpredictable, which was bad enough, but since Dunnsy's death, Kirk hasn't hit anyone or even cracked up at anybody, which is the really worrying thing. There's been no vent to whatever's going on inside his head. Hardly saying a word to anybody. And increasingly fucking fixated by Matt Wilson, for no greater apparent reason than Barker isn't around to take the blame.

Dazza notices Adnan dancing with Marianne. That's when he remembers. The telescope.

'*Check that. Opportunity knocks.*'

*   *   *

Kirk paces it out, finds the spot. Last night's wee trip was worth it for the practice. Not easy to find it in the dark, which was why he needed a dry run. He'd also needed the reassurance of checking that it was still there and hadn't been discovered. He shifts the boulder and lifts the ziplocked bag carefully, taking hold of it by a fistful of polythene until he can safely determine which end is the handle.

This established, he removes it from its protection and takes it in his hand, feeling the weight, placing a finger on the freezing cold steel of the blade. He feels a surge of something, some kind of higher energy running through him.

He's always thought knives were shitebag weapons: a sneaky edge for vicious cunts who couldn't really fight. He doesn't need this to take on Matt Wilson, but they both know that. It's not about victory and defeat, pride and humiliation: it's about fear. That weirdo cunt has never shown him any.

To Kirk, there's always been something intimate about violence: you and your opponent, locked together to the exclusion of everything around you in something more sincerely personal than sex. Which is why it's at its best if you're both into it: well matched in terms of physicality, anger, fear, desire. It means fuck-all to batter somebody who won't fight back, which is why there's never been any point in just going up and leathering Matt Wilson.

Who overcomes by force hath overcome but half his foe.

He remembers them discussing that line in Miss Ross' English class, and like everyone else, he initially took it to be merely the usual platitude about not solving your problems through violence. However, he sees a deeper truth in it now than most people will ever understand. He could punch fuck out of Matt and he wouldn't even be close to overcoming a tenth of his foe. Something in him— by far the greater part of him—would be undefeated. Matt knows Kirk could hammer him: it's a given. Not even a starting point for the fucker. He is not afraid of him, not intimidated by him, not even remotely acknowledging of him.

322

Which is why he wants to look deep into Matt Wilson's eyes and see the impassive cunt feel something.

*   *   *

Oh.

This is so very, very different to kissing her cousin's wet and weedy little next-door neighbour Carl. It isn't something she merely feels in her lips or even her arms: it's like some heightened vibration that is tingling her skin, melting her insides, threatening to explode her from within. Caitlin's always thought Rocks looked intimidating, even harsh, but his lips are surprisingly tender, and though his arms are soft around her, there are places beneath the skin that feel like they won't give.

He is warm, delicate, gentle, and just a little too polite. She recalls Carl's wandering hands, the ongoing struggle to keep his paws from her chest without breaking off and completely ruining the minor excitement of getting a snog. Tonight, she *wants* Paul to touch her chest, and not through two layers of cotton and Lycra. She's waited a while, altered her position incrementally to try and bring his hand closer without being too overt, but he's not taking the hint. So much for subtlety, she thinks, undoing a couple of buttons and leading his hand through the resultant gap.

He breaks off, looking uncertainly at her as if to say 'You sure about this?'

She nods, giggling a little.

*   *   *

Theresa draws on the joint, the resultant glow from the tip lighting up her face as they stand huddled in the lee of the biggest outbuilding. Looks like a barn or a stable or something. Fuck knows. Closest Beansy ever gets to the countryside is when Celtic are away at Kilmarnock. Might be warmer inside but he's afraid it's full of fucking hay or fertiliser or petrol and they'll end up setting the thing ablaze. He's still warm from the dancing anyway: they all are. And when they start to get cold, then the lassies might be that bit more amenable towards the idea of a wee cuddle.

*   *   *

The track is searing now, guitars screaming as 'Mogwai Fear Satan' reaches another crescendo. Radar's alone on the stage but he's got about thirty dance partners, and five hundred more in his head. Everybody's having it. Adnan and Marianne: get in there, mate. Deborah and Cameron. Deso and Fizzy are dancing together, right next to Carol-Ann, Michelle, Ruth and Roisin, and close by that crowd, even Rosemary and her pals are up.

*   *   *

Ewan takes a long draw and holds the smoke. Matt is working the controls, going to find Saturn. The music sounds both distant and immediate at the same time: loud enough to move him, far enough so as not to intrude. It's all just . . . out there. He'll remember this forever, man.

Caitlin breaks away from the kiss for a second. Rocks opens his eyes, staring back, checking everything is okay. It is. She just wants to look at him, see all of his face. This time it's *his* shirt buttons she undoes before kissing him again. She senses the tautness of muscle beneath his skin, runs her fingers over his nipple and down on to his stomach. She feels very pleasantly, very slightly out of control. It's like she's drunk, like she's high, though she hasn't touched a drop since a sole glass of champagne at her mum's fortieth in June.

* * *

Deso and Fizzy are seriously going for it, the girls all around forming a circle or maybe just giving them a wide berth. They're pouring water over each other, spinning in a binary orbit, then they pull off their shirts and dance on, stripped to the waist. Looking over their heads, Radar can see steam coming off them as they pass in front of the outside door.

* * *

It seems so isolated down here. The music is muffled and consists mostly of bass sounds: throbs and thumps.

 Caitlin's hand runs along Paul's abdomen, feels the rigid bumps of his six-pack, then her fingers brush against a different kind of rigid bump altogether. *How can it be flesh and yet so rigid? How can the softness of a kiss, the tenderness of*

325

caressing, give a willing place to this brutal, unyielding thing? If she could touch it, hold it, it might put her mind at ease. She undoes the button on his waistband. The voice that would normally warn her she'll regret doing this is barely audible beneath the one telling her she'll far more regret not doing it when she had the chance.

*   *   *

Eyes accustomed now. Picking up speed. Got his bearings, a fix on his target. He's moving through the trees, closing in.

*   *   *

Liam's heart is racing as he closes the door. It's like a shot of adrenalin straight to the heart. In fact, no drug could do this, and you never need to escalate the dose. He twists the key and locks it. By the time he turns around, Rebecca already has her top off and starts kissing him, popping studs as she tugs his shirt.

*   *   *

'Hear that?' Ewan asks.

Matt nods, mumbles agreement.

Ewan nips the joint and slips it back between his fingers, out of sight, so he can show a clean palm. Not throwing it away until he sees who's coming. If it's Guthrie, it's gone. Moving too fast to be Guthrie, though. Moving *very* fast.

*   *   *

It's stripped right down now, down to just the bass drum. Beat. Beat. Beat. Beat.

Deso and Fizzy, stripped right down.

Beat. Beat. Beat. Beat.

Rocks and Caitlin, stripped right down.

Beat. Beat. Beat. Beat.

Liam, Rebecca, kissing, clasping.

Caitlin's hand. Gripping, moving.

Beat. Beat. Beat. Beat.

Light. Heat. Flesh. Faster.

Sees him now. There's the bastard.

Music. Souls. Prey. Closer.

Beat. Beat. Beat. Beat.

Theresa toking. Yvonne giggling.

Draws the knife. Grasps the hilt.

Gripping, sliding, faster, harder.

Beat. Beat. Beat. Beat.

Eyes on target. Dead ahead.

Sounds behind him. What the fuck?

Something grabs him. Knife goes tumbling.

Wheels around. Sees his hunter.

'Fuck you doing? Was that a blade? A fucking blade? You want the jail?'

Matt's eyes widen. 'Jesus Christ.'

Dazza raging. Kirk's mist lifted.

'Make him scared. That's all I wanted . . .'

Smashed aside, sent to ground. Something sprays him, wet and warm. Blinds his vision, fills his mouth. Tastes like metal. Feels like oil. Wipes his face, opens eyes.

Beat. Beat. Beat. Beat. Beat. Beat. Beat. Beat.

Throat is open. Chest is open. Stomach open. Eyes are open.

Knife plunging.

327

Beat. Beat.
Blood spurting.
Beat. Beat.
Come spurting.
Beat. Beat.
Jesus Christ. Jesus Christ. Jesus Christ. Jesus
Christ.
Beat. Beat. Beat. Beat. Beat. Beat. Beat. Beat.

*   *   *

Radar fades up 'Cloudy Room'. Brings it in above
the beat.

*There's no going back from here. There's no going
back from here.*

XIX

Merrick had never truly understood the word
carnage. He thought it was just another term for
chaos, one he'd heard used to describe a bad rush-
hour, Christmas Eve at the supermarket. Now,
though, he fully comprehends its meaning, and in
particular why it derives from meat. He has never
seen so much rent flesh.

That it appals the eyes is merely the beginning:
its true horror is what it conveys to the mind, to
the soul. Billions of years it had taken, since that
first twitching flagellum, millions of generations,
minutely developing, expanding, adjusting,
refining, to bring forth these constructions, the
most astonishingly complex machines in the known
universe. And in a matter of seconds, they had

been reduced to quivering, glistening chunks of lifeless matter.

He doesn't know whether it would have made much difference had he been able to sound the alarm. They have torn through the place so quickly, overwhelming anything in their paths. Along each corridor, decoherence rifles sit serenely in their locked cabinets, surveying the scenes of bloody devastation they were intended to prevent. He sees severed arms still gripping pistols, soldiers' own knives buried to the hilt in what could barely even be described as their corpses.

With a cacophony of screams cascading pell-mell through the corridors and the slap-slap sound of their inescapably fleet footfalls seemingly all around, he comes very close to taking one of those pistols and just using it on himself. It would be quick, would be easy. But just as he bends down to prise it free, Colonel Havelock appears, along with three other soldiers, grabbing hold of his trembling arm and hauling him onwards.

They make it only a matter of yards before they are attacked, demons bouncing off the walls with deadly agility to blindside soldiers who had seen them coming half a second ago. Havelock gets off a couple of shots from his side arm, but it doesn't seem to stop any of the creatures. He and Merrick survive, though, because the demons are so intent upon slaughtering the other three men they've brought down first.

Havelock hurls Merrick towards a door off the passageway and urges him just to keep running down the tunnel ahead.

'We've got to make for the back door,' Havelock yells breathlessly at him. 'The main elevator shafts and all the emergency exits are cut off.'

'Back door?'

'Access walkway, north-west ventilation duct. Maintenance details sometimes use it as a short cut.'

'To what?'

'*To the surface*,' Havelock urges.

Merrick hasn't the breath to ask if it's far, doesn't want to know the answer anyway, doesn't want to think about how long these tunnels run, blocks the echoes of voices quoting how many kilometres the accelerator chase extends beneath this mountain. He concentrates expressly on running, breathing, blanking out the fire in his muscles, the pain in his lungs.

His breath is loud inside his head, amplified, like their footfalls, by the narrowness of the passage. It's a clattering, irregular tattoo, two non-synchronised gaits, but within it is syncopation enough to detect the interference to it of a new sound, approaching from behind. It echoes from all sides and seems to be coming sometimes from above, sometimes below. Havelock hears it too.

'Don't look back,' he hisses. 'Just keep running.'

He feels like his chest is going to implode, but somehow he keeps his limbs pumping, the hot air scorching his dry throat, his eyes fixed on Havelock's back. The colonel is fitter than he is, has to be holding back so as not to abandon him. That may change if he can't maintain this pace.

The other sound is getting closer. He daren't look back. If he looks back, he's dead, he knows it.

Havelock knows it's gaining. He accelerates, starting to put distance between them. Oh no. A voice in Merrick's head repeats an old punchline,

330

he doesn't remember the rest: 'I don't have to outrun the lion, I just have to outrun you.'

Then he sees why Havelock has sprinted: there's a ladder up ahead, leading to a hatch in the ceiling of the tunnel. He's run on to climb up and get it open.

Merrick is a few seconds behind as Havelock scales the ladder and gets a hand on the hatch. He twists a spindle to unlock it, then starts banging the metal plate, first with his arm and then, with growing desperation, his shoulder. Finally it bursts open as though spring-loaded, and Havelock hauls himself up out of sight as Merrick reaches the foot of the ladder.

Havelock re-emerges through the hole immediately, leaning down to offer Merrick an arm. As he stretches his hand up to reach the colonel's, he feels something slam into his side, trying to haul him away. Merrick grips the rung with all he's got and thrusts his free arm once more towards Havelock, whose eyes suddenly widen in shock. Merrick feels arms about his legs, pulling him down, as blood suddenly erupts from Havelock's neck, preceding the emergence of a blade from inside his throat. Merrick's horrified recoil causes him to lose his grip on the rung, and he is pulled downwards as the blade yanks sharply to the side, semi-decapitating his erstwhile protector.

Merrick hears screaming as he is dragged along the floor of the tunnel; realises it's his own only when a hand is clamped over his mouth. Up above, he sees the demon descend the ladder, head first, moving like liquid. Whatever's got him changes its grip and rolls him into a cavity he hadn't seen at

331

the foot of the wall.

He drops, free-falling for what turns out to be about four feet but at the time feels like a thousand, landing with a dull bang on a metallic surface. It's suspended, though, not solid, so there's a bit of give, for which he's all the more grateful when his abductor lands on top of him a second later. The hand returns to his mouth: a human hand. He sees a whirl of black material as the figure kneels up and pulls a metal grate back into place with his free arm before sliding an aluminium panel out of the way, revealing a further drop into one of the maintenance ducts attending the accelerator chase.

The figure then turns around and reveals himself to be the man Merrick most wants in his corner right now.

'Oh thank God,' he whispers, and truly means it.

'Indeed,' replies Tullian archly. 'No disrespect, Dr Merrick, but if either of us gets out of this place alive, I sincerely doubt we'll be thanking science.'

XX

Gillian endures a moment of panic, fearing Julie is going to let out one of her signature indiscreet guffaws as they hasten along the corridor. Gillian wonders whether it was wise to tell her beforehand rather than wait and just show her. Probably safer this way: better she blurts now than pressed up against the bedroom wall.

Gillian puts a finger to her lips as they approach their room.

'Total silence,' she whispers. 'Tiptoes, don't bump the furniture, no sound, got it?'

Julie nods.

Gillian leads her up to the wall and nudges the mirror aside, revealing the spyhole. Julie leans against the cornflower plaster and closes one eye. She squints, wiggles her head unsatisfactorily.

'Cannae see anything,' she whispers. 'Too dark.'

'Let me try.'

Gillian presses her head to the wall, keeping the mirror levered away with her elbow. The lights have been switched off next door, right enough. She gestures Julie to flip off their own switch. 'Quietly,' she mouths.

She looks again, shapes gradually forming in the dark, black becoming minutely distinct shades of grey. There is something moving, writhing, definitely, but with one eye and limited depth perception, it remains shapeless. They must be under the bedcovers. Just have to be patient, and all will be revealed.

Julie's nudging her.

'Let me.'

'Just a sec.'

'Come on.'

'Just a sec.'

She hears a slapping sound, a guttural breathing, deep and masculine. There are more pronounced stirrings, a peak appearing in the bedclothes, which seem imminently about to fall off and finally reveal what they are covering. Then Julie uses her bulk to shove Gillian out of the way, side-swiping her with her hips. There's delight, disbelief and mirth in Julie's eyes.

Gillian stumbles, off-balance from the way she

was leaning. Stupid cow's probably given the game away doing that. She looks up, sees Julie shove her face against the plaster, mouth open slightly in concentration. Then just behind her, through the darkened window, she thinks she catches a glimpse of movement. How ironic would that be: getting spied upon while spying upon Liam and . . .

Gillian feels her entire body seized and shaken as though by some invisible giant as the window shatters and something hurtles through it, smashing into Julie with a crunch of bones. They end up on the floor a few feet from where Gillian has collapsed, having lost her footing in fright and slid backwards down the wall. She sees limbs tangling, clothed and bare, two heads, one Julie's, one bald, a thousand fragments of glass glinting in the moonlight on the floor.

Julie ends up face-down, the intruder on top, his head bowed so that Gillian cannot see his face. She can see Julie's, though, suddenly racked with pain and fear as he grips a long, jagged splinter of wood and drives it into her back.

Julie reaches out a hand to Gillian, but though she'd only have to come forward a foot to reach it, she cannot move, will not draw an inch from where she is pinned against the wall. He tugs and twists at the splinter, Julie screaming, reaching, Gillian paralysed, morbidly entranced.

Then the intruder lifts his head and looks at her.

It is as though white light and white noise have filled her head, some kind of information breakdown inside her brain. Though she doesn't close her eyes, she sees nothing for a few moments, hears nothing. When sound and vision return, it is to show the intruder thrusting its claw

334

inside the wound in Julie's back, a scaly knee pressed into the base of her spine. Then it lets out a roar that shakes the room as its muscles tighten, commencing a wrenching action that silences Julie's cries forever.

The sound of the roar awakens something in Gillian, something so deep and automatic that she feels suddenly possessed, as though it is not her own will or even her own energy that moves her, scrambling backwards on her hands, feet, bottom, out of the room and into the corridor. Her body is no longer her own, but she is condemned to remain inside it, like a helpless passenger. Control of her eyes has been surrendered also. She wants to look away, wants to turn her head, wants to close them, cover them, but she cannot take her gaze from the creature. It climbs slowly to its feet and begins moving forward, rendered a dark silhouette now that she is in the light of the corridor. There is something in its hand, something dripping.

She has to climb, has to get upright, but it's almost as though she's forgotten how: as though whoever has possessed her needs to learn how to walk again. She pushes herself against the wall as the creature fills the door frame. Light hits it.

Oh Jesus.

There was no breakdown, no brain malfunction. She imagined nothing in the half-light. It really is a demon. And it's holding Julie's spinal cord in its fist, her head still attached, dangling like a mace.

Something inside reconnects, her own consciousness abruptly thrust back into the driver's seat in her brain. She's on her feet. She runs. She makes it to the first corner then slams into Liam, naked but for a towel wrapped around his waist, come to investigate. He reels, grabs her shoulders to steady himself and tries to hang on to her. She struggles to throw off his grip, wants to shout, to scream, to tell him, but her brain reboot hasn't fully completed. Instead her eyes convey the message. Liam turns to look just as Julie's head smashes into his face, crushing it like a bowling ball hitting a coconut.

As the demon rains down a second blow, Rebecca emerges, also towel-clad, through the fire door connecting the boys' and girls' corridors. She suffers no similar disconnect between eyes, brain and vocal cords. As Gillian runs, flat out, it feels like the entire passageway is vibrating with the scream.

*   *   *

'Did you hear that?' Blake asks. 'Sounded like a window breaking.'

'Heard glass, yeah,' says Kane.

'I'd better go and check.'

'More likely somebody dropping a bottle outside. Just stay put—it won't be the last tonight, and we can put the kids on clean-up duty in the morning, when they can actually see what they're doing.'

'Yeah, okay,' Blake agrees. 'It didn't sound like a bottle to me, though.'

They hear some screams, muted slightly by the music from the dining room, but audible nonetheless.

Blake looks concerned. Hasn't spent quite enough time around kids, then. If you reacted to every shriek, thinking it was a scream of distress,

336

you'd never be at peace.

Kane sighs, Blake once again very effectively hot-wiring his conscience.

'Should probably check it out,' he says, getting up. 'About time we relieved the others anyway.'

As he opens the door, a female voice echoes down the corridor, and Kane feels every hair on his flesh prick up in response.

'That *was* a scream.'

*   *   *

Caitlin felt this odd sense of achievement when she realised Rocks was coming. She had to stifle a giggle as inappropriate and possibly insulting, but there was something simultaneously elating and comical about it, to say nothing of laughing at her own startlement when she felt the spasms and looked down to see the resultant jets.

She looks in his eyes, knows she won't be able to stem laughter if she sees it in his face too, but instead he seems disoriented, like she's just shaken him awake.

He looks down.

'Oh God, I'm sorry,' he says.

*   *   *

The now palpably doped-up Theresa puts two fingers down the collar of Marky's shirt and leads him towards the door of the outbuilding.

Marky languidly complies, though one of his hands is also holding one of Yvonne's. Giggling, she moves off too, three in a chain, reaching a hand out to Beansy. Now this is promising.

337

The jay is done and disposed of, the remains of the roach ground into the frozen-hard earth. No danger of conflagration, but better watch they don't trip over a lawnmower or walk into a big steaming pile of freshly laid cowshite.

Theresa stumbles a little, causing their wee chain to halt and disconnecting Yvonne's fingers from Beansy's. Beansy jogs ahead a wee touch, making it to the door first and sliding the heavy wooden crossbeam out of one of its joists. One side of the door swings open slightly. Theresa releases her fingers from Marky's collar and steps unsteadily into the gap, where she stops with a shudder.

Must have seen something she doesn't fancy. Maybe there *is* a big steaming pile of freshly laid cowshite. But then she jerks her head back and stretches, as if on tiptoes, except that when Beansy happens to glance down, he sees that her feet aren't touching the ground. The lassie is fucking levitating. Mental.

'Check oot David Blaine,' Marky says. 'How are you doing that?'

She rises higher, just a few inches, then Beansy hears this bubbling noise, followed by a dripping. Something's running off her feet on to the ground. Something dark.

She begins to turn in mid-air. That's when Beansy sees that she's got a pitchfork driven through her stomach and is being pivoted on it by . . .

'God in Govan.'

The light is very dim inside the barn, spilling in through high windows and the open door, but it's enough to make out what is holding the pitchfork: to see it from head to . . . tail.

338

Horned head. Pointed tail.

With a sudden swing of two powerful arms, it hefts the pitchfork from side to side, whiplashing Theresa off her impalement, then drives the fork through Marky as he stands there, helplessly gawping.

Beansy, instantly sobered, slams the door closed with his shoulder and pulls the crossbeam back down on to both its joists. The blood-soaked points of the pitchfork splinter through the door as he does so, the nearest spike stopped a centimetre from his eye.

He throws himself back, lands sprawling on the hard earth, then scrambles to his feet, grabs Yvonne by the waist and drags her off, running.

'Fuck me. Fuck me. Fuck me.'

'Oh Jesus. Theresa. What was that?'

'I don't know. I don't know. But I'm no' slagging Marilyn Manson ever again.'

*   *   *

In the three-quarter darkness of the outbuilding, Marky lies on the floor, transfixed and paralysed by injury, pain and fear. Hyperventilating, convinced he's dreaming or delirious, he watches the demon pull the implement from the door. It stands there for a moment, pitchfork in hand, a tableau of one of the images he saw in that book Marianne was passing around at lunchtime. That's good. He's seen the image before. That means he is dreaming. But dreams never hurt like this. In dreams, you couldn't feel the chill of the earthen floor and your blood turning cold as it soaked your clothes.

The demon strides across to where Theresa is crawling, laboriously and quivering, leaving a blood-streaked trail on the ground. She's heading away from the door, no destination in mind, knows only that she has to move. The demon drives its weapon through her head, pinning both to the floor, then steps away, leaving the pitchfork standing upright, towering over the twitching body.

Marky enjoys a moment's hope that it has abandoned its weapon. Then he sees the demon stride towards the far wall, upon which hangs another pitchfork, a spade, a rake, a hoe, an edging tool, a fire-axe, a baling hook and a chainsaw.

*   *   *

Kane hears the screaming abruptly stop as he and Blake hasten along one of the link corridors, replaced by the sound of running and gasping, desperate, panicking breaths. They emerge into the main corridor leading from reception to the dormitory block, and are almost bowled like skittles as Gillian clatters headlong into them. Kane just manages to stay on his feet, putting his arms out to help Gillian retain her balance too, but she immediately starts struggling to get away. Her head is down, pressed against Kane's chest as though she's trying to charge through him, her breathing a series of anxious whoops.

'Gillian, keep the heid. What's wrong?'

'No, no,' she gasps, her legs thrashing as her feet seek better purchase to wriggle free and push past him.

'Gillian,' Kane says more firmly, taking her chin

340

in his hands and raising her face so that she will look at him. That's when he sees that her face is spattered with blood. Her eyes are like headlights, stretched wide and flitting restlessly, unable to focus on any single thing, almost like they're attempting to escape from her head and flee on their own.

'Jesus, what happened?'

She's still struggling. Blake puts an arm around her, starts talking softly just so that she'll hear his voice.

'Gillian, it's Mr Kane and Father Blake. It's all right now, you just need to catch your breath, then you can talk to us.'

Kane hears more footsteps in the corridor, turns to see Heather walking briskly towards them.

'Just calm down,' Blake continues. 'Breathe slowly.'

Gillian's eyes focus on each of them just long enough to convey that she thinks they're insane.

'Let me go. Let me go.'

'It's all right. You're all right. Just breathe—'

'It's not all right,' she shouts, her limbs suddenly still. 'It's coming. It'll kill us all.'

Kane, Blake and Heather look at each other. Kane's thinking booze and teen hysteria, but there's the blood.

'What's coming, Gillian?' Blake asks.

'The Devil. We've got to run. Let me go. Let me go.'

With this last, Gillian's voice crumbles into sobbing and her legs give too, like an act of exhausted, hopeless surrender. She clings on to Kane, crying and trembling. Definitely teen hysteria.

341

Heather steps in, putting an arm around her and tugging her gently away from Kane.

'Come on with me, we'll get you a seat,' Heather says.

Gillian lets go of Kane, leaning into Heather now for support. Then she suddenly shoves Heather aside and bolts down the hall towards reception.

'I'll go after her,' Heather says. 'What do you think?'

'Prank gone wrong? Bang on the head?' Kane replies. 'We'll check out the dorms.'

*   *   *

Heather has never seen Gillian move so fast. The girl is normally slowed by equating enthusiasm with dweebdom, as much as her pal Julie is by her bulk, but tonight Heather knows she's not catching her before she reaches the end of this corridor. In her haste, one of Gillian's legs catches the end of a sofa in the sitting area and she goes sprawling to the floor. It buys Heather only a couple of seconds, as Gillian's on her feet again very quickly, heading for the dining room, shouting. Her voice can't compete with the music, but Heather can hear it well enough, and so does Sendak, who is just emerging from the double doors along the passageway beyond the far end of reception.

'We've got to get out of here! We've got to get everybody out of here!'

Sendak looks to Heather quizzically over the approaching Gillian's head. Heather gestures to him to grab her.

'Hey, hey hey, let's just settle it down,' Sendak

says, intercepting her before she can reach the party, then forcibly escorting her back towards Heather.

'You've got to let me go. We've all got to get out or we're all dead. It's inside. It's coming.'

'What's coming?'

'The devil. The devil is here.'

'She's hysterical,' Heather says redundantly, as Sendak sits Gillian down on one of the armchairs, crouching in front of her so that she can't run.

'What about the blood?' Sendak asks. 'Are you hurt?'

Gillian begins shaking her head, more than merely by way of answering the question. It is increasingly trance-like, catatonic, saying no to absolutely everything that is currently assailing her.

Sendak examines her, running a hand over her scalp and down her face, smearing the blood on her forehead.

'I can't find any injuries. Whose blood is this?' he asks.

Still she shakes her head.

He takes hold of her face, his powerful fingers firmly cupping her chin, forcing her to look at him.

'Gillian, I need to know: whose blood is this?'

She can't shake her head any more, but Heather can still see the word 'no' repeating on a loop in Gillian's eyes. She knows but she will not, cannot say.

'Father Blake and Mr Kane have—' Heather begins, but is halted by a shuddering crash and a shower of glass as one of the huge windows is shattered only feet away.

Lying on the floor, sticky and glistening amid the

thousands of tiny blinking fragments, is Dazza's head.

Heather stares at it, the enormity of its consequences too great for what she is seeing to quite add up. She looks instead to Gillian, who she now understands to be a few chapters ahead. Gillian is balled up, trembling and jerking.

'I take it that answers my question, at least,' mutters Sendak, getting to his feet, but the loop playing in Gillian's eyes hasn't altered. She shakes her head again, more slowly and pronounced than before, and manages a single whispered issue, the only word she can say, and in answer to Sendak, the only word that can make this worse.

*   *   *

It fair gets the blood pumping, Radar would have to admit, the old Fratellis. Didn't want to play it, to be honest. Got a bit fed up with it a wee while back, and feared everybody felt the same way—familiarity breeds contempt and all that—and he reckoned it would be a wrong move. However, he thought he'd be getting inundated with requests all night, and instead they've generally been content to leave the music to him, so it seemed churlish not to stick on the only song anybody asked for. He had a replacement cued up in case it was going down like a brick budgie, but it's entirely the opposite. The whole place is bouncing now, and he fancies piling in. The last twenty times he's heard that song it must have passed him by, but something about it tonight just reconnects him to Big Jan's last-minute winner against the Huns to reignite three-in-a-row, and suddenly he's down

344

from the decks and birling on the dance floor.

He can barely make out who he's dancing with, but the vibe's so good, nobody seems to care: they're all just going for it. The dry-ice machine has held up better than the disco lights, though he suspects that the former may have played a part in fusing the latter. There's still the UV and the spinning laser-ball, with the welcome overall effect that all you can see is this pulsing throng of dancers unless you're up close enough to make out any individual's face.

Radar spots a couple of figures in silhouette, identifiable as Deso and Fizzy via their naked torsos. He bops his way over, passing Adnan and Cam, still forming a tidy wee foursome with Marianne and the new Goth version of Deborah, who is kind of an emo in reverse as she seems to have learned how to smile since undergoing her makeover. He feels a wee pang of what-might-have-been over the fact that his pals appear to have scored while he was alone at the controls, but he wouldn't trade it for the time he's had; and besides, the night's still young.

He reaches them just in time for another round of the chorus. Looks like he's seeing double, though: there appears to be another skin-headed figure in silhouette behind Fizzy, steam rising from the bloke despite being well inside the door.

Then Fizzy moves his head aside just enough for Radar to see that his doppelgänger has horns, and a face like he's been dooking for chips. Fizzy clocks Radar's look of alarm. He turns around but doesn't seem remotely perturbed by what confronts him.

'Nae luck, Beansy,' Fizzy says. 'You shot your

load last night. You're never getting us twice with the same—'

A taloned hand silences Fizzy by clutching his neck, then lifts him bodily off the floor before repeatedly driving a knife deep into his stomach.

Radar watches this like it's happening behind glass. The music seems to fade out, the image to retreat. There's folk still dancing just behind where Fizzy is being gutted, oblivious through facing away, unsighted by the dry ice or, in the case of Jason and Samantha, steadfastly ignoring whatever immature high jinks their classmates are up to. Then there's this eruption of blood from Fizzy's mouth that arcs across the room, spraying clothes, hair and faces. At first they assume it's Deso and Fizzy firing more water about the place. A number of irritated faces turn around, intending to tell whoever it was to fuck off.

They're not telling this to fuck off.

Radar's glass wall shatters as the air fills with screams. The music floods back into his ears and the hall floods with panic as everyone tries to flee. Not all of them make it.

*   *   *

A precipitate keening of terrified voices rises above the music, playing an overture to stampede. Heather looks up from where she is all but cradling Gillian and sees kids pouring out of the dining room, buffeting Sendak as he hastens to investigate.

Guthrie stands at the side of the entrance, urging the evacuees through and preparing to pull the doors closed against whatever is loose in there. It's

346

just a melange of shapes, flickering in steam and laser-light. He won't admit to himself what he thinks he saw: it was merely something that he assumes his own troubled mind has projected. But what he can see for sure is that there are bodies on the floor and there is blood on every face that passes him. Blood and horror. He's seen these faces before: this panic, this revulsion, this mortal fear, and once again, he has got there too late. Whatever else has to be confronted, he first needs to get the kids out safely.

He sees Michelle stumble, Carol-Ann having caught her heel. They both go down. Two more kids trip over them, the rest managing to swerve around the growing tangle. Guthrie rushes to assist, and as he does so he sees, undeniably, what they are fleeing from.

'Holy Mary, Mother of God,' he whispers, then launches himself into its path before it can reach its next prey.

Sendak hauls the girls to their feet and all but throws them through the doorway into the corridor. He slams one of the double doors closed, grabbing hold of the other as Guthrie emerges from the steam and the flickering semi-darkness. He's blood-soaked and stumbling, but upright, the creature nowhere to be seen.

'Dan! Come on!' Sendak yells.

Guthrie stretches out a hand. Sendak does too, but he's keeping hold of the door with his other, aware he cannot let go under any circumstances. It has to close, even if they both die closing it, but for now, he's got a second's grace. Guthrie staggers closer a step, then his legs give out and he drops to his knees, but he falls forward just enough for

Sendak to reach his hand. As he takes hold of it, the demon hurls itself over Guthrie's head and crashes into Sendak, knocking him backwards on to the floor of the corridor.

Oh fuck.

The creature scrambles to its feet less than a yard away, just inside the dining room. To his left and right he can see terrified kids who literally don't know which way to turn. It's quicker than him. He can't even sacrifice himself by charging the thing because it will be through the gap before he's even upright. Then the second door suddenly swings closed as Guthrie throws himself against it in what will be his final conscious act.

There's a clunk as the doors latch together. Sendak leaps to his feet and seizes both handles, using all his muscle to keep them in place. A blood-streaked blade juts through the tiny gap where the doors meet, stopping just short of his face, followed by a resounding thump as the creature tests their integrity.

Sendak shouts to the nearest kid, one of the girls who fell. Michelle, he thinks her name is.

'I can't let go of these handles. I need you to take the keys from my pocket and lock this door.'

The girl looks at him as though he's the monster. She just wants to run.

The blade is wiggling, the creature trying to work it free, Sendak keeping the doors pulled tight to prevent precisely that.

'Now, goddamn it. *Now.*'

The girl shudders in response to his shout, but obeys nonetheless. Figures. When people are scared like that, they'll follow orders simply because it's the only thing that makes sense, a way of telling themselves that there is still some kind of process in control.

She extracts the ring of keys and starts fumbling though them. They all look alike.

'Blue tag on the end. Says DR.'

There's another thump, the reverberation enough to drive the doors slightly apart and free the blade. It comes through again a fraction of a second later, lower down, close to where Michelle is trying to fit the key into the lock. It cuts her wrist: nothing serious, but enough to draw blood and cause her to drop the keys.

'I need this door locked,' Sendak shouts. 'Someone help her.'

'It's okay,' Michelle says, tremulous. 'I'll manage.'

She reaches down to the floor and discovers that the keys are lying in a puddle of blood seeping under the doors.

'Oh God.' She starts to weep but doesn't flinch from lifting the keys.

'Mr Guthrie,' she says, picking out the right key a second time and twisting it in the lock. 'He saved me.'

'He saved everybody,' Sendak corrects. 'And now you have too.'

He steps away from the door and looks at the milling shambles in reception. Mrs McKenzie, Heather and himself are the only adults present.

'We need to get to the games hall,' he announces, but they're barely listening. They all stand and look at each other, not responding. Some of them are very close to losing it. Nobody wants to go first.

'It was a demon,' one of them says, almost

hysterical. 'A fucking demon.'

'Come on, people,' Sendak urges. 'Let's keep it together.'

He makes his way towards Heather, still squatting protectively beside the trembling and catatonic Gillian. She represents precisely how 'together' everyone else is likely to be very soon. They need someone to take the lead.

'What the hell is in there?' Heather asks frantically. 'She said the Devil killed Liam. The kids are shouting about demons . . .'

Sendak holds up a clenched fist: signal for Stop.

'The games hall has no big windows, and just two exits to control. We secure it first and deal with the weird shit that don't make sense later.'

Heather nods. Got it. She gets to her feet and puts on her practised teacher voice. 'Games hall. Everybody. Now,' she commands. 'Two abreast, but don't run.'

'Mrs McKenzie, you help Gillian get there,' Sendak orders. He turns again to Heather. 'You, come with me: double-time.'

XXI

Deso's running, flat out and blind, into the darkness and the trees, and it's only as he feels the cold of the air shorten his breath that he realises he has no idea where he's running to. He's just been following the figures in front, couldn't even say for sure who they are. There's people running behind him too, doing the same. He doesn't know who they are either because he hasn't dared look back, hasn't risked slowing down. None of them knows where they're going: they only know where they don't want to be. As a cloud blows in front of the moon and dims what little light they can see by, Deso is aware that while they may have escaped the building, they have given no thought to what they might be running towards.

'Hang on,' he urges the two in front. 'Slow down.'

They either don't hear him or simply aren't minded to take stock quite yet. A scuttling sound from not far beyond their periphery abruptly changes their minds. They pull up, turning around. It's Rosemary and Bernadette. Deso looks back now too. He sees Cameron and Marianne. Beyond them, way beyond them, he sees the outbound facility, flickering lights and music still spilling from the side door they escaped through. It looks as though nothing happened. He doesn't know what he was expecting to see—flames and pentagrams and shit, maybe—but it's almost possible to imagine the party still going on, people inside laughing about some elaborate trick.

Except he can still taste Fizzy's blood from when it sprayed his face, can still see the knife going into Fizzy's naked flesh. It was dark, the lights were flashing, but he knows he saw Fizzy die just as surely as he saw Dunnsy die.

They all just stare at each other for a few moments. Nobody wants to say anything: it's as though they all know what they witnessed, but it will only become real if someone verifies they saw the same thing.

'We need to find some cover, some shelter,' Deso says. 'We're wide open out here, and I'm fuckin' freezin'. We should head back towards the buildings.'

'Back?' Bernadette asks. 'That's where that *thing* is. Or did you miss Philip getting carved up by a bloody *demon*?'

Deso wipes some of Fizzy's blood from his face and holds his palm up to Bernadette.

'I didn't miss that, no,' he says, trying his best to swallow his anger.

There is another scuttle in the blackness, the sound of a threatening low growl.

'Deso's right,' agrees Marianne. 'We can't stay out in the open. We need to get back inside for protection.'

'I've got my protection right here,' says Bernadette. She reaches inside the collar of her blouse and pulls out a crucifix, suspended on a silver chain around her neck.

'Oh for fuck's sake,' Deso says. 'What's that meant to do? It's monsters we're up against here, not fuckin' Protestants.'

'I know what I saw,' Bernadette insists. 'We all know what we saw. Father Blake was wrong: there *are* demons. I don't know what brought them down upon this place, but I do know that faith is the only thing that can save us.'

'Have you any holy water on you as well? I'm sure they're shit-scared of that too.'

Deso starts to walk towards the facility. Marianne and Cam are turning back that way also. Rosemary is left next to Bernadette, looking unsure which option to take.

'Come on,' Marianne urges the pair of them. 'You'll be sitting ducks out here.'

'I'd rather place my trust in the power of God

than in the integrity of those buildings,' Bernadette insists.

Deso turns around. 'Walls can be breached, it's true,' he concedes. 'But *nothing* fails like prayer.'

Rosemary shakes her head. 'I can't believe you're reckless enough to be . . . blaspheming after what we've just seen.'

'And after what we've just seen, I can't believe you'd want to be standing out here, just waiting to be—'

Deso hears a scrambling sound and senses movement in the air, just too late to react as something pounces from the darkness, knocking him to the ground with a startling snarl of aggression.

He feels a pain in his back: sharp but shallow; a pre-pain, in fact, only the hint of how much it's going to hurt in a few seconds from now. He's been slashed by its claws, a glancing blow when it battered into him. He's hit the deck with a bone-jarring wallop, the frozen ground biting into his bare skin. He rolls on to his side, but the demon is too quick. It pounces again, landing on his chest, and swipes a talon towards his neck. Deso throws up an arm. It gets batted away by the impact, but it saps the momentum enough to prevent the intended effect, that of ripping his fucking throat out. The demon reaches off to Deso's left and locates a stone, about the size of a grapefruit. It raises it as high as its scaly arm will reach, and is about to bring it down when it suddenly hears something and glances to Deso's right.

Bernadette has stepped forward, thrusting her crucifix towards the demon with her outstretched hand, chanting:

'*Pater noster, qui es in caelis, sanctificetur nomen tuum. Adveniat regnum tuum. Fiat voluntas tua, sicut in caelo et in terra . . .*'

The demon seems almost hypnotised by her voice, its gaze fixed upon the out-thrust statuette. Its eyes flash, a low growl beginning to grow in its throat. It sounds angry, but to Deso's ears, it could also be fear.

Over Bernadette's shoulder, Deso can now see a second demon converging on the group. It is also seemingly hypnotised by the crucifix, also very agitated by the sight, to the extent that it stalks past the frozen figures of Cameron, Marianne and Rosemary, to take up position on the other side of Bernadette, equidistant from where its partner is straddling Deso.

'*Panem nostrum quotidianum da nobis hodie,*' Bernadette continues, her voice tremulous but clear. '*Et dimitte nobis debita nostra sicut et nos dimittimus debitoribus nostris. Et ne nos inducas in tentationem, sed libera nos a malo. Amen.*'

Upon this final word, both demons—plus two more Deso was unaware of—suddenly attack Bernadette with a yowling, hissing, rending ferocity. They tear her apart in a blind rage of claws and teeth and knives and stones. There's something worse than primal brutality here: there's fury, there's bloodlust, there's hatred.

Suddenly rendered invisible to the brood, Cam and Marianne take their cue and flee. Deso gets to his feet and grabs Rosemary, spinning her away from the awful sight and dragging her along with him.

'Just keep running,' he tells her. 'Don't look back. Don't look back.'

354

'I hate to admit it,' says Kane as they approach the dormitory blocks, 'but I'm starting to think Guthrie was right about not cutting them quite so much slack. We opted to turn a blind eye to the booze, allow them to let off some steam, but these kids are all suffering various degrees of post-traumatic stress disorder. They've got some seriously horrible emotional effluent backed up. It shouldn't surprise us if one of them flips out and starts talking about the Devil—despite your best efforts.'

'Yeah,' agrees Blake. 'One of those occasions when your intention backfires because instead of defusing an idea, you realise you've inadvertently introduced it to the mix. If I'd been talking about ghosts up on that hill today, then that's probably what we'd be hearing about from overwrought and tipsy teens.'

'Speaking of which . . .'

Kane tilts his head to indicate the double doors, from beyond which they can hear the sound of female whimpering.

'Let's go and find out who threatened to scratch whose eyes out, shall we?' Blake says.

'Probably over a guy, too, who's oblivious of the pair of them.'

Kane pushes the left-hand door but it jams only a few degrees in, something blocking it. He gives the right one a try, same result. He pushes again, more forcefully, senses some give and slides it open a few inches. He can see a pair of legs on the ground.

355

'Way pished,' he says. 'Guthrie is going to be serving up the biggest helpings of I-told-you-so for—'

Which is when he notices the blood smeared along the tiles behind the sprawled body.

'Fuck,' Kane says. He shoulders the door and slides the legs out of the way just enough for them both to step through the gap.

'Roll him on to his side,' Blake suggests. 'Make sure the airway's open.'

They crouch down and take hold of the body, hauling it a half-turn and revealing its face. Kane thinks it's Liam Donnelly, but he honestly couldn't say for sure, even though he's known the kid since he was twelve.

'Jesus Christ,' Blake says. 'Jesus Christ.'

Kane gets back to his feet in a daze. He looks at the blood trail, sees it smeared along the floor for a few yards. It ends—or presumably begins— against the wall opposite the tributary corridor, leading to one further bedroom and the emergency exit. Kane walks slowly, reluctantly closer. Still he can hear the whimpering. He reaches the junction. There is more blood outside the bedroom door: drops and pools rather than smears, a few fragments of glass scattered among them. He takes a few steps further, looks inside the room, and promptly throws up.

Blake arrives behind him. Kane signals for him to get back. One look at Kane bent over a pile of puke is enough to convey that he doesn't need to see what precipitated it.

Still they hear the whimpering. Blake pursues the sound, passing the tributary corridor. Kane steadies himself and turns to follow. It's only as he sees his oldest friend pass out of sight around the corner that it occurs to him that they both ought to be scared.

*　　　*　　　*

'Repeat: there are confirmed fatalities and we are under savage and lethal attack. We need armed back-up and we need medics . . .'

Sendak has the phone cradled to his neck, speaking as he flips through a ring of keys. He finds the one he's looking for and unlocks a drawer in his desk, on top of which sits a white box marked 'Medkit', alongside an aluminium baseball bat. After rooting around in there frantically for a few seconds, he gives up and sets about locating another key. There's a look of exasperation on his face, and Heather suspects it's not because he can't find whatever he's searching for.

'Two . . . ? They're what? You gotta be kidding me. You gotta be fucking kidding me. Fuck.' With which he violently slams the phone down.

'Two what?' Heather asks. 'Cops?'

'Two *hours*. That's for armed back-up. Would be close to ninety minutes by road from Inverness even if they were ready to roll out right now.'

'Can't they take a helicopter?'

'They *are* taking a helicopter. But they have to wait for it to come up from Edinburgh. And don't even ask about the paramedics. Pile-up on the goddamn A9 at Kingussie, so they're all a half-hour south of dispatch, and Raigmore Hospital's air ambulance just left for Shetland. Isolation ain't so splendid now, huh?'

Sendak finds what he's been hunting for, which

357

turns out to be another key. He uses it to unlock a heavily padlocked cabinet on the wall behind his desk, revealing a pump-action shotgun and a box of shells.

'I'm gonna do a sweep, see if there's anyone else left alive.'

'What do you need me to do?' Heather asks, and hopes it doesn't sound too much like she's dreading the answer.

He holds out the shotgun towards her.

'Get your ass to the games hall and hold the fort.'

Heather recoils like he's holding a snake.

'I've never . . .'

'Don't sweat it,' he says, thrusting the stock into her hands then reaching for the carton of ammo. He places the box in the crook of her arm and slings the medkit around her shoulder by its strap. 'Pick yourself a spot in the room with a clear view of both doors. Then you make sure the safety's off and shoot anything that don't knock politely.'

*   *   *

How the fuck did that happen? Rocks is left asking himself. Girls truly are incomprehensible. He'd been specifically intent upon *not* trying his luck, planning to take it slow, let her know with all sincerity that he's not just after a bit of winching, and the result is he ends up going *way* further than he's ever been with any lassie before.

He just wishes he had stopped her before he came—though to be honest, nothing on this earth was going to make him stop her before he came. He never wanted to come so much in his life, and

358

doesn't think he ever *did* come so much. It nearly hit the ceiling, felt like it was jolting through his entire body rather than just his knob. As soon as it was over, though, he suddenly felt really self-conscious, like the private world the two of them were cocooned inside just evaporated and they were left with a slightly squalid reality. He can hear the muffled music again, it having faded out while they were, well, you know.

He has this awful feeling of failure. He's afraid he's cocked it up: literally. It's got to hit her too, surely. She's going to be affronted, think he's a creep.

'Oh God, I'm sorry,' he says.

'Don't be,' she assures him. 'Unless this is the part where you dump me.'

'I was more worried it would be the part where you dump me—or at least run away screaming. I'm sorry. I shouldn't have let you do that.'

'Says who?'

'I don't know. It just feels . . . I don't know. Not wrong, but it's like there's something telling me I *ought* to feel it was wrong.'

'It's called Catholic guilt. *As the caterpillar chooses the fairest leaves to lay her eggs on, so the priest lays his curse on the fairest joys.* That's how Blake put it.'

'Father Blake said that?'

'No, William Blake.'

'Who's he?'

'Poet. Painter. He painted *The Ghost of a Flea*, that picture Mr Hazel has on the wall behind his desk in the art department.'

'Oh aye. Gave me nightmares in first year. Big baldy scaly bastard, with a mirror.'

'That's the one.'

Caitlin's face darkens a little, suddenly very serious. 'You can't tell anyone about this,' she says. 'I hope you realise that.'

'I wouldn't,' he insists. 'God, not for a second, seriously, I wouldn't . . .'

'I know you wouldn't. I'm saying you can't, even if you wanted to.'

'Why not?'

'Because nobody would believe you.' She grins again. 'There have to be some benefits to being the wee quiet lassie.'

'Unless they'd heard about Bernie's big sister,' Rocks replies.

Caitlin gasps a little and they both laugh.

She begins buttoning up her blouse.

'We'd better be getting back to the party,' she says.

'Yeah.'

They both make themselves look respectable, then head for the door. Rocks stops just before opening it.

'So you're definitely all right about this?' he says. 'You're not feeling . . . a bit awkward.'

'Oh, I've got plenty of Catholic guilt too, but once you know what's making you feel a certain way, it's easier to resist it. They fill your head with such useless shite. We had fun. Nobody got hurt. It's not like we're going to Hell for it.'

Rocks holds the door open for Caitlin, then they climb the short few stairs back up to the corridor. He hears a clatter of swing doors being thrown open, accompanied by a bowel-trembling roar. They both look to their right, where a big baldy scaly bastard is lumbering towards them: the

360

Ghost of a Flea but with horns, dangling in one hand a human head suspended by its ripped-out spine.

* * *

Kane finds Blake in the female shower room, crouched down over the shivering figure of Rebecca. She's hunched against the tiled wall, clutching her knees to her chest, eyes staring away into some point far beyond.

'Is she injured?' Kane asks.

'Not physically,' Blake replies. 'What did you find in that room?'

'Something I'll take to my grave. We need to get Sendak, get everybody out of here. Got to get on the phone and bring every cop in the Highlands to this place, because I think the fucking Manson family are making a comeback.'

Blake puts a hand under Rebecca's arm and urges her to get to her feet. She just balls up tighter.

'No. The beast will kill us. It's going to kill us all.'

The word 'beast' jumps out at Kane. Its implications are horrible but curiously consoling. If some sort of animal is loose in here, then for some reason that seems less disturbing than the thought that what he has seen was wrought by a member of his own species.

He joins Blake in his crouch.

'What did you see, Rebecca?' Kane asks, softly but firmly, trying not to back her further into her withdrawal while conveying that she needs to answer. 'Take your time, but you have to help us here. What did you see? What kind of beast?'

361

Rebecca swallows, tries to calm herself. Her voice is but a whisper:

'Not . . . *a* beast.'

Kane and Blake trade glances but say nothing, Gillian's earlier reference to the Devil now the elephant in the room.

'We really can't stay here,' Kane tells Rebecca. She pulls her arms tighter about her legs.

The nearby fire exit door bangs with a deep, ominous impact out in the corridor. Rebecca shudders, her state of withdrawal broken by the return of immediate threat.

The door bangs again and they all get to their feet, moving back into the passage, Blake with an arm supporting Rebecca around her waist. Kane hauls a fire extinguisher from its strapping on the wall, hefting it to use as a weapon.

It bangs once more, this time accompanied by a voice.

'Fuck's sake, some cunt let us in.'

Kane puts the cylinder down and runs up the tributary corridor, closing the door on Julie's corpse before he opens the fire exit. Beansy and Yvonne burst through it and make their way towards the main corridor, blood-spattered and terrified. They take in the red-smeared walls and floor, the quivering Rebecca, and it is apparent to all parties that they are on the same page.

'It killed Marky,' Beansy says, almost disbelieving his own words. 'Theresa too.'

'Oh God,' sobs Rebecca, bending forward like she's been punched in the gut.

'What did?' Kane asks. 'What did it look like?'

Beansy searches for the words and the composure. He looks at Kane, then over Kane's

362

shoulder, whereupon his eyes pop.

'That!'

They turn around to see Caitlin and Rocks running flat out towards them. Bursting through the swinging fire doors at their backs is a vision that makes Kane come over all nostalgic for the homely and comforting sight of Julie Meiklejohn's corpse.

XXII

Kirk can still hear the beat of the music out there beyond the trees: it's muted and distant, but it's the only bearing he's got with regard to his location. He's scrambling along, close to the ground, not daring to go too fast but too scared to slow down either. His breathing is heavy, giving him away as much as the patter of his footsteps and the banging in his chest. His eyes are darting, trying to scan the darkness for movement but doing well even to pick out a path to follow between the trees.

He can feel himself start to panic again. It's like waves, small at first but growing each time, his awareness of the process no impediment to its escalation. Similar to vomiting: you can feel it coming, know it might even be a couple of minutes yet, but it's got control of your body until it's done.

Something's closing in on him, he can sense it, but he has to ask himself: is he panicking because he can sense it, or is he sensing it because he's panicking? Don't look back, he keeps telling himself. Don't look back. Don't look back. But if there's something approaching, he needs to know where from, needs to check his six as well as his three, nine and twelve.

Okay. He can look back, but he can't stop. Must not stop. He turns his head, feels his legs slowing in response despite his determination otherwise: some instinct overriding his conscious intentions, telling him it's bad enough running about in the dark without ceasing to look where you're fucking well going.

He sees nothing on his tail, but his eyes can only penetrate a few yards into the gloom. He turns his head again, thinking it's now safe to accelerate, but instead he pulls up to prevent himself running into Ewan.

Jesus fucking Christ.

Poor bastard has been pinned to a tree by the leg of a tripod ripped from Adnan's telescope. It's been driven through his neck. His eyes are open but he is dead, must have been killed almost instantly. Just as well, because he's been mutilated. Looks like something has been biting chunks out of him. *Eating* him.

Kirk can feel tears coming now. Fuck. This is him losing it. This is what he can't run from, can't prevent. He feels like a fucking wean, a lost wee wean that wants its mammy. It's not just tears. It's the whole, shaking, sniffing, snottery greeting he hasn't done since his maw died when he was eleven.

He does want his mammy.

He's scared. Really, really scared. Nobody thinks you're ever scared when you're the big man, and after a while you start to believe it, because most of the time it's true. Most of the time. And when

364

it's not true, you can hide it better than anyone, because nobody is looking for it in you. Problem is, when you are scared, nobody helps. Most of the time. Nobody notices. Nobody sees it, sometimes not even yourself.

He was scared of Barker. He hid that from himself, more effectively than he's tried to hide . . . aye, that. Told himself it was dislike, contempt, when it was plain fear. Something in that boy was feral: untamed and unfeeling. Something in that boy wouldn't care what you did to him, which was scary enough, but it was what he might be capable of doing in return that spooked Kirk deep down.

He had read somewhere that the average prison fight lasts less than ten seconds, and from his own experience he understood why. In that ten seconds, even the first two or three, that's when you can know you're already defeated. You realise almost instantly that you're up against superior mental force and aggression, so something primal kicks in, a species memory that your tea's out. He's seen it himself: guys who were bigger and physically stronger than he was, offering precious little resistance beyond the first few blows. They know it's over. With Barker, though, maybe it would have been Kirk whose strength folded. That's what he was secretly afraid of.

Other times he'd tell himself that such a situation would be the making of him: overcome the fear, get in the moment, retreat into technique, feel the thrill running through his limbs as they delivered each punch, each kick. But in all of those imagined scenarios, the cunt never turned up with a knife. That was what really fucked him up about the whole thing. He wasn't ready for that, but it

365

was precisely that kind of ruthlessness, that kind of vastly heightened aggression that he feared Barker capable of.

The morning Dunnsy died, Kirk had a dental appointment: a fucking loose filling. He kept telling himself—and everybody else—that it would have been different if he'd been there: Dunnsy would not have died if he'd been there. But what he's been running from ever since is the fear that it would have been different simply because *he* would have been the one who died.

He'd been ducking it, chasing it out of his head, diluting it in fantasies where he saved the day, wrested away the knife and punched the wee fucker's cunt in. But when he saw that thing killing Dazza, he saw the truth. Taken by surprise, then ripped apart with merciless ferocity: that would have been his fate.

Maybe, in fact, it still is his fate. That thing was smaller than him, wiry and feral, just like Barker. What if it *is* Barker: some visitation of his inner self, the soul of a demon? Then he remembers whose knife killed Dazza, and wonders what if the demon is his *own* inner self: the thing he was about to become if he stabbed Matt Wilson?

This thought, to his surprise, jars and chills him more than the first. He observes himself as though from above, stalking though the woods with that blade in his hand, and he thinks: wanker. He sees with absolute clarity how pitifully shallow this whole hard-man act is, understands how easily Kane saw through it, and wonders how much more the teacher saw.

Kane was the only person to ever accuse him of being a shitebag: the only person to recognise he

366

was scared of something. That was when he realised Kane had his number.

He had done better in his exams than anybody expected: did it to shut a few folk up, particularly some of the sarky fuckers among the staff. He thought it would buy him some slack, keep them off his case if they were content he had bagged a few qualifications. Then one day Kane asked him to stay behind after class. Kirk thought it was just the usual kind of bollocking about his attitude or not paying attention.

Wrong.

'I learned something quite surprising about you when I saw your exam results,' Kane said. So not a bollocking: a wee bit of humble pie maybe, washed down with a helping of congratulations.

Very wrong.

'You're a shitebag and a waster,' Kane went on. 'That's what I learned. You've sat here in my class, in every class, doing the bare minimum, and I'm sure when it came to your exams, you did the bare minimum of studying for those too, if any.'

'Aye, and yet despite that, I did okay,' Kirk replied, trying to sound cocky.

Kane wasn't impressed.

'When you could, it turns out, have done brilliantly, which is what makes you a waster. But wasters can change their ways. It's being a shitebag that's a greater obstacle.'

'And what am I meant to be shiting it from?'

'Being who you really are.'

That got his attention. What came next was almost a relief.

'Do you know how many bright Scottish boys from places like Gleniston end up making the least

367

of themselves, just because they're afraid getting the head down and scoring good grades would clash with their hard-man image? Too fucking many. And our unis end up full of overprivileged mediocrities from Fettes and fucking Hutchie Grammar and the like, who rise way above their abilities because they're not afraid someone's going to call them a poof for getting their sums right.'

Kirk looked up at that point, involuntarily telling Kane he'd scored a point, and hoping to fuck he didn't realise which one.

'In your year, there's some bright kids: there's Matt, there's Adnan, there's Caitlin, and it turns out that Kirk Burns could be the smartest of the lot. Even if you're not, you've got other qualities that could take you further than any of them. You could have it all, son. You could do anything. But you'd rather pish it away in exchange for acting the big man for a few short years, in front of a bunch of folk who will never respect you for that; the most they'll give you is fear. You *could* have people's respect, though, if you wanted it. You're a born leader. And if you start shining in the classroom, who's going to dare give Kirk Burns any shite for it? But that's not what you're afraid of, is it?'

Kirk found it hard to look him in the eye, worried about what he'd give away, worried about what Kane already knew, and aware that everything he'd said so far was true.

'It's a scary prospect, taking on a new mantle. Owning up to what you really are, and admitting you've been deceiving everybody for so long. We both know the easy option would be to keep up the

368

pretence, keep being Big Kirk. But this is your notice, Big Man: you can hide what you are from your pals and your classmates, but you can't hide it from me any more. If I see you trying to, I'll know it's because you're a shitebag. But worse than that: *you'll* know it's because you're a shitebag.'

He *is* a shitebag. He's fucking pathetic.

He's not been hiding this as long as Kane thinks. He didn't realise he was good at his subjects until late in third year. It didn't seem important back then, though—not as important as being the big man, having a laugh, causing a bit of mayhem. By fourth year, he'd started to realise he was limiting his options if he didn't screw the nut, but old habits died hard, and it felt like certain behaviour was expected of him. So not hiding from it, but definitely running from it. Kane got that right.

Wanker.

Shitebag.

Scared.

Scared of Barker. Scared of dying. Scared of what he is. Scared of living.

He's about the only person here tonight who wasn't tanning drink. He'll do a bit of hash, but he has to watch the booze: it disinhibits. Threatens to reveal the aspect of him he prefers to keep hidden. He told Dazza that once, when he was nagging him to get jaked. Dazza thought he meant it brought out his violent side.

Quite the opposite, Daniel, dear boy.

Dazza. Poor fucking Dazza. Pals since they were nine. He wants to cry some more, wants to totally lose it in weeping, but he hears the slap-slap of footsteps nearby and he knows the crying is over for now.

The grief leaves him in an instant as he feels a quickening within. He'd say it's a survival instinct, a reflex, but it feels like something greater.

He's not the big man any more, and he's not scared either.

'Come on. You want to do something for Dunnsy? Let's party for Dunnsy.'

Aye.

For Dunnsy. For Dazza. For Ewan, and for whoever else this Howson-looking fucker has killed.

Let's fucking party.

* * *

It is Kane's first look at what wrought the sight he witnessed behind that closed bedroom door, and by simple deduction he understands what it is wielding in its hand. Disbelief is drowned in more compelling reactions: instincts telling him that, however little he can make sense of it, this apparition represents greater danger than he has ever faced in his lifetime. A tiny part of him wants to stand and stare, conditioned by a thousand movies, TV shows and video games to passively admire a gruesome spectacle that will safely pass before his field of vision but never break the fourth wall.

Rebecca, Beansy and Yvonne, perhaps having been through this process the first time around, engage less nuanced responses upon their second viewings. The latter two take off instantly, fleeing headlong down the corridor, while Rebecca simply loses the place. She starts screaming 'no, no, no', staring fixedly beyond the departing Rocks and

370

Caitlin at their pursuer, her legs buckling as she attempts to assume a despairing, hopeless crouch.

Blake, understanding that this is hardly the time for counselling, drops a shoulder, slams into her and picks her up in a fireman's lift, carrying her off in time to see Beansy and Yvonne turn the corner out of sight.

Kane, by dint of that moment's aghast fascination, has faced the rear long enough to witness Rocks tumble to the deck. He's courageously trying to keep himself between the monster and Caitlin, but in attempting to check his pace and not run into the back of her, his feet have kicked together and brought him down.

Caitlin stops and turns, aware of him tumbling at her heels. She bends down to help him, but from Kane's lengthened perspective, he can tell the creature is going to get there either before Rocks is vertical again or only a couple of paces later.

Almost everything inside Kane is telling him to flee. Maybe it's only the spark of disbelief that presents an alternative course; from a lifetime's experience, he knows it can't be courage. He hefts the fire extinguisher again and runs in the opposite direction to the one his survival instincts are dictating.

'Caitlin—get clear,' he calls, just as all four of them are about to converge. Caitlin throws herself to one side and Kane drives the cylinder forward with all of his momentum, smashing it into the creature's face. He feels it in his shoulders, in his abdominals, and in his own rattling teeth as something crunches, something breaks on the end of the metal.

The creature reels, staggering backwards, then

371

collapses against a wall before dropping to the floor. Kane turns to assist Rocks, but he is already up and running, Caitlin a couple of paces ahead.

Kane glances back as he reaches the corner. The creature is climbing to its feet, black blood and what looks like teeth pouring from jaws that don't appear to connect properly any more. He can still feel an echo of the impact in his hands. It is the only act of violence he has committed in his adult life, and despite what he committed it *upon*, the memory of the sensation makes him feel sick. Nonetheless, he knows the whole guilt and self-disgust package would have been a worthwhile price to pay if the fucker was actually dead.

He turns the corner into the corridor leading to reception, and is dismayed to find his fellow fugitives heading towards him, rather than away with all possible haste. He can't see beyond the fire doors behind the rearmost figure of Beansy, but he's guessing that this means the mystery guest didn't come stag.

With Blake burdened by the weeping weight of Rebecca, it is Rocks who is leading the retreat. He and Kane soon converge, midway along the passage, upon the door to the executive dining room. This has been unused and out of bounds during their stay, so they have no idea what is in there or where it leads. All they know is that it is their only option.

Kane grabs the handle. It jerks down freely enough but the door itself fails to budge.

'Fuck's sake.'

He tries the handle again, pulling back against the door in case it's just an awkward catch, but there is no way this thing is shifting. The rest of the group has gathered behind him.

'It's locked,' he reports. 'It's fucking locked.'

He looks to either side, finds a creature filling the corridor to left and to right. The one with the sore face doesn't look inclined to sit licking its wounds, nor to forgive and forget, while its counterpart lets out an ear-splitting roar, preparatory to a charge.

Einstein said that 'religion is an attempt to find an out where there is no door'. Kane has never understood this quite so acutely as now. There are no more fire extinguishers, no weapons to be improvised.

Rocks shoulders it, stepping back to the opposite wall and hurling himself against the solid wood. It doesn't give. Kane reflects bitterly on how reassuring that would be if they were safely locked on the *other* side, when suddenly it swings open twenty degrees.

They all pile into the narrow gap, Kane shoving Blake and Rebecca through it with the creatures flanking him mere yards away. The door slams to, the second Kane is clear. He sprawls on the carpet, looking up to see the key being turned by the determined figure of Sendak, who then slides a formidably heavy sideboard back into place as a barrier.

Breathless and choking with the sheer impossibility of what has transpired over the past two minutes, Kane stands up, turns to Sendak and tries to speak.

'It was, it was . . .' is as far as he can get. He points back at the door, eyes wild, unable to articulate.

Sendak, grim but calm, silently puts his fists to

373

his temples and extends his index fingers.

Kane nods in frantic affirmation.

XXIII

Adnan feels like he has simply materialised in the games hall. Though it was only seconds ago, he has barely any memory of the journey through the corridors to get here, and his recall of the dining room feels like it's been censored. He has a vague recollection of his hand on Deborah's arm as she hurried along beside him, but beyond that, no details. By contrast, his awareness of his current surroundings seems heightened, extra sharp. It is as though his mind has diverted all resources to processing the present, non-essential peripheral systems temporarily shut down.

He was in this room briefly yesterday, saw only a games hall: various court lines on the floor, blank walls, high ceiling. Right now he sees something else: a space they can control, can fortify, the place Sendak knew they could best hold out. Three doorways, only two of them exits, the third a storeroom. One set of double doors opening inward on to the corridor they entered through; the other pair comprising the emergency exit, opening outward on to a short staircase and disabled access ramp. No windows on any of the walls for the creatures to break through, just a small mesh-reinforced pane of glass in each of the emergency doors.

The only article of non-functional decor is a yellowed and tattered head shot of George W

Bush taped about seven feet up on one wall. That the gormless fucker is smiling down upon a scene of chaos and total disaster is almost reassuringly familiar.

There's a clock a few feet along from George. Adnan reads that it's dead on eleven, then realises that the second hand isn't moving. WTF? That's what his watch read when it died on him this morning. He checks his mobile, as he has been doing since: the only thing it's good for, the paltry signal it achieved yesterday but a memory in the face of today's flatline. The phone tells him it's ten past ten. It feels much later, and he fears it's going to be a very long night.

Everyone is just standing around, some dazed, some hysterical, all of them waiting for someone to tell them what to do. The only adult, Mrs McKenzie, seems fully occupied by tending to the quivering wreck that is Gillian, slumped on the floor against a wall with her arms clutched around her knees. Anxious glances are directed towards the corridor, searching for Sendak, or at least for one of the teachers.

Those doors have to be closed, Adnan thinks. He understands this with a primal need, like they're letting in poison gas. They have to be closed, and now, but he feels as though he doesn't have a voice to demand it, like if he opened his mouth to speak, nothing would emerge. He's just waiting, they're all just waiting, helpless children, crying for the grown-ups to come. He sees Maria with her hands clasped and her lips moving, recognises that she's saying Hail Marys. That's the first thing to jolt him out of stasis: gods or grown-ups, they would die if they kept waiting for either to show up and save them.

The second jolt is more physical: a reverberating thump against the emergency doors, accompanied by a slap of feet and a low growl of frustration. The doors hold, but the whole frame is shaken. They open outwards, which makes them all the harder to breach, but this also means they're only as good as the hinges holding them up and the wood those hinges are screwed on to.

Adnan takes hold of a badminton net-stand and carries it to the emergency exit, where he slides it through the handles for further reinforcement.

'We need to barricade this fucker, right now,' he announces. 'And get those other doors shut as well.'

One or two of them look at him like he's raving incoherently, but for most, the message gets through and the spell is broken. Maria unclasps her hands and helps Deborah in putting a shoulder to a set of five-a-side goals, looking almost grateful to be taking action. Radar arrives at the emergency exit with a second net-stand. There is another wallop at the outside doors as he and Adnan pass the shaft between the handles, but it's duller, the added metalwork absorbing part of the blow. It will hold.

Satisfied, Adnan glances towards the corridor doors and sees that one side is still open, Jason Mitchell stood beside it. Adnan is about to ask what's causing the hold-up when he sees Miss Ross hurry through the gap. She has a shotgun in her hands, but she's holding it out in front, palms up, like it's covered in slime and she can't bear to touch the thing.

She places it on the floor, alongside a box which

she had been cradling between her upper arm and her side. A second, larger box is suspended from her shoulder by a strap. She places this down also, then pulls a piece of paper from a pocket and hands it to Deborah.

'I want a list of who's missing and a list of who's here.'

'Yes, miss,' Deborah responds.

'Now,' she says, very gingerly lifting the shotgun. 'I don't suppose any of you lot knows anything about . . .'

Adnan grips it by the barrel and takes it from Miss Ross' hand. 'Tannhauser twelve-gauge. Combined gas-ejection and pump-action. Ghost-ring sights.' He bends down to retrieve the box of shells and begins loading them into the gun. 'Takes eight in the breech, one in the tube. Gas ejects the spent shell and the pump chambers the next.'

He pumps the gun to chamber the first shell, inserts the ninth round and hands the weapon back to the slightly awestruck teacher.

'Who says you learn nothing from video games?' he adds.

Deborah leans on the side of a ping-pong table and quickly scribbles down her list of who is present. She scans the hall, counting heads, checking the figure tallies with the number of names, then starts a new column headed by the word 'Missing'. The tears come on as she begins to write. Despite what she saw in the dining room, it's only as she puts names on paper that the truth of it seeps through. Philip O'Dowd. Dan Guthrie. Liam Donnelly. Julie Meiklejohn.

This last makes her shiver, sends something through her that starts as terror and ends as ice, stemming the tears and putting emotions on hold. She glances at Gillian, or rather at the blank-eyed husk that remains of Gillian, and glimpses another reality, not so far away. In that parallel world, it was she who went off with Gillian during the party, back to *their* bedroom, where it was she, not Julie, who died at the hands of a demon.

In this reality, however, she is still alive, and a very different person, all because thirty-odd hours ago, a bag slid a few feet inside a luggage hold. And why did it slide? Because the bus swerved. The bus swerved because the driver turned to look at the fire, the fire started by a hastily discarded fag, the fag discarded because Guthrie was on the warpath, the deputy on the warpath because Cameron's music was too loud, his music having been turned up because Deborah had turned up her own . . .

'You okay?' asks a voice, hauling her out of this vortex. It's Adnan. She wipes her eyes and nods in accompaniment to a breathy 'yeah'. Then she clears her throat and feels a cold sense of determination take hold. These parallel worlds could regress infinitely behind the present reality for every one of them. They are not lucky, they simply *are*, and the only thing that matters is keeping it that way.

'I'm compiling a list of who's missing,' she announces to the group. 'Everyone who's not here, I need their names.'

Adnan and Radar have a look at who's already on the sheet. Marianne and Cameron are the first to be listed below the ones they know to be dead.

'Rosemary and Bernie,' says Maria. 'And Caitlin.'
'Ewan,' states Adnan. 'Matt.'

'Rocks,' offers Radar. 'Dazza too. And *Kirk*,' he adds pointedly.

'At least that makes me feel a bit better,' Adnan mutters, almost but not quite under his breath. Deborah gapes at him, can't believe he said this.

'No, I just mean it's some comfort to think these monsters aren't the scariest thing out there.'

*   *   *

Kirk is moving steadily and deliberately now: slower than before, picking his steps, taking care over his balance, mindful of the weight of the large and formidably solid stick he's carrying. Got a bead on the fucker. Aye. Changes everything when you're the one doing the stalking and it's your prey that's unmindful of your approach.

Silent. Picking out each step. Steadying his breath, letting each exhale come gently from an open mouth to minimise its sound. Clouds overhead are on the move. The moon breaks through again, bringing hard edges to the greys and shadow shapes, picking out the figure of Matt Wilson crouched beneath a tree like it's some celestial spotlight.

This is it. He has to move now, strike before his approach is detected. He alters his grip on the stick, scans the forest floor, chooses his path, takes a breath and begins to accelerate.

Matt senses the movement, turns in time to see Kirk emerge from cover. His face is a picture of hate, his mouth wide to issue a roar, a battle-cry. Matt knows he has no time, Kirk is moving too fast. He covers his head with his arms, the sight of the swinging stick the last thing he sees before

379

closing his eyes. There is a crunch of contact, a howl of pain, but he feels nothing except the vibration of falling weight upon the ground nearby, followed by scrambling sounds and urgent breath. Matt opens his eyes and removes his arms from view, in time to watch Kirk circle around, placing himself between Matt and the demon that had been about to pounce upon him.

Kirk has lost the stick. He got a good crack in there, but couldn't keep hold of it as they tangled on the deck in the aftermath. He touches his face, feels warm dampness, glances down at his shoulder where it is stinging. Claw marks. He looks across at his foe: crouched, circling, keenly returning his scrutiny, its tail moving with each step, clearly an aid to balance.

A phrase leaps to mind, something from a wildlife documentary: ambush predator. Aye. That's what he's looking at. Something that likes to surprise its prey: less cocksure when it finds itself facing a square go. It doesn't look as big as he remembers. Either his fear had blown the creature up in his mind or he's not looking at the same thing as killed Dazza.

He checks the horns. They're small: not truncated like Hellboy's, but wee, budding, trainer-bra efforts. Definitely not the thing that killed Dazza. In demon terms, he's looking at a midget or a wean. He recalls the ten-second rule, and though they only clashed for a moment, it was more than enough. He understands. He has the measure. There will be no paralysis by fear. There will be no subconscious surrender to superior mental force and aggression.

In short, he can take this cunt.

Kirk touches the wound on his shoulder, glances at the blood on his fingers, then stares back at the demon.

'You fight like a fuckin' *lassie*,' he shouts.

The demon charges in response, as much in panic as in anger, and hurls itself towards him with an inhumanly impressive leap. Kirk stands his ground and sends the head in. He can feel as well as hear the crunch of breaking bone as his forehead connects with the demon's face.

Kirk reels, a little dazed from the impact, but nothing compared to the demon. It staggers drunkenly, struggling to get back on its feet, black blood spurting from its nose and mouth.

Kirk doesn't hesitate. He kicks it in the face with everything he has, knocking it on to its back. With it lying there stunned, he kicks and stamps on its head—again and again and again—until he feels a hand on his arm, tugging him back.

'It's dead,' says a voice. It sounds miles away, but that's because his ears are filled with the whooshing of his blood around his head as he thrashes away with his feet. 'Let's go.'

Kirk wheels around and sees Matt standing beside him.

He looks down at what's left of the creature's head, realises he's trembling with the adrenalin, sweating despite the cold.

He's never killed anything before. Christ, look at it. What a fucking mess. He looks at Matt, thinks of what he felt less than an hour ago, thinks of what else could have been lying at his feet, thinks of what he wanted for Barker, thinks of Dunnsy, thinks of Dazza, thinks of Ewan. He feels something welling up, something he knows he can't stem. He pulls Matt closer, throws his arms around him and starts to cry.

*   *   *

Marianne tugs on Cameron's arm and urges him to slow down. She's breathless, she needs to get her bearings, and the intervening events have thoroughly vindicated Deso's suggestion of hiding out somewhere indoors. She doesn't know where Deso and Rosemary ended up, and more to the point, nor does she know where she and Cameron have ended up. When the creatures converged on poor Bernadette, they all just scattered.

The music is distant now, though still bloody playing: Radar must have had a whole default set-list cued up on his laptop. It's easy to imagine the party still going on in one of Adnan's parallel universes: all of them are still dancing, none of this horror has happened, and the only thing she's anxious about is whether either she or Adnan will get up sufficient nerve to initiate a snog.

By a dim glow of light through the trees, she is able to deduce that they are just north of the Fort Trochart compound. From memory, the barn should be the first thing they come to, as good a place as any to fortify themselves.

'I'm guessing if Adnan was here,' Cameron says very quietly, 'you'd be finding it pretty hard not to say "I told you so".'

'Why?' she asks, with pronounced consternation.

'You're the one who already believed in all this stuff. Demons, I mean: that's what we saw, wasn't it?'

'I'm into Tolkien as well. Doesn't mean what we

saw were orcs. I believe in the power of myth, but that's not the same as believing the myths themselves. Reality is what you're left with when you *stop* believing in things, so it doesn't matter what these fuckers are: what matters is how we keep them from killing us.'

'Don't suppose you've got any pointers on that score: do we need stakes through the heart, silver bullets . . . ?'

'Pointers? Yeah.' She glances towards the dark grey shape of a two-storey structure just distinguishable against the black of the night. 'We barricade ourselves inside there and wait for the cavalry.'

'Okay,' Cameron says. He strikes her as too scared to dissent, even if he did disagree. The one good thing about the blind leading the blind is that the follower is unaware that the leader can see fuck-all either.

Having caught her breath just enough, they both set off at a cautious jog, trying to cushion their footfalls as they proceed. While they were aimlessly running, it never occurred to them to exercise any such stealth, only to put as much distance as they could between themselves and whatever was tearing Bernadette apart. As soon as they had a goal, however, despite neither making an entreaty to that effect, they were both instinctively endeavouring to conceal their movements. There is a palpable fear of being set upon from any angle at any moment, ramped up the closer they get to their destination, a thought that hadn't crossed their minds either of the times they fled in panic.

They reach the outbuilding at its rear, Cameron

accelerating when he sees the narrow door at the left-hand corner of the gable end. Marianne can't shout, so she has to draw upon the last of her reserves to catch up with him before he can open it.

'No,' she says. 'We need to do a circuit. We don't know what's already in there.'

They make their way cautiously around to the front, where they can examine the main entrance.

'It's okay,' Marianne concludes. 'It's still locked from the outside. Give us a hand with this crossbeam.'

They lift the beam from its brackets and lower it to the ground as quietly as possible, before Cameron tugs the door open. Marianne glances back, anxiously looking out for possible pursuers, then follows him inside. They both stop as they feel a squelching underfoot.

'Shite,' Cameron says.

'Probably.'

'Hang on, is that a light switch there?'

'Yeah. Let me close the door first, though.'

'Got you.'

Marianne pulls the door to, then Cam flips the switch. They look down and see that he is standing in a puddle of blood, more dripping into it from above. Slowly, reluctantly, they look up, just in time to see a baling hook swing down into Cameron's chest. He gets hauled rapidly upwards out of sight, blood spraying around his wildly kicking legs.

Marianne turns and runs, pushing the door open only to slam into another creature, who grips her around the throat and lifts her up. The image of Fizzy's death flashes into her mind and she wets herself as she spots a knife in the creature's other clawed hand.

Marianne closes her eyes but the blow doesn't come. Instead, she hears a guttural issue that she deduces must be speech. She looks again and sees another, larger creature approach, gesticulating towards the main building as it talks. The one holding her gives a growled response, then carries her, still by the neck, into the building, where she is thrown against a pillar and drops to the floor. She feels the ground cold and tacky under her hands and looks to her side where she sees two bodies lying close by, naked and mutilated beyond recognition. The larger demon looks overhead and growls some form of command. This prompts movement above, and she glances up to see a third creature perched on the overhang of the upper level, blood smeared all over its mouth and chest, the baling hook in its hand.

There is a discussion, or possibly an argument, after which the one with the baling hook briefly disappears from sight, then rather angrily shoves Cameron over the drop. His arms flap as he falls, thrust out in front just before impact, then he cries in agony as snapped bone rips through muscle and skin. Marianne instinctively gets up to run to him, and is promptly sent reeling back against the pillar by a blow that lifts her feet off the ground. The creature then seizes her by the left wrist and drives its knife through her palm, pinning her in place.

Her scream threatens to shake the barn, shake the night.

Then the creature giving out the orders looks at her thoughtfully, very thoughtfully indeed, and says something in what sounds unmistakably to be

Latin.

*   *   *

Kane fears they may be approaching feeding time in the executive dining room. Every five seconds brings another crash against the door, with the creature outside enjoying more success than Rocks in attempting to force it open. The sideboard and other furniture piled in front slides forward a little with every impact, before being shouldered back again by Sendak. The lock has already given, splintered out of its frame. The blockade is preventing the door from opening more than an inch or two each time, but the door itself is cracking horizontally at around chest height.

Sendak digs his heels into the floor and uses himself as a human wedge, addressing the room as he does so.

'Okay, people, the good news is that I made a call and help is on its way. The bad news is we'll be lucky if it gets here inside two hours, and as you are all aware, party crashers never come alone.'

'Where are the rest of the kids?' Kane asks, though he's dreading the reply.

'Games hall. It's the best place to defend. Two exits, no windows. Creatures took the dining room, killed at least one of the kids, I couldn't see for sure. Some of them ran outside. It's sealed off now. Guthrie didn't make it either.'

Sendak fires it out, blank and neutral. No sorrys, no platitudes, just pertinent information. Kane understands: they can't afford anything else right now.

There's another crash at Sendak's back.

'What about Heather?'asks Blake.

'She's in the games hall, got my shotgun. And that's where we gotta fall back to. This door's not gonna hold much longer.'

A section of veneer tears away, sprinkling sawdust beneath it as the plywood starts to crumble.

'That door opposite leads to the kitchen. I need some of you to get inside, get hold of something heavy and stand by to barricade it as soon as I get through.'

'The kitchen?' asks Kane. 'But you said they took the dining room. Aren't they connected?'

'Only by serving hatches, and they're sealed by roller-shutters. There's a door leading back out to the corridor, then round one corner we've got a clear run to the games hall.'

'How long a run?' asks Blake, mindful of having carried Rebecca on the last mercy dash.

'The longest one you'll ever make,' Sendak replies.

'Hey, don't sugar-coat it, give us the truth.'

Sendak offers him a grim smile, then shakes as the next crash impacts.

'Get moving, people.'

Blake helps Rebecca through to the kitchen. She still seems dazed, but she has resumed the ability to perambulate herself from one spot to another, which could be the difference between life and death for both of them. She and Yvonne stand out of the way as the others assess what kitchen appliances would make the best barrier. The consensus is the huge double-doored Maytag fridge opposite the hobs. It takes Kane, Blake, Rocks and Beansy to manoeuvre it across next to the door, and they all hold their position as they wait for Sendak to make his move.

The Sergeant waits for the next crash, forces the sideboard back one last time, then sprints for the kitchen, Caitlin slamming the door as soon as he's clear. They shuffle the fridge in front of it, but Sendak directs them instead to tip it on its side.

'Less likely to topple, and we can pile some more shit on top of it,' he explains.

As they set about further bolstering this barricade, they can hear the rending and splintering of wood as the adjacent dining room is breached. The first slam against the kitchen door follows seconds later, accompanied by a horrible guttural roar that vibrates through all of them like pins and needles.

'What . . . are . . . those . . . things?' asks Caitlin, shaking.

'They're fuckin' demons, man,' Beansy replies, his tone implying it's an astonishingly stupid question. 'Demons from Hell.'

Caitlin turns to Blake and forces the question that, like the demons themselves, he's been able to evade so far, and which he still hopes to remain a step in front of.

'You said there were no demons, Father.'

He is resolute and grave, answering to more than Caitlin and Beansy.

'There are monsters, of that there can be no dispute. But we don't know what they are, and we damn sure don't know where they're from.'

Kane happens to catch a glance at Sendak, whose expression betrays that he just might have an idea regarding this latter question.

XXIV

Deso can see light again through gaps in the trees. They lost sight of the buildings after fleeing from the attack on Bernadette, and having run blindly for who knows how long, the effect was similar to doing somersaults underwater: you no longer know whether the direction you are headed is actually taking you further from the surface.

He's still got a hold of Rosemary's hand. He remembers grabbing her because he feared she was going to freeze in the sight of Bernadette's death, and she hasn't let go since. It's the only part of his body that isn't cold. Running made him warmer but he couldn't keep it up, and after the initial panic, he didn't feel inclined to drive forwards at anything above the most cautious pace. They've both been staring into blackness, starting at shadows, flinching from every whisper of wind. Now they can most definitely hear something close by: a low, rumbling animal sound.

'There!' Deso whispers, and points towards the outline of a small, one-storey structure only twenty or thirty yards away. It's a storage shed on the gravel path that skirts the boundaries of the compound, which means they've come around two hundred and seventy degrees.

They maintain a cautious pace through the last of the trees, then can't hold back from sprinting the last dozen yards across open ground. It is indeed a shed: a reassuringly sturdy-looking concrete-and-aluminium affair. It is also, less reassuringly, padlocked shut.

'Oh God, it's locked,' Rosemary whimpers, threatening to lose it.

'Shhh.'

They hear more movement in the trees: that low rumbling again, and the sound of heavy footfalls.

'You got a hairpin on you?' Deso whispers. 'A kirby grip?'

She shakes her head.

'Fuck.'

He is clutching his naked torso against the cold, delicately fingering the shallow gouges where the demon's claw dug in. He enviously eyes Rosemary's top, which gives him an idea.

'Take your bra off.'

'What? Listen, if this is the "don't want to die a virgin" routine, you picked the wrong girl.'

'Fuck's sake, I need the wire. I'm working on the "not dying" problem rather than the "not dying a virgin" one. Take it off. It's not like you need it anyway.'

Rosemary lets out a tut of indignation but complies nonetheless, pulling her bra out through her sleeves. Deso bites into the material to tear it, slides out one of the underwires and begins attempting to pick the lock.

'Have you done this before?' she asks him anxiously.

'Yeah. Just don't tell Big Kirk in case he works out who it was stole his bike that time in second year.'

They hear the guttural growl again, sense more movement. Rosemary sees Deso's face betray growing desperation, not conducive to the task at hand.

'Mother of God, please, hurry.'

'Hurry? I've a regulation tea-break to take yet. Fuck's sake, what do you think I'm doing here?'

'I don't care, but do it faster.'

Deso bites back another retort, realises he's getting himself in a state. He pulls the wire out of the lock for a moment and takes a breath. As he does so, he glances at Rosemary, who is anxiously scanning their surroundings. He catches sight of her chest, the material of her top now clinging tightly to the outline of her breasts. When he said she didn't need the bra, he'd meant to imply she'd no tits, but having seen the results of her taking it off, he realises it was an accurate, if unintentional compliment. Talk about a way to find your centre. He's calmer now, the moment of fluster passed. He passes the wire delicately back into the slot and a few seconds later, the padlock pops.

They slip quickly in and close the door. It's dark inside, almost completely so, with only a few slivers of light admitted through a single transparent plastic window that is largely obscured by the contents of a shelving unit. Rosemary pads her palm around the wall until she finds a light switch. She is about to turn it on when Deso's hand intercepts hers and stops it. With his other hand, he puts a finger to her lips.

Outside, they hear the sound of footsteps on the gravel.

His eyes adjusting to what little light there is inside the shed, Deso gets a grip on the shelving unit and drags it against the door as quietly as he can. The footsteps continue their approach. Their gait is irregular, broken, unsyncopated. It makes Deso think of a lizard on hot stone: quick bursts, pauses, scuttling: definitely not human.

He hears more moving gravel, then another, growing silence. Has it stopped again? No. It's on grass. Closer.

Fuck's sake. It's right outside. He can hear it breathing.

The door moves, given a trial push. It comes in only a centimetre before being blocked by the shelving unit. A second push follows, this time with greater intent. It opens a fraction further: enough to betray that there is something blocking it: something that can be shifted. He holds himself steady against the shelves, keeping his centre of gravity low. Rosemary crouches alongside, also leaning into the blockade. The outside pressure on the door relents: he worries it's ahead of a more determined charge. Then a scream carries through the air from not so far away: a human scream of pain.

The third push never comes. There are more footsteps on the gravel, hurried this time, retreating. Deso breathes out, his long sigh rendered vibrato by his shivering and the tremulous chattering of his teeth.

Rosemary stands up straight again next to him and places a hand on his shoulder, getting a guide on where he is in the near-darkness. He can barely see her, but her face is only inches away, close enough for her breath to feel warm.

'You're freezing,' she gasps.

'Least of my worries, I'd have thought,' he whispers.

'But one I can do something about. Just don't take this the wrong way.'

With which she presses herself against him and puts her arms around his back.

It's like stepping into a bath. Deso feels warmth envelop him immediately, but after a few seconds he's afraid he's sapped the lot and transferred the problem, as he can feel Rosemary begin to tremble. Then he feels a wetness against his bare shoulder and understands that she's crying. Instinctively, he puts a hand to the back of her head and strokes her hair as a gesture of comfort. Her shudders continue, near-silently, as she lets out just some of her grief, and Deso is strangely grateful, because the role of consoler serves to dam his own straining reservoir.

He says nothing, knows there's nothing he *can* say: just strokes her hair and holds his other arm against the small of her back, keeping her pressed against him. He can feel it when the sobbing subsides, the last of the shudders replaced with quiet sniffs. He just hopes she doesn't break apart now, and not merely for the sake of staying warm. When she pulls her head back from his shoulder, he feels a surprisingly deep moment of loss and regret, but it only lasts for the half a second it takes for her to turn her face upwards and kiss him.

*   *   *

There's a horrible silence about the games hall as the time grows since the last failing assault on the emergency doors. They're all just standing there, waiting again, but waiting this time for they know not what.

'I think I preferred it when they were still screaming outside and trying to batter their way in,' Radar says. 'At least you knew where they were.'

'No,' Adnan corrects him. 'At least you knew where *one* of them was.'

'Aye, true enough. Cheers for the thought. How's that atheism hanging, by the way?'

'Tell you the truth, I'm shitting it in case I die and it turns out the Muslims were right. I think I could take dying, but I couldn't face an eternity with all my relatives smugly saying they told me so. I'd rather be in Hell.'

'We *are* in Hell,' says a voice: low, convinced, dreadful, resigned.

It's Gillian, raising her head to speak for the first time since they arrived in the games hall.

'We're going to get through this,' Deborah tells her. She's trying to sound reassuring but one look at Gillian tells her it's an impossible sell. Her eyes are hollow, like something inside her is already dead.

'No,' Gillian says flatly. 'I've worked it out: the bus crash. We didn't survive it. We only think we did.'

'Stop upsetting yourself,' says Miss Ross softly, but it's clear that Gillian's words are having more of an effect on her than hers are on Gillian.

'I know the truth,' Gillian insists. 'I know what I saw. We died but somehow we've not accepted it, we've created this dream world for ourselves, but now the demons are coming for us and the dream is over.'

Deborah wishes Marianne was here, sure that she'd have some better vision of this: turn it into myth and poetry, shine a light on a simpler path of truth. In the event, Adnan proves an adequate substitute.

'Bollocks,' he says. 'Fuck all this *Sixth Sense* crap. My five senses are telling me I'm still alive, and listening to them—and only them—is what's going to keep me that way.'

Heather bids herself a smile. It's laughter in the dark, and it has to be pretty dark before you are needing buoyed up by the defiance of your teenage charges, but it's welcome nonetheless. The effect lasts for about a second, up until the hall is shaken by another scream from outside, one that this time sounds all too human.

'God almighty,' Heather asks. 'What was that?'

She hurries to the emergency doors and peers through one of the windows, several of the kids at her back.

'Jesus,' declares Radar, more appositely than he could have possibly intended.

About twenty-five yards away, to the north-west, they can see one side of the two-storey barn where Sendak stables his horses. There are three demons in view, one of them standing over a figure cowering on the grass; the other two busy with a second human upright against the wall. Another scream pierces the night as one of the demons raises an arm and strikes a blow with what Heather deduces must be a hammer. Further strikes follow, then the two demons step away, clearing the view to reveal Marianne nailed to the wall through her hands in crucified pose.

Deborah splutters, unable to cry, unable to speak, barely able to breathe.

'Crucifixion. They really are demons,' says Maria.

'Fuckin' bastards,' Adnan declares. 'We've got to do something.'

395

Heather changes her grip on the shotgun. It feels different now: no longer alien and cold, but an instrument of singular purpose.

'Open the door,' she tells Adnan.

'No!' screams Gillian, getting to her feet. 'That's what they want. They'll get in here. That's why they're doing it. Can't you see?'

Heather looks at the assembled survivors: safe so far, gathered where Sendak told them they could hold out.

'They're doing this because they can't get through these doors,' adds Jason. 'They're not wild animals: they know what they're doing.'

'And I guess that's just too fucking bad for Marianne and whoever else is out there?' challenges Adnan.

'If we open those doors, we *all* die,' Gillian counters.

Over at the barn, the demons begin dragging the cowering figure towards the wall, evidently so weak as to require propping up.

'Fuck, it's Cameron.'

One of them holds out Cam's left arm at the shoulder in preparation to be nailed. It flops unnaturally, bending where it shouldn't. It's hanging off, a compound fracture having sent the bone through muscle and skin. A second demon straightens the arm against the wooden wall and drives a nail through the palm. It's too high. Cameron struggles against the grip of the first demon and loses his footing. He slips, his weight consequently suspended from the nailed arm, which rips free somewhere between wrist and elbow. He drops to his knees screaming, leaving the nailed hand and forearm in place.

Adnan moves for the doors and Jason steps in front of him, at which point Deborah kicks Jason full-force in the balls, yelling: 'Open the fucking door!'

Adnan and Radar take hold of a net-stand each, hauling them clear of the handles.

'You close these as soon as I'm through,' Heather tells them. 'And don't open them again until I'm on the steps. No sooner. Got it?'

'Got it, miss. Just remember, you pump to reload. And don't forget to turn off the safety.'

Heather checks the weapon again, resting her thumb against the catch now in case she can't see it so well outside.

'On go,' she says. 'Three, two, one, GO!'

Adnan and Radar each push the unlocking bar on their doors, Heather rushing through between them.

'Now fucking close it again,' growls Jason, grabbing one of the net-stands. Adnan and Radar grip the handles above the unlocking bars and pull the doors back into place.

Heather runs towards the barn, shouting to get the demons' attention. One of them is already looking her way, having heard the doors opening. The others immediately turn away from Cameron. There is no question but that Gillian and Jason were right. All that remains to be resolved is whether Heather could make the risk worth it.

The first demon begins marching towards her, the other two taking up flanking positions. Smart tactics if she was carrying anything other than a gun. She steadies herself, holds it at waist height and pulls the trigger.

Heather is immediately knocked backwards by

the recoil, losing grip on the gun as she falls. The demon flinches in fright and surprise, but is otherwise unscathed. She scrambles to her feet and picks up the weapon again, this time holding the stock against her shoulder and bracing herself for the kick. She pulls the trigger. Nothing happens. The demon resumes its approach. She pulls the trigger again: no resistance; it's just sliding freely back and forth.

Then she remembers: pump to reload. She pumps the slide. The action is stiffer than she anticipates, and it takes a second attempt, by which time the demon is yards away, its fellows also closing in. She feels the trigger lock forward, knows the shell is primed. She blasts again. Once more the demon flinches; once more the sound and the flash are the only things to impact.

'Oh Jesus fucking Christ.'

She pumps it again, by which time the demon is now running towards her. The gun reports once more, but in this instance not even the bang halts the demon's charge. A second later it is upon her, the last thing she sees a gnarled claw sweeping towards her face.

'What the fuck?' asks Radar.

Adnan just keeps staring through the window, watching as Heather is dragged by her feet towards the barn. Her arms start to thrash. She's coming around, dazed but not unconscious. They're going to nail her up now too.

Jason lifts the second net-stand and prepares to thread it between the handles, content that the ill-advised rescue mission is over.

Adnan puts a hand on one of the metal shafts and prevents its progress.

'Open it again.'

'Are you suicidal?'

'They left the gun. They don't know what it is. I can get it.'

'They left it because it's no threat,' Jason argues, almost yelling. 'Jesus Christ, were you not watching? Guns don't fucking *work* on them. What the fuck is that all about? How can that be?'

'Because they're not of this world,' says Gillian.

*　　　*　　　*

Sendak is opening drawers and slapping knives and cleavers down on an island worktop in the centre of the kitchen. The toppled fridge is doing its job, but the door frame is already giving warning that it will eventually come away from the wall. He tucks a knife into his belt and picks up his baseball bat again in one fist.

'Arm yourselves with anything you can carry. If you can't find something that stabs or slashes, just grab something you can hit the fuckers with, long as it won't slow you down.'

'How about a rolled-up dish-towel?' asks Beansy. 'My mammy always said you could take somebody's eye out with one of them.'

Sendak sighs, trades a look with Kane. Kane can tell they're both grateful for anything that might lift morale.

'Well, there's a Cuisinart too,' Sendak tells him. 'You think you could get one of them to stick its hand in there out of curiosity?'

'Maybe just stick with a meat cleaver,' Beansy replies.

'Yeah. That'd be my call too.'

Sendak moves to the door, beckoning Kane forward with him. Kane lifts a long, metal-handled kitchen knife and does as he is bid.

'Gonna check the coast is clear. Need you standing by to close this thing again if there's any surprises in store.'

'You got it.'

Sendak turns the handle and pulls the door ajar, Kane resting a foot against it, ready to drive it home if required. Sendak sticks his head out and looks left and right down the corridor.

'We're good to go,' he reports, pulling the door all the way open. 'Here's how it's gonna be. You go first, I'll be holding the rear. You take a right out of the door, first left, then it's a straight run to the games hall. You don't stop, you don't look back, no matter what you hear behind you. Your job is to get the folks in there to open the doors at the other end and be ready to close them again once everybody is through.'

'You go first' to run the demon-infested gauntlet doesn't sound like the best offer Kane ever heard, but he wouldn't trade it for what Sendak's dealt himself: closest to any pursuers, able to move at no greater pace than the slowest of the group. Yeah, he'd settle for 'you go first'.

'Any questions?' Sendak asks him.

'Just one,' he replies. 'What is it you're not telling us? There's something you know, isn't there. Or at least suspect.'

Sendak acknowledges the question with a look that gives nothing away.

'The compass going crazy out on the hike. Everybody's watches stopping. It's all connect—'

Kane is cut off as an arm appears above him,

snatches the knife from his hand and drives it into his throat.

He staggers backwards into the kitchen, blood spraying the walls as it jets from the wound. Sendak hurls a blade towards the attacker, suspended from the corridor ceiling, staring upside down at what it has wrought. It dodges, leaping to cling to the wall as the knife embeds itself to the hilt in the roof tiles. It keeps its eyes on Sendak throughout, then sets itself to spring. He kicks the door closed a fraction of a second before the creature slams into the wood, then slides the island unit in front.

Blake is cradling Kane's head as blood continues to gush from his neck. He's got a dish-towel pressed to it but it may as well be a paper hanky.

'I can't stem it,' he says, though he doesn't know to whom; may as well be talking about his own precipitate grief. 'There's just too much.'

'Fucker was on the ceiling,' Sendak says, dismayed and apologetic. 'I checked left and right. I didn't look up. I didn't look up.'

Through his forming tears, Blake can see that Kane's eyes are losing their thousand-yard stare of shock and confusion. There's weakness in them, but an attempt to focus. He's looking up at Blake. They both know he's dying.

'Don't . . .' Kane says, his speech a faltering hollow whisper. 'Don't dare . . . try and give me . . . last rites.'

Blake shakes with a sob: laughter and grief, released by the pain of glimpsing all that he's going to miss.

He sniffs back his tears, has to hold it together for Kane, the last, the only thing he can still do for

401

him.

'What about Pascal's Wager?' Blake asks, forcing a smile through his tears.

Kane's head shakes, just enough for Blake to feel it in his hands.

'How the bookies . . . get rich. Shitey odds . . . not worth . . . the stake.'

With these words, Kane dies and Blake collapses inside, clutching his friend's head in his lap while the blood seeps into his trousers from the cold kitchen floor.

XXV

Tullian is looking left and right along the maintenance tunnel, referring back and forth to a square of paper with a rough schematic etched out upon it.

'If you're trying to get your bearings,' Merrick tells him, 'the bad news is that the shortest route to the surface is back the way we came.'

Tullian satisfies himself regarding his orientation and leads off in the opposite direction.

'No, we really, really don't want to head for the surface,' Tullian says. 'I have a grave fear that Elvis may have left the building. We're probably safer down here than above ground. We need to secure ourselves and wait for the military to send in their emergency lockdown team.'

'Well, there's bad news on that front too, Cardinal. No alarms were raised. I tried myself, but the systems had been disabled. Sabotaged, I have to assume.'

'Sabotaged? By whom?'

'Steinmeyer.'

Tullian sighs regretfully. 'I had my fears,' he says.

'The guy's been slowly losing it for weeks, and when the military said they were taking his toys away, it pushed him over the edge. That said, I have to ask what could possess him to do something as catastrophic as this.'

The Cardinal grimaces.

'Unfortunately, I rather think you may have answered your own question, Doctor. What indeed could possess him?'

Merrick didn't think he could feel more scared, more ill, but he does now. It makes sense, in ways that have consequences too horrible to dwell upon right now. He has to stay focused on the immediate.

'The bottom line is, nobody along the military command chain knows anything has gone wrong here. The cavalry aren't coming.'

'Then we have to alter that,' Tullian declares. 'We will make for Security Control. If the damage isn't irreversible, then that's where we can get the systems back online. We can raise the alarm and perhaps reactivate the mag-locks.'

'There are CCTV feeds in there too,' Merrick adds. 'We can spot where the demons are and maybe isolate them. At the very least we can relay their positions to the lockdown team so that the demons don't get the drop on them.'

'We'll be their guardian angels, watching from above,' the Cardinal states drily, picking up the pace.

Tullian stops to examine a sign on the wall, next to an access hatch leading to the accelerator chase.

Merrick estimates they've travelled about half a kilometre along the duct. They haven't heard anything for a few minutes: no gunfire, no screams, no slap-slap of approaching feet.

'The next ladder,' Tullian indicates. 'That should take us to the coolant monitoring chamber. Security Control is up one level after that.'

Merrick glances reluctantly down the passage towards their goal.

'I'm still recovering from the last ladder,' he says.

'Don't worry, I'll go first,' Tullian is assuring him, when an access hatch further back along the duct explodes open, almost unhinged by the force behind it.

Merrick's reluctance to approach the ladder is thoroughly dispelled. He overtakes Tullian as they sprint towards it, the Cardinal encumbered by a stiffness to his gait perhaps resultant of his robes. Merrick scales the ladder like a spider monkey on PCP and finds the overhead hatch to be in mercifully smoother working order than the one where Havelock met his doom. He twists the release and flips it open, barely thinking about what might be waiting for him above it as he hauls himself through the gap. Without pausing to check his new surroundings, he twists himself around and leans through the gap to assist the ascending Tullian. He can hear the slap-slap approaching as he reaches an arm down, and can't resist a glance to check the distance. There's time yet, so stay calm: more haste, less hurry.

Then he hears a clattering sound as Tullian's hand stretches up and clasps his own. Once Tullian has cleared the hatch, he can see what it was: his iPhone, with the AV files stored on it. It's at the foot of the ladder, apparently intact; even if it's damaged, the data should be recoverable.

The demon still has ground to cover. He can make it. Those files represent everything he has done here, as well as the sacrifice of everyone who has been lost. He has to make it.

'What are you doing?' Tullian asks in breathless disbelief as Merrick climbs back into the hatch and slides, fireman-style, down the outsides of the vertical poles. He grasps at the iPhone, his nervous fingers scraping the concrete and failing to grip it properly. It spills again, slides a couple of feet. The slap-slap is becoming pound-pound, the weight of the approaching creature palpable as it shakes the floor of the duct. Merrick reaches for the iPhone again and gets hold of it this time, then throws an arm towards the ladder. The demon is yards away, gaining pace, preparing to hurl itself. Merrick's foot slips on the second rung in his panic. The slap-slap has ceased, the demon in mid-air. He closes his eyes and grips the shaft.

Merrick hears a squealing, grinding, radio-static pulse that stings his eardrums and makes every filling in his head feel like it's been connected to the mains. A wave of dust buffets him, strong as the wind behind a juggernaut lorry, and he senses a tiny precipitation on his skin. He can taste blood and metal, like licking a battery, a tingling in his sinuses too as the wind fills his nose.

He opens his eyes and looks up. Tullian is staring back at him through the hatch, along the barrel of a decoherence rifle.

'I guess that's why you were walking funny,' Merrick says, by way of acknowledgment.

'How do you think I stayed alive long enough to

save you back there?' Tullian responds, offering him a hand up.

'Couldn't you have used it a bit sooner?'

'Limited charge. I'm only using it when I absolutely have to.'

'Where did you get it? I thought the cabinet locks had been sabotaged too.'

'Not all of them, presumably, though I had to prise it from the proverbial cold, dead hand of a fallen soldier. The poor soul must have been overwhelmed before he could use the thing. Now, are you going to tell me what is so important about that phone that you were prepared to risk both our lives to retrieve it?'

XXVI

The demon dragging Miss Ross has almost reached the stable wall.

'I can see the gun,' Adnan says, calmly and quietly. 'I can reach it before they reach me.'

'Fuck, would you forget about the gun?' Jason tells him. 'You're always on about empirical evidence, Adnan, well trust the evidence of your own eyes: Miss Ross shot that thing three times from close range and it barely batted an eyelid. Gillian's right: we're dealing with supernatural beings. The normal rules don't apply.'

Adnan turns to Radar.

'One word: parsimony.'

Radar nods, understanding. He barges Jason aside and grabs the net-stand.

'Radar, you open that door and you're as good as

killing him,' Jason argues.

'You definitely up for this?' Radar asks.

'It's my funeral,' comes the reply.

Deborah steps up and mans the other door, her hands on the unlocking bar.

'Same deal as before,' Adnan advises. 'Close it immediately. Don't risk opening it for a second longer than you have to. On three. One . . . two . . .'

'No!' shouts Gillian, rushing to stop them, but Adnan completes his count and disappears through the doors.

'Why did you do that?' Gillian asks, tearful and uncomprehending as she stares at the pair of them. 'Why did you let him do that?'

'Faith,' Radar replies blankly.

*   *   *

Adnan feels the fear slowing his legs as soon as he hears the doors closing behind him. As the cold air hits his face, so does the stark realisation that he may have just made a fatal mistake. From inside, it looked different, felt different. There was this irrepressible compulsion within him to take action, partly driven by the desire to save his friends, and partly by the simple belief that he *could*. Knowing he could help seemed to relegate all other considerations. He wasn't a brave person, though he tried to be a selfless one, but the thought that he could make the difference had somehow muted the sense of danger. It's been bloody well turned up to eleven now he's outside, though.

He can't see the gun: lost it when he had to take his eye off the windows as the doors were pulled open. He thinks he knows roughly where Miss Ross was standing, and is heading that way, but if he doesn't spot the weapon again, he's fucked.

He comes close, he comes really close to turning on his heel, racing back and hammering contritely on the doors to be let back inside. Then he sees it: a dark sheen of metal catching the light differently from the frosted grass.

One of the demons has heard the doors open and begins moving towards him. The others turn briefly but are not diverted from their task, content that their comrade will deal with the situation as before. They proceed with hauling the scared and struggling Miss Ross to her feet and preparing to nail her to the wall. Cameron they have temporarily given up on, and he remains where he fell, curled up in a shivering pile on the ground.

Everything is simple now. No decisions to be weighed, no morality to consider: only instinct, only survival. A race, in which second prize is death.

Unlike Miss Ross, he doesn't stalk his way steadily towards his enemies. He's sprinting, low to the ground, arrow-like, and he's going to make it. The demon facing him is in no greater hurry than the one that took down his teacher, failing to comprehend what is at stake should he reach the strange black stick that flashed and banged. Perhaps they think it's a totem, some witch doctor's charm that wields power over the human credulous and devout, but holds for them no fear.

Miss Ross shot that thing three times from close range and it barely batted an eyelid.

There is a reason why the demon wasn't injured,

and he's betting his life that it isn't the one Gillian suggested.

Adnan reaches the shotgun with the demon half a dozen yards away. He's never fired one before, but he's watched Miss Ross make all his mistakes for him, so he knows what not to do. He pumps the slide, chambering the next shell, and raises the gun to his shoulder as the demon lets out a vicious roar and prepares to lunge.

The roar is cut off as the demon's head flies apart in an explosion of black blood and splattering tissue.

Adnan stares, frozen, for a breathless moment as the decapitated body remains upright before him, wondering if this is also what Miss Ross saw, whether it will impossibly reconstitute itself before resuming its attack. Then the corpse drops limply to the grass and he knows it's game on.

Oh yeah.

The HUD comes down as he pumps the shotgun. His health is at 100. Ammo reads five. Frags: one. And counting.

Watching inside the games hall, Radar turns to Deborah with a relieved smile.

'Chalk one up to parsimony,' he says.

'What do you mean? I thought parsimony was being tight.'

'It's a scientific precept stating that the simplest explanation is usually correct. Either, as Jase suggested, the laws of physics don't apply to these creatures—even though the ones involving doors seem to apply pretty effectively—or there's a simpler explanation.'

'Which is what?'

'That Miss Ross couldnae hit a coo's arse with a

banjo.'

Back outside, the other two demons have clocked that the clash didn't run to form and their pal has undergone a nasty bit of entropy, but they don't appear to understand why. They let go of Miss Ross and begin moving towards Adnan, spread apart in flanking formation.

Adnan takes careful aim and blasts the one on the right, blowing a hole through its stomach. It drops, doubled over and gurgling, unable to scream. The remaining demon gets the picture now. It turns and starts to run, but Adnan shoots it in the back.

He sees Miss Ross get up and begin running towards where it fell, wonders for a moment what the fuck she's doing. When she reaches the demon, she bends down and prises a hammer from its grasp, then returns to the barn wall.

Adnan hears a noise behind him and turns to observe that Radar and Deborah have ignored the directives and are charging out to help. He's not sure whether the bigger risk is in their leaving the building or in leaving Jason in charge of the door.

'Keep us covered,' Radar says, rushing past to make for Cameron, who has passed out. He and Deborah lift him between them, she gripping his ankles, Radar under his arms, while Heather embarks on the equally onerous task of pulling Marianne's hands free from the wall with the hammer. She leaves the nails stuck through the flesh for now, just using the fork-tail to grip the nail-heads and help tug the points out of the wood.

'What about the rest of Cam's arm?' Adnan asks.

'Best where it is. It's freezing out here. That'll preserve it. Let's just get everyone inside. There's morphine in the medkit.'

'*Morphine?*'

'It's Sendak's medkit.'

*   *   *

Another loud bang echoes above the trees, once more causing Kirk and Matt to stop in their tracks. Kirk has a look around, gripping the heavy stick he retrieved from near the corpse of the thing that attacked him. Matt takes the moment to rest, leaning his backside against the fallen trunk of a dead tree.

A second bang follows, then a third.

'More gunshots,' Kirk says. 'Sounds like there might be a fightback on the cards.'

'I thought you had already started it,' Matt replies.

'Only technically.'

He opts to take the weight off his feet, sitting on the trunk a few feet along from Matt. He's still shaking from the fight, his heart rate well up. 'Better lie low for a minute,' he says. 'Don't want to head back to the building if we're just gaunny get plugged.'

Matt nods, looking distantly into the darkness, still visibly trembling also.

'You okay?' Kirk asks him.

Matt nods again, without turning around. Okay's kind of relative, Kirk realises. He looks at his wounds. On any other night, the gouges on his shoulder would constitute quite a battle scar. Trip to casualty for sure. Right now he can barely feel them for the adrenalin; that and the fact that he's half numb with the cold.

'Thanks, by the way,' says Matt after a few seconds of silence. 'For, you know . . .'

'Never bother.'

Kirk opens his mouth to say more, but pauses to reassess. He feels he ought to confess, but what fucking good would that do? Actually, mate, I came out here to put the living shiters up you, if not to actually carve you open. Fuck that. But still, he is sorry, and he should say so.

'Least I could do, in fact. I owe you an apology. I've been a total cock lately.'

Matt finally turns to look at him. Kirk thinks for a second that he's going to say 'Lately?', but maybe that's just what he deserves to hear. In fact, Matt says nothing.

'I've been a pure shambles, tell you the truth, and not just since Dunnsy died. That's maybe just brought it to a head. I'm not making excuses here, but . . . there's stuff I'm having a hard time trying to handle. Stuff it's impossible for anybody to understand.'

Matt's nodding, looking away again. He seldom, if ever, looks you in the eye. That has always pissed Kirk off, but right now it makes it easier to talk, makes it feel like the guy is listening and not judging. That's what made it impossible to talk to Rocks or Dazza: because he knew they'd offer advice, they'd try to help, and though he couldn't say why, he didn't want that; couldn't *take* that. He didn't need help. He just needed to be heard.

'I've been acting the hard man as long as I can remember, but it's only recently I've come to realise it's the path of least resistance. It's an easy part to play when you're actually feart of the tougher ones. And it's a very good cover for what I

412

don't want anybody to suspect about me.'

'Being gay, you mean,' Matt says, and gives Kirk a bigger fright than anything else that's jumped out at him tonight.

Jesus.

That wasn't what he was talking about, but by fuck, there it is out there now. Matt says it flatly, matter-of-fact, in a way that would sound like a sarcastic throwaway insult from anybody else. But Matt says everything flatly and matter-of-fact. He's not coming the cunt, trying to be obnoxious: he's stating the truth.

Kirk finally gets him, and it would very much appear that he gets Kirk.

Kirk's impulse is to deny it, explain that he was actually talking about being brighter than anybody knew, but he can see this is futile. Matt *knows*, which nudges denial off the list of options and prompts him instead to ask himself therefore how obvious it is, and who else has tumbled.

'How did you know?' he asks.

'I'm qualified to recognise it,' is Matt's reply.

'You're qualified to . . . ? Oh. *Oh*.'

'Quid pro quo.'

'Or mutually assured destruction.'

'Neither of us has much to lose. I'm not exactly covetous of social cachet and who the hell is going to give *you* a hard time?'

Kirk thinks of Mr Kane's words that day: *if you start shining in the classroom, who's going to dare give Kirk Burns any shite for it?* What was true then is even more true of this.

'Doesn't make it any less frightening, does it?'

'No,' Matt agrees.

'Though this fair puts it into perspective. When

413

there's fuckin' monsters loose in the world, it seems crazy that anybody should give a fuck whether you're into girls or guys.'

'Heresy, dear boy. Pope Benedict said homosexuals are as great a threat as global warming.'

To his surprise, Kirk finds it in himself to laugh, and glances instinctively into the trees in response to having made an involuntarily loud sound.

'Just goes to show,' Matt adds, 'you can take the boy out of the Hitler Youth, but you—'

Kirk feels another warm spray, accompanied by a dull thud that shakes him through the tree trunk. When he looks again at Matt, his head has been split down the middle by an axe, buried in his skull all the way to the bridge of his nose.

Kirk barely has time to react before he sees a second demon coming at him, swinging a heavy, awkward object. He throws himself over the side of the tree trunk as the object crashes into the wood where he was sitting. Its weight and solidity would have surely been enough to smash his skull, but its ungainliness bought him the fraction of a second that kept him alive.

Kirk looks for the stick, realises it's on the ground on the other side of the trunk. The demon lifts its weapon again, its partner meanwhile struggling to disembed the axe from Matt's head. Kirk sees the object clearly now and recognises two things: one, that it is a chainsaw; and two, given that said chainsaw isn't turned on, he's not looking at the dux of Beelzebub High.

Kirk takes a short run and dives at the bastard, hurling himself over the tree trunk and slamming into the demon on the other side. They both crash to the ground and roll over a couple of times in a thrashing tangle. Kirk takes a couple of slashes from its claws, but when he rolls free, he can see that he has disarmed his opponent.

The other demon has now got Matt on the deck and has a foot on his head to increase its purchase in removing the axe.

Kirk springs up into a defensive crouch, keeping his eyes on his foe. Both his stick and the chainsaw are lying on the ground between them, his position several feet closer to the latter. The demon rushes forward and picks up the stick. It brandishes its new weapon as Kirk hefts the chainsaw, letting out a sneering hiss that suggests it is pleased with this turn of events.

To each his own.

'Jolly sporting of you, old chap,' Kirk says.

He pulls the starter cord, prompting the chainsaw to buzz into life.

Vengeance follows.

*   *   *

Sendak is crouching down beside Blake with an arm around his shoulders.

'Gotta let go, okay?' he says.

There is another wallop against the door, shuddering the upended contents inside the fridge.

Blake nods. He's reluctant but he understands. As long as this moment endures, this moment of holding Kane's head and weeping for him, then he doesn't have to deal with the next one. The assaults on the kitchen door, however, deny him the luxury of prolonging it.

He lets Kane's head come down gently to rest on

the floor and climbs to his feet, Sendak close by to steady him if needed. He looks around, sees a room full of scared people. It feels like he's been away from them for ages, in some other place: somewhere calm where he didn't feel fear, only grief. Now that he's back, he sees their fear but doesn't feel his own. He's not quite ready yet to feel anything at all.

Sendak taps his chin, makes him look into his face.

'How you doin', man?'

'Been better,' he replies. 'Yourself?'

'I'm having limited fun right now.'

'Copy that, as I believe the expression—'

Sendak puts a hand to Blake's mouth and casts an urgent glance towards the windows.

'Shit. Kill the lights. Now.'

Rocks reaches quickly for the switches and complies. The room doesn't plunge into complete darkness, but is instead sparsely illuminated by the windows, transformed from black mirrors into providing a dim view of the grounds outside.

Demons are emerging from the gloom, making their way directly towards the kitchen, which until seconds ago must have looked like a shop window to these bastards. They're tooled up. One is carrying a pitchfork, one a machete, another an axe; one of the fuckers even has a scythe.

'Been raiding my barn,' Sendak says grimly. 'All *we* got is fuckin' sports goods and kitchenware. *God damn it.*'

'No such thing as an atheist in a foxhole then,' Blake says. It's about all he can manage by way of gallows humour.

Sendak nods, keeping his eyes on the windows.

'That's right,' he says in a low register. 'Everybody converts when their life is at stake. Everybody. No matter what they profess to believe. When the shit hits, they all convert.' Then he glances briefly at Blake with the most grimly serious face the priest has ever seen, and adds: *'To atheism.'*

Sendak checks his grip on the baseball bat and stares at the approaching horde. 'Anybody who truly believes there's a better world waiting for them just as soon as they leave this one ain't gonna take evasive action to put that off. If you believe that shit, then you go throw yourself out there and buy the rest of us some time, because I sure ain't trusting you to get my back. What do you say?'

Blake swallows and picks up a sharpening steel, the only weapon left.

'I've got your back,' he tells Sendak.

'Good man. There are *only* atheists in foxholes, Father, because that's when you realise this is all you got, and if there's gonna be a solution, it's gotta be man-made.'

The approaching demons are less than ten yards away. Another shuddering impact shakes the upturned fridge, a section of the door frame coming loose in a cloud of exploding plaster dust.

Yvonne and Caitlin shove the fridge back hard against the door while Beansy and Rocks stand facing the window, weapons in hand. Every one of them looks terrified; even Sendak's face betrays that he doesn't fancy their chances, though only Blake is close enough to see this.

Through the windows, the nearest two of the demons is close enough for Blake to make eye contact.

Then from outside, there comes the quite

417

implausible sound of someone singing.

'Iiiiiiii'm a lumberjack and I'm okay . . .'

Blake wonders for a second whether he is really hearing this, then receives his answer when the creature he'd been staring at turns to investigate where the sound is coming from. The moment it does, a severed demon head smacks it in the face with bone-shattering impact, before a human figure comes charging out of the darkness, revving a chainsaw.

The nearest demon lunges at him and is promptly disembowelled with demonstrable and vocal alacrity. Then he moves on to the one reeling from its recent concussion, relieving its headache by the non-prescription expedient of relieving it of its head.

Blake gawps in a kind of gruesome awe at this spectacle of fervent carnage.

'Jesus Christ,' he mumbles.

'Naw,' corrects Rocks in elation. 'Kirk Burns.'

Sendak pats Blake on the shoulder. 'Man-made solution,' he says.

Outside, the remaining demons have sussed the odds and are making for the trees, Kirk shouting after them.

'Aye, yous better run, ya Hun-lookin' bastards. You kick the arse out of bein' ugly.'

Sendak puts down his blade and swings open one of the windows.

'In here, come on,' he calls.

Kirk switches off the chainsaw and hands it across, then retrieves the abandoned axe also before clambering through the gap. His clothes are spattered with black blood, his top ripped at one shoulder.

'You all right?' Sendak asks.

'Aye, but I'm no' sure I'll get a second day out of this T-shirt.'

Then Kirk spots the body on the floor.

'Aw, fuck. Fuck.'

He kicks out in anger, booting an oven door. 'Fucking bastards. They got Matt. Ewan . . . Dazza.'

'Christ,' says Rocks. Caitlin takes his hand and he's grateful for the feel of it, though it's not enough: it's like a trickle of water that only lets you know how thirsty you are. He pulls her against him. No more, he thinks. They're not getting anyone else.

Kirk is shaking his head grimly.

'I'll never kill enough of these cunts. Never.'

Sendak grips him around the uninjured shoulder.

'I hear you, man. I hear all of you. But we got work to do right now.'

On cue, the door leading to the executive dining room takes another thump. Kirk picks up the chainsaw again.

Sendak nods towards the other door.

'Need to get down this corridor to the games hall. But we got a visitor waiting out here, okay?'

Kirk yanks the starter cord.

'I'll introduce him to my wee pal.'

Sendak and Blake remove the barricade, shoving the island unit back into the centre of the room and clearing a space for everyone to assemble, ready to run. Sendak counts down with three fingers and grips the handle.

He opens the door, revealing the corridor to be empty. This time, however, he sticks his head out and checks above. It's all clear.

'Okay, everybody, let's move it out, fast.'

Kirk leads the way. Sendak remains at the door, ushering the others through and protecting the rearguard once they are in the corridor. He's ditched the bat for an axe in one hand, a knife in the other.

They move steadily but cautiously down the corridor, not going flat out because of what they might run into. Kirk keeps his eyes darting around, ready to react to movement.

There is a crash from behind.

'Keep looking forward, people,' Sendak shouts, though it's his duty not to heed his own instruction. He glances back to the kitchen: a demon has smashed through one of the windows and landed awkwardly on top of a cooker. Its feet scramble for purchase, kicking—and, he fears, turning—a couple of the gas taps in the process.

A second demon clambers through the jagged gap, letting out a defiant roar. Yeah, you're all real tough when the chainsaw's out of range.

Rocks can't prevent himself glancing back when he hears this noise. Though it won't make any difference, he needs to know how close it is. As he turns his head, he's aware of a frantic movement at his side and sees Caitlin lifting into the air, screaming. A demon has burst through the ceiling tiles and grabbed her around the neck.

Rocks gets one hand around Caitlin's waist and plunges his knife into the demon's arm with the other until he feels the blade strike bone. The creature lets go and retreats, shrinking rapidly back out of sight.

'Fuck, they're in the crawl space,' Sendak warns. 'Could come from anywhere. Just run. Fast as you can, run.'

A ceiling tile explodes in front of Kirk as he reaches the corner, a demon dropping from it a few feet past where he is supposed to turn left. It didn't get the memo about the chainsaw. Kirk lets his momentum take him beyond the turn and rips into it while the others hurry past at his back.

Sendak tugs him away from his work. The creature is not dead, but it's not posing a threat either, and he won't be feeling any guilt about not administering a *coup de grâce*.

Another tile explodes from the ceiling behind Sendak. Kirk starts to turn, but the Sarge screams at him to keep moving. Sendak checks back, as the incursion sounded very close behind. Sure enough, one of the fuckers has hit the floor only a few feet away and is preparing to spring. Sendak alters his stance just a little, adjusting his weight, and lets the creature's own lunge take it into his axe. He knows immediately from the impact that the weapon is not coming back out again, so he abandons it, letting go of the shaft and resuming his sprint. Just before he turns, he sees two more demons scramble around the corner, coming from the kitchen.

Rebecca reaches the games hall first, her long legs having retained their memory of when she was the girls' fastest sprinter in the days before she discovered make-up and charge cards. In her previous catatonia, however, she must have missed enough of the discussion as to be incredulous to the point of despair at finding the doors locked against her.

She bangs her hands against them in terrified frustration and turns around with a look of

421

anguish on her face, seemingly unable to speak.

Fortunately Caitlin, the wee quiet lassie, has voice enough for both of them.

'OPEN THE DOORS. OPEN THE FUCKING DOORS RIGHT NOW!' she yells as she covers the last few yards along the passage.

She can hear movement from within, the sound of a heavy object scraping the floor, but for an excruciatingly enduring moment, the doors remain fast. Caitlin looks back at the stampede heading towards her, seconds from being cornered. She can see demons in avid pursuit, one of them leaping from wall to wall, gaining momentum like a pinball zig-zagging against spring-loaded buffers.

The doors give an anticipatory shake as a bolt is slid free, then finally begin to swing apart. Caitlin, Rocks and Rebecca burst through the widening gap, almost flattening Maria and Roisin. Just behind them, Jason and Radar are standing next to a set of five-a-side goals, ready to slide them back into place. Yvonne gets through next, escorted by Beansy.

Caitlin's relief at the doors opening lasts only long enough for her to begin worrying about how long they must stay that way. She glances back down the hallway in time to see the wall-bounding demon overtake Sendak and evade Kirk's chainsaw by crawling above his reach along the ceiling. It is bearing down rapidly on Father Blake, who is not going to make it to the door in time.

Caitlin is about to close her eyes when she is barged violently aside. She reels, steadies herself and finds Adnan standing where she had been, viewing the corridor along the barrel of a shotgun.

'Get down,' he commands the approaching

422

priest.

Blake dives and Adnan fires, splattering the demon.

'Owned,' Adnan declares.

Kirk stops at the doorway and waves Sendak past him, keeping his eyes and his chainsaw pointed down the passage before stepping backwards into the games hall.

Adnan pumps the shotgun and takes aim at the next demon, but before he can shoot, the doors are slammed closed and the barricade restored.

*   *   *

Rosemary is somewhere else now, somewhere better, somewhere wonderful. The horror and the danger are still nearby, close enough for her not to be oblivious of them, but she can keep them out of range while she immerses herself in this: in taste, in smell, in feeling.

He's warm against her. The skin of his back is cold in each new place she touches, but wherever there is contact, heat seems to spread, like sparks to her fingers around a plasma ball.

She didn't hesitate to worry whether he would respond, whether he would permit this: it was as though they both knew in one sudden moment that it had to happen. She doesn't know how long ago that was. Time is suspended here, and while she is in this moment, she knows she is not in the horror of the immediate past or the terror of the immediate future.

It's not some gentle embrace, some delicate, tender kiss. It didn't even begin that way. It is both a hunger and a feast, a thirst and its slaking, a need and a fix, but there is no satiation, only escalation.

She pulls his hand to her breast because she wants to feel it there, but it's not enough. She tugs her top up so that her chest can press against his with no material between them, but it's not enough. Then she takes his hand and pulls it between her legs, holding it in place with her own as though she's afraid he'll take it away.

Deso's not complaining, but what with demons running around, he is genuinely wondering whether Rosemary might have become possessed. He quite liked the girl, thought there was more to her than she let people see under all the holy-wullie stuff, but he didn't realise how much he fancied her until she kissed him. At that point he became immediately aware he was experiencing something unlike with any previous lassie he's got off with. If what passed between him and the others was a nine-volt battery, then this was like being plugged into a hydroelectric power station. However, when she put his hand up her skirt, it was as if she was no longer in control, no longer quite here. She stopped kissing him then too, just buried her face in his neck as she held his hand still and moved against it. There were bangs in the distance: three, then a little later, three more, but she didn't even seem to hear them.

She lets out a series of shrieks muffled by his collarbone, her whole body shuddering, the fingers of her free hand gripping him like she might fall off the world. Then she lets go of his fingers and he feels her go loose with a long sigh. She's back now.

Uh-oh, he thinks. This is where it turns to dust. This is where Titania sees that Nick Bottom has a donkey's napper.

Rosemary steadies her breathing, still resting her head against his shoulder. Somewhere in her mind's horizon she can see a storm of embarrassment and shame, but it's a splinter in a kaleidoscope, and it belongs in the old world where demons never came, where she would never have had the nerve to even kiss Deso.

In this dark new world, the guilt doesn't come. There is clarity instead, clarity like she cannot ever remember. She understands that this world, this universe, is something far different and far more complex than that which she had so long believed.

Within this greater complexity, however, she knows three things for certain.

If there is such a thing as sin, then what she just did most definitely wasn't it. If there is such a thing as God, presiding over such an infinite domain, then He cannot possibly be concerned with what a girl did with her genitals.

And if the demons are already out there, then it's way too late to worry about damnation.

'Thank you,' she tells him, finally pulling away from his shoulder and looking him in the face. His eyes glint a little in what meagre light there is, the only features truly distinguishable.

'Eh, any time,' he replies uncertainly, a little taken aback. 'I mean . . . you know . . .'

'I do,' she assures him. 'So we have to make sure there is an any time. Let's have a look around at what's in here.'

Rosemary reaches for the light switch again, but Deso stops her once more.

'I'm sure there's nothing out there,' she argues.

'I think I saw a torch. If we use that, we won't be

so blind when we switch it off again.'

Deso locates what does indeed turn out to be a small Maglite. He switches it on and plays it around the shed, revealing a tractor mower to be taking up a great deal of the floor space. The beam then picks out a number of plastic cylinders containing pesticide, next to a high-pressure spray lance with back-pack mounting. Deso continues to scan the walls but Rosemary grabs his hand and directs the torch back towards the pesticide sprayer.

Deso doesn't get it.

'What?' he asks.

'It says it's an eighteen-litre tank, and it doesn't have to be pesticide that's in it.'

'What, then? You think we could get Father Blake to bless it and it'll turn into a holy-water gun?'

Rosemary takes the torch from his hands and picks out another large plastic container on the floor to the rear of the mower. It has a pressure-seal cap, a detachable filling nozzle thrust through the carrying handle, and the words 'highly flammable' etched on it in several different places.

'I was thinking infernal rather than divine,' she says.

XXVII

With the doors closed, it takes those who were already in the games hall only a short few seconds to deduce the implications regarding those who didn't come through them. Heather looks to

Blake, whose apologetic expression serves as confirmation about Kane.

As the long-fought tears finally take her, she lets herself fall against the priest, whose arms close around her. They remain in this clinch for a while, Blake allowing himself to close his eyes and shut out everything else just for a merciful moment. It feels like the only good thing left in the world. The warmth of Heather's body, the smell of her, the wetness of her cheeks against his neck: it feels vital, the essence of being human. It feels like something to stay alive for.

He opens his eyes again and catches sight of someone else's gaze: one of the girls looking briefly across then turning away again. He is reminded, minutely, that such an embrace would have been the talk of the steamie mere hours ago. Now it seems bizarre to care about things like that. Nonetheless, it's important to believe that there is a normal world for everyone to return to: a world where these kids get to go back to school and have a future. He has to focus on getting them there, but he's starting to ask himself what he wants his own role in that world to be.

Sendak gives the hall a quick survey, checking the fortifications. Kirk stands alongside him as they look through the small windows in the emergency doors.

'Anyone else still out there, you think?'

Sendak shakes his head. 'Never seen anything like it, not in man nor beast. A bloodlust that's beyond feral, and yet they're intelligent, coordinated. More like warfare. War *crime*.'

'They leave nothing alive,' says Adnan. 'Fuckers only spared Marianne and Cameron to use as bait.'

'They crucified them,' adds Radar.

'Crucified?' Sendak asks.

Blake glances across, over Heather's head.

Marianne holds up her bandaged hands, red soaking through at both palms. She and Cameron have been laid out on exercise mats, having had morphine administered by Mrs McKenzie. Marianne is groggy, but she has sat herself up against the wall, partially resting against Deborah. Cameron, however, is mercifully unconscious.

'Fair to say they've got a serious issue with crucifixion,' Marianne says bitterly. 'We were ambushed by several of them, and we only got away because Bernadette pulled out a crucifix.'

'They shrank from the crucifix?' Blake asks.

'No. They went fucking postal. Ignored the rest of us and all fell upon Bernie. At least it was quick,' she adds, glancing towards Cameron. 'I saw some other bodies in the barn. I'm not sure who. They'd been eaten.'

'Marky and Theresa,' says Beansy, his voice dry.

'Didn't kill the horses, though, for what that's worth.'

Blake doesn't understand why, but he feels relief at Marianne's response to his question, despite it discounting a possible means of defence. While his faculties can still comprehend this, he knows he can ward off complete despair. He knows he may be clutching at straws to be still searching for what would be termed a 'rational' explanation, but those straws are the only thing he *can* cling to if he wants to believe that the normal world still exists.

Sendak casts an eye over Cameron, taking in the makeshift tourniquet Mrs McKenzie has fashioned from ripped-up clothing.

'This boy's lost a lot of blood,' she reports. 'He needs hospital treatment soon or he's not going to make it.'

Sendak scans the room, calculating.

'Twenty-three,' Deborah tells him, anticipating what he is about. She holds up the sheet of paper bearing her lists of names.

'Okay. Gonna be snug on legroom, but I can't see anyone whining about it.'

'About what?' Blake asks.

'Got two Land Rovers outside.'

Heather finally pulls away from Blake and looks at Sendak like she can barely dare to believe it.

'But this is the part where you tell us the keys are in an office at the other end of the corridor we just escaped down,' Blake says.

Sendak holds up two sets of car keys.

'Oh, thank God.'

'Thank me,' Sendak tells him, 'but maybe not yet. The Land Rovers are parked all the way on the other side of the compound—hundred and fifty, maybe two hundred yards from here. Not to mention the five miles of single track we gotta drive through the forest before we hit the open road and are literally out of the woods.'

'I've got faith,' Blake tells him.

Sendak permits himself a smile.

'Okay, people,' he announces. 'We're launching Operation Get the Fuck Outta Here. Heads up. Let's look sharp.'

Adnan reloads the shotgun with the last shells from the box and hands it to Sendak.

'Six rounds left,' Adnan reports. 'That's it.'

Sendak nods in acknowledgment, then turns to Kirk.

'Can you drive, big guy?'

Kirk shakes his head regretfully.

'I take it you can, Padre?'

'Sure,' says Blake.

Sendak tosses him a set of keys. Heather looks at him like she wishes he'd kept this to himself.

'I'm coming anyway,' Kirk declares.

'Damn straight. These fuckers are *scared* of you.'

'Scared of this, anyway,' Kirk replies, picking up the chainsaw.

Sendak casts an evaluative eye over Kirk's black-spattered weapon.

'How much juice you got in that thing?'

Kirk frowns.

'Petrol? Don't know. How?'

Sendak goes over to the five-a-side goals that are wedged against the door to the corridor and unscrews a length of tubular metal from the stanchion.

'Gimme your jacket,' he tells Blake.

Blake hands it over and Sendak begins ripping it into pieces. He wraps several strips tightly around the metal tube at one end, before soaking the binding with petrol poured from the chainsaw. Then he taps Beansy for a lighter, sets the torch ablaze and hands it almost ceremonially to Blake as Adnan and Radar prepare to open the doors.

'We know they ain't scared of crosses, but I never encountered any creature dumb enough *not* to be scared of getting its ass barbecued.'

*　　　*　　　*

They move briskly but tensely, eyes darting to seek out unseen dangers in the darkness. Blake forms

430

the forward point of a triangle, flanked a few feet behind by the others. They stay close to the wall for the first stretch, then, on Sendak's command, drift wider as the corner approaches, in order to have the widest field of vision upon anything that might be waiting for them around it. Blake can feel the metal pole get gradually hotter. It's tolerable right now, but he hopes it steadies soon.

The purr of Kirk's chainsaw is the only noise to be heard, drowning the sounds of their breathing and their footfalls on the frosted grass. They can't hear their own steps, so there will be no aural warning of attack. Blake strains to see beyond the flickering corona extending around his torch, trying to resolve shapes out of shades. Around the corner, the side of the building ceases to present any clean lines: walls advance and retreat as dictated by the facility's blocks and link corridors, with fuel tanks, bins and hoppers also looming haphazardly in the darkness, each potentially concealing an ambush. Matt-black panels denote the kitchen's broken panes, distinct from the sheen where other windows remain intact. But there, a dozen or so yards right of the building's far corner, their goal is in sight. Two Land Rovers sit parked on an apron of frozen dust, a narrow track leading around to the open ground where the coach dropped everybody two days ago. Beyond that is the road through the forest: it's less than a hundred metres off, but that part of the journey is a long, long way distant.

'Fuck,' mutters Kirk. 'Here they come.'

Blake turns to his right and looks up the gentle slope towards the treeline, where silhouetted figures are emerging from the shadows. There are

431

only a couple at first, then more and more become visible, cautiously intent upon the exposed trio. Their guttural voices sound out across the air, calling instructions. There is no mass charge, but as their numbers swell, they begin to spread out, forming a noose that they will inevitably tighten.

Blake holds the torch a little higher, keeping the brightness above his sightline. There must be a dozen of them. Fifteen. Twenty. God knows. He can't count, can barely retain focus in his fear.

'Stay tight,' Sendak commands. 'Keep it together. We can do this.'

The triangle closes, the three of them now almost back-to-back in a defensive formation. Some of the demons are holding their ground, maintaining a perimeter; others are closing in, slowly, cautiously. Kirk holds aloft the chainsaw, revving it as a warning.

Nervously, Blake gives the torch a wave too, sweeping it to convey that it is a weapon. The flame flickers, then starts to fail.

'Oh, bugger.'

He waves it again, like the air will help reignite it. It dies.

'Oh shit. Sendak . . .'

'Keep it together,' Sendak states, his tone indicating that even for him this is a bigger ask than the last time he said it.

'Should have used more petrol,' Kirk moans.

The trio keeps moving, but the approaching demons are now less cautious and are starting to stride forward with purpose.

Kirk revs the chainsaw again. It cuts out.

'Oh for fuck's sake.'

He tugs the starter cord. It growls briefly then

432

splutters out again.

'Used too *much* petrol,' he revises, sounding close to panic.

'How many shots are in that thing?' Blake asks.

Sendak pauses before responding, long enough for Blake to fear the answer will be one.

'Six.'

Blake looks at the ring of demons surrounding them: there must be at least twice that number ranged between them and the vehicles.

'But these fuckers don't know that.'

One of the demons launches itself at them. Sendak fires, blows it away, spraying matter all over the creature behind it. Sendak pumps the shotgun just in time to repel a second assault. The demons close by retreat, but only a few yards. Then there sounds out a rumbling growl from up the slope, prompting human and demon alike to look towards the trees. A dozen more horned creatures are emerging into the moonlight: blades, teeth and claws at the ready.

One of them lets loose a deafening, defiant, gut-shuddering roar, the cue for what will be a decisive final assault. The members of this second wave break into a run, the first group holding their positions to prevent any escape.

Then a human voice pierces the sky.

'HAAAW!' it shouts. 'Creatures of the Eternal Darkness?'

Deso stands with the lance gripped in both hands, the backpack strapped around his shoulders, and Rosemary at his side.

Some of the demons turn in response, mostly those of the first wave. The second group continue charging, undistracted.

Their mistake.

Deso squeezes the trigger on the lance as Rosemary flames up his trusty Ronson Triumph.

'Let there be light.'

The lance sends an arcing blast of flame towards the nearest demons, training it on the first of them and then sweeping it steadily across the line of attackers. Several of them are completely engulfed and fall, burning, to the ground, while others run off, flames dancing about them, crashing into each other and spreading panic.

'Oh yeah,' declares Sendak. 'Oh yeah. Oh yeah.'

Deso twists the outlet valve, cranking up the range and the pressure as he sends the spray towards the demons on one side of the enclosing ring. He strides forward as they scatter, pursuing them with his deadly jet as they flee. Unfortunately, they are fleeing past the nearer of the Land Rovers.

'Oh no,' gasps Sendak. 'Oh no. Oh no.'

One of the flaming demons crashes through the windscreen as Deso's plume of flame also engulfs the vehicle.

Deso lets go of the trigger immediately, cutting off the fire like switching off a light, but he can only extinguish the blaze at one end.

'Oh-oh,' he breathes.

The Land Rover burns for a few seconds, then explodes, consuming the vehicle alongside it and triggering a second blast almost before the first one has ended. It obliterates what was left of two more blazing demons and sends a pulse-wave through the air that Deso can feel in his chest. He hauls the backpack off lest it detonates, and steps hurriedly away from it, dragging Rosemary clear also.

Sendak, Blake and Kirk look on in horror as flaming debris from the blast is sent flying against the walls of the building; and more distressingly, against the tanks abutting the walls of the building.

'Get down,' Sendak shouts. 'Now!

The three of them hurl themselves to the deck just before the fuel tanks go up. The explosion rips open the side of the building, blowing demons apart like cinders.

Another explosion follows instantaneously, the leaked gas in the kitchen igniting in a flash that sends a spurt of flame towering into the sky and several objects hurtling out through the windows. One of them looked like a body. If it was Kane's, Blake hopes he wanted to be cremated.

Deso stands open-mouthed and stares at what he has wreaked. Retreating demons are scuttling for the shadows, ready to regroup. The vehicles are mangled, twisted and burning. The complex is ablaze in two different places and there is flaming wreckage everywhere.

'Well, that's annoying,' he says.

* * *

Sendak supervises a retreat back inside, keeping the shotgun raised to cover them as they retrieve the fallen demons' weapons and hasten to the emergency doors. The blast damage looks enormous but the fires don't appear to be spreading. The games hall will remain a safe haven for now.

Deso sits disconsolately against a wall, casting a baleful eye over the spraying apparatus, which

Kirk has retrieved in order to refuel his chainsaw.

Sendak walks over and kicks him gently on the soles of his feet to get his attention.

'Head up, son, you just saved all our asses.'

'Then bollocksed up our chances of escape,' Deso argues.

'He giveth and He taketh away,' says Rosemary, sitting down beside him and giving his hand a squeeze.

Just along the wall, Marianne is wincing, cradling her hands in her lap and looking very white.

'Morphine's wearing off,' Mrs McKenzie says. 'There's no more. I gave the boy the lion's share, but he'll be feeling everything soon enough too. He's still losing blood.'

'How long for the paramedics?' asks Heather. 'You said two hours, that had to be at least an—'

Sendak looks reluctant to answer. Heather clocks this and cuts herself off.

'Two hours was for the armed response. Paramedics were all at a crash, an hour south of Inverness. They ain't comin'. Not in time, anyway.'

'An armed response team will have medical supplies and transport, though,' she suggests.

Sendak sighs grimly. 'They ain't comin' either.'

'But you said . . .'

'I know what I said. That's what they *told* me. I didn't believe them but I had to talk like the glass was half full at that point. It's no-bullshit time now, though, and the no-bullshit reality is that they don't just send out an ARU on a member of the public's say-so. At most they'll send the local beat-cop from Tornabreich to check it out, and that ain't happened either. Which means best-case scenario is Hamish Macbeth shows up soon and we evacuate five, maybe six people, while the rest wait who knows how long for back-up.'

'And what's worst-case?' Blake asks.

'PC Macbeth got here a little while back but encountered resistance.'

His tone is flat, indicating to Blake that he is strongly inclined to believe this the more likely. However, having just admitted he gave the glass-half-full treatment to Heather earlier, there has to be a reason he's laying it all out so straight now.

'Give it up, Sergeant,' Blake says. 'What aren't you telling us?'

All eyes are on Sendak now; whether they be anguished, desperate or daring to hope.

'There *is* somewhere we can find some meds,' he reveals. 'More wheels too, maybe.'

'What's the catch?' asks Blake.

'It's also most likely where these freaks have come from.'

'MoD—Keep Out,' states Kirk.

Sendak nods: half confirmation, half confession.

'Underneath Ben Trochart is a rabbit warren of tunnels and caverns. Used to be a secret nuclear command bunker. Post-Cold-War, it's been turned into an R&D facility: ten times as secret.'

'So how does an ex-US-serviceman know this about a top-secret MoD facility?' Blake asks.

'The MoD are only holding the note. They ain't running the show.'

'You were posted there,' Blake deduces, trying—and failing—to keep a tone of accusation from his voice.

'Yep,' he confirms unapologetically. 'Two years I was in that place. Saw some funky shit . . .'

He could go on, but who is that going to help,

and besides, there ain't the time.

'I never saw any goddamn demons running loose, if that's what you're gonna ask. What matters is I know my way around—including a short cut to get in. That's the good news. The bad is that we're talking a mile and a half through the woods to get there—*before* you step into the heart of darkness. For that reason, I don't expect to be inundated with volunteers . . .'

'I'm in,' Kirk interjects.

'. . . which is why I'm just gonna tell you how it's gonna be. You just told me you can't drive, didn't you?'

Kirk sighs.

'That's okay, because I want you minding the store until we get back. This fire should keep 'em away, and it's gonna burn plenty yet, but anything comes calling . . .'

Kirk pats the chainsaw.

'I'll send them away with a flea in their ear,' he says.

'My man.'

Sendak then turns to Adnan.

'How about you?'

'Failed my test last month,' he confesses. 'But I *can* drive.'

Sendak checks the safety and tosses him the shotgun in a gentle arc. Adnan catches it one-handed.

'Good enough. Four shots, four kills, way I heard it. That ratio puts you on this detail. I don't need you to parallel park.'

'Fair enough,' Adnan agrees, already picturing the frag count on his HUD.

'I'm in too,' Blake declares. This prompts a look

of grave concern from Heather, but they both know there's no choice.

Sendak produces another set of keys from his pocket and strides towards the storeroom. Blake makes his way over to the pile of weapons recovered from Deso's fiery rout. He crouches down alongside them and picks out a long-handled axe. When he stands upright again, he finds Heather beside him. She weaves the fingers of her right hand through those of his left and brings her face close to his: close enough, but not close enough.

'Stay alive,' is all she says. He's sure she's going to kiss him but she doesn't. His heart is thumping. He's disappointed, but also relieved. He's not sure he could have left here if she had.

Sendak emerges from the storeroom with two bows, a long box full of arrows and a roll of tape.

'Anybody knows how to use these things—and I mean really knows, not just which part you hold and which end you point—then be my guest.'

He then squats down next to the improvised flame-thrower and goes to work with the roll of tape. By the time he's finished, it has Deso's lighter strapped just beneath the nozzle at the end of the lance, the lighter itself rigged so that this little pilot light remains permanently burning.

Sendak stands up with the rig strapped to his back and gives a nod to Rocks and Radar, who are manning the barriers on the emergency doors. When he turns to make sure his detail are ready and assembled, he finds Rosemary standing in front of him with a bow in one hand, a knife in the waistband of her skirt and an improvised quiver round her shoulder, fashioned from a tennis racquet cover she found in the storeroom.

'My family goes to Crieff Hydro twice a year. I've been doing archery there since I was nine. I'm in.'

'That's great,' he says. 'But I meant for here. When you see them coming, take out as many as you can, but make sure you get back inside and let these guys close the doors way before—'

'I can drive,' she says.

Sendak's expression is equivocal. She can tell this didn't quite sell it.

Rosemary fleetly draws an arrow from the bow and plugs George W Bush from close to twenty metres away at the other end of the hall.

'You're hired,' he tells her.

Having added a driver, Sendak beckons Blake across. He addresses him quietly, glancing towards Heather as he speaks.

'You know, you don't have to do this, Father. I got what I need in terms of personnel, and I think that lady back there needs you more than either of you is entirely prepared to own up to.'

'You could be right,' Blake admits. 'But the greater our numbers, the better everybody's odds. Besides, there's something *I* need too.'

'What?'

Blake stares portentously at him.

'Same as you. Answers.'

Here Be Dragons

XXVIII

They have an unseen escort for the first stage of their journey, taking them through the forest: a constant sound of footsteps out of sight amid the trees.

'They're stalking us,' Blake observes.

'Yeah, but they ain't gonna attack,' Sendak asserts with calm conviction. 'They've seen enough to understand what a shotgun and a flame-thrower can do. They just want to know what we're up to with these things, and they'll be content to see us take them away, because then they can get on with trying to break into the games hall and eat our friends.'

Vindicating Sendak's judgement, their escort falls away, even before their route takes them out of the trees and on to open land. They pick up the pace now, their path clearer and more direct, though Sendak appears to be leading them towards a rock-face. When they make no diversion to skirt around it, Blake starts bracing himself for the prospect of a climb, though he doesn't see how any of them are going to manage it while carrying their weapons.

'Okay, everybody take a second, catch your breath,' Sendak tells them.

Adnan checks the time on his mobile. It's quarter past one. They've been travelling almost an hour. He wonders how long Cam's got; how long any of them's got. They found a blood-streaked police motorcycle at the edge of the road only a few minutes into their trek, confirming

Sendak's fears. The local bobby's failure to report in may or may not trigger a reponse—who knows how much radio traffic is normal for round here in the middle of the night?—but at most it's not going to be swift and it's not going to make any difference. It's all about the four of them now: no one else.

There is some thick vegetation growing along the foot of the rock-face, bushes and creepers climbing seven or eight feet in places. That will get them an easier start, but there's at least twenty feet of bare rock to scale after that.

As the others wait in place on the coarse grass, their breath spiralling steam into the moonlight, Sendak strides on, heading straight for the wall. Blake watches keenly, assuming the military man is going to demonstrate some kind of climbing technique. Instead, Sendak takes a machete from his belt and begins hacking at the bushes in front of him. He tosses away a few branches and beckons the group forward.

'Demon-hunters, party of three?' he says, turning on a torch and directing it through the gap he has created, revealing the walls of a concealed crevice.

They venture in slowly behind Sendak, his torch now the only source of light in a very, very dark place, the passage before them disappearing into complete blackness. Adnan raises his shotgun, taking each step tentatively, while Rosemary notches an arrow against the bowstring and tugs it back.

The passage widens after a few yards, the torch playing back and forth steadily across the floor of what turns out to be a large cave. Sendak then draws the beam along one wall, looking for where it ends. The torch suddenly lights up a twisted and bloody face, its mouth open to scream. Adnan pulls his trigger in fright, finding it locked as he's forgotten the safety. Rosemary, having no such obstacle, looses an arrow that goes through the mouth, pinning the head back against the rock. Sendak draws the torch down beneath the neck and picks out a military uniform.

'Oh my God,' Rosemary gasps. 'It's a soldier. I've killed him.'

Sendak brings the beam down just a little further, then cuts its path short when it briefly discovers the glistening viscera spilling out from the soldier's abdomen.

'No,' Sendak assures her. 'You're a few hours late for that, but nice shot all the same.'

He resumes his scan of the walls and ground, then finds what he's after. The beam focuses upon a metal panel lying on the floor of the cave, then he sweeps it a couple of feet to one side and picks out the hatch it was previously covering.

'This is where they got out, I'm guessing.'

Adnan keeps his weapon trained on the hatch, remembering the safety this time, while Sendak crouches down and points the torch through it.

'Let me check it out,' he says, disentangling himself from the spraying apparatus. 'Gimme the gun.'

Adnan hands over the weapon and guesses he's not the only one to feel that bit more vulnerable as Sendak disappears out of sight, leaving them in almost total darkness.

There is almost total silence too, a long few seconds of listening to each other breathe, before soft sodium light erupts from the aperture. It is followed shortly by Sendak's face.

'Step into my office,' he says.

They follow Sendak along a narrow, concrete-walled passage, which takes them to another, wider hatch and another ladder, this time plunging a long, long way down through an enclosed shaft.

'We must be miles from where Kirk found that MoD sign,' Blake says quietly as they descend. 'How big is this place?'

'Big,' Sendak replies.

'Bloody typical,' Adnan mutters. 'Why is it that when the military have to host something dangerous, they stash it in bloody Scotland?' He puts on a fake upper-crust accent. ' "What's that? Polaris? Thames Estuary? No thank you." '

'Adnan?' Sendak interrupts him.

'What?'

He puts a finger to his lips.

Adnan cans it, and the ensuing silence is filled with a pulsing sound, low and powerful, which gets steadily louder the deeper they go.

At the foot of the shaft, they reach a sturdy metal door, which is visibly vibrating on its hinges with each throb.

'Brace yourselves,' Sendak says, and Blake thinks for a moment that he's talking about how much louder the noise will get when the door opens. However, it's not the sound that Sendak meant them to prepare for, but the sight.

They emerge into a wide corridor. The lighting is low: a few fluorescents are flickering, but most of them are completely smashed. What light there is illuminates a scene of true Stygia. There are body parts scattered across the floor: arms, legs, torsos, heads, a couple of slain demons, and blood everywhere. The walls are sprayed; the floor is awash with it.

Rosemary sucks in a loud gasp, feels her head swim.

'Keep it together,' Sendak tells them. 'We've seen worse shit tonight, and we'll see worse yet.'

Rosemary reaches out a steadying arm against a wall and closes her eyes. She puts herself back in that shed, with Deso. It's just for a second, but it's enough. When she opens them again, she's ready to go on.

Sendak is standing amidst a pile of butchered flesh. Instead of mere disgust, it is consternation that is writ lividly upon his face.

'What's wrong?' Blake asks, like there could possibly be anything *right* about this scene.

'Where the hell were these guys' weapons?'

'They must have been taken by surprise,' Adnan suggests.

'Yeah, but . . .' Sendak examines a single bullet hole in one wall, probing it with his finger. 'Looks like all they were carrying were side arms. I don't get it.'

'Father,' says Rosemary. 'You need to see this.'

Blake turns to observe that she has progressed a few yards down the corridor and is standing over another mutilated body, lying halfway out of a doorway. As he approaches, he sees the dog collar, just like his own, around the corpse's neck, but that's not why she has alerted him. On the half-open door is a coat of arms: cross keys beneath a triple-crowned mitre.

'This is a Vatican symbol,' he announces, glancing from the insignia to the sign above the door frame stating: 'Authorised Personnel Only'.

447

Blake nudges the door open further, but Sendak grabs his arm. Blake moves aside to let the Sarge go first, the spraying lance and its twinkling cigarette lighter preceding Sendak's entry.

Blake is about to step over the body and venture through the doorway when his progress is halted a second time, this time by Adnan scuttling low to crouch over the dead cleric and wrest something from his hand.

'What are you doing?' Rosemary asks in disgust.

Adnan holds up a keycard, wiping blood from it on the thigh of his jeans.

'Sharp thinking,' Sendak approves.

'I play a lot of *Doom*,' Adnan explains. He opts not to add that he is actually playing it in his head right now, it being the only way he can get through this without turning into a gibbering jelly.

Sendak leads them along a narrow blank passageway with a sliding double door at the end, also marked with the Vatican symbol, this time above a bar of printed text. He nudges at the barrier and finds it locked.

'Looks like the Church were running the show,' he states with some disquiet. 'How does that work? "Congregation for the Doctrine of the Faith",' he reads aloud. 'Mean anything to you, Padre?'

'That's the Vatican arm in charge of investigating the supernatural,' Blake informs him.

'Figures.'

'Though it's what it used to be called that's most ominous.'

'Do tell.'

'The Holy Inquisition.'

XXIX

Merrick needs a lie to give him; even one Tullian can see through will sound less awkward than simply refusing an answer. He comes up with a good one. Naked girlfriend pictures. Can't afford this phone to get found later and her nudie shots to end up on the web. It's thin, but being a priest, Tullian's sexual squeamishness should make him want to drop the subject soon as.

'It's . . .'

Merrick sighs, his hand on the door leading out of the coolant monitoring chamber. He can't lie, no matter the consequences. If it wasn't for the Cardinal, twice, he'd have lost more than his secret back there, so perhaps it's appropriate that it should be Tullian's call.

'I owe you my life, Cardinal, so I can't grudge you the truth. The phone is full of video files. Proof of what happened here, specifically regarding my work on holy water and its effects on the specimens. I'm a scientist. I couldn't bear the idea of it all being lost, of the military erasing my work from history for the sake of their own convenience. Knowledge sometimes is inconvenient.'

'Where did you get the files?'

'I snuck into The Little . . . the Alpha labs. That's where I was when the breakout happened. Forgive me.'

'In my line of work, Dr Merrick, forgiveness is all part of the service. You have more than my forgiveness. You have my gratitude.'

449

Merrick is puzzled.

'I was under the impression that you didn't want the outside world knowing anything about these creatures, for fear of the resulting hysteria.'

'I didn't,' he replies. 'But that was when I still believed that this operation was under control.'

Tullian goes first through the door and checks the passageway, sweeping the rifle back and forth. The stairwell they need is a couple of dozen paces away. The path is clear; or at least clear of threats. Blood, limbs, offal and excrement are strewn from wall to wall.

Merrick spots an ID badge attached to a lump of something dark and moist. 'Avedon', it reads.

Christ.

Tullian recces the stairs and beckons him to hurry. They advance to the next level, where the Cardinal dashes across the passageway and holds open the door to Security Control.

Merrick makes his way inside, where he staggers dizzily to one corner and vomits into a wasterpaper bin. He's sick again and again, then the dry heaves take him until he wishes there was something, anything else in his stomach so that he could vomit that too. Tullian hands him a half-drunk bottle of water from a desktop and Merrick takes a swig, slumping weakly into a chair. He feels a lump in his throat, the onset of tears. Grief hasn't had a look-in against fear and horror these past few hours, but seeing that name badge has finally kicked it off.

He wipes his eyes when he thinks the tears are receding, his vision cleared to reveal Tullian busily working two different keyboards in front of the bank of computer monitors and CCTV screens.

Tullian is alert to his resumed attention, and looks round with an expression of both sympathy and resolute intent.

'They'll do all this again,' the Cardinal says sorrowfully. 'I've sent the call. They'll dispatch a lockdown team.'

Merrick then hears a series of dampened thumps from the door and the corridor outside. He looks across in alarm, but Tullian puts him at ease.

'That's the mag-locks coming back online. Some of them, anyway: the restart doesn't appear to have fixed them all. The ones in this block are functional, though. We're safe for now. But understand this: the lockdown team will do their job, the military will mop up the mess, they'll spin a story . . . And then after a while, they'll do all this again. As a scientist, you know this to be true.'

Merrick nods regretfully. No matter the price of that glimpse: someone is always going to be willing to pay it.

'Which is why your files could be an invaluable bargaining chip.'

'Generate a public outcry, you mean? But at what cost in terms of panic?'

'We wouldn't release the files. Just let them know we have them, and *threaten* to release them if they ever reprise this experiment.'

'I can't see that deterring many scientists.'

'That's not who we'd need to deter. This disaster was only possible through proprietary military technology. What's inside that phone could ensure they don't try and rebuild this abomination. Can I see it?'

Merrick produces the device. 'It's damaged,' he reports. 'The LCD's a mess, but I can hook it up to

451

one of those PCs.'

'Fine. We should back it up anyway. I'll find some blank disks.'

Merrick connects the phone and, to his great relief, is able to access its memory. He copies the data across to the local drive.

'There's not many files,' Tullian observes with disappointment.

'I didn't have much time. I just grabbed everything I could with a time- and date-stamp that matched my experiments. I haven't had the chance to even check what's on this stuff,' he adds, selecting three files at random and launching them in different windows. A simple drag-and-drop on the multiple-monitor control interface puts them up on separate screens, then Merrick begins sliding the progress bars on each in turn, in order to find himself in shot and confirm they constitute the evidence required. He's there in all three: standing over a strapped-down demon, undertaking his own personal deal with the devil, his trade-off for that glimpse.

'Hold on, where did this—' Tullian begins, cutting himself off.

Merrick looks at what has grabbed the Cardinal's attention and instantly understands why there is nothing more to say. One of the files has no soundtrack, evidently a CCTV feed supplementary to the cameras Tullian's men had set up. It's from high on the wall ahead of Merrick, facing back towards the other cameras: an elevated angle showing him smaller in shot, but for that, displaying the bigger picture.

He turns around to confront Tullian, who has picked up the decoherence rifle and is pointing it

452

at him.

'Knowledge sometimes *is* inconvenient, isn't it, Doctor?' he says, almost apologetically. 'I wish you hadn't just seen that, but in your own words, you owe me your life. And I'm afraid I do, vehemently, grudge you the truth.'

Merrick sees the trigger twitch. Then there's light. Lights everywhere, flickering and indistinct: white shapes stretched and pulled by random refractions in the rain and spray before being temporarily shrunk to points and discs by the wiper blades. Nothing holds its form or position long enough for him to focus. The closest thing to a constant is the perforated blur of lines on the road, stuttering just out of syncopation like a slowing zoetrope.

His eyes are closing; it ought to frighten him how involuntary this seems, but it feels so beckoning, so comfortable. It'll be okay. Just a few seconds' rest, ten seconds, three hundred and thirty-three metres, surely he can risk that. NO. He snaps them wide, breathes extra deeply a few times, sourcing oxygen, gives his head a shake. The windscreen is a membrane, fluid and warping, stretching the light, smearing the shapes, blurring the white lines. He's squinting, narrowing his eyes in an effort to shield the pupils, keep them from contracting so that he can see better into the rain-filled darkness. Maybe if he closes one eye and thus keeps it dark-adapted, then he can open it and close the other next time the oncoming lights are too bright. He tries. Yeah. Closing one eye feels good. It feels too good. He wants to close the other one too.

He hits a straight length of road, an interchange. There are streetlights for the first time in however many miles. He can see the road stretch out, unbending, must be half a mile. Six hundred and sixty-six metres would be twenty seconds. He can close his eyes for twenty seconds. The road is straight. He doesn't need to steer for twenty seconds, doesn't need to look for six hundred and sixty-six metres. He can just, yes, that's it, just . . .

XXX

Adnan unlocks the door with a swipe of the card, then Sendak takes point again briefly before calling them through. When he does, his voice is hollow and weary.

'You might think it'd be redundant for me to say brace yourselves again, but trust me on this.'

A few moments inside the cavernous laboratory beyond and they all understand that it was not redundant. There are further corpses littered about the place, more clerics by the look of it. Blake would guess six, maybe seven. It's impossible to tell precisely how many, as it would require an extensive retrieval operation and subsequent limb count. There's only one that looks comparatively intact, though its head is obscured. It is slumped backwards over a packing crate next to a formidable cylindrical door, this barrier's strength and solidity rendered moot by the fact of it lying half open. The clinical whiteness of the walls and floor tiles serve to make the blood and viscera all the more lurid, but it's not that which has him spooked more than the first gore-spattered corridor.

'What in the name of God happened here?' Blake asks in a dread-struck whisper.

'Due respect, Padre, I think you answered your own question.'

In the centre of this antiseptically pristine slaughterhouse, there is a dead demon laid out on a cross-shaped wooden board, its face contorted into an agonised, screaming grimace. Its wrists and ankles are held by steel clamps, but it has had nails driven through its palms and feet. Its skin is flayed and blackened where it has not been cut away completely by dozens of stab wounds.

With all of this to hold their appalled attention, it takes a while for anyone to notice the TV monitor sitting on a desktop next to a jar containing a demon's claw suspended in fluid. Once noticed, however, it has all of them silently rapt.

It shows another demon secured to a similarly shaped fixture, a steel one this time, with the further precaution of a neck restraint holding its head in place. A figure in black robes approaches, carrying a small vessel of clear fluid.

'*Let these waters be sanctified by the power, the agency and descent of the Holy Spirit,*' he incants. '*Let descend upon these waters the cleansing of the Three who are One . . .*'

'It's a rite of exorcism,' says Blake. 'Blessing holy water to drive out demons.'

'*. . . that Satan may be crushed under our feet, that every evil counsel directed against us may be brought to naught, and that the Lord our God will free us from every attack and temptation of the enemy.*'

Then the robed figure opens the vessel and gives a flick of his wrist.

'Holy water burns their skin,' says Rosemary in tremulous awe.

Adnan is standing furthest from the monitor, which is why he is able to notice a slight motion off to his left. He whips his head around, convinced the body slumped over the packing crate moved one of its legs.

'Sendak, I think this one's alive.'

Adnan hurries closer to it, and as he does so, the figure definitely moves again, apparently trying to sit up. Then its torso rises enough for Adnan to see that half of its head is missing above the jawline, a millisecond before a demon leaps out from behind the crate. In his panic, Adnan shoots the demon three times and pumps the gun for a fourth before Sendak restrains him.

'Adnan, easy. You can only kill it once.'

The blood is rushing around Adnan's ears, its sound almost as loud as the constant pulsing. He needs to get it back. His HUD displays an increase to his frag count, but his ammo level is looking less healthy. It was true what Old Man Murray said: first-person shooters go downhill from the moment you see a crate.

'Shit. Sorry. One shot left.'

'That's okay. Bound to find some more twelve-gauge shells in this . . .'

Sendak is distracted by a clatter of metal from the other end of the lab, and turns around in time to witness Blake disappear, hauled backwards down a hole in the floor next to a punched-out grate.

Sendak grabs the shotgun from Adnan and rushes to the gap, but when he looks down it he can see only shadows. He pulls out the torch and

456

points the beam into the shaft. It drops a couple of metres to a passageway below.

He could crawl down there, but he knows it could be suicide. Blake is gone, and he can't risk himself while there are so many others relying on this expedition coming through.

'FUCK!' he roars in anguish, kicking the grate. 'MOTHERFUCKING . . .'

He lets out a deep sigh, feels his discipline take the wheel once again. 'Okay,' he says. 'Okay. We gotta keep going.'

'Which way?' Rosemary asks. 'Back to the main corridor, or . . . ?'

Sendak indicates the cylindrical door.

'They didn't have nuclear blast shit when I was posted here. I want to know what's on the other side of that.'

*   *   *

Blake is in semi-darkness, a few slivers of light coming through tiny slits somewhere above. He is in a duct of some kind, pipes and cables running along both walls. His captor has suddenly stopped dragging him, but keeps a hand clamped to his mouth. There have been no blades, no claws, only the blind fear of being hauled helplessly down into blackness.

A human voice speaks very softly, calm but firm.

'Shh. Quiet, Father. Be still.'

Blake tries to turn his head but it is too awkward given the position in which he is being held.

'Don't move,' the voice tells him, a concerned warning rather than a command.

Forced to stare ahead, it is now that Blake

notices an air vent low in the wall to his right, its grille straining as something pushes it from behind. Suddenly, the grille gives and a demon's head and shoulders burst through. Before it can fully emerge, it is disintegrated completely by a blast from something close to Blake's side.

His captor then releases his grip and allows Blake to turn. He sees the robed figure he just watched on the monitor, though his face and garments are now bloodied and dirty. Blake's gaze is drawn irresistibly to the sight of the futuristic-looking rifle slung around his shoulder.

'You get further with a holy word and a ray-gun than just a holy word,' he says. 'I'm Cardinal Terrence Tullian. Peace be with you, Father . . . ?'

'Blake. Father Constantine Blake. My friends . . . I need to . . .'

'I'm sorry, Father Blake. I know how difficult this will be to hear, but you're going to have to summon your deepest faith and believe me when I tell you that as men of God, you and I are the only ones who can still end this evil.'

*   *   *

They venture cautiously through the circular portal and emerge into a vast vault, high-ceilinged and extensive in dimensions but nonetheless cramped by virtue of the sheer multitude of its contents. It is like a warehouse, Adnan thinks at first, seeing only the side view of so many rows of cube-shaped boxes, stacked three high. It smells like a zoo, almost bringing tears to his eyes. Then as he glances along the rows, each fronted by steel bars, his impression is revised until he realises he is looking at a prison.

'This used to be a weapons testing range,' Sendak says.

'So many,' Rosemary says. 'Dozens of them. Hundreds, maybe.'

'All these cages are open, every one,' Sendak states. 'Computer error maybe, some kind of malfunction.'

'Oh, fuck,' Adnan reports, having proceeded one row further along and encountered more mutilated remains.

'What?'

'Think I found the screws.'

Adnan steps away carefully from this latest discovery, mindful of his most recent encounter with a corpse. Blood has coated the wall above the bodies, and almost but not quite obscured the existence of a glass cabinet attached to the stonework. He tugs up his sleeve and wipes the spray from the front panel. The blood smears slickly across the glass, but is cleared enough for him to make out the contents.

'Whoa. Sarge, you have to see this.'

'I've seen me enough corpses today to last a lifetime. I'll take a rain check.'

'Not the bodies, Sarge. Weapons.'

Sendak and Rosemary retreat from the row they had entered and come around next to Adnan. As they approach, there is a burst of noise from high up on one of the walls, and they turn in startlement, only to be met by the sight of steam venting from a broken pipe.

'Shit. This thing's gonna give me a goddamn heart attack before—'

There is another sudden noise heralding

459

movement behind and above, but this time it's no false alarm. Two demons are bounding along the tops of the cages, gaining speed and preparing to pounce, each gripping some kind of sparking blue pole in its claws.

Rosemary and Adnan react instinctively, each getting off a shot and hitting their target. Unfortunately they both pick the same target. The surviving demon checks its approach, coming in now from a different flank as it bears down on Sendak. He swings around to point the lance and squeezes the trigger, but sprays only liquid, the sudden motion having snuffed his makeshift pilot light.

'Ah, shit,' he breathes, figuring this is it as the demon launches itself from on high. He hears a sound that seems to grind electrically at the inside of his skull, like when the dentist is drilling his teeth, then feels a wave of dust on his skin and a taste in his mouth of blood and metal. It's a sound, a sensation and a taste he's encountered once before, and in this very room.

They all look for the source and locate a solitary figure at the far end of the row of cells, gripping a rifle similar to the ones locked in the cabinet. He limps towards them, his clothes torn, his face caked with dust, grime and blood.

'Nice shooting, soldier,' Sendak hails him. 'What's your name?'

'I'm not a soldier,' he replies. 'And my name is—'

'Steinmeyer,' Sendak interrupts, recognising the face that's under all that shit.

Steinmeyer is taken aback for a moment, then he also recognises who he is talking to.

'Sergeant Sendak.' Steinmeyer looks at the two

460

armed teenagers in Sendak's keeping, like *that's* the weirdest thing going on around this place. 'What are you doing here?'

'I still live in the neighbourhood. But if you mean what am I doing down here right now, well I think the answer to that has more to do with whatever the fuck *you're* doing here. I see you never scrapped those guns you were working on. What other little experiments might have gotten out of hand?'

Steinmeyer bows sheepishly.

'Those guns were the price of my soul, which I sold to fund my other work. I never got to apologise personally for what happened to your comrades and yourself. They kept the accident from me, and I didn't even find out about it until months after you—'

'The price of your soul just saved my ass, so consider the debt paid. I think you better keep back the act of contrition for your subsequent work. What's been going on in this place? How come there are demons running loose on my property, slashing up my paying guests?'

Steinmeyer shakes his head.

'Not demons,' he says.

'What the fuck else could they be?'

'I don't know what they are. Only what they're not.'

'Holy water burns their flesh,' Sendak argues. 'They have horns on their heads and they have some pretty fucking serious issues with crucifixes, to say nothing of the whole ripping-people-apart thing they got going on.'

'Come and see this,' Steinmeyer says. 'All of you. Follow me.'

461

He leads them back along the row of cages and swings open one of the barred doors.

'There.' He points.

They draw closer, despite being repelled by the smell. On the walls of the chamber, etched in claw marks, blood and excrement, are a series of pictures.

'It looks like cave paintings,' Adnan opines.

'I've found several just like this,' Steinmeyer says. 'It's a narrative. The occupant of this cell telling his story, in some despairing attempt to express himself.'

He points to what now appears to be the first picture in a sequence: a rendering of a horned figure standing over another. The artwork is crude but recognisable, enough to make it clear that the creatures are clothed. The next shows a group of them before two isolated individuals: one boasting a headdress, the other identifiable as the standing figure in the first image.

'A murder,' Steinmeyer says. 'Followed by a trial. This is a civilisation: primitive, possibly fifty thousand years behind our own, possibly a hundred thousand, but a civilisation nonetheless. If you look at the drawings in other cells you'll see that they were *all* prisoners: some of them convicts, others captured in battle. Their punishment is always the same, however: they are stripped naked and cast into this black portal. Sometimes it appears as a cave, sometimes a pool, sometimes a pit. But it's what happens next that is truly revealing.'

'Oh shit,' says Sendak, reading ahead.

'I'm interpreting some of these marks as religious symbols. At this point they believe they're

462

dead, and have passed through into the next life.'

'And this is their Hell,' states Rosemary, having reached the parental-discretion-advisory parts of the narrative. She sees torture, crucifixion and . . . 'Is this cannibalism?' she asks.

'They were fed only their own dead,' Steinmeyer confirms. 'And those who didn't eat simply starved. But you are right: this is their Hell. We are their demons, and they have learned to recognise those who carry crucifixes as the worst of their tormentors. They are murderers and warriors, starved and brutalised, and they will kill on sight any and every human being they encounter, because they believe us to be capable only of evil.'

*   *   *

'I think the monsters have finished their fag break,' Kirk announces, staring through the window in one of the emergency doors. 'Could be game on again. Aw fuck,' he adds, his tone suddenly less laconic.

'What?' asks Rocks, then he sees it. 'Bollocks.'

Heather rushes across to join them, equally impatient and dreading to discover whatever could have inspired such gloom in anyone with Kirk's apparent appetite for the fray.

In that respect, the view doesn't disappoint. There are four demons moving towards the games hall carrying a long and formidable-looking section of timber, several others attending on the fringes.

'Must have cut away one of the open joists from the barn,' Kirk suggests. 'Gaunny use it as a battering ram. Anybody got some boiling oil?'

From what Heather can see, the closest they

have is an outside tap attached to a garden hose.

'Naw, but we do have an archer,' Rocks replies. 'Beansy, I hope you werenae lying about having used one of those things on holiday, because you're up.'

'I wasnae lying,' Beansy insists. 'But I didnae say I was any good.'

'Well, you don't need to hit a fuckin' bullseye,' Rocks assures him. 'You just need to plug a few of these bastards.'

Rocks and Kirk open the doors and Beansy takes a pace forward on to the top of the steps. Caitlin is standing beside him, ready to hand him more arrows.

Heather feels suddenly very ashamed. These mere kids are out there defending everyone's lives while she's barely holding herself back from hysterics. She didn't want Blake to leave because she literally wanted someone to hold on to, and because she knew that if he left, she might well be losing him forever.

All fear and desire is naked now, all pretences and façades stripped away. She can admit to what she wants. She doesn't want to die. Life is all that matters. Life is all there is. She wants to hold Blake again. She wants to tell him the truth. She can admit to that truth. But whatever she wants, she needs to make it happen.

She steps back from the doorway and rushes to the storeroom, looking for anything that might yet be put to use. Alongside footballs, team bibs, hockey sticks and assorted racquets, the only item of any weight is a buffing machine for polishing the floor, yards of flex wrapped around its handle. On the wall beside it is a large grey circuit box.

464

Heather crouches down and flips it open. Like everything else around here, it's a modern affair, with the lights on a different circuit to the power points, and its express purpose is something she knows how to circumvent.

Beansy looks out across the grass towards the barn where everything turned to shite a few hours back. One minute he's heading in there, healthy buzz off a jay and in with a serious shout of a wee footer with Yvonne; the next minute . . .

Aye. Payback, ya bastards.

Beansy tugs the string between his fingers and draws a bead on his first target. The fuckers with the battering ram seem worryingly near when you're just looking at them, but become a lot further when you're taking aim.

He lets fly. The arrow sails into the darkness to no apparent effect.

'Arse-candles.'

'Steady, Beansy, don't get flustered,' Kirk tells him as Caitlin hands over the next arrow.

Don't get fucking flustered. Aye, nae bother, big yin. Demons heading towards them lugging a battering ram, but nae fucking pressure, eh?

He takes aim again, holds his breath, remembers this time what that instructor woman told him when she was standing right behind him with that lovely perfume in his nostrils and her tits occasionally just brushing against his back. *Fire as you breathe out.*

He lets go the arrow as he lets out his breath, and this one thunks into the demon's belly, downing the fucker and causing the other three to drop the timber.

'Get in,' cheers Rocks.

Caitlin feeds him again. He scores a second, shooting his mark in the thigh.

The demons start growling at each other, then the remaining two ram-bearers abandon the thing and go haring off.

'Ya fuckin' dancer,' Rocks declares, but the congratulations are premature. A few moments later, four replacements retrieve the timber, while the two who had scurried off return, carrying wreckage from the exploded vehicles to use as shields. They take position in front of the battering ram, which can now proceed at will.

'The legs. Go for the legs,' Rocks suggests. Beansy fires off another three arrows, one hitting a car door and the others biting harmlessly into the ground as the rudimentary siege engine continues to progress.

'If they get to these doors with that thing, we're fucked.'

Kirk pulls the rip-cord and starts the chainsaw again.

'Not gonna happen,' he states defiantly, but Rocks can see the doubt in his face, the bravado he's summoning for the benefit of those around him. Recent months haven't been the best of times between them, but he's seen what the big man is truly made of tonight. Unfortunately he's also seen quite literally what several other folk were made of, and that's the thought he can't suppress as Kirk gets ready for what could be his final charge.

'Stop right there,' orders a voice, and they turn in surprise to see that it's Miss Ross, holding a hockey stick with something threaded around it.

'Grab the hose out there and turn that tap on, full bung,' she tells Rocks. He complies unquestioningly, though he's a little baffled as to what she has in mind. Under her direction, he floods the stairs, the disabled ramp and the concrete apron in front of both.

'Great plan,' Kirk says, equally confused. 'If we make the path slippy enough, one of the monsters could have a nasty fall. Just need to hope the water freezes in the ten seconds we've got before they get here.'

'Ready the doors,' Heather commands, as the siege engine reaches the concrete. Rocks drops the hose and steps back inside, which is when he sees that whatever is wrapped around the hockey stick is also plugged into the mains. He catches a glimpse of bare wire on the curled end just as Heather lets it fall into the puddle.

'Hey, check it,' says Beansy. 'They're dancing.'

XXXI

We must be ready, Parducci had told him.

Tullian was prepared, but he could never be ready for what he saw when he was summoned to the Orpheus Complex.

They said very little beyond formal greetings as they escorted him down inside the elevator. He guessed their thinking: they were telling him nothing because they didn't want to prejudice the experiment. Or maybe they were just so scared that they didn't feel there was anything helpful that they could say to him. He was, after all, the expert in this particular field.

He remembers the heat, the way it caught in his

throat the second the doors opened. It was like the blast that could hit you momentarily as you passed directly under a large space-heater, except that there was no ensuing relief of passing out of range. It took only minutes to walk to the brig, where the holding cells were accommodated, but he was sweating heavily by the time they arrived. At least it covered up his apprehension: he'd have been sweating anyway. He was trembling, drawing upon all his strength to steel himself for what he was about to witness, the sight that had driven the king of this same land to murderous obsession four centuries previously.

He was escorted by General McCormack and Colonel Havelock, but they waited outside while he examined the specimens. One soldier, armed only with a pistol holstered at his hip, accompanied him inside the brig, remaining at the door as Tullian approached the first holding cell.

He thought nothing could have prepared him for confronting a live demon, but as he gazed through those bars, he realised he was looking at something far more disturbing.

The creature was seated on the floor, almost balled up. It stared at him anxiously for a moment, taking him in as he stood there in his robes, then looked away, glancing up furtively every so often. It seemed, if anything, relieved to recognise that he was not a soldier. He held up his crucifix. It tracked the movement of his hand initially, but once again seemed at greater ease once it had established that what he held did not appear to be a weapon.

He advanced to the second cell, where his presence elicited much the same response.

Tullian felt genuine, chest-tightening fear. He saw what Parducci predicted the scientists would see, and saw that they would be *right*.

These were not demons.

He considered all that he thought might be proven when he had stood in that vault and wondered aloud why the Church did not show the world their proof. The corollary demonstrated all his forebears' wisdom in keeping it secret.

Then he saw the malign brilliance of the Morningstar, of Lucifer's charade. Convince man that there are no demons by giving him scientific proof that they are instead mere visitors from another world. More exotic than mistaken glimpses of horse's breath in the morning mist, but finally explicable, and explicable in a way that will further exalt scientific exploration over the spiritual. With demons thus dismissed, so would follow Satan, so would follow Hell, and this would be catastrophic. These creatures, wherever they were from, were not demons, but their presence on Earth was Satan's work nonetheless: instruments of a plan to destroy faith. Though they might not even know it, they were all the more dangerous agents of his evil for *not* being demons.

'The pillars of Heaven have their base in the abyss'. So said Jules Michelet, esteemed French historian and author of the seminal *Satanism and Witchcraft*. 'The heedless person who denies this base could shatter paradise . . .'

Who would understand this better than Satan himself?

These creatures were in fact the first wave, dispatched to sow confusion and disguise the true threat. The real invasion would only come when the last bastions of resistance were at their weakest, and what shape might the Church be in a few years after a blow to worldwide faith such as this?

Tullian understood then that he had to beat the Devil at his own game: counter deceit with deceit, meet subterfuge with subterfuge. *To wage by force or guile eternal war.*

The military asked for his help because they feared they had brought forth demons from Hell. Well, he would give them demons from Hell, and continue to confirm their worst fears until they finally saw sense and closed this thing down forever.

In time, though, he came to understand that this would never happen. The place would be 'mothballed', operations merely 'suspended'. Inevitably, they would resume. Even if it took years to repeat the anomaly, eventually Steinmeyer or his successor would do this again. He had to destroy it. And not just destroy this machine so that it could not be rebuilt—for anything could be rebuilt—but destroy it in such a way that no one would permit the building of another. A few casualties would not be enough: this had to be a full-scale disaster, to put fear into both army and government that these were unstable forces they were dabbling with.

He had understood even sooner that keeping this whole thing under wraps was an impossible dream. This was not like the vault beneath the Vatican and the trusted few who kept its secret. Information would leak. Soldiers would talk. Scientists would definitely talk. The world was going to find out about these creatures, one way or another, which was why he had to shape the message. That, he realised, was where this could become more than mere damage limitation; that was where this could become a victory. He could take Lucifer's charade and turn it to the Church's advantage. For despite Parducci's reservations, if this abomination was unavoidably to be revealed, then what a renaissance of faith might it inspire, to learn that there truly were demons and there truly was a Hell? What a revolution might ensue were it to be demonstrated that the tenets of science had been shaken, with verified experiments showing the unique effects of holy water upon these creatures?

That was why he had gone to some lengths to ensure Merrick lived to tell his tale, and could have kissed the man when he revealed that he had salvaged some video files. Despite Tullian suggesting that they could be used as a bargaining chip, he knew Merrick would not be able to resist leaking them, especially in the face of any cover-up. A leak from a Church source would be damaging to the point of self-defeating, but coming from a scientist, it was perfect. Unfortunately, there had been that cursed CCTV feed, which had left him with no choice.

He felt dreadful about what he had been forced to do to Merrick, as he had felt dreadful throughout the many sleepless nights of prayer and contemplation as he prepared himself for his awful task. He knew there would be loss of life, and he regretted that profoundly. However, this would mostly be among soldiers, and it was the highest nobility of their vocation that they always knew they might have to lay down their lives for a

471

greater good. What greater good was there than this? If Satan was showing his hand so dramatically, then that demonstrated how high the stakes truly must be.

What might this be the precursor of, he barely dared ask himself. And thus what price a few lives against thwarting the crucial first foothold towards establishing Hell on Earth?

He had engineered this disaster and he had shot Merrick, but it was not sabotage and it was not murder.

This was war.

XXXII

'We need medicine and we need transportation,' Sendak states. 'Got twenty-odd people, including injured, holed up down the valley, surrounded by those things.'

'There's armoured personnel carriers top-side,' Steinmeyer replies. 'At the surface compound. Medkits on board. But we need to go via the Cathedral. Shut down the machine. Follow me, we'll have to go through the labs.'

'The Cathedral?' Sendak asks as they set off behind the professor.

'The great cavern housing the beating heart of this place. That's the sound you can hear all around you. The machine is out of control. All the systems have either shut down or gone haywire. The armoury codes appear to have malfunctioned same time as the cages. When the creatures broke loose, nobody could get hold of anything heavier than pistols. Surprise attack by overwhelming numbers . . .' He nods towards a pool of gore. 'This is the result.'

'So where did you get *that* bad boy?' Sendak asks.

'My desk drawer. This is the prototype. The others required code clearance for use because, quite frankly, the military were more worried about the technology ever getting out than they were about security inside the facility.'

'No shit,' observes Sendak bitterly.

'Yeah, yeah, so that's the boy-toys,' Rosemary interrupts. 'What about the bloody creatures? Where did they come from? How did they get here?'

Steinmeyer stops at a sliding door and fumbles through a selection of bloodied keycards. He swipes the appropriate one and leads them through into another carnage-strewn passageway.

'I don't have an exact answer for either of your questions,' he tells Rosemary with the awkward over-courtesy of one unused to addressing young females. 'But I will tell you what I know. The "how" part involves the technology we've been developing here. This facility houses a particle accelerator that is a hybrid between a conventional radio frequency atom-smasher and advanced plasma-laser technology. My work here has been principally to do with developing a theory of quantum gravity. I—'

'Oh my God,' Adnan interrupts, a realisation belatedly dawning on him. 'You're *Lucius* Steinmeyer.'

'I am,' he confirms, a little surprised by the recognition.

'I'm only familiar with your older work, sir, but I'm totally geeking out here.'

'Well I'm overfamiliar with his newer work,' Rosemary chastises. 'And so are a few of our late friends.'

'Indeed,' Steinmeyer says regretfully. 'Though in my defence, like many great discoveries in science, this one came about unintentionally. The machine created an anomaly: an unforeseen and, to be entirely honest, inexplicable effect. A portal, though we didn't know that until something came through it.'

'Inside the accelerator?' Adnan asks, reining in his excitement for fear of drawing further disapproval.

'No. Even more curiously, the anomaly appeared *outside* the impact observation chamber: precisely 16.16252 metres from the dead centre of the octant. And when I say precisely, I mean very precisely. Measured by laser.'

'Precisely 16.16252,' Adnan says. 'So the distance is a ten-to-the-power-thirty-six multiple of the Planck length.'

'What does that mean?' Rosemary asks.

'Nothing that sheds any light on what was created. We had no idea what the anomaly was, and I was still deliberating how to probe it when the first of the creatures came through. As to the question of from where . . .' Steinmeyer sighs with a deep and enduring frustration. 'There are three possibilities: that they are from somewhere else in our universe, and the anomaly is a bridge or gateway via higher dimensions; that they are from a completely different universe, and the anomaly is a rupture in the membrane separating theirs from

474

ours; or even that they are from right here, a parallel version of our Earth, where the path of evolution developed differently. In which case the anomaly—'

'Is like a way of tuning to a different reality,' Rosemary says, glancing at Adnan in acknowledgment.

'Quite,' says Steinmeyer. 'The curtain between worlds, between universes, is gossamer-thin; it's possible there may even have been naturally occurring breaches in the past, hence these creatures' previous excursions into our world may have given birth to our demon myths. I would know more if we had been able to study the effects properly, but that didn't happen. When the first specimens came through, the military people freaked. They brought in Cardinal Tullian, and in their superstitious, cowardly panic, they let him order off the menu in terms of his remit. He and his staff have had absolute control over the creatures ever since. I can say with some authority that what happened here has quite comprehensively given the lie to the phrase "non-overlapping magisteria".'

'So why didn't the military just shut it down?' Rosemary asks, prompting an ironic snort from Sendak.

'They never know whether to fish or cut bait,' the Sarge adds. 'Also known as a wait-and-see policy. With so much invested, my guess is, no matter how spooked they got, they weren't gonna pull the plug just like that. Am I right?'

'Very astute, Sergeant Sendak. We would need years, decades to work on this, but Tullian was angling for a shutdown from day one. All

475

developments in cosmology have been obstructed by Tullian's church, from Copernicus onwards, because they threaten its own explanations. They can't burn you at the stake any more, but they still have their methods of applying pressure. I knew a shutdown was inevitable. That's why I raised my counter-concern that if we turned off the machine, we might never be able to recreate the anomaly. Thus it was only military indecisiveness that postponed the shutdown so long.'

'But that shutdown order *was* given?' Sendak asks.

'Yes. General MacCormack ruled that it be mothballed.'

'Which would effectively close the portal forever, because the anomaly might not be replicable.'

'That was the impression I gave him.'

'The impress— You knew otherwise.'

'There was a power surge one night, a few weeks back. I had to reset all systems and the anomaly was lost. But when I restored the previous settings, it reappeared. I decided to keep this to myself and pretended to be desperately opposed to any suspension of the operation. I was protecting years of work. I had to make everyone think that shutting down the machine and closing the anomaly would be the end of it. Then, I hoped, we could later resume proper, unhindered research once we had dampened the hysteria and regained control of our own operation.'

'But somehow the freaks got loose before the shutdown could commence?' Sendak suggests.

'No. The shutdown sequence was well under way. I was packing my bags. The creatures got loose when all of the magnetic locking systems

476

failed, which could have been caused by the machine suddenly being flipped to inverse polarity. That's not something that just happens by itself. And nor do all of the armoury cabinets spontaneously malfunction.'

'You think this was sabotage?'

'I think my beaten-man performance didn't fool everybody. I suspect there's somebody in here for whom mothballing isn't enough. Listen to the sound of the machine.'

Sendak is finding it increasingly difficult to hear anything else. The pulsing has been getting louder and stronger with each corridor Steinmeyer leads them down, each doorway they pass through: disproportionately so, in Sendak's estimation. It's not just a pulse, either: it's a cycle of pulses, and it seems to intensify with each new round.

'It isn't getting louder simply because we're getting nearer,' Steinmeyer confirms. 'The pulse is getting stronger. It's the inverse polarity. It allows things to go through from our side instead of vice versa.'

'What would happen if something tried to go through at normal polarity?' asks Adnan.

'It wouldn't get near it. All of the specimens try when they first come through, but it's repellant, similar to bringing together two like poles of a magnet. Basically, it's not a two-way street. We reversed the polarity so that we could try sending probes through the portal, but we couldn't devise a way of retrieving them remotely . . .'

'And I'm guessing you struck out on volunteers to do it manually,' Sendak suggests.

'Quite. Our efforts were further limited because we found that the machine can't stay inverse for

477

long without becoming unstable. Security protocols were put in place to ensure the polarity could only be inverted under highly controlled conditions. That those protocols have been overridden is how I know this wasn't an accident. If we don't intervene, the machine is going to destroy itself.'

'Given how this shit has worked out so far, you want to tell me why that's a bad thing?'

'The machine is powered by a fission reactor connected to the biggest nuclear train set outside of CERN. If we don't shut it down, it'll blow the mountain apart and kill everything within five miles of here.'

*   *   *

Blake was a God-send: literally a God-send.

Even as Tullian stood there, contemplating the enormity of having just broken the most sacred of commandments and killed a man in cold blood, he had glanced at one of the CCTV screens and read the message the Lord was sending. It could not have been less ambiguous: in his moment of greatest doubt, no less than a priest had been delivered into his midst.

But no sooner had he noticed the collar on one of the four figures picking their way along a corpse-strewn corridor than a movement on another of the screens told him what work was still to be done. Steinmeyer had survived, and was making his way through the Alpha labs. In a matter of mere minutes, their paths would surely cross. It was imperative that he be the one to apprise his fellow clergyman of the situation before Steinmeyer delivered his version of events.

Fortunately, he knew a few short cuts, and by feeding the test chamber's monitor with one of Merrick's video files he had a means of causing the new arrivals to tarry there a while: a means that would throw a large spoke into Steinmeyer's 'rational' explanations.

'Like "a gossamer curtain", that was how he always described it,' Tullian tells Blake. 'Someone should have strangled him with one.'

Tullian opens a security lock and checks the path ahead. He spots a shock-pike lying abandoned on the floor and hands it to Blake as he ushers him through the doorway, demonstrating the charge button with a push of his thumb.

'Make no mistake, Father, I am no Luddite. Quite the contrary. I love science. In fact I owe my position in the Church to my passion and dedication to it. But here, in this place, is where science met its limit, and Steinmeyer refused to face that. Science could not account for some of the phenomena we were encountering. This was the advent of a paradigm shift of cosmological proportions, but Steinmeyer was effectively still saying the Earth is flat and the sun orbits around it. Steinmeyer is the most dangerous kind of zealot: a scientist who cannot accept what the data is telling him. Everyone in this place could see what was plain except him: he had opened up a gateway to Hell.'

'You're not using that as a figure of speech, are you,' Blake asks rhetorically. 'How do we close it?'

'The machine is out of control. It's going to consume itself. No one must prevent that. Unfortunately, Steinmeyer is still alive and will give anything to do just that. If he encounters your friends, he will use them, lie to them, and if it serves him, he will sacrifice their lives to his ambitions like his zealotry sacrificed all these others.'

*   *   *

Marianne lets out a strained moan and winces, the pain in her hands throbbing with her pulse now that the morphine has worn off. Cameron is still unconscious, which may be a mercy, but she suspects it's not down to his continuing analgesia.

'You okay?' Deborah enquires. 'Sorry, I know I keep asking that. It's just . . .'

'It hurts,' Marianne says, her voice strained. 'A lot. I'm worried about infection too. Think I'm getting a temperature. My head's thumping and it looks like the lights keep pulsing.'

'That's not your headache,' Deborah assures her. 'The lights *are* pulsing.'

Kirk glances up at the fluorescents, watching their glow fade and intensify, fade and intensify. He's convinced the latter phase is getting marginally brighter each time, but it could just be the effect of the contrast.

He glances towards Miss Ross and indicates the hockey stick, now disconnected from the mains.

'Wasn't me,' Heather insists. 'Sockets are on a different circuit. Anyway, this doesn't feel like power fading. This is power growing.'

'How long have they been gone?' Radar asks, casting a concerned glance at Cameron.

Kirk looks instinctively at his watch. It still reads 11:00, as it has done since the hike. He hauls it off

480

in frustration and casts it to the floor. Instead of hitting the ground, it whips away sideways through the air and sticks to the wall, drawn by irresistible magnetic forces.

He looks at Heather, like he needs a corroborative witness that this just happened. Her expression does the job.

'Did I dog Physics the day we covered this?' he asks.

*   *   *

'My fear is that Steinmeyer has in fact been possessed,' says Tullian, leading Blake through another sodium-lit service duct. 'And that is why he is, literally, hell-bent on preserving this infernal gateway. He was always a driven man, admirably so, but not like this, not to the exclusion of reason. However, perhaps this very drive was what made him a suitable vessel. He has certainly proven an effective one.'

Tullian turns and places a hand on Blake's forearm, gripping it as he looks intently into his eyes.

'I have to warn you, Father, that there is a strong possibility, should your friends come into his sphere, that they will be contaminated too. I'm telling you this in order that you may prepare yourself and understand that, if this is the case, then they are no longer your friends.'

Tullian advances into the duct, Blake following. This one is only a few yards long, housing a ladder at the end. An aluminium plate beside it reads 'Observation Platform Emergency Access'.

Tullian puts a foot on the first rung and then

481

stops, turning around to face Blake, something having occurred to him.

'There is another thing I need to tell you, in case anything should happen to me.'

He reaches among the folds of his robes and produces an iPhone, which he holds up momentarily for Blake to see before popping it back whence it came.

'If for any reason I don't survive, it's imperative that you recover this.'

'What's on it? The Pope's mobile number?'

'Evidence that I can use as leverage if any government, any organisation, ever attempts to repeat this madness: evidence proving that what was brought forth here was not merely some unknown species, but the forces of Hell. This phone contains video files and test data demonstrating that holy water burns their skin, while ordinary water does not. There is no chemical explanation for why mere water, once blessed, can do that to living tissue. This constitutes proof that the scientific paradigm has met its outer boundaries. This constitutes proof that what we have been telling the world for two thousand years is true.'

Blake had seen the footage in the lab, simultaneously amazing and appalling. He saw holy water burn living tissue: the tissue of a living creature, restrained and helpless, unable to resist or retreat as its skin blistered and burned. He also saw a corpse alongside: a demon that had been tortured and crucified.

He understands a terrible truth. Kane was right about him: he never truly believed. All these years, he's just been searching for a reason to. Well, now he's been given one, and he doesn't like how it feels. If Hell exists, then so must Heaven, but he finds them two sides at war: battle and slaughter, enemy prisoners tortured and executed. Didn't he already have this in the old world yesterday?

*   *   *

'Gimme a hand here,' calls Sendak, beckoning Adnan to help him clear the doorway of bodies. They're only feet apart, but he has to all but shout above the sound coming from beyond the doors.

'This is the Cathedral,' Steinmeyer announces, swiping a keycard. 'Once we get inside, I don't need to warn you to stay back from the anomaly.'

Sendak spots a pistol gripped in the hand of a dead soldier. He tries to wrest it free, but it is locked solid.

'Sarge,' Adnan yells, using his head to indicate the floor by his feet, his hands occupied by dragging what's left of some poor grunt.

Sendak looks across and sees the shotgun lying beneath the body Adnan is shifting. There are also two boxes of twelve-gauge ammunition by the wall, one of them spilled open.

They both begin loading shells into their weapons' breeches, which is when Sendak notices that Adnan looks concerned.

'What?'

'Fresh weapons and spare ammo just outside a big door. End-of-level-boss and a major battle up ahead.'

'This is real life, kid, not a video game.'

'Yeah, and in real life, somebody stashed this hardware for a fight—and still never made it.'

XXXIII

Blake emerges behind Tullian on to a platform above the main body of a vast cavern. The pulsing noise is deafening, the air filled with wind and light. He feels like he is on the bridge of a ship in a lightning storm. There are monitors, control panels, switches and dials on console banks either side of the platform, effectively forming barriers against the thirty-foot drop below. Waist-height railings fill in the gaps. They don't look very substantial, but Blake is guessing the weather up here is usually calmer.

He looks over the side to observe, if not the source, then the epicentre of the energy storm. He sees two great black cubes, like nuts on a giant bolt, separating sections of a huge steel cylinder that disappears into the live rock at either end of the cavern. In front of the central section, between the cubes, floats a black ellipse that appears to exist in only two dimensions. It has no depth, and though Blake can't see through it, he can see either side of it. Flashes dance around it like a corona, fading before they can resolve into being for any length of time. There is vibration all around, every object shaking into a blur with each pulse, their oscillations so intense that it looks like solid matter is having difficulty holding its shape too.

Tullian points towards a section of the console bank on Blake's right, where there is a large lever under a Perspex cover, marked 'Emergency Shutdown'.

'We can't let anyone near these controls,' he shouts above the noise. 'Not anyone! The horrors you've seen already are nothing, Father, nothing. If this gateway is not destroyed, the dark legions will have unopposed passage into our world.'

Sendak is first through the door. He has barely emerged into the deafening, teeming chaos of the Cathedral when a demon comes hurtling towards him, scampering over a pile of crates. He blasts it with his shotgun as the others file in quickly at his back.

Steinmeyer rushes past and stops in his tracks, aghast, as he takes in the view. The floor of the hall is strewn with debris: mostly the contents of the soldiers' interrupted packing-up exercise, but much of it the remains of what used to be his control and monitoring HQ. He scrambles amidst the wreckage, looking frantically for any terminal that might still be running, but what hasn't been shot up or smashed has been fried and scrambled.

'What the fuck do we do now?' asks Sendak.

'I need to get to the manual shut-offs on the observation deck. They're a built-in failsafe, they override all online systems. They're just up . . . oh, fuck, no. Tullian.'

Sendak looks towards the elevated deck jutting out of the cavern wall opposite the cubes, where he sees Blake standing alongside a guy in black robes.

Steinmeyer raises his decoherence rifle and takes aim. He gets off a shot just as Sendak throws up an arm to deflect it. The blast vaporises a section of console as the two figures dive for cover.

'The hell you doing?' Sendak demands, keeping hold of the barrel of Steinmeyer's weapon. 'That's our friend up there.'

'You don't understand. He's with—'

Steinmeyer is cut off as a creature erupts from the wreckage by their feet and sends both men sprawling to the floor, Sendak's weapon clattering from his grip as he falls. Steinmeyer keeps hold of his, but only at the cost of an agonisingly awkward landing that snaps his ankle.

Blanking out the pain for one last desperate second, Steinmeyer manages to roll on to his back and fire his rifle, but only hits an upturned stack of servers, inches from where Sendak has righted himself into a crouch.

Sendak feels the wave of dust just before he sees the creature leap upon the professor, an army-issue Ka-Bar knife gripped in its teeth as it wrests the rifle from his hands and tosses it far among the rubble. Out of the corner of his eye, he locates the shotgun's stock, only inches from his right hand. He stretches to tug it from where it is wedged amid the debris, only to discover, when he pulls it, that the stock is all that remains. The creature yanks back Steinmeyer's head with one claw, exposing his throat and roaring out a battle cry as it raises the blade in the other.

The battle cry turns to one of pain as Adnan's shotgun and Rosemary's arrow make their interventions. The assailant is thrown backwards off Steinmeyer like a rag doll, its head exploding in a cloud of black.

Sendak watches Adnan step across to where the creature lands, pumping his weapon to finish it off if need be. Then his warning cry is swallowed by the storm as a second demon, larger than anything he has seen so far, emerges from cover and grabs

Adnan from behind. It lifts him off the ground, gripped around both his upper arms, and hurls him into the black disc just as Rosemary fires her final arrow.

The arrow lodges in the creature's back while it stares in apparent confusion at the portal, into which Adnan has disappeared instead of being violently repelled, as was presumably the creature's intention. It then breaks off the arrow contemptuously, turns and begins stomping towards Rosemary.

Blake watches this unfold from above, his own warning cries lost in the tumult. He turns to Tullian, gripping the barrel of the Cardinal's rifle and directing it below.

'Shoot it. Shoot it, for God's sake.'

Tullian hauls the weapon clear of Blake's grip and shakes his head gravely.

'This weapon has charge left for one shot, and I'm saving that for anyone who tries to reach these switches.'

Rosemary turns and looks for another weapon, but sees only Steinmeyer crawling hopelessly amid the wreckage, looking for his lost prototype. The creature halts briefly to pick a knife from the body of a dead soldier, before resuming its progress with singular intent. It is two yards away when a flat-screen monitor smashes into its head, dropped from somewhere above. This doesn't floor it, but by the time it has recovered from the blow, it finds itself looking at Sendak as well as Rosemary.

Sendak moves in large sideways steps, waving his arms, drawing it away from the girl, towards where they came in.

'Yeah, that's right,' he shouts. 'Over here, you

Gollum-looking sonofabitch.'

Sendak steps back through the doorway, brandishing a blade of his own. His opponent follows, at which point he hits a button on the wall and brings the doors together with a servo-assisted whine, locking the creature away from Rosemary and Steinmeyer, but also locking himself in a tight corridor with the thing. He scans his surroundings. All he sees is body parts and dead soldiers. The creature gives a roar, towering over him. Fucker's eight feet if it's an inch.

They both have Ka-Bars. Other than that, it doesn't look like a fair match. He almost died here once before, long time ago. Maybe some things are just meant to be. Maybe you can outrun your fate for a while, but you can never escape it.

*   *   *

Blake leans over the console bank, having lost sight of Rosemary when she disappeared beneath the platform. Tullian is also intent on what he can and can't see below, happier when he had Steinmeyer in his line of vision and knew he was safely isolated away from the controls. With the elevator out of commission, the only way up here is via the emergency ladder they just ascended, and that requires a journey back out of the Cathedral. Thus he's searching the view beneath, but casting a regular eye back towards the door behind him, inset in the rock.

Blake thinks he hears a voice and strides across to the front of the platform, looking over the barrier closest to the portal. He sees Rosemary staring up, an arm around Steinmeyer, who looks

488

racked with pain as he struggles to remain upright. Blake's guess is he's broken his leg.

'You have to shut down the machine,' Rosemary shouts.

Blake turns to look at Tullian and finds him right alongside, also staring down at these supplicants.

'No,' Tullian responds. 'It must be destroyed.'

Steinmeyer summons up whatever strength it takes to shout through the strains of his agony.

'Damn it, man, this thing isn't just going to short a few fuses. It's a nuclear device. It's going to take out the entire mountain.'

'Christ,' Blake appeals. 'I left twenty kids less than two miles from here.'

Tullian's eyes bulge briefly but his expression remains intent.

'He's lying,' he tells Blake. 'He'd say anything to keep the gateway open. And even if he isn't, then that doesn't matter either. This is more important than individual lives. Their souls will be saved. And for their sacrifice, for our sacrifice, the reward will be truly great.'

Tullian steps away backwards, raising his weapon at Blake as he moves to protect the shutdown controls. That's when Blake understands that Tullian's belief is absolute. He is prepared to die for it; for and through his faith.

The question for Blake, the question he can no longer evade, is what does *he* believe?

He believes Steinmeyer isn't lying, and he believes Tullian's logic is correct in that God would reward anyone who made the ultimate sacrifice to defeat evil in His name. If Blake truly believes what he has so long professed to, then he will very soon be granted paradise, and reunited with those he has lost. Reunited with Gail. Reunited with the kids who died tonight. Reunited with Kane.

He offered Kane Pascal's wager, and he refused, even in his final throes. Now Blake is facing Pascal's wager as inverted by Sendak: Do you truly believe there's an afterlife, and are thus content to sacrifice the life you've got here?

There are only *atheists in foxholes.*

No bet.

Blake flexes his thumb and powers up the pike as he swings it, sweeping it upwards and into Tullian's rifle just before he pulls the trigger. The rifle fails to fire, blue sparks dancing around it for a moment before its LEDs fade to black.

'Now step away from the controls,' Blake tells him, waving the pike.

Tullian sighs gravely and bows his head in defeat, but it's a feint. He changes his grip on the rifle, grabbing it by the barrel, and lunges at Blake, swinging it like a club. Blake reads it all the way, shifting his footing so that Tullian's momentum sends him off-balance, spinning from a glancing impact against Blake's side. He sprawls at speed towards the railings and tumbles over the edge, but Blake is able to extend the pike for him to grab on to. He levers it against the steel barrier, leaving Tullian dangling by one hand, thirty feet above the Cathedral floor.

The pulsing intensifies further, shaking loose rocks from the walls. This place really is going to go up, and soon.

'Shut it down,' Steinmeyer calls. 'There's no time to waste.'

Blake looks back. He can't reach the console

490

without letting go of the pike. The Cardinal stretches up with his other hand, seeking a second grip, and as he does so, something falls from his robes. A glass phial tumbles and spins towards earth, smashing against a metal crate.

The liquid proceeds to eat through the metal in a fizzing, steaming fury, the droplets that sprayed the concrete voraciously eating that too.

'Oleum,' shouts Steinmeyer. 'Concentrated acid. He faked it. He switched the fucking phials.'

Blake stares down at Tullian, who has now established a second hold on the pike: clinging on to this life with both hands.

'They aren't demons,' Blake shouts. 'You brutalised them. You *made* them demons.'

'I know what they are,' Tullian calls back. 'They're Satan's agents just the same. Don't you see? He's the Deceiver. It's Satan's gambit that we drop our guard while his minions invade. The very fact that they are *not* demons is *greater* proof of his scheming. That's why I had to convince the military to shut it down, at all costs.'

Blake thinks of Kane's words to Guthrie, two lives tallied among Tullian's 'costs'.

If scientists found indisputable proof that there was no God, the Church wouldn't miss a beat. It would simply say that this emergent proof was merely a fabrication to lead man astray . . .

'He sabotaged the place,' shouts Rosemary. 'He let all of this happen. He killed everybody.'

'You lied about everything. *You're* the one who wouldn't accept the evidence.'

'It is the measure of our faith to believe *in spite of* evidence, Father. Satan is using science to seduce you. And only faith can save us from him.'

491

Another pulse sends more rocks tumbling, one of them smashing into the platform only feet away. Time's up.

'Science says you fall at ten metres per second squared,' Blake tells him. 'Let's see if faith can save you from that.'

Blake lets go of the pike and lunges for the console.

Rosemary watches Tullian fall, looking away before he hits the ground, only he doesn't; at least not directly. There is a flash of movement from close to one of the cubes, and Tullian is intercepted by a demon pouncing upon him in mid-air. They land in a tangle in front of the anomaly, the blue light of the pike crackling the air around them, before the demon rights itself and hurls Tullian, pike and all, through the portal.

The creature then turns to face Rosemary and Steinmeyer, roaring its vengeful intent as it charges forward.

Its head suddenly explodes in a splatter of black blood as several shots rip into it from the side. They both turn to see Sendak standing in the doorway, pointing a pistol: still gripped in the now severed hand of its previous owner.

Blake locates the Emergency Shutdown Sequence lever and flips it. An LED then lights up on a button close by, stating: 'Confirm Emergency Shutdown?'

'Damn straight,' Blake says, and hits it.

The pulsing sound ceases immediately, the portal vanishing like a shadow when the light that cast it is snuffed out. There is still a powerful thrumming in the air, but it sounds steady, controlled and, most crucially, receding.

Blake takes a walk back to the barrier to check on those below, and on the floor at his feet he spots something else that must have fallen from Tullian's robes during their struggle.

After a few seconds, the thrumming has died and the place is almost silently at peace. Then there comes a reverberating crash from the steel doors at the opposite end of the Cathedral.

'Find cover,' Sendak orders, raising his weapon, attached hand and all.

There is another crash, something very powerful bringing itself to bear upon the metal. Then, upon the third, the doors buckle and several soldiers storm through the gap: visored and faceless, carrying machine guns.

'Drop your weapons and get down on the floor,' the first of them commands.

Another of them spots Blake looking down from the platform.

'You, hands in the air and come down here, now.'

Blake puts up his hands to indicate compliance, but is preparing to explain why he's reluctant to undertake the second part when something occurs to him.

'Say, you didn't get here by helicopter, by any chance?'

*   *   *

'Listen,' Kirk says. 'You hear that?'

Rocks nods. 'Choppers.'

Upon this word there is an immediate clamour around the emergency doors.

The sound gets louder, then a few moments later

493

they can see the lights of two aircraft coming over the trees.

The helicopters split paths and touch down either side of the wrecked compound. Soldiers spill out and immediately begin scouring the perimeter, taking down the last stray demons with machine-gun fire.

Then a group of four emerges belatedly from one chopper and proceeds towards the games hall.

Kirk drops the chainsaw and grabs one of the net-stands, dragging it from its lodging place through the door handles as Rocks removes its partner. He goes to throw the emergency doors wide apart, but finds they won't budge. A glance through one of the panes reveals that two of the soldiers are barring the exit, and Kirk has to duck out of the way as the other pair use their rifle butts to smash out the glass.

The panes removed, it is the other ends of their weapons that are thrust through the resulting gaps. Kirk grabs one by the barrel, Rocks the other, angling them upwards while everyone scrambles back deeper inside the hall. Then the guns issue a series of hollow popping sounds and a number of grenades pinball around the walls and ceiling before bursting open in clouds of gas.

Kirk ducks down and picks up the chainsaw again. He's got hold of the rip-cord when his legs give, and is unconscious by the time he hits the floor.

XXXIV

Lieutenant Rodriguez, the head of the lockdown team, climbs back aboard the helicopter and takes a seat opposite Blake, Sendak and Rosemary. Steinmeyer is lying on his back behind them, across a row of his own. As the chopper begins rising into the dawn sky, Blake looks below to the other side of the FTOF complex, where he can see soldiers carrying unconscious survivors out of the games hall and placing them aboard the second aircraft. Cameron and Marianne are distinct among them by having already been hooked up to IV bags.

'They'll all wake up in hospital,' Rodriguez states. 'Where they'll be told there was a massive gas leak and subsequent explosion. The gas had hallucinogenic effects, manifest both before and after the blast, resulting in vivid memories of bizarre events which, clearly, couldn't possibly have happened.'

'They all had the *same* hallucinations?' Sendak asks. 'That ain't gonna fly.'

'Mutually reinforcing hysteria. Somebody shouted "monster" amid the chaos, and in their minds they all saw it. Cross-contamination of their recollections. They can't be sure a memory is what they actually saw or what someone else claims to have seen. I'm betting it wouldn't be a tough sell to suggest drugs and alcohol played a part too.'

Rosemary shakes her head with bitter disapproval.

'I know it sounds shitty, but it's for their own

good,' Rodriguez insists. 'What would you rather they believed happened to them? Wouldn't you prefer to wake up later and be assured the world still makes sense the way it used to?'

'It's not that I don't wish someone could tell everyone the weird stuff never happened; it's that I don't believe it'll work.'

'It'll work. It'll work because they'll *want* to believe our version.'

Rosemary looks down for a moment, her way of conceding the point. He's right. They'll resist it initially, but soon enough they'll succumb to the reassurance the official explanation offers. She just wishes there was such an option open to her. She went into the lions' den for her classmates and thought it was the hardest, bravest and most selfless thing she's ever done, but she understands that a more arduous task still lies ahead. It is her burden now to know the truth but tell no one; her duty to maintain their mass delusion, to reinforce the security of a comforting belief she knows to be false.

She glances across at Father Blake and wonders if he's been carrying the same cross.

'And what about those of us right here who know different?' Blake asks.

'Professor Steinmeyer and Sergeant Sendak are bound to secrecy. I can't stop you and the girl talking, but I'd strongly advise against it. It won't help your friends any, but if that ain't a good enough reason, I can give you a starker one, which is that nobody's going to believe you. You don't have any proof.'

'And thus you wave your magic wand and this all goes away,' Blake says.

'Don't you want it to go away, Father? Get on with your life?'

'No. Because it isn't over. My young friend Adnan went through that portal, and we all know there's still a chance we can bring him back.'

'I hear what you're saying,' Rodriguez assures him sincerely. 'And I give you my word I'd volunteer *personally* for that particular S&R mission, but we both know it ain't gonna happen. It would take a lot more leverage than one missing kid to get the brass to even *contemplate* firing that thing up again.'

'Yeah,' Blake concedes with a sigh, hoping he sells his defeated act better than Steinmeyer. He slumps back in his seat and pulls out the iPhone.

'I'm sorry, Father,' Rodriguez tells him. 'Usual aircraft rules. No cellulars in-flight.'

'Just checking it's still intact. I'll be needing it later.'

'You can use it soon as we land. Thinking of getting one just like it myself. You reckon they're pretty hot?'

'This one's dynamite.'

*   *   *

Blake looks out of the window once more as the chopper descends towards Raigmore Hospital. He can see dozens of staff lined up close to the landing pad, waiting to attend to the casualties arriving in two helicopters.

As the wheels touch down, Rodriguez leans across to him again.

'Now, before I let you out of this bird, assure me one more time that we're all straight with this.'

497

'I'm straight with it,' Blake replies.

'Good. Now get busy forgetting: that's the best way to help your friends and to help yourself, not to mention your church.'

'Don't worry, I'll be keeping this strictly to myself.'

He pulls off his dog collar, which is, frankly, beginning to chafe.

'I swear to God.'

Bonus Level

XXXV

Adnan waits until they're long gone before making his move. He's trying not to even allow himself to think about how scared he is, how lonely he feels. He calls up the HUD as he stalks through the strange vegetation, shotgun raised. It's just a bonus map, he tells himself. A secret level. You complete it and then get back to the main arc of the game.

From his hiding place among the rocks, he had watched with some disquiet as they carried Tullian away.

The Cardinal came through the portal only a few minutes behind, tumbling to the rocky ground amidst a sudden lightstorm before an awed and fearful gathering. The flashes and noise accompanying Adnan's own entrance must have been what drew the creatures, alerting them that something dramatic was afoot, but he had exited stage left and taken cover before any of them showed up. Thus the initial disturbance had served merely as a harbinger of this subsequent advent.

Tullian lay stunned on the ground at first, taking a moment to gather himself as he recovered from what had preceded his arrival, not to mention the rigours of the journey itself. Then he stood up, prompting gasps as his great robes swirled about him. Despite the rips and frays and smears of blood, they must have looked luxuriant beyond the imaginings of these observers in their crude and muddied rags.

Tullian stared for a few seconds, wild-eyed, at the assembly before him, then turned back towards

501

the portal, which chose this unfortunately coincidental moment to close, prompting another round of terrified amazement.

Then their leader approached him, a huge demon in a headdress just like Adnan had seen depicted in claw marks, blood and shit on the walls of that cell: the tribal chief or holy man. Tullian reached out and zapped him with the pike, sending him flying backwards through the air with a flash of blue sparkling light that outshone the sum of their flaming torches.

Within seconds, they were prostrate in worship. Every last one.

Four of them brought up a litter, the chair suspended on poles that the chief had arrived aboard, and very soon, Tullian was being carted off, shoulder-high, like fucking Threepio in *Return*.

Major lossage. The stupid fuckers think he's a god.

That's how this shit starts.